FRONTIERS OF CHAOS

A PALLAS GROUP SOLUTIONS THRILLER

Peter Nealen

CHAPTER
1

"Here he comes." Ken Mack was looking up while I lounged in the opposite chair in the outside dining area of Matsu.

In most places, that wouldn't have been a great position for surveillance. Sitting out in the open like that wasn't giving me a warm and fuzzy about our tradecraft.

That was assuming a couple of things, though. The first, that our target had the situational awareness to notice us, which he hadn't in the last two days, and the second, that anyone looked at anyone else for more than a passing glance in this city, anyway.

We weren't a mile from where the Alaska Way Viaduct had once stood, which had been a notorious homeless camp in a city that was increasingly becoming one big homeless camp. The cops only went certain places, and the rest of the city was on its own. In fact, there were two obvious vagrants just down on the corner, one of them aggressively gesticulating and yelling inarticulately. So, the urge to not make eye contact with anyone was even stronger there at the moment.

That actually made life easier for us. Sucked to be a Seattleite, though.

I would have thought that a sushi restaurant on the side of the street within spitting distance of Lumen Field would be nonpermissive as hell, but despite the camera on the streetcorner a few dozen yards away, no one had approached us or asked us any questions. Hell, we hadn't even gotten any weird looks, and we'd been hanging out for a while.

"He coming here again?" I didn't look over my shoulder or otherwise show any particular interest. The bums on the street corner might be holding everyone's attention, whether they were being obvious about it or not, but that didn't mean we didn't still need to be careful.

Ken didn't look up, though he was still watching our subject. "Yep. Seems to be his favorite lunch spot." Ken, getting as long in the tooth as he was, usually wasn't the sort to get annoyed by the boring parts of the job, but even he couldn't keep the vaguely sarcastic sneer out of his voice.

After all, we'd already spent most of a week watching a pencil-necked dweeb of a small-time journalist, who worked in a rental space belonging to a company called WeWork and was about as interesting as the spots on the table in front of me. We were both starting to wonder just what the hell we were doing there.

"Pattern of life." I was just as bored but tried to keep my tone unbothered. It was a part of the job, on surveillance. If the target really was up to something nefarious, usually it only could be picked out when he or she did something out of the ordinary, and people, in general, are weird enough that you have to establish a baseline for what "the ordinary" is. That can take a long time, which is why surveillance and private investigator work—which really boil down to the same thing—usually involve long hours of mind-numbing boredom.

Ken snorted. "What the hell are we following this guy for, anyway?"

I shook my head as Ernest Wise walked past and into the restaurant, not paying the two of us any mind. He seemed completely distracted, which probably wasn't good for him. Not that he could probably do much even if his situational awareness had been on point. He was the very image of a stoop-shouldered "skinny-fat," with a pronounced gut but scrawny as all hell otherwise. His hair hung down over his eyes, making it seem unlikely that he could have seen much even if he'd been paying attention.

He probably should have been. Even as he walked by and into the restaurant, I looked up and made eye contact with the bum sitting on the street corner.

Neither of us had intended it. He sure as hell hadn't. His eyes widened as I took in his body language, and rapidly reassessed what I was looking at.

It took about half a second to see through his disguise. It was good, mostly thrift store clothes, just ragged and dirty enough to sell the idea that he'd been living on the streets, and he hadn't shaved in a while. His hair, sticking out from under a dingy watch cap, was dirty and long. But there was an awareness about him that belied the appearance. Most of the vagrants on the street were either drugged out of their minds, mentally ill, or just eager to find a handout. There's a certain alertness to be found in the last one, but this guy wasn't that kind of alert.

This guy was a predator.

I could say that with a fair bit of confidence because so am I.

There's a certain edge to a predator's awareness. A panhandler is looking for marks, while a predator is looking for prey and threats. It's hard to describe the difference, but if you've been there, you know it.

He recognized me, too. Not me personally, but the fact that I was as out of place in that sushi restaurant as he was on the street.

Fortunately for everyone around us, he didn't panic, but looked away an instant later, going back to his play-acting. It was too late, though. He might hope that I hadn't noticed, but I had.

Why was he here? Because of us? I felt myself start to tense, my eyes darting to the other bum, who was yelling nonsense at a light post. That guy seemed to be genuinely out of it, and the three other people I could see on the street, a pair of young women and a single older guy, walking in opposite directions, were all just trying not to look at either of the street people, the older guy pausing to cross the street to keep away from them.

Hardly the enlightened ideal of Seattle, but probably common sense.

None of them read as the kind of meat eater the guy on the corner was. I wanted to check my six, but I couldn't turn around like that without potentially giving the game away. Right at the moment, the man on the corner couldn't be entirely sure that he'd been made. Let me start scanning intently, and he might figure it out.

We'd had a couple of run-ins with guys in our own line of work, hired by a shadowy network of hitmen—or a single facilitator; we still weren't sure which—who contacted contractors like us via anonymous, encrypted emails and farmed out high-paying hits, most of them aimed at undermining American security and helping those who profited off that same decline.

Was this guy one of that network? Phil and I had successfully infiltrated it for a few operations, but before we'd been able to get deep enough, we'd had to act to protect our actual client from a hit squad hired by the network in Indianapolis. We'd done what we could to cover our tracks, but they had to know that we were attached to Pallas Group Solutions—the fact that Carr & Sons Chemical had hired us wasn't a secret, though it also wasn't advertised—which made us all targets.

"What have you got?" Ken had noticed my heightened alertness.

"Homeless guy on the corner." Ken shifted his phone. He was using the camera as an over-the-shoulder mirror. Smart idea, as long as the bad guys didn't see themselves in the screen. "The one sitting down."

He watched for a moment. "Seems like a normal bum."

"He was watching us. Definitely not a homeless guy." The fact that Ken just nodded and took my word for it was thanks to a lot of rough times and hard-earned trust. I hadn't known Ken nearly as long as I'd known Drew, my previous partner. Drew and I had been brothers from the Basic Reconnaissance Course onward, the better part of twenty years. But Drew was dead, killed in a raid in Mazatlán, and Ken and I made a good team.

Ken, shorter than me by half a head, his hair and beard more salt than pepper these days, scanned over my shoulder at the other end of the street. It's an advantage to using a two-man team. You can cover a lot more territory with two sets of eyeballs instead of just one.

"Might have another one." His eyes were momentarily fixed on a point over my right shoulder. "It's genius, if you think about it."

"It is." My admiration was tempered by the fact that we were dealing with what were most likely professional killers every bit as effective and well-trained as we were. At least, if my paranoia wasn't just running away with me. "But we are not in a place I'd like to be if this is gonna go down."

"No argument here, brother." He shifted slightly in his seat. To someone watching, he might just be adjusting, but I could see that he was repositioning himself to be able to get at his Glock quickly.

If this was going to go down, it was going to go down fast. Especially if they thought they'd been made.

We didn't move from there, though, as desperately as every nerve in my body wanted to. Old boy on the corner there hadn't made a move yet, and while I was a firm believer in the axiom, "When in doubt, attack," this wasn't quite the time or the place.

After all, I couldn't be *sure*. They might not be there for us. They might not be who we thought they were. I'd been in enough insurgency environments over the years, where it had been awfully difficult to pick out the actual spotters and IED triggermen from the ordinary people. I knew all too well how important it was to be sure before you pulled the trigger, especially in a place like Seattle, which wasn't exactly an active warzone—despite the high, and climbing, levels of violent crime—and was actively hostile to ordinary citizens simply defending themselves.

This could get ugly with a quickness, so we had to be very, very careful. We stayed where we were, all the more alert, trying to watch our potential predators as well as maintain contact with Wise. The contract was suddenly of secondary importance, but both of us were professional enough that we weren't going to just drop it because of a perceived threat.

So, things got quiet again, even though both of us were now keyed up to a considerable extent.

At least, I was. Ken had always exuded an aura of unflappableness, though sometimes I knew it was a bit of an act. Still, he liked to say that he was far too old to get too stirred up, since it was bad for his heart. He was as calm and expressionless as ever as he kept looking over his newspaper, that he had to have read through about three times already.

I glanced inside. Wise was almost right on the other side of the window, sitting at a table and staring at his phone. He was every bit as oblivious to his surroundings as he had been before—either that, or he was better at this countersurveillance thing than I'd thought.

The next hour crawled by. The homeless guy who'd been yelling at a light post drifted away, but the guy on the corner stayed in place. I was increasingly convinced that he wasn't what he appeared to be, but he wasn't doing anything overtly threatening, so there wasn't much of anything I could do about him. Just keep an eye on him until he did something.

Maybe they were just there on surveillance, in which case we might have a chance to break contact once we moved off. I could hope.

An open city street was not where I wanted to get into a gunfight, especially not when I hadn't had a chance to pick the time or place.

Time seemed to slow to a crawl as I endeavored to act casual, perusing my phone to cover my scans of the area. Nothing else had changed, and the eerie quiet and calm continued, even as the man on the corner and I tried to watch each other without appearing to.

I could tell that was what was happening. He wasn't looking at me, but once I'd picked out that he was alert and watching, I couldn't miss it anymore. He was good, but he was definitely in the same line of work.

The question that really started to weigh on my mind was, what was he waiting for?

It made sense that a professional would take his time, especially in the operating environment we found ourselves in. Seattle might not be permissive for us, but that meant it was just as nonpermissive for them—unless they had political connections that they could leverage against us.

That seemed likely, but for whatever reason, they weren't acting with complete impunity, like I might otherwise have expected. It bore thinking about, even as I tried to keep track of our opposition and mentally prepare and visualize what I was going to do once things went pear-shaped.

Not *if*. *When*.

We were starting to run out of time. There's only so long you can dawdle in a sushi restaurant, even in Seattle, without it looking off to somebody. We'd already picked where we'd relocate to, before we'd even walked in, but with that fake bum on the sidewalk, I was starting to get antsy.

Then, almost without my realizing how much time had really passed, Wise walked out of the restaurant and headed for WeWork again.

That was when I realized that I'd misread the situation. Because the guy on the corner wasn't watching me. He was watching Wise as the reporter crossed the street, already starting to get up—though he was doing a reasonably convincing job of looking stoned or drunk while he did it—and talking to himself.

Or to the Bluetooth earpiece in his ear.

They weren't after us after all. They were looking for Wise, the same way we were.

The question now was, what the hell were we going to do about it?

That question was answered for me when I caught a glimpse of the knife in the man's hand as he started across the street toward Wise.

CHAPTER 2

Seattle wasn't the place for an armed Good Samaritan, but I couldn't exactly let the guy murder our mark, either. Not that I had any particular attachment to Wise, but I also didn't know for sure why we were supposed to be surveilling him in the first place. The client had been almighty close-mouthed about that part, and only the fact that I trusted Thad "Goblin" Walker as much as I did had led me to accept the mission as briefed. He had to have a reason for accepting as vague a tasking as this one, so I'd play along.

That meant, though, that without knowing for sure that Wise was a bad guy, I couldn't just sit by and watch him get stabbed to death in the street.

Wise wasn't paying attention to anything but the traffic, angling across the street, probably mainly to avoid the homeless weirdos on the corner. So, he didn't see the hitter in disguise as the armed bum moved toward him, his hand dropping low, the knife now concealed in his palm and sleeve. The man was speeding up, the façade of chemically-enhanced vagrant falling away as he closed in on his prey.

This definitely wasn't just another surveillance job. This was a hit.

I was already out of my chair, vaulting over the railing, realizing that I'd just committed myself and burned our surveillance. Not that that was going to stop me at that point.

Plans of action were flipping through my head as I moved, though most of them were just slight changes on the theme I'd been thinking through since I'd noticed the guy with the knife. I hadn't been able to form a complete plan while he'd still been sitting there, but now that I saw what he was doing, the contingencies collapsed to a point right there on the street.

Over two decades of Recon and clandestine operations habits meant that I rebelled at the idea of yelling in the street unless there were already bullets flying, but the situation meant I *had* to draw attention to myself.

"Hey, buddy! You dropped something!"

Wise looked around, confused, as if he wasn't sure if he even should look toward the sound of my voice. This part of Seattle being the haven of drugged-out vagrants that it was, looking around at a shout could attract attention that no sane person wanted. Yet my tone hadn't been the grating screech of a homeless guy on meth, so he looked around.

The guy with the knife did, too, and he stutter-stepped as he realized that I wasn't walking toward Wise, I was walking toward him. I hadn't drawn a weapon, though I was sure ready to, and every instinct was *screaming* at me to pull my Glock and go to work. Seattle might be a hellhole for self-defense, but I still had the paperwork I needed to carry concealed in Washington State, and if this guy gave me a reason, I'd drop him like a bad habit.

It wasn't as if I was particularly attached to the Glock 19 in my waistband. It's a good reason to have multiple guns, though.

He made eye contact for the second time, and I could see the wheels turning. Unfortunately, he sized me up and decided I was a threat that needed to be dealt with instead of avoided.

I was about ten feet away at that point, and he turned and charged.

To this day, I'll never know what prompted him to do that. Maybe he thought that if he'd broken off, it would have burned his cover as a homeless guy, and he'd have been rolled up. Maybe he thought that he could cover the ground fast enough—after all, the twenty-one-foot rule is a thing—to put me out of action and still get to Wise.

Maybe he was just one of those guys who gets into the profession for the sake of killing, and now that he was somewhat more unsupervised, he figured to add a couple more Stateside kills to the scoreboard.

Since it is a truism that if you're going to get into a knife fight, you should expect to get cut, I was already braced for it. I knew I probably wasn't going to get my weapon out before he reached me, especially at that distance, so I didn't try. He was too close.

Instead, as he lunged at me, coming in low with the knife aimed at my guts, I sidestepped, blocking the knife thrust with the heel of my palm to his forearm. That's not a comfortable thing, and he almost dropped the knife as he staggered, the shock running through his arm at the impact, giving me an opening, at which point I kicked him in the knee.

His knee almost bent sideways, though he rotated just enough with the impact to keep me from snapping the joint. He was already recovering, though he dropped the knife and reached for his waistband, just as I took a long step back, my shirt already clearing as I gripped my Glock and ripped it out of the holster.

My backstep had given me some space, and fortunately, I hadn't lost track of my surroundings in the sudden confrontation. A car sped past, the breeze plucking at my sleeve, as I leveled the weapon at the ragged man on the side of the street.

Wise was running, I saw through my peripheral vision, even though I was as focused on the bad guy in front of me as I needed to be. Probably just being smart and trying to get away from the violence. Nothing I'd seen so far made me think that he had any idea he was a target.

The man in front of me knew he was fucked. I could see it in his eyes as he froze, my 9mm leveled at his face. I was out of his reach, and his own handgun was too far from any position where he could bring it to bear before I shot him. This guy wasn't like some of the others we'd run into in this shadow war we were in, who had apparently decided that death was better than capture.

Unfortunately, he wasn't the only one in play.

An engine revved, tires squealed, and there was a *bang* behind me. I started to involuntarily look toward the noise, and he started to make his move.

Fortunately, I saw the shift just in time, and my finger tightened on the trigger as I flicked my eyes back toward him, my focus settling on the front sight just as his SIG cleared his clothes.

There was no way I could hesitate. I shot him through the skull from less than six feet away, the bark of the 9mm deafeningly loud in the concrete and glass canyon of the street. He stiffened and fell over onto his side, his skull leaking red onto the pavement.

With a curse, more at the fact that I'd just had to smoke somebody in fucking Seattle, of all places, I shifted and turned, checking the rest of the street and our surroundings, looking for the next threat. I hadn't heard any more gunshots, but even as I moved, tires squealed on the pavement and a car roared away toward the intersection and through, heading north. Something made me look at the plate. I was still in that combat awareness mode, so details jumped out at me. It was a Washington plate, though that meant less than the number, which I dutifully noted before turning back toward the other side of the street, just as the screaming started.

"Someone call 911!" At first I thought they were looking at the man I'd just killed. This could be very, very bad, but the clinical part of my mind told me that holstering and running were the wrong reaction. We had damned good lawyers at PGS, I was carrying an Idaho Concealed Carry Permit, which was honored by Washington State, and, provided there were no shenanigans on the part of Seattle PD, there was no way that I should get burned for shooting a man who'd just tried to stab me and then tried to shoot me.

While there were quite a few people staring at me and the gun, though, the 911 call wasn't for the dead man at my feet. It was for Wise.

The car that I'd seen had veered onto the sidewalk, leaving dark streaks of burned rubber, and hit Wise as he'd shrunk away from the confrontation on my side of the street. They hadn't slowed down, either; that much was obvious. Wise lay crumpled in a growing puddle of his own blood, about fifteen feet away where he'd been thrown by the impact.

The whole thing came together in my mind at that moment. The "homeless" guy I'd shot had been the primary, but he'd had backup, and when I'd intercepted him, the backup had swung into action.

Whatever the reason that the client wanted us watching Wise, apparently we weren't the only ones, and now he was dead.

I cursed as I holstered the gun, glancing at Ken as he looked at Wise's body. He met my eyes, his mouth thinned to a narrow line, and nodded slightly.

It was a hell of a situation, and I thought that both of us were probably thinking the same thing. We'd just been thrown into an extremely dangerous situation without even knowing it. If we got clear of the Seattle cops in any sort of reasonable amount of time, there were going to be questions. Lots of very pointed questions.

What the hell had we just stepped into?

CHAPTER
3

The phone buzzed, and Nick King grimaced as Vicky sighed. It wasn't an angry sigh. While she looked like a supermodel, and could sometimes sound about as vapid—though Nick was pretty well convinced that those instances were her version of sarcasm—she had made it clear that she knew what she was getting into, and while she might not *like* sharing Nick with the job, she was more willing to do that than not have any of him at all.

For Nick's part, he was still desperately holding off on thinking through her hints that he needed to meet her dad.

It's not that I'm scared. I'm just wondering just how fast this is really going. After all, they'd only been dating for a couple weeks. She seemed to have plans, and he was still figuring out just where he stood.

After all, he'd seen some pretty horrific drama over women in his day, and he was wondering where the catch was.

He grabbed the phone. "Sorry, babe." He almost flinched at using that term, but Vicky just rubbed his arm with a smile. She liked it when he called her that.

His eyebrow went up as he looked at the screen and saw that it was Matt Patric. He and Matt had been partners when he'd first started with Pallas Group Solutions, just after the hit on their first client in Atlanta. Matt had been shot up badly during the fight for the Bowman Ranch in New Mexico and had been on the bench because of it for months. Last Nick had heard, Matt was about ready to come back, but that didn't explain why he was calling *now*.

Levering himself up off the couch, Nick brought the phone to his ear. "What's up, man?"

"Hey, Nick, are you at home right now?" The two of them lived less than fifty miles apart, Nick in the small town of Lyons, and Matt in Fort Collins.

Nick's frown got deeper as he went completely still for a moment. Something about Matt's tone was off. Something was wrong.

"Yeah. What's up?"

Matt sighed. "It might be nothing. A guy I know from way back reached out to me yesterday. Started asking some very pointed questions about the company."

Nick felt his blood run cold. Matt was right. It might be nothing. It might also be a fishing expedition by one of several enemies they'd made over the last year or so.

"Now, from what I've been able to find out, he retired a few years ago, and he's been doing some off-and-on contract work. It might just be that he's interested in joining up. *Might*." Nick could almost hear his friend shake his head. "Something doesn't feel right, though."

"You think somebody's digging." It wasn't really a question.

"I think it's entirely possible. Especially after that intel brief we got."

Nick grimaced, already heading for his back room where his go bag was waiting. Vicky was watching him from the couch, with concern written all over her features. She wasn't asking questions or hounding him, though. She just waited.

That was slightly unnerving all by itself.

"Does he know where you live? Do you need me to come over?"

Matt hesitated. Nick could imagine what his friend was thinking. He'd probably be in the same spot. None of them wanted to be wrong. None of them wanted to be easily stampeded. If it *was* nothing, Matt was afraid that he'd never live it down. The job required a certain amount of paranoia, but that wasn't the same thing as jumping at shadows.

"I mean… Yeah. He knows where I live. I had him over a few years ago, before he retired out of Group." Matt got hesitant again. "I don't think there's necessarily a threat, though. Not yet. He was just asking questions, and he lives quite a ways away. Last I heard, he was moving out of Colorado Springs and heading to Florida."

Nick stopped, standing over his go bag, staring at the far wall with narrowed eyes as he thought it through. Matt didn't want to panic or get the rest of the company stirred up for nothing. If it was nothing. "Okay, bud. Just let me know."

"Thanks, man. Just thought I should pass the word that somebody was asking around. I know Goblin hasn't exactly advertised." Matt sounded a little relieved. He was concerned, but without a smoking gun, he didn't want to go overboard. "See ya at work in a week."

"Yeah, man. See you soon." But as he took the phone away from his ear, Nick remembered the brief that Matt had mentioned. He'd been a little involved with securing a chemical plant down in Honduras at the time, but a few guys from the A Team had infiltrated a network of special operations trained hitmen, coordinated through the dark web, and had gotten fairly deep until they'd had to break their cover to stop the same network from kidnapping or killing their principal.

Somehow, he doubted that the sudden interest in PGS after that was coincidental.

He was still standing there, his phone in his hand, thinking, as Vicky came to the door behind him. "What's wrong, baby?"

"I don't know." He looked down at the phone and the go bag at his feet.

"Is somebody in trouble?" She was leaning against the doorjamb, her voice quiet.

"Maybe." He sighed and looked down at the phone again. "I'm sorry, babe. I've got to look into this."

"It's okay. I've got the week off." He could hear the warm smile in her voice, and he almost didn't make the next call. "I'll be here, waiting."

With an enormous effort, Nick kept his eyes on the phone and called Doug.

"You know it's our time off, right, Nick?" Doug Chen wasn't what Nick would have ever considered lazy. He was a former Delta operator, though Nick had no idea just how long he'd been in The Unit. Judging by his performance under fire, Nick was guessing he'd been there for a long time.

He was, however, old enough and wise enough not to want to borrow trouble, and he'd made it clear more than once that time off was time off. Not because he was difficult about it, but simply because he recognized, from long years of experience, the risks that burnout presented to men in this profession.

"I know, and I wouldn't call, but I heard from Matt. Seems that somebody he knows from way back contacted him and was asking a lot of questions about the company." He hadn't kept his profession from Vicky, but he also hadn't gone into a lot of detail with her, either.

That got Doug's attention. "Was he, now?" He sounded pensive. "You're in Colorado, right?"

"Yeah." Nick felt his game face coming over him. He wasn't crazy; Doug thought this was a threat, too.

"Shit. I can't get there in any less than forty-eight hours. Hold on." The phone went quiet, though the call was still open.

Nick dropped into a crouch to double-check his go bag, mainly just for something to do while he waited on Doug. He knew that everything was there, but if he was busy, Vicky wouldn't be asking him questions he wasn't sure he could answer.

"Okay. I've got a buddy out that way. He's in Colorado Springs, so it's gonna be a minute. Can you get over to Matt's place?"

"Yeah." It would mean going alone, because if there really was a threat, he didn't think he could wait until a former Special Mission Unit operator got all the way up from Colorado Springs. That would take at least two hours. If this guy knew where Matt lived, and his questions were meant to gather intel for a hit, then things could get real, fast. "I'm on my way now."

"Watch your back, Nick."

***

Matt Patric's house wasn't all that fancy. One story, brick, with an attached garage, it looked more like a middle-class factory worker's house than a GWOT contractor's house, but that was probably why Matt still had it. The good money in the contracting world hadn't lasted forever, and as the pay had steadily dwindled—along with some of the jobs—those who had lived high on the hog, playing at being "contractor rich," had often found things tightening. Matt had been careful with his money, and so he was better off than some guys Nick knew.

He stopped his old Bronco just down the street and sat behind the wheel, just observing the neighborhood. It wasn't the sort of place that anyone would usually expect terrible violence to happen, in contrast to some of the gang-riddled barrios where they'd worked recently, especially in Mexico and Honduras. He'd been at this long enough, though, that he could sort of see through the illusion. The manicured lawns, the neatly trimmed trees, the well-kept-up houses, and the nice, clean vehicles on the street and in the driveways weren't an impenetrable shield toward the forces of crime and violence.

Especially if those forces had the sort of funding, training, and political backing that some of the people PGS had found themselves up against did.

Nothing jumped out at him. He checked every vehicle and nook and cranny he could see, but if there were real pros involved, he knew that nothing might stand out. There were no out-of-place vehicles in front of Matt's house. No one loitering on the street who didn't belong there. Everything was quiet.

Something didn't feel right, though.

He pulled across the street and parked in front of Matt's place. Maybe he'd gotten there in time. But something was telling him that something was wrong.

He wasn't carrying his PGS Glock; he was off work and so he was still carrying his own personal carry handgun, a P365. He made sure that it was still concealed but easy to reach, and got out of the vehicle, starting toward the door. The fact that he was circling around toward the garage and staying out of direct line of sight from the door and the windows was *mostly* unconscious at that point.

He took one more glance around at the quiet neighborhood. No sirens, no surreptitious faces in windows. There was no outward sign that anything was wrong. But he could feel the hairs on the back of his neck going up.

Only a carefully considered, professional caution kept his handgun in its holster as he moved to the door, reached out, and knocked, still not *quite* standing in front of it.

The door swung partway inward at the impact. It hadn't been latched.

He thought he heard a faint noise from inside, but his pistol was immediately in his hands as he pushed through the door. Maybe the "right" answer would have been to back off and call 911, but that was Matt and his family in there.

He cleared the door quickly, sweeping the living room over his pistol's sights. There wasn't a *lot* out of place, but there was one overturned chair.

More sounds came from the back bedroom. Almost like a faint scuffle, and then he heard a low voice. "Shut the fuck up."

Every impulse told him to drive straight to that room, but he knew that he needed to be *really* careful, since he was on his own. Single-man CQB is a nightmare by any metric. The average man only has about a hundred twenty degrees of peripheral vision, and three hundred sixty degrees of security are needed in a combat situation, especially in a close-quarters fight. CQB is a game of angles, and with only one set of eyes and one gun to cover every angle, it gets complicated, fast.

Keeping his back to the wall as much as possible, avoiding full exposure to the next door, he moved to cover the kitchen first, seeing no movement there, though there was enough wreckage in there to suggest a struggle. He saw some red spatter on the counter and his blood would have run cold, if he hadn't already been deep in the zone.

He noted it and moved on, his muzzle moving to the next danger area.

The kitchen was set toward the back of the house, just across from the short hallway between the garage and the two bedrooms. Nick paused at the corner, taking a deep breath as he brought his pistol back to his chest, the muzzle pointed at the opening next to him, then pivoted around the corner, punching the weapon out as he searched for targets.

One bedroom door was closed. The other was open, and he saw movement, quickly shifting toward it even as someone hissed an epithet.

Common sense might suggest that this was the time to take it slowly and carefully, pieing off the door and engaging targets as they were exposed. That was leaving aside two details, though. The first, and most obvious, being that his friend and that friend's family were currently being held hostage, and if these bad guys smoked either Matt or Linda, Nick knew that he'd never be able to live with himself. The first tenet of hostage rescue is that the hostage is worth more than the rescuer's life.

The other factor was that most American interior walls will not stop bullets. They'll barely slow them down.

So, as soon as he saw the man pointing a gun at Linda, almost out of sight through the narrow bit of doorway he could see through, he shot the man through the cheekbone and plunged into the room, pivoting toward the corner, his finger still on the trigger.

The man he'd shot was already falling as he cleared the threshold. Even as his eye and muzzle tracked toward it, there was an explosion of movement, the *thud* of a body hitting the wall, a curse, and then the bed was knocked almost a foot to one side, almost taking Nick's knee with it. He shifted quickly, bringing his SIG to bear, but he didn't have a shot.

Matt Patric was on the floor, fighting with another man in a balaclava for control of what looked like a CZ P10. Nick didn't dare shoot for fear of hitting Matt, so he quickly grabbed Linda and got her down on the floor, even as he briefly checked the man he'd shot on the way through the door. That guy was down, hard, but Nick snatched the pistol out of his limp hand and pressed it into Linda's palm before he turned to where Matt was wrestling with his assailant.

The P10 fell to the floor with a *thump* as the gunman stifled a scream, Matt now in full control of his wrist and torquing it, hard. In the next moment, Matt threw himself onto his back on the floor, kicking one leg up and over the gunman's neck and putting him into an armbar. The man did cry out then, because Matt wasn't going for submission. He was trying to do damage.

The gunman's arm broke with a nauseating *crunch*, and then, even as the man let out a muffled scream, Matt twisted again, putting him into a scissor choke and bearing down.

He held the choke as the gunman frantically tapped. Nick hesitated, then accepted that Matt seemed to have things under control, so he pivoted back toward the hallway. That other bedroom and the garage still needed to be cleared.

That took seconds. When he came back, Linda was on her feet, the dead man's gun in her hands, and Matt was getting up, having scooped up the other gunman's weapon. That guy was limp on the floor, though after a moment, Nick could see he was still breathing.

"Call 911, honey." Matt's voice was a rasp, though it seemed more from exertion than any injury. He looked up at Nick. "Thanks, brother. Didn't think anybody was going to get here in time." He coughed. "Hell, I didn't think I was going to need you, until I did."

Nick holstered his pistol. "How much do we need to worry about the Fort Collins cops?"

"Some, but not too much." Matt was already reaching for his own phone. "I'll call the office and get some lawyers moving." He shook his head. "Good thing Goblin keeps the ones on retainer that he does."

"Good thing," Nick agreed, even as he looked down at the two gunmen, one incapacitated, one dead. They probably weren't going to get a chance to interrogate the one, but it was abundantly clear to him that they were going to need to take steps.

That network that Chris and Phil had infiltrated might have disappeared after they'd blown their cover to protect Gage Romero, but that obviously didn't mean they'd gone away.

And Pallas Group Solutions was, apparently, squarely in their crosshairs. Nick didn't believe for a moment that this had just been a burglary, and he suspected that, if they were to remove the balaclavas, they might well find that one of the two hitters on the floor was Matt's old acquaintance.

He pulled his own phone out and called Doug. Even if he and Matt got wrapped up dealing with the Fort Collins PD, the word needed to get out to the rest of the company, and fast.

CHAPTER
4

Goblin was already on the teleconferencing app when we finally got loose from the Seattle PD and got back to our hotel. It was early the next morning; the whole thing had been grueling. The local DA seemed to think that compassion entailed allowing drugged-out vagrants to stab you, but then the police had found all the weaponry and comm gear that the dead "homeless person" had been carrying. That had thrown one hell of a wrench into her gears, and the fact that Goblin already had one of our on-call attorneys there in Seattle, locked and loaded, had finally gotten us the go-ahead to leave, sans our weapons—even though Ken hadn't even drawn his—without charges, though we'd been sternly cautioned that we needed to be available for further questioning in the "ongoing investigation."

Something told me that the investigation was probably going to dry up fast, if the hitmen were as connected as some of the others like them that we'd encountered recently. These guys weren't *mareros*, *sicarios*, or other thugs for hire. They were professionals, like us in just about every way but ethics.

So, I was tired as hell and still stressed when Ken and I sat down across from the computer and its built-in webcam in my room, having already equipped ourselves with our backup weapons. I hadn't had a chance to call Julie and let her know that I was all right—we'd been doing that on a daily basis when I was deployed for over a decade—and I was still struck by the sense of impending threat that was not only due to the presence of the hitters in Seattle, apparently focused on the same target we'd been watching, but also just the fact that local law enforcement was probably looking for something to pin on us.

The pensive look on Goblin's face when the video window opened didn't help much.

He didn't wait for us to ask him what was going on. "Well, I've run your report past the client, Ken. His response was…interesting, to say the least."

We both waited quietly. The report had been short, as it had been made up of about what Ken could put over the phone while we'd waited for the cops, but Ken was an old enough hand at this that he hadn't left anything important out. We really didn't have much of anything to add right at the moment.

"It seems that he's somewhat upset that you weren't able to save Wise."

Maybe it was because it was well after midnight, but that immediately pissed me off. "Wait a damned minute. The contract was for surveillance, not protection. Those are very different taskings, and if this asshole wanted us to be doing more than just watching Wise, he should have fucking *said* that in the first place."

Goblin was looking out of the screen with a raised eyebrow, as if to ask if I was done. There was a faint, sardonic smile on his face that told me I was preaching to the choir, and I subsided.

"I told him all of that, albeit *slightly* more diplomatically. Fortunately, he's accepted it, though that took about an hour's discussion. He's been playing this contract very close to the chest—which is why I haven't told you who he is—but up until this point, the money's been good enough to let some of that slide. I'm now drawing some hard lines on how much we'll accept working in the dark, though some of those negotiations are still underway."

Ken let out a quiet sigh. Generally speaking, he was pretty blasé about some of this stuff, but even he was tired and frustrated.

"So, what's next?" I decided that if Goblin had opted to continue with the contract, no matter how shady it seemed to be, then I needed to trust him and get onto the next step.

For one thing, as tired and pissed as I was, it was probably the best way for me to keep on an even keel, and losing my shit and tossing tables in a hotel room wasn't going to accomplish anything.

"Well, that gets complicated." Goblin leaned back in his chair a little, revealing slightly more of the office in Dallas, as bland and corporate as it was. Thad "Goblin" Walker had maintained his priorities when it came to the corporate versus the operational side, with as much of the company's resources as possible going to operations. We'd both known companies that had gone pretty far in the other direction. "We've got a couple of issues to deal with. The client still hasn't revealed what, exactly, his interest in Ernest Wise was. And even if he does eventually tell us, I don't think we can entirely trust him to be one hundred percent open about it. So, that means we need to look even deeper into Wise, and what might have made him a target. That's your long-term objective. Ziggy and Drizzle will be backing you up.

"Unfortunately, we also have a rather more pressing security concern, and we need to address it first." He sighed. "There was an attempt on Toe-Tag and his wife yesterday, and I just got a call that somebody attempted a drive-by shooting on Hybrid's house. Both incidents were preceded by contact from old acquaintances asking questions about the company.

"We're on someone's target deck, and I think you know whose, Chris."

I nodded, even as my blood ran cold. We'd known this was coming as soon as Phil and I had decided to intervene and stop the shadow network hitters from kidnapping or killing Gage Romero. We'd showed our hand that time, which was why the

27

network had gone completely silent even as we'd abandoned the identities of Walter Callahan and James Kelly. Even if they hadn't realized just who the two of us were, they had to know that we were either Pallas Group Solutions or connected to them.

"Now, before you panic, I've already got people moving to cover your families. If you need to go check on them, though, I'll make sure you still get paid. This is important."

He didn't need to say it twice. So far, I'd managed to shield my family from what we'd been doing, but the thought of the bad guys coming after our loved ones had hovered over PGS like a thundercloud ever since we'd first crossed swords with the cartels. It was the whole reason we'd gone on the offensive in Mexico. We'd moved quickly to take the war to the Sinaloa factions who'd been involved on the Bowman Ranch before they could take the war to us.

But that our families could be used as leverage against us had always been a Sword of Damocles over our heads. Now, it seemed that threat was coming to fruition.

"Unless you've got anything else pressing, Thad, I need to make some calls and get some flights lined up." I fought back the fear and dread that were clawing at my throat as I desperately wanted to get home *right then.*

"Don't worry about flights." Goblin's expression was serious, his voice low and calm. "They're already booked, and as early as I could get them. It means you won't get much sleep, but somehow, I doubt you were going to sleep much as it was."

He had that right. "Okay. Thanks, Thad." I still couldn't quite relax, though. "I still need to call Julie, though."

"Get on it. I'll pass along any other info I get, as soon as I get it. I expect the same from both of you." Goblin looked back and forth between us. "This is probably going to develop fast. The quicker we can disseminate information throughout the whole company, the faster we can react, and hopefully get inside the bad guys' OODA loop." The Observe-Orient-Decide-Act loop had almost become a cliché in our community, but it was still a legit concept, and we were already outside the enemy's loop from the sounds of it.

We signed off quick and Ken headed for his room while I dialed Julie.

***

It wasn't Julie waiting for me at the airport, but I'd been expecting that. Bob Horner was a younger guy, just out of the Army, and wasn't part of a main team yet. So, he'd gotten supernumerary work, which in this case meant he was available, so Goblin had sent him, along with a lot of the guys who were lining up for the E Team, to cover our families until one or more of us could get where we were going.

I didn't have hard and fast numbers, but probably about half the company's contractors were single, without kids. Of the rest, most were still married, though a few had kids but no wives, as such. I didn't know where Bob fell into that, but he was there, and he didn't hesitate to put the pedal to the metal on the way out of the airport parking lot.

I was already on the phone, calling Julie. She was going to have more up-to-date information than Bob did, no offense to Bob. He didn't seem to take any, keeping his eyes on the road and getting us on the way to my place as fast as he could without getting us pulled over. "Handgun's in the glove compartment, with two reloads," he said, as I waited for Julie to pick up the phone. "It's one of yours. Your wife gave it to me. Same with the carbine in the back." He jerked a thumb over his shoulder, and I saw one of my weapon bags on the back seat. "Nobody had showed up yet when I left, but we both figured it was a good idea."

There were some guys who would definitely not be comfortable with another dude being in their house with their wife. Not really knowing Bob, I shouldn't have been, but I knew my wife. If he'd gotten out of line, she wouldn't have hesitated to kick him out, and she'd have backed it up with a pistol, if need be. She sure as hell wouldn't have given him my guns to pass along to me.

She answered the phone before I could do much more than nod. "Chris." There was noted relief in her voice. "I'm so glad you're back."

"Anything going on?" There was only so much I wanted to say over the phone, even though we were encrypted. It was still a third-party app, and if the bad guys had the resources they'd demonstrated so far, there was only so far we could trust it.

"There might be. Tyler noticed a truck on the road just about a hundred yards away. It's just sitting there, has been for half an hour." She sounded nervous, though since it was Julie, she wasn't losing her head. "Tyler wants to go confront them and see what they're doing here, but I talked him out of trying it until you got here."

I glanced at Bob. I'd put the phone in speaker mode so that he could hear. Young as he was, new as he was, he wouldn't be there if Goblin hadn't vetted him. He just nodded his understanding.

"Good call. We'll be there in about forty minutes." I cringed a little as I checked my watch. There *were*, occasionally, drawbacks to living out in the sticks. It was a long drive to and from the airport.

To be honest, if I didn't need to fly for work, we'd be living a lot *farther* out.

Bob had us flying down the road just fast enough to get there without getting pulled over. He had a feel for the area, at least. There are places where the local highway patrol will watch for anything more than a couple miles over the speed limit, and they're usually pretty well hidden. Traveling the speed of traffic, give or take a couple miles per hour, is usually a good way to disappear into the noise.

It was actually a little less than forty minutes before we were pulling up the dirt road in front of my house. I spotted the truck Julie had been talking about immediately.

We had neighbors, but they were all pretty well spread out. Most plots around our area were a minimum of ten acres, with quite a few being twenty or thirty. It spaced us out pretty well, and also meant that a truck just loitering on the side of the road stood out pretty badly.

It was a relatively new Chevy Silverado, white, with tinted windows, and it was sitting off the side of the road. Since it was a dirt road in the middle of relative nowhere in the hills south of the Snake River, that meant that the truck was sitting on a slope, halfway in the brush. There was no movement around it, but I thought I could see silhouettes of two men, sitting back in their seats, away from the windshield.

And it was facing my house.

Bob didn't slow as he passed the truck, momentarily blinding them in a cloud of dust, but that was decent tradecraft, and I couldn't fault him for it. I wanted to make sure my wife and kids were okay, though I still did what I could to watch the truck as we went by. I might have seen a phone lifted to snap a photo as we passed.

Tyler Rutledge was waiting at our place in his old Bronco. Julie was up on the porch, watching the truck, and the boys were just visible in the living room window, doing the same thing.

I knew from bitter personal experience that the more I tried to get them to stay out of sight and away from the windows, the harder they'd try to get to where they could see. I still needed to try, but it was going to be an uphill battle.

"Boys, get in the back." I used the full force of Dad Voice, developed further by my time as a Marine NCO back in the day. Julie's head snapped around and she glared at Sammy and Rick while they disappeared hastily from the window. I didn't doubt that she'd already told them to go to the back room or the barn and stay there.

Tyler got out of his vehicle and joined us on the porch. Bald and bearded, he was showing a bit more gray in the shaggy spade of hair on his chin, though when I thought of how much older he was than me, just how little more became slightly depressing. We shook hands, as he spat off the side of my porch.

"Those two were hanging out near my place yesterday. I think they just now figured out who was where." He didn't take his eyes off the parked Silverado. "I thought they were casing the area for a robbery, until I came over to warn Julie, and she said somebody else you worked for had been hit, and that it was looking like you guys were being targeted." Tyler didn't know everything about what I did, but he knew enough. We were old friends, albeit not from the military or the contracting world, and he was effectively the boys' uncle, even though we weren't related.

"We are. Nobody's died yet, but things are getting a little sporty." I wasn't counting the guy that Nick had smoked. Nobody who mattered had died.

"Yeah." Tyler looked through the settling dust, and I followed his gaze. The truck hadn't moved, though they had to know they were the target of some significant scrutiny by then. "How do you want to handle this?" He folded his arms. "I was about to go down there and have a little powwow, but figured I should wait for you."

"I can go down there, if you want to stay with your family, Chris," Bob offered, squinting up at me from the base of the steps beneath the porch.

I shook my head, still watching the Silverado. "They're here for me. I wouldn't want to disappoint them." I'd already strapped on my Riptide C .45 under my shirt. I carried a Glock for work, but when I was at home, I got old fashioned. I glanced at Tyler. There was no way he was going to stay back. "You want to take your Bronco, or my Dodge?"

Tyler didn't even hesitate. I knew he had a Smith & Wesson 457 in his waistband. I wasn't a huge Smith guy, but Tyler was, and he loved that old gun. It had been his dad's. He just turned toward his Bronco, slapped the hood as he went around the front, and swung in behind the wheel.

I hauled myself into the passenger seat, looking back at Julie. She had her own pistol, a full-sized Springfield 1911, at her side, though it wouldn't be immediately obvious to the men in the Silverado. She just nodded, her phone in her other hand.

Sometimes we needed to talk. Other times we didn't. I think, deep down, in a part of her mind she never talked about, she'd been preparing for this since we'd first started dating. While the jihadis had never really made a concerted effort to attack servicemembers at home, there were psychological warfare attempts and harassment. We'd always known that it *could* escalate to this point, even if it usually didn't.

Some contingencies are so out there that they don't even deserve the time to think through them. Others are unlikely, but still need to be thought about.

Tyler gunned the engine, and I had to motion for him to slow down. "Let's not just charge 'em. I want to catch them by surprise, if we can. Make it look like we're just going back out to the store, or over to your house. Like we're going to pass them by."

"Then we stop when we get right next to them?" Tyler might not have been the greatest tactician, but he was a hunter, and he had some common sense.

"That's the plan." It might not work, but I was short on ideas, and I wasn't sure just how much the sheriff could do about a rando vehicle just sitting on the side of the road, because the locals thought it looked suspicious.

He nodded, letting off the gas just a bit, and we headed back down the road toward his place. Dust billowed from the tires, and I had my Riptide out, just in case. I was leaning back a little in my seat, trying not to expose myself in the windshield too much, even though it was probably a futile gesture. They already knew I was in the vehicle, and they probably knew we were coming for them. Try as we might to play the game, if they had two brain cells to rub together and any experience at this kind of surveillance—not to mention any knowledge of their target—then they'd know what was up.

Still, they didn't move until Tyler suddenly braked, bringing the Bronco to a quick but smooth stop right next to the

Silverado. He rolled down his window, leaning toward the Silverado, his hand down by his side, where he'd stashed his 457 in the door.

The two guys in the Silverado might have panicked. Things could have gotten ugly right then and there, but while they didn't quite panic, they didn't play it smart, either. The smart thing to do would have been to play it off, pretend they were lost or looking for a friend's house.

Instead, they suddenly gunned the engine, spinning the rear tires in the gravel and racing away, the tinted windows still all the way up. I couldn't see much more than vague shapes on the other side of the darkened glass, but they were watching us as they pulled away, as fast as possible.

Tyler cursed, throwing the Bronco into a three-point turn to go after them. "I'm not letting those sons of bitches get away."

In a lot of places, getting into a high-speed pursuit with potential bad guys as a private citizen would be a bad idea. The law tends to frown on it. In rural central Idaho, though, especially where we had a relatively close relationship with the sheriff—he was Tyler's cousin, actually—sometimes it could work.

I already had my phone out, calling 911. I *could* call Sheriff Rutledge directly, but it might go better to go through dispatch, especially if there was another deputy closer.

Besides, while I might not fully explain it to Tyler, who was probably wondering why I wasn't just calling his cousin, we were in a position where we had to step very carefully. If they couldn't get us one way, our adversaries would come at us from a different direction, and we'd already been targeted by lawfare as it was.

"Nine-One-One, what is your emergency?" I thought I recognized the dispatcher's voice, but this wasn't the time.

"There's a white Chevy Silverado that appears to have been casing my house." I rattled off my address and the plate number. It was an Oregon plate. "We came out to see if they needed help, and they ran. We're tracking them south on our road."

"Okay." I was still half expecting the dispatcher to warn us to let them go and not follow, but she didn't. Maybe Julie had already called. "We have a deputy in the area. Please stay on the line and keep me informed what the vehicle is doing, and I will pass it along to the deputy."

That was somewhat surprising, but then, like I said, we'd deliberately cultivated a relationship with the sheriff's department in our neck of the woods.

So, as we twisted and turned our way down the dirt road, following the dust cloud ahead of us as the Silverado tried to get away, turning north, over the ridge and toward Highway 26.

"He should have tried this in town." Tyler had cooled off a little and was being a bit more clinical as he closed some of the distance on the truck, though he was smart enough to stay back just a little. We were out in the fields and the hills, but that didn't mean we necessarily wanted to get into a running gunfight. "Ain't nowhere to hide out here. Not for a vehicle."

I shook my head. "Too much urban work over the last few years." Not that I was complaining about the bad guys being incompetent. Made it easier for us. "Old skillsets have atrophied."

"Should be common sense." Tyler might not have been military, but he was a hunter. He understood cover and concealment. "Don't try to hide out in the open in a place where everybody knows you don't belong. Works with deer and elk, works with people."

We were over the ridge and out into the fields, heading toward the highway as fast as the driver could get that Silverado to go without losing control. If you haven't been driving on dirt and gravel roads in a while, it can get tricky, keeping the back end of a pickup from breaking loose and sending you into a spin. While the dust made it hard to see, I was still pretty sure I spotted at least one fishtail as we sped toward the highway.

My phone buzzed. I pulled it away from my ear, where I'd been giving the dispatcher a running commentary so she could walk the deputies in. When I glanced at the screen, it was a call from Deputy Andy Beck, a man I'd helped out with some training off and on over the years since Julie and I had moved out there. Putting the phone to my ear I quickly told the dispatcher, "Hey, Deputy Beck's calling me."

"Okay, sir, I'll let you talk to him. He probably wants to cut out the middleman." She hung up, and I quickly answered Beck's call. "Talk to me, Andy." I wasn't on the force, so I could be somewhat more informal.

"Is that you in the big cloud of dust coming down off the hill?" Andy didn't much care about formalities, especially after what I'd taught him. I'd been frankly appalled at the level of training some of the deputies displayed.

"That's us." I held on as Tyler hit a bump. Some of that was unavoidable on those roads, especially after the rains we'd had that month.

"Okay. I've got three more deputies down here on the highway." They were taking this seriously. I just hoped that it wasn't going to turn out to be a wild goose chase just because the bad guys had good lawyers. "We're keeping the lights off until they get here. If you can close off the road behind them, do it, but Chris? Put your weapons away, keep your hands where we can see them, and leave this to us. You're going to be downrange, and not all of my guys know you."

"Roger." I'd somewhat expected that, as soon as I'd cooled off a little from my initial, rage-monster reaction to these bastards stalking my family. "We'll stay out of your way."

But I am going to get the intel I need from these sons of bitches.

The road curved toward the highway, and while there were two rows of low junipers on the left side, there wasn't a whole lot of concealment for the sheriff's department vehicles on the side of the highway itself. That wasn't as big a problem as it might have been, though, since there was enough of a ditch on either side of the road that these guys weren't going to be able to make a fast getaway across the fields if they tried it, and we were right on their tailgate at that point.

The red and blues lit up, and the Silverado suddenly braked, hard, skidding on the dust and gravel. Tyler was right behind them, and by the time they came to a complete stop, we were so close that they couldn't back up. They were boxed in.

Deputies in dark blue uniforms and plate carriers leveled shotguns and carbines at the Silverado. "Get out of the vehicle with your hands up! You are under arrest!"

A part of me wondered what the paperwork for that was going to look like. We might know what they were up to, but proving it, even for the sake of booking them, was going to be difficult.

They played it smarter this time, stopping and getting out of the truck with their hands held out to their sides. One was blond and beefy, looking like he'd gone to seed a little, while the other was lean and muscular, darker and black-haired. Neither one was visibly armed, though from the way the smaller guy's shirt was partially untucked, I suspected that they'd hastily disarmed in the truck as soon as they'd been stopped.

"What's the deal?" The smaller guy sounded confused and a little angry. "We were just driving, and these assholes started following us."

"That's not what they told us when they called 911 about somebody casing their houses." Andy stepped out, barrel-chested and straw blond. "Turn around and put your hands on the hood. We'll sort this out at the station."

They did as instructed, playing it smart. Mostly smart, anyway. The little guy turned and looked at us over the hood as he did so, and there was pure venom in his eyes.

I met his gaze coolly, standing next to Tyler's Bronco, my Riptide within easy reach but out of sight, just in case.

Keep mean-mugging, jackass. You'd have to be one hell of an idiot to push this now.

37

Somehow, though, my own glare felt a little hollow. We'd intercepted these two, but how much information had they already passed?

We needed to get home and make some preparations.

CHAPTER
5

Julie had never gone for my half-joking suggestions that we should mount ballistic glass in the windows and back them up with steel shutters. She had pointed out—correctly, I might add—that we had a regular frame house, not a log blockhouse, and so hardening the windows wouldn't really help that much. Bullets would still go through the walls.

Of course, she'd been even more aesthetically against the idea, which I couldn't blame her for. The house was an old farmhouse, and making it look like a mutant cross between that and a hardened apartment building in the Baghdad embassy was probably not what any wife would want to live in.

It still left us trying to figure out just how to make it a lot harder to get into the house and wreak havoc.

While they might not be ballistic, the windows were still pretty solid, double-paned and heavy. The doors were equally heavy-duty, though that was more for the sake of keeping the cool in during the summer and the heat in during the winter.

I knew enough about breaching not to trust any of them to keep a determined hit team out. If they wanted in, they were going to find a way in.

The trick was in making it far too costly.

Tyler, Bob, and I had already added a couple extra lights and motion sensors out front. While it meant Julie and I might not get a whole lot of sleep—there were plenty of coyotes around that might set off the motion sensors—we'd get plenty of warning if somebody was snooping around. Of course, we could still get some warning from Rex, our big German Shepherd, but he was getting old and was a little hit or miss on whether or not he'd hear anything while he was snoring.

"There's got to be something more." While he was new, and he didn't live here, Bob seemed to be taking this almost personally. With his hands on his hips, he looked around the yard.

"Short of digging fighting positions and putting in machinegun nests and concertina wire, I'm afraid there's not much." I looked around, double-checking the lights and where we'd put the motion sensors. We'd needed to put them back from the road at least a bit, lest one of the neighbors set them off driving by—including Tyler, on his way home—and then we wouldn't get *any* sleep. In which case, I might welcome a home invasion with open arms. *At least get it over with.*

Bob, for his part, tilted his head a little as he looked over the yard. "Have you *got* concertina wire?"

"No." I couldn't help but chuckle a little. "My wife would kill me, anyway." I shook my head. "I don't have any 240s to stick in machinegun pits, either. Nope, I'm afraid this is about as good as it's going to get." I started back up toward the house. "You staying here tonight? We've got a guest room."

I have to admit that I sort of hated myself for asking, because I knew—and I was pretty sure Bob knew—that I wasn't just being hospitable. While it *would* be the hospitable thing to do, to put up a teammate who'd come out to cover our security, so that he didn't have to pay for his hotel room, I was pretty sure PGS was already paying for such a room. No, this was as much about having another set of eyes and ears—and another gun—in the house if those guys got out and came looking for us.

I didn't doubt they'd be out shortly. Whoever was doing this, they were prepared, and that meant that they'd have legal representation on call, just like we would. While Phil and I hadn't gotten deep enough into the network's operations to hear about that part, even the mob had good lawyers.

We hadn't had a smoking gun, and I knew that Andy was well aware of it. There was suspicion, there was probable cause, and the fact that they'd lied to the deputies when they'd been stopped added to that, but the justification to keep holding them was almighty thin. We *knew*, and I was including Andy in that "we," but we couldn't necessarily *prove* it.

Which meant they were coming.

If he knew that I was mainly looking for a Plus One, he either didn't object or just didn't care. "Sure. I hadn't checked into a hotel yet, anyway." He glanced toward the house. If I'd been there, Julie might have offered already, but I knew she wouldn't. Not without me there. She was a stickler about what was appropriate, even if she'd been armed to the teeth—which she was—and ready and willing to feed him his guts if he tried anything with her or the boys. Which she also was.

Tyler stopped in the driveway. "Well, I'd better get home." He stuck out a hand and I shook it. "You guys stay safe, all right?"

"You, too." I was getting a nasty feeling that Tyler might have put a bullseye on his own back that afternoon. If they'd noticed who that Bronco belonged to, Tyler and his family might have just become targets.

In some stories, the hero was supposed to start to get all angsty and worried about that. It just pissed me off, and it made me all the more determined to find these bastards and give them a dirt nap.

I watched Tyler climb into his Bronco and head up the road, while Bob waited, apparently uncomfortable with the idea of going up to the house and making himself at home while I was still outside. Decent of him.

"Come on. Let's get some sleep while we can." I didn't know if they were coming that night, but it was never a good idea to assume that the enemy *wouldn't* be coming.

***

I wasn't sure what jerked me awake. Julie was still sound asleep beside me, breathing softly. I listened for Rex's bark, but he was quiet.

No, he was growling, softly. He sensed something. Not enough to raise the alarm, but he was awake, and he didn't like what was out there.

Careful not to rouse Julie, I swung out of bed, pulling on my jeans and shoving my feet in my boots before scooping my Riptide C and my light off the nightstand. It might be nothing—Rex had growled at shadows before—but I didn't feel like taking the chance.

Bob was already up when I came out into the living room. "Quiet, Rex. We've got it." I spoke as much to make sure Bob didn't think I was a threat as he watched the yard from beside the living room window as to shut my dog up.

I realized that Rex might have been growling at Bob. "What's up?" If it turned out that the new guy just couldn't sleep, and had set my dog off, then I was about to get grumpy.

"Something going on down the road." He had his carbine in his hands, and I realized he was looking up the road toward Tyler's place.

"Shit." I turned back toward my room, where I had my rifle and my gear staged. *So, that's the play.* They were going to go after Tyler first. Maybe to take him and his family hostage to draw me out.

I wasn't as worried about making noise, mainly because I was going to need Julie to be up and ready to provide covering fire if things went sideways. I pushed through the door, grabbed my plate carrier—yes, it was the same one I used at work, because I'd started getting and carrying much of my own gear while I'd still been contracting overseas for the US government—and flipped it over my head. I had my placard attached to the front, with mags, radio, blowout kit, and all the other little tools and bits of gear that go in a chest rig. It was heavy and not exactly silent as I put it on, though I'd taken steps to keep the worst of the rattles down.

Julie was already awake, though, and her own light came on as I settled the plate carrier on my shoulders. "Are they here?" She was reaching for her Springfield as she spoke, already swinging her legs out of the bed, ready to move to stand in front of the boys' room, mama bear already awake and looking for something to maul.

"Not yet, but something might be going down over at Tyler's place." I was thinking through the possibilities and contingencies as my sleep-fogged brain started to clear, the adrenaline pushing the cobwebs aside. "It might be a diversion. Get the boys locked down and hold the fort. If they're just trying to get Bob and me out of the house, then we'll be coming back in hot."

She just nodded. There was no panic, no hysterics. She might never have had the training or the experience that I had, but my wife had a head on her shoulders, and when her family was threatened, she got cold. She headed for the boys' room, her pistol in her hand, and the small go bag that I'd put together for her over her shoulder.

For my part, I scooped up my own Frankengun carbine and pulled my helmet on, PVS-14s mounted. I hadn't been able to afford—actually more like I hadn't been able to *justify*—the twin-tube PS-31s, as much as I might have wanted them. I'd done multiple combat deployments with 14s, though, so I figured they would work fine.

Then I moved out to join Bob, who ducked away from the window to gear up. That took seconds, and then we were moving out.

We didn't take the front door, since that was bathed in light from the porch lights and the additional floods we'd installed. There was a single gap out behind the garage, and that was only there because I'd figured we might need some cover and concealment if we were going to do exactly what we were doing right then. Always have a plan for a sortie, even in defensive works.

It meant that there might be an opening for the bad guys to exploit, if they were thorough enough in their reconnaissance, but sometimes you've got to take the chance. I'd never been a believer in turtling.

Besides, I had some contingencies wired up to that door, along with early warning setups in the weeds. I knew where they were, but an attacker wouldn't.

Momentarily disabling the alarm on the door, we slipped out. Julie could turn the alarm back on, and she probably would. Then, moving around and stepping over the tripwires I'd set up, we slipped into the brush and headed up the hill behind the house.

We moved quickly, without taking too much effort at staying silent. Getting out and up onto the hillside, I could hear more of what was going on down by Tyler's house, and it didn't sound good. There was some yelling and the occasional gunshot. Tyler and Marie were holding their own from the sounds of it, but somebody was putting up a hell of a disturbance out there.

That made me hesitate, slightly. If this really was a diversion, then whoever was down there at the Rutledges' was just trying to draw us out, and as soon as we engaged, Julie was going to be fighting for her life. At the same time, I couldn't just hunker down and let Tyler fend for himself. He was a neighbor and an old friend, and to the boys, he was essentially family.

I held up on the military crest of the next finger. Bob was following my lead, so he just stopped and took a knee in the sagebrush as I carefully scanned the road and the hillside below us.

There. The vehicle was blacked out, probably shut off, but I could see four men in the brush next to it. And they were facing my house, not Tyler's.

So, the attack on the Rutledges *was* a diversion. It was intended to draw me out and get me out of position for their main attack.

Pallas Group Solutions guys were their targets, not their neighbors.

Signaling to Bob, I pointed out the hit squad next to the Jeep. He peered at them—Bob was running nicer NVGs than I was, so he had binocular tubes—and signaled that he understood, then moved up closer to where we could whisper without being overheard.

"You think those guys are the main effort?"

"Pretty sure." I looked up toward the north, but the crest of the finger was in the way. Hustling a little bit higher, I peered over the crest toward my neighbor's house.

The lights were on out front, which made things a little difficult with my NVGs. The PVS-14s don't like artificial light that much, and there's some bloom, though I was far enough away that I wasn't getting whited out. I could still see enough to spot the unfamiliar truck out front, and the figure gesturing and waving a weapon from behind it.

So, it looked like there was one down there, and four closing in on my place. That decided things. Tyler could deal with one armed shithead. I had these four who were gunning for me, my wife, and my kids to worry about.

Besides, dealing with them might well take the heat off Tyler.

I pointed down the hill, at where the four of them were starting to move, stepping away from the Jeep and spreading out into a wide V as they approached the side of my place.

We had to move fast, since they were going to be directly between us and the house in another couple of minutes. That would put Julie and the boys downrange from our own rifles. So, while we maintained our spacing, instead of bounding like we should have under better circumstances, Bob and I started moving down the hill, keeping to a half crouch to stay low—I was sure those guys had night vision, too—while moving to close in and get into an advantageous position as quickly as possible.

I had no intention of challenging these punks. They were approaching my property under cover of darkness, armed and geared up for war. They were going to get all the war they could stomach, and then some.

We hustled down the slope toward a small shelf that overlooked the greenhouse. That would give us some microterrain cover and put us within twenty-five yards of the hitters as they approached the house. They had just crossed the road, staying back from the glow of the lights out front, and were starting to push into the sagebrush and up the hill, making for the same gap that Bob and I had used to push out.

I got down first, Bob following suit a couple yards to my left. I couldn't see him through the brush, but while we hadn't talked all that specifically about this before we'd turned in, we'd gone over the possibilities enough that he'd made it clear he was going to follow my lead.

Settling in quickly behind the rifle, I canted it to bring my offset red dot to bear. I'd never gotten an IR laser for that weapon. Night vision goggles were getting far too common. I'd come to prefer passive aiming on NVGs. Besides, lasers are *expensive*.

The brush made for some difficulty, as I suddenly only had a narrow window through which I could engage. For a second, I felt the fear in my chest that I'd miscalculated, and was looking at the ground behind them, and was out of position to engage before they got to the house, but a moment later, the silhouette of the first man on our leg of the "V" came into sight between the two short bushes.

Letting my breath out, the dot went still, and my trigger broke just as the man's silhouette came across that little spot of bright green in my PVS-14s. The rifle bucked backward in my shoulder, the suppressor spitting with a hissing *crack*, echoed a split second later by Bob's similarly suppressed weapon. The man jerked, stumbled, and fell, dropping out of my sight picture as he rolled down the slope.

I shifted my hips, moving my point of aim back toward the next man, even as Bob just started to rake the hillside with fire. Through my narrow window in the brush, I could see figures diving for the dirt, and I missed a shot before I heaved myself up onto a knee, dropping my muzzle as I leaned into the gun, looking for targets.

Two of them were still moving, though they were trying to get low to the ground and get out of the line of fire. Their mistake lay in the fact that they didn't know where the fire was coming from, and seemed to assume that it was coming from the house. One was shooting wildly toward the lights, making me eternally grateful that the boys' room was at the back.

Suppressors can be worth their weight in gold sometimes, especially at night.

Bracing my weapon, I tracked in on the far figure and dumped about ten rounds at him. It was hard to see hits in the dark, even on NVGs, but he stiffened and dropped.

When I scanned the hillside next, I couldn't see the fourth man, but I could hear him. At least one dude down there was still alive but in a whole hell of a lot of pain.

I had zero sympathy, but I was somewhat glad that we hadn't killed all of them. There was one we could interrogate.

Rising to my feet after carefully scanning the ground around us, I started down the hill toward the bodies, my rifle held ready to engage if one of them was playing possum.

I had a rage building in me that I knew was dangerous, but as I moved down toward the four men who'd come to kill me and my wife and kids, I hardly cared.

CHAPTER
6

If the first man was playing possum, he was doing a hell of a job of it. He lay crumpled up against a bush about ten yards downhill from where I'd hit him, his head down and almost completely tucked under his body. It looked uncomfortable as hell, and the only reason his rifle was anywhere near him was because the sling was wrapped around his neck.

The one still making noise was down in the draw on the other side of the finger, with a fair bit of terrain between him and the house. His groans were getting worse, and there was a decided liquid rattle to them. He'd probably been lung-shot, and he wasn't going to have a good time.

Turning the stricken man in front of me over wasn't an easy task. I didn't want to get too close to him, in case he really *was* that dedicated to playing possum, so I'd need to turn him over with my boot, but the way he was lying against that sagebrush, there was no easy way to do that.

Finally, crouching down next to him, I got my still-warm suppressor under his helmet and prodded his eye.

Nothing. He didn't flinch, didn't move at all. He was dead.

Bob had already moved on toward the next one, and when I looked up at him, he gave me a thumbs down. Same there. I started moving down toward the man who was gurgling in the draw.

It took a minute to find him in the dark, even with the moon up in the east and on NVGs. He'd fallen down between two clumps of sagebrush, and was curled halfway into the fetal position, moaning, half out of his head with pain.

I looked around once more, but there was no sign of any others, aside from the one dude who'd been taunting the Rutledges, so I turned on my white light. I didn't flip my NVGs up, but just closed that eye to keep from getting blinded. I wanted to see this son of a bitch.

He'd been lung-shot, all right. There was pinkish froth around his mouth, and blood was dribbling down his chin and his neck to soak his black combat shirt under his plate carrier. That plate hadn't saved him. Either Bob or I had shot him through the armpit. I could see the puckered hole just above his plate carrier's cummerbund, and that side was soaked with blood, as well.

"You've got a choice." My voice was a harsh rasp, from a combination of hard movement to contact and the rage that was threatening to choke me. "You tell me every fucking detail about who sent you here and why, and I'll call 911 for you. Otherwise, I'm going to stand here and watch, and tell the sheriff and the paramedics that I was just too late."

On a deep and quiet level that I tried not to pay too much attention to, the fact that I was entirely sincere in that threat kinda scared me.

He looked up at me, and I could see the panic in his eyes. There are a lot of different kinds who get into the profession, and not all of them are the warriors they think they are. I've seen guys who worried constantly before their first firefight turn into tigers. I've seen the guys who talked the most shit before the bullets started flying turn into quivering bowls of jelly once the first shot cracked off. Knowing some of the sort who turned to this particular kind of work, I expected that this dude had thought he was tough as hell until that bullet had ripped through his lung.

"Please…" The rattle was getting worse. He didn't have long. He might not have until the ambulance got there. While I could treat him, and probably save his life, I wasn't going to lift a finger until he talked.

"I've got chest seals and fourteen-gauge needles. The price is information."

He was having increasing trouble breathing. I realized I was probably going to have to treat him just to make sure he didn't strangle to death from a tension pneumothorax before he could talk.

Bob loomed out of the brush. "Last one's dead. This is the only one left." He looked down at the dying man. "Might want to stabilize him first."

While I felt a flash of anger at his interference, a quiet voice in the back of my head told me I should probably be grateful to him. I still grumbled. "Cover him. If he *twitches* wrong, shoot him again."

Slinging my rifle to my back and cinching the sling down tight, I bent down, taking the wounded man's weapons and flinging them up the slope. His knife, too. I got some blood on my hands, searching him for any holdouts, but by the time I was satisfied, his labored breathing was getting worse. I was starting to see the distended tendons on the side of his neck, too, as his pleural cavity filled with air and blood.

It took another minute to get his plate carrier off, his combat shirt cut open, and a chest seal over the entry wound. I searched for a few more seconds for an exit wound, before finding it just beneath his shoulder blade. I confess I wasn't gentle as I moved him around and checked him, and if he'd been able to breathe a little more easily, he would have screamed as I moved him around. Finally, with both holes plugged, I pulled a fourteen-gauge needle, found the right spot between his ribs, and jabbed it home, letting some of the built-up air out and easing the pressure in his chest, which was slowly squeezing his heart and remaining lung to death.

He sucked in a deep breath as the pressure eased, and I stepped back. "Now, talk."

It took a second for him to get his breathing under control. "It was supposed to look like a home invasion gone bad. I don't know why, and I didn't ask."

"Where'd the contract come from?"

"An encrypted email. I don't know who's on the other end of it, either. Whoever it is, they pay really well, though." Without the building pressure in his chest, he was starting to get back on something of an even keel, and the panic was receding. That concerned me. From what Phil and I had seen, there hadn't been a lot of backstopping on the hitman network, but this guy was acting like he wasn't that worried, considering he was admitting to planning to murder my family in the middle of the night.

"What's the email?"

He hesitated. I was tempted to rattle off the contact email we'd used to get into the network a few months before, but I couldn't be sure he wouldn't just agree that that was it, letting us go down a rabbit hole that led nowhere.

Finally, he recited the same, familiar email address, through a service based in Luxembourg, that we'd used before. It interested me that they were still using the same email, but that might have been simply because there was no way I knew of to trace it to them. It wasn't like the service provider was going to cough up names. Privacy was the heart of their business model.

When he didn't elaborate beyond that, I shone my light a little more directly into his eyes. "Going to need more than that."

For as much pain as he was in, the shock already starting to take hold—and that could kill him as surely as the tension pneumo would have—he was still hesitant, his brain starting to catch up. He knew what I was demanding. It would amount to a full confession, and while a lawyer might be able to make the case that it was inadmissible—having been coerced in return for medical care—he had to know enough about our outfit to know that Pallas Group Solutions wouldn't care. Even if we were going to try to build a criminal case to hand over to the cops, we'd just use this as a first opening.

Still, he must have decided that it was better than being left to die on the hillside while waiting for the sheriff's deputies. He started talking.

CHAPTER
7

"Well, now." Goblin had called us in, and while I was still a little nervous at being away from my family that close to a hit that had targeted us for a killing, we now had much more extensive security on our homes. Much of it was local, friends with some experience and willingness to step up and keep an eye on things, even when we weren't there. Goblin had also made some other arrangements. Nothing like having us actually defending our own homes, and I suspected that a lot of the guys he was bringing in—probably on less pay than we were getting—didn't have quite our training or experience levels. It was better than nothing, though, and we couldn't exactly just stay home and fort up. Not against a threat like this.

That had been a tense conversation with my wife. Julie was one of the most level-headed women I'd ever known, but even she got upset that I was leaving so soon after the attempt on our lives. Even my explanation that I needed to go hunt these fuckers down hadn't gone over that well. It was a remarkably civil argument, all things considered, especially when I heard some of the other stories in the team room about the same discussion, but she was *not* happy.

I couldn't say I was, either, but I didn't see any other option. And that wasn't because Goblin was saying I *had* to go back to work. Going on the offensive, taking the fight to these bastards…that was the only way forward that I could see.

Otherwise, we'd be looking over our shoulders and hunkering down for the rest of our lives.

Julie understood that. I knew that she did. It was just going to take her a little time to work it through. Unfortunately, we didn't have that much time, so I had to leave while she was still upset.

Sammy, as young as he was, thought it was cool. There'd been a *real* firefight, right outside *our house!* Fortunately, he hadn't seen any of the bodies, and Julie wouldn't let him go over to the hill where the bloodstains were still soaking into the dirt.

"What have we got?" KG had a dip in, and sounded about as level-headed and calm as he ever did. I didn't know much about KG's family life, but I didn't doubt he'd been targeted, too. From what I'd heard, the bad guys had gone for a pretty clean sweep on the A and B teams. They'd failed, across the board, but that was mainly because we'd had some advance warning thanks to Matt Patric, and, well, we're not quite the ordinary guys that our adversaries thought we might be.

We were all professional paranoiacs, after all.

"Well, Chris's lone survivor sang like a canary, so we've got a lot more intel than we did a couple days ago." Goblin had a dip in, too, though it didn't take away the bags under his eyes. The man was tired, and it showed. Not that any of the rest of us had gotten much rest lately, either. "We did turn it all over to Sheriff Rutledge, and while he says he can't use it, given the way it was collected, he also doesn't figure he needs to, since he's got everything he needs to charge the man with attempted murder, aggravated assault, and about half a dozen other things. *With* a fair bit of certainty that he can make it stick and send him away for a *long* time."

He spat some dip juice into a paper cup. We were in the company office in Dallas, so I would have expected him to have a regular spitter, but when I thought about it, I'd never seen Goblin use anything but a plastic bottle or a paper cup as a dip spitter.

"Of the hitters who went after our teams, we got about ten. Four more were arrested. The rest were either warned off or chased off and their E&E plan was apparently successful. This was, apparently, a fairly major operation, with four to five men assigned to each target. We've done enough damage that *somebody* wants us off the board, badly.

"Here's where it gets interesting. Of the four arrested, only two were Americans. One was a Brit, and the other was an Aussie. These guys are going pretty far afield for their operators, though GWOT veterans seems to still be a common thread. So far. We've still got a pretty small sample size."

I figured that included my identification of Skyler Pertman in Indianapolis. I'd known Skyler on contract, and it hadn't surprised me as much as I might have hoped to find him working for a criminal syndicate, though one far more underground and secret than the cartels.

"The guy that Chris grilled spilled a bit more than just that part, though. He gave us a little more of an overall picture." He spat into his cup again. "While the clients have been hidden from the boots-on-the-ground shooters, they do know that they're generally cleaning up messes from high-level business magnates and politicians. Most of these guys are the sort who don't really care, as long as the check clears, so they'll do whatever as long as the pay's good." He spat into his cup again. "I get it. We all cash our paychecks, too. I do hope that we've cultivated a bit more of a sense of professional ethics in this outfit, though."

There was a bit of shifting of weight. I thought that more than a few of us were wondering just how far we were all willing to go, all things considered.

"As we were already aware, due to their activities in Nashville, St. Louis, and Indianapolis, some of their missions are also intended to apply pressure through kidnapping, assassination, and sabotage. Maybe some good old domestic terrorism to go along with it. Once again, we're dealing with functional sociopaths who have decided that the pay is everything." He brought up a photo of Wise, before he'd been pulped by a fast-moving vehicle. "Now." He sent another squirt of dip spit into his paper cup. "We don't have a smoking gun that these guys were responsible for taking Wise out. We don't have a roster, and the Seattle cops have still not publicly identified the man that Chris smoked. *However.* There are patterns to be observed, and so far, the pattern is matching.

"We did some digging on Wise. Turns out he was working on a story about a small town in Southern California that's essentially the property of the Tijuana Cartel and is being used as a major human trafficking hub. We don't know which one, because apparently his story was encrypted, and the password apparently went with him to the grave. We've contacted the small internet newspaper he worked for. Either they don't have the story, or they just didn't want to tell us.

"There is a possible connection that we can follow up on, however. Wise, it turns out, started his latest project after investigating a story about a massacre near Shelter Valley, California. About twenty-seven people were found dead near an extensive campsite in the hills just outside the town. Actually, it's technically an 'unincorporated community,' not a town, but you get the idea. Given some of the recent reports of cartels essentially taking over desert towns in Southern California and using them as north-of-the-border bases of operation, this bears some looking into."

"Cartels hiring American hitters?" Custus sounded skeptical. "Why not use MS-13? Or their own *sicarios*?"

"Couple of possibilities." Goblin had clearly been expecting the question. "There are American SOF dudes who have gone to the dark side—and I'm not talking about Officer Candidate School. There are documented cases of contractors and just former SOF guys going to work for the cartels. Not a lot, but enough.

"The other possibility is that there's someone else who stands to lose a great deal if the Shelter Valley operation is exposed, and *they* hired the network."

That drew nods. There was no one in that room who thought that was particularly outlandish.

The fact is, our military and contract service had already shown us in no uncertain terms that most people can't be trusted with power—or money, but those boil down to the same thing, at a certain level—and that there are always corrupt people with money and influence who will stoop to any depth to get what they want. Sometimes it's ideological. Sometimes it's just plain, old, ordinary greed. The end result is the same.

"So, what's the plan?" It was getting late in the day, but I had a cup of coffee in my hand, because I'd crossed two time zones in a week, and hadn't gotten a hell of a lot of sleep along the way.

"Well, that brings us around to our clients." Goblin hesitated, as if thinking over just how much to tell us. That was concerning all on its own. Goblin usually pushed all the info down the chain he possibly could. "There's still non-disclosure stuff up my ass, and that's leaving aside the fact that they're not telling us much, but the picture is starting to become clearer. The initial pitch we got was that they represent a major risk assessment and mitigation firm, and that they're looking for specific information about specific places and people in the interests of their primary mission. That's the official story, and while it does generally check out—we researched the company extensively before taking the contract—I also suspect that there's someone else working through the company for another agenda. I think I know who it is, and what that agenda is, as well, but right at the moment, I'm not at liberty to speculate too much.

"At any rate, we've got another set of targets. More strict surveillance. Hopefully we don't get bitched out again if something happens this time, since I made it abundantly clear what 'strict surveillance' means. If they want us to be prepared to intervene, they'd damned well better let us know ahead of time." That drew a couple of shakes of heads. Everyone had heard about the complaints about the Seattle job.

"I'm not going to hand those assignments out to the A or B teams." He folded his arms as the room got still. None of us wanted to be shut out. "The C Team will take over, but only because we've got bigger fish to fry. Don't worry. I've made sure that we're getting paid enough to go around. Everybody's going to get to pay their bills this month."

He looked around the room. There had to be a reason he'd only brought in the A Team for this brief. "The B Team is going to California, to follow up on this Shelter Valley massacre, and see what Wise was really interested in. If it was worth killing him, it might be worth ripping the mask off and getting some more bad guys dead." Goblin was *pissed*. He was usually a bit more subtle than that, even with us.

On some level, that worried me. I'd been around enough to know that, for one thing, Goblin didn't lose his temper easily. Even when we'd been worn out, getting jerked around by the client in a warzone, he'd always kept his cool.

The other matter was that even a cold anger can cloud thinking and make for bad decisions. I didn't necessarily think this was a bad decision. Somehow, it looked very much like that massacre was linked to our current contract. Still, emotion is a bad guide to action, and we all had to be careful about it, especially when we carried guns for a living.

"Now, we don't have a contract down there, even though there are a few logistics ride-alongs to be had, but we won't be able to bid and pick one of them up in time. Fortunately, this is CONUS, so we don't really need a reason to be anywhere. California's a non-permissive environment for a lot of our hardware, so they'll have to maintain a low profile, but we're all pretty good at that."

He pulled up a file on the laptop set up on the desk and projected it on the wall behind him. The image that came up was of a relatively bland-looking man with a slightly receding hairline and a pronounced overbite above a protruding Adam's apple. He stared out of the screen with a bored, heavy-lidded expression.

Goblin turned to us, his face set. "Now, I told a few of you that I had my suspicions about who was running the covert network of hitters that Chris and Phil infiltrated. It was somewhat slim, based on a bit of a linguistic tic that I recognized in the encrypted emails that Chris got, but I've seen a couple more indicators since that solidify the connection, at least to me. Most of it is circumstantial only; just little things that add up to me."

He pointed to the image on the wall. "This man was introduced to us as a 'consultant' named Caleb Slobodian. I'm sure it's not his real name, nor is it likely that he's still using it now. He is politically and financially connected all over the world and has extensive sources of information inside dozens of governments and transnational corporations."

His eyes were hard flecks of granite. "The fact that this guy was brought in as a 'consultant' should have been an indicator that something wasn't copacetic to begin with. The few times I had to deal with him, while he was polite and professional at all times, I couldn't shake a bad feeling about him. Like he was probably one of the most morally flexible people I've ever seen, and you guys can agree that, given some of the people we've worked with, that's fucking saying something."

He wasn't lying. We'd all known some good people in the intelligence and special operations communities, though we'd seen more than our fair share of stupidity and arrogance, which tended to be our primary gripes with them. Some of those people, though, had been the lowest form of white collar scum, for whom "honor" and "integrity" were dirty words.

"While I have to admit that I don't have a case that would stand up in court—we all know that's relative, but I'd rather have a smoking gun before we drop the hammer—but given the attacks that have already been launched against our families, I think we've got enough to go hunting."

The image changed to a map of Belize. "Slobodian is or was a US citizen, but to the best of anyone's knowledge, he's been living as an expat in Belize. That's where we're going to start.

"Pack your bags, gentlemen."

CHAPTER
8

Belize wasn't all that far from Honduras, where we'd conducted a very kinetic evacuation from a burning chemical plant not all that long ago.

Not that the atmosphere around Placencia was anything like San Pedro Sula, half of which was ruled by the *maras*. If anything, this place was the polar opposite of that benighted city. From what we'd seen so far, the greatest threat in Placencia was alcohol poisoning.

This was the heart of expat territory in Belize. This was where reasonably well-off Americans who wanted the tropics and relatively cheap real estate tended to retire. The town was little more than one big resort, from what I'd seen so far.

It wasn't a fancy or rich place. Most of the roads were still dirt—packed sand, really—and I hadn't seen a building more than three stories tall since we'd gotten there. The houses were better kept-up than most of what I'd seen in gang-ruled Latin America, with bright paint touched up regularly—which it probably needed to be, that close to the ocean. The Caribbean might not be as harsh as, say, the North Atlantic, but there's still weather, and saltwater does a number on manmade materials.

I walked out of the Lazy Palm Suites, a single, three-story house painted what might have been an eye-searing blue anywhere else, but here it almost blended with the sky and the water. Padding out onto the sand—the hotel's back porch opened up right onto the beach—I squinted as I put my sunglasses on.

It felt weird. Disturbing, even. Not that there was some sinister undertone to the tourists, sand, sun, and water. Nothing *Twilight Zone* like that. No, it was that I was standing on a beach in the Caribbean, in cargo shorts, a t-shirt, and sandals, not all that long after someone had tried to hit my house and kill me, my wife, and my kids.

It galled me to be standing there, in a vacation spot, far from my family while they were under threat.

You ain't here to take a vacation, though. This is work. It just doesn't look like it, because you're in a peaceful place built for relaxation.

I should be used to the fact that war can take some strange shapes, but some things you just don't get used to. Even though I'd spent the better part of half my career as a paid gunslinger staying low-profile and generally avoiding trouble as much as possible—the job of a close protection specialist, even working for a government intelligence agency, is more to spot and avoid fights than get into them—but some of that hard-wired aggression that I'd learned as a Recon Marine just never goes away. It can't. When trouble becomes unavoidable, then that aggression and skill with weapons and tactics become vital.

You've just got to learn when and how to turn it on and off.

I knew guys who hadn't been able to learn that lesson. Guys who'd simply gotten bored and quit. I couldn't necessarily blame them. There had been plenty of times where I'd wondered if there wasn't some modern-day equivalent to the mercenary companies that had formed and gone to Africa back in the '80s, not a few of them with a lot of Vietnam veterans signed on. The older I got, and the more I saw the wreckage that had followed in the wake of the declaration of the end of the GWOT—which I still didn't quite accept—the more I understood those guys.

Ah, to pack a duffel bag with a couple of rifles, a submachine gun, a bunch of ammo, and some socks, and fly to Angola or somewhere. Those were the days.

Of course, I was a husband and father now, so I couldn't just cut ties and run to the nearest war. Even as I thought it, some guilt crept in, exacerbated by my current surroundings, along with the little thought that there were plenty of wars to go volunteer in, especially in Ukraine and Syria.

Syria had sure fallen off the radar as soon as Ukraine flared up again…

I shook off the brooding. I had a mission, as boring as it was. We were at war, as quiet and shadowy as that war might be.

Even as I tried to clear my thoughts and start to head for my target for the day, that word kind of popped out at me. "War." There would be those who insisted that we, at Pallas Group Solutions, couldn't be at war. War was a state thing.

I would challenge anyone to say it wasn't a war when their family and friends were targeted for death. What would *you* call it?

I turned north and started along the beach. It was still early enough that there were only a few tourists and expats sunning themselves on the sand. Not that Belize was quite the destination where we could expect the sort of crowds you'd see in, say Miami. That was a combination of blessing and curse for our mission there.

We weren't actually looking for Slobodian. Not yet. Goblin didn't have any information as to *where* in Belize he might have settled down, and the odds that he was even in the country were pretty slim. From the limited profile that Goblin and our resident team-attached intel nerd, Noah Radford, had put together, the man was a bit of a wannabe jet-setter, often flying halfway around the world on a whim. He certainly had no shortage of money.

He also was very good at information security. There was no sign of "Caleb Slobodian" anywhere. Not even Radford, with his considerable skill with computers, had been able to find any digital trace of him. We needed to locate someone who knew him, who could get us some updated information about where he was and what he was calling himself.

That could be a tall order. If Slobodian really was the sort of operator we thought he was, then he'd be *extremely* cagey, and between people who would know what we wanted to know, and people who would likely talk to us, would be a very small Venn diagram.

Goblin thought he had a thread to pull on, though, and that was who we were looking for.

Alex Bolus was an old hand in the intelligence game. His resume, when Radford looked it up, had been bland as all hell, and if you didn't know what you were looking for—or didn't have somebody who knew him, like Goblin—you'd think he had been nothing but a GS-14 desk jockey, for entirely too long, before he'd retired to Belize, to soak up the sun and the ocean air. Goblin didn't even know all the places Bolus had been, or what he'd done in most of those places, but he'd been around when Slobodian had been "consulting," and from Goblin's recollection, Bolus had been up to his neck in whatever had been involved.

And from what Goblin knew about Bolus, he figured that there was no way the older man *wouldn't* have kept an eye on our target, one way or another. He might be retired, but he was the kind who kept his ear to the ground.

At least, that was what Goblin assumed from what he knew about the man. There hadn't been any contact in years. We'd have to find him and make sure.

That was why Ken, Phil, Marcos, KG, Goblin, and I were in Placencia, all of us in different hotels and rooms, acting the best we could like tourists, operating on local cell phones. We weren't entirely defenseless, since the yacht that Goblin had somehow finagled into a floating operations platform was just off the coast, cruising along and keeping its distance from most other vessels on the Caribbean, just in case. All our gear was there, weapons included. We didn't *expect* the hunt for Slobodian to end in Belize, but we were ready if it did.

In the meantime, we had to play tourist, keep our eyes open, and see if we could find Bolus.

I'd never have thought that it would take so damned much effort to act nonchalant and casual, but it really did. I'd gotten wired pretty tight through the events of the last year or so and, knowing that someone had come after my family less than a week before, it was hard as hell to just act like I was on vacation, in a tropical resort where there really wasn't much of anything beyond sunburn to worry about. Even the water was pretty safe. There was gang activity and violent crime in Belize City, as was to be expected in this part of the world, but for the most part, the rest of the country was pretty calm, comparatively speaking. With fewer than half a million people in the entire nation, it was somewhat insulated from the *mara* wars and even some of the narco traffic from Colombia and Venezuela.

Somewhat insulated. I had no doubt that there was still cartel presence in Belize. Sometimes, the quietest places are just as useful to those monsters as the open battlefields. The only question was which cartel was in the country?

I had to force my mind away from that line of thought. I was already eyeing the other people on the beach, wondering which one was a cartel shot caller. It wasn't that it wasn't a possibility. I just had to maintain my cover, which required some outward relaxation, even if I was still watching everyone I could see.

So far, all I'd seen were retired expats and tourists. The town, built on a long peninsula that was practically an island by the time you got to Placencia itself, was basically one big resort, and as such, everything seemed laid back and relaxed. Nobody really paid much attention to anyone else, but it was a lackadaisical sort of thing, not the furtive atmosphere of carefully minding one's own business that we'd seen in countless warzones, of the acknowledged and unacknowledged variety.

Despite my best efforts, being in mission mode in a tropical paradise was still throwing me for a loop.

Reaching the Cozy Corner, I found a table, ordered breakfast—while several of the other clientele were already well into their morning drinks—and settled in for the day's surveillance.

***

Under different circumstances, it might have been a relaxing day. As it was, it was just boring.

I floated up and down the beach, checking in at most of the gathering places and watering holes throughout the day, hanging out on the beach, getting into more than a few fairly inane conversations with locals and a few thirsty middle-aged women, most of which I was able to extricate myself from without having to get too grumpy.

I was still coming up empty. It might have just been my timing, or else I wasn't covering Bolus's usual haunts. We didn't know for sure that he lived *in* Placencia in the first place, of course. Goblin was pretty sure he lived in the vicinity, but he could even be ashore, somewhere around Independence and Mango Creek. He might even be out of the country at the moment.

Without having been in contact for several years, Goblin didn't want to risk reaching out to him to start with. If he really was still talking to Slobodian, then he might spook the prey if we weren't careful. That meant that the mission at the moment was simply to find him, put him under surveillance, and build a pattern of life.

We just had to find him first, and since the man wasn't a social media butterfly, that got a little more complicated.

The sun was starting to dip toward the mainland in the west when my phone buzzed. The number wasn't in contacts, but we'd made sure to memorize the rest of the team's cell numbers so that we didn't need to have them input with names and other indicators, just in case one of us got rolled up. We were taking precautions that were probably unnecessary in

Tourist/Expat Central, Belize, but good tradecraft is good tradecraft, and getting lazy tended to lead toward disaster more often than not.

I was by myself, at a table on the deck of the Tipsy Tuna Sports Bar, so I scooped up the phone and checked it. The message was to the whole team, a jumble of phone numbers, and included a photo.

It was straightforward. *Eyes on. At the Placencia Beach Club.* The photo showed a slightly overweight, deeply tanned man with a receding hairline and his hair buzzed short—he probably shaved his head to embrace the baldness, and just hadn't touched it up for a few days—in a white shirt, blue shorts, and sandals, sitting at one of the weathered wood tables on the deck, nursing a cocktail.

I actually relaxed a little, putting the phone back down and picking up my own drink. I didn't usually indulge on a mission, but in a bar in Placencia, dressed the way I was, it would look out of place if I didn't have something, so I was nursing it.

We'd made contact. Now it was going to take a few days to establish his patterns—and determine whether or not he was compromised to a degree where we'd need to either snatch him or break off altogether—but that was okay.

I felt better knowing we had a target and weren't just wasting our time. Saying a quiet prayer that Julie and the boys would be safe while we took the fight to the sons of bitches that had tried to have us all murdered, I settled in for a long few days.

CHAPTER
9

Shelter Valley wasn't much of a town, but none of them had been expecting it to be. An unincorporated community in the middle of the Mojave Desert wasn't ever going to be an appealing destination, especially not after the couple of NTC rotations Nick had been through at Fort Irwin. He'd seen enough of the Mojave to last him a lifetime there.

The last time he'd been in that desert, he would have preferred to be in Afghanistan.

The team had debated trying to stop at either the RV park at the south end, the guest house at the north, or both, and see if they could get any intel. Josh, who apparently was originally from California, though that was a detail he tended to keep on the downlow, had opined that it would be a waste of time. He'd seen a few of these little desert communities, and he might have mentioned *The Hills Have Eyes* in his assessment.

Tim Coleman, their new team leader—Nick would have pulled for either Doug or Saul to take over the job, but in Pallas Group, the team leaders needed to be actual employees of the company, not just contractors—had weighed their options carefully, then decided to send Matt and Manny to the guesthouse while Mike and Saul went to the RV park. That meant getting a trailer, but fortunately, they'd had enough advance warning that they were able to add that to mission prep.

In the meantime, the rest of the team drove through the town, getting as much of a feel as they could from the highway before heading up to a rendezvous point in the hills around Granite Mountain.

It had been a long drive, and as the trucks circled up in a rocky draw about five hundred yards from the Cool Canyon trailhead, Nick had to stifle a groan. They'd hardly been out of the vehicles since crossing the border from Arizona. Some of that was simply caution, as most of the route before they'd hit El Centro had been along Interstate 8, which was solidly in cartel territory. There was Border Patrol and State Police presence along the freeway, but none of the contractors expected that presence to deter much. Not anymore. Especially not once they got across into California.

The other factor was that they were armed to the teeth, and most of what they were carrying was illegal in the state of California, and that was making them a little more paranoid than usual.

Stretching, Nick took in the surrounding desert as the sun started to go down behind the rocky hills. Doug, for his part, already had his rifle in his hands as he got out of the passenger seat, scanning the desert carefully. He glanced over his shoulder, past the bed, at Nick, who ducked back inside, pulling his own carbine out with some chagrin.

Doug had been a Delta operator. Even after all this time, he was still switched on, and always managed to make Nick feel like he was still playing catchup. Not that Doug ever seemed to go out of his way. He just had internalized certain things to the point that they were second nature, things that even after over twenty years, Nick still had to think about.

Dust rose to the northeast, and both men turned toward it, Nick already measuring the distance to the chest rig on the back seat, but then the radio came to life. "Thumper, Croak, this is Gameshow. Inbound to your pos, five mikes."

Nick leaned back into the truck and grabbed the handset. The radio wasn't as well installed as some of those they'd used overseas, but it was still wired up so that they could get an amp attached inside the vehicle. "Roger, Gameshow. We have eyes on you. Bring it in."

While Doug maintained security, Nick proceeded to shoulder into his chest rig and pull his ruck out. The message had been received, even though there had been no words spoken.

They were in enemy territory. They needed to act like it.

By the time the last truck had pulled up with Josh and Abaeze in the cab, Nick and Doug had changed over to tan fatigues, chest rigs, and boonies, with skullcap mounts for NVGs. Carl and Durand were almost dressed, while Nick and Doug held security.

"Boy, this brings back memories." Josh's voice seemed unnaturally loud in the twilight quiet of the desert, accompanied as it was by the slam of his truck door. All eyes turned to him, and he cringed. "Sorry." His stage whisper seemed almost as loud, and Durand shook his head as he finished shrugging into his chest rig. Chastened, Josh turned back to the truck and started pulling out weapons and gear.

It was still light, though the sun was already half set, by the time the full team was geared up and ready to go, gathered in a tight circle, on a knee, a few yards away from the trucks. The desert seemed achingly silent, even the wind having gone still.

Josh seemed to be feeling chatty, though, possibly because it had been almost a half an hour since they'd met up, and they'd seen no movement at all aside from a couple of vehicles on the highway, most of a mile away. "So, where's this Tim dude? Vern would have been out here with us. Hell, even Frank would probably have come along." He kept his voice low, remembering some of his fieldcraft, though the part of Nick that would always be Special Forces wondered just how much fieldcraft the former SEAL had ever gotten.

Some rivalries die hard, even if personal relationships were fine.

"No idea." Doug was perhaps more laid back about it than some teammates might have been, including Saul. Saul wouldn't have yelled, but he'd have been audibly disappointed in Josh for breaking the silence. "I didn't hire the man."

Josh got the message and subsided.

They waited, watching and listening, for another half an hour, as the sun went down and darkness fell. Finally, while they'd heard nothing but the distant passage of vehicles on the highway and the plaintive howls of coyotes somewhere in the hills, Doug got up, pointed to Abaeze to take point, and then pointed up over the ridge.

With a nod, his NVGs in front of his eyes, the shorter contractor got up and led the way toward the OP.

**

The whole movement was less than a mile and a half, but it still took over two hours. That was necessitated by the terrain, the loads they were carrying, and the caution that becomes absolutely necessary on a combat patrol.

None of the PGS contractors were under any illusions that this was anything but a combat patrol. Some guys would have considered this sort of a thing Stateside to be LARPing, play-acting at being cool. For some people, that was exactly what it would be.

Every man on that hillside had several CONUS kills, and knew that they were, in fact, in a warzone, even if no one of the powers that be would admit it.

It was getting on toward midnight when they finally filtered into the OP, a hollow in the hilltop overlooking Shelter Valley. Below, the community was a scattering of lights against the dark gray of the desert floor, backed by more hills, dark against the sky. A couple of headlights moved on the road, but otherwise the valley was still and quiet.

The desert didn't provide a lot of options for cover and concealment. A glance told Nick that they weren't going to be able to put the whole team up on the hilltop facing the town, not without taking a significant risk of detection once the sun came up.

Doug tapped Carl and Durand first. "You guys have been in the middle, so you get first watch." It wasn't a perfect way to figure who was the most smoked, but the guy on point was usually working the hardest, with the men in the rear having to catch up, especially if they paused to check security more often.

Carl's shoulders might have slumped a bit beneath his ruck, but Durand just nodded stoically and turned toward the peak.

Nick lowered his ruck to the rocky ground, almost put a spiny desert plant into his knee as he followed it, shifted his position, and set in to hold security while Carl and Durand got the observation post established.

It was going to be a long couple of days.

***

Things started moving before very long, though.

He'd just been shaken awake, Josh looming over him to whisper that it was time to switch out. Both positions had gone down to fifty percent security. For every man up, the other was down getting some rest. They'd stay that way for the duration of the operation, unless something popped up that would require all hands on deck.

Sitting up, he nodded groggily. Even if Josh couldn't see the signal, he could see that Nick was up, which was enough. He moved back to his own position next to his ruck.

Shaking off the cobwebs, Nick gathered up his rifle, pulled his NVGs on, and slipped his arms through his ruck straps before levering himself to his feet. Rule One in an OP: always be packed and ready to move. There was no telling when something might clack off and you'd have to run.

He'd seen some OPs where that hadn't been followed. Most of those guys had been lucky that they'd been in relatively permissive places. Some of them, however, hadn't been. There were some dudes in the ground that he'd known who'd gotten sloppy and paid the price.

75

John Taliban didn't screw around when you got sloppy.

Trudging up toward the OP, he saw that, naturally, Doug was ahead of him. If the other man wasn't such a generally good dude, Nick could see where he might start to resent the way his partner was always two steps ahead of him.

And the day I start to is the day I need to check myself. He'd seen what those sorts of resentments could do to a small team. Hell, it had happened with Frank Moretti, which was why he was no longer the B Team's manager, or team leader, or whatever PGS was officially calling their direct employees assigned to run teams.

The slope wasn't bad, even in the dark, and the PS-31 NVGs they were using provided enough clarity and depth perception that he didn't stumble more than once or twice, usually because he'd misjudged where a rock was.

When they got to the OP, both of them moved in to join Carl and Durand. The two contractors had done a pretty good job of building up their cover, stacking rocks and doing some strategic digging in so that they could get good and low while still having line of sight on the town and the highway. They'd even set up a good spot for rucks to rest.

Stowing his ruck, Nick moved to join Carl and Doug at the parapet of rocks and brush they'd built. He'd seen some of the objective area from the little saddle where the rest of the team was set in, but there was a much better view from up here.

And there was more to see than he would have expected in Shelter Valley.

While it hadn't been easily visible from the highway, from up on the hill, they could see a sprawling compound built in the shelter of two shoulders of the hills, behind most of the community as seen from the highway. It would be invisible to anyone on the ground during the day, but during the night, it was lit up with floodlights.

Enclosed in cyclone fencing, the place was divided up between tents, a couple of trailers, and what looked like three large Quonset huts. No, not Quonset huts, Nick realized, as he looked closer. Those were greenhouses.

He'd heard about cartel grow operations in California. The state had legalized marijuana several years before, but it hadn't had the desired effect of putting the cartels out of business. Instead, they'd simply adjusted, and their illegal weed, still untaxed, was less expensive than the legal stuff, in many places.

"Those three vehicles by the east gate just came in about fifteen minutes ago." Carl was giving Doug the data dump. "At least five armed men, and what looks like two bigwigs got out and went inside the north trailer, with one of the two dudes who came out to meet them." The pair of binoculars balanced on a rock looked about big enough to study Mars, but that was what you wanted on surveillance, particularly at any healthy range. Same with the equally enormous telephoto lens on the digital camera next to the binos.

This OP was a little close, but still far enough out that they shouldn't be easily detected, unless the cartel had security patrols out on the hills.

"Any patrols?" Doug asked. He'd been thinking the same thing.

"Maybe. There was a truck that rolled out about an hour and a half ago, kinda moseyed around the town, then came back in. Sure looked like a security patrol to me." Carl wasn't finished, though. He pointed. "See those two big tents?"

"The ones that look like GP Larges?" The General Purpose, Large, Tent was a military standard that they'd all had some experience with over the years. Usually with far too many men inside of one.

"Those." Carl shifted his pointing finger slightly. "If you look at the end, you can see that they're being heavily guarded. At least four shooters each, and those are the ones we can see."

Doug just looked for a long few moments. "There's something in there they don't want anyone getting into."

Carl nodded. "Or there's something or someone inside they don't want getting out."

Nick's eyes narrowed as he settled in next to Doug and found the tents in his NVGs. Sure enough, there were knots of men on the ends, near the doors. They were too far away for him to see much of anything else through his PS-31s, but they were definitely there.

"Well, we'll keep an eye on things. You guys head back down and get some rest." Doug gripped Carl's shoulder, and with an answering squeeze, Carl moved down to the rucks, hefted his, and followed Durand down to the hide.

Doug and Nick set up quickly, Doug taking the first shift on the OP, while Nick settled in to cover rear security.

***

They'd just switched out when things started to get interesting.

Doug had given Nick the quick rundown. There had been a couple more vans coming in during the last hour, with some of the passengers going into the tents, and a couple more into the trailer where Carl and Durand had seen the apparent bigwigs go. Nothing had really stood out, except that there had been an apparent increase in traffic with the coming of night.

That's sure not suspicious at all.

Now, as Nick got settled behind the low-light binoculars—they weren't night vision, exactly, but they were designed to pull in as much light as possible, making them useful in twilight conditions or moderate nightly illum—headlights caught his attention. Swiveling his optics to check, he spotted a convoy of about four trucks, five vans, and a bus turning off the highway and heading through the residential roads toward the compound.

He watched as the convoy wove between houses. A dog started barking outside one of the local residences, only to be suddenly muffled, as if pulled inside, just before the outside lights were switched off. That was a tell, right there.

The convoy pulled up at the gate, met by more of the men with guns. Most of them were in jeans and t-shirts, several wearing ball caps and with bandanas or balaclavas covering their faces.

Several more armed men got out of the trucks and moved to the vans and the bus. From there, they started herding people out of the vehicles and into the compound. Several more groups were inside, hastily separating the men, women, and children into groups, some of them shoved into one tent, the others into the next.

He couldn't help but notice that one of the groups was entirely made up of young women.

This is interesting.

From what he was seeing, it looked like this was a two-pronged operation. On the one hand, there were greenhouses that appeared to be a cartel grow operation. It was also being used as a hub for human trafficking. Some of those people were probably going to be held there as slave labor for the greenhouses. There was plenty of documentation of such things. The coyotes would charge tens of thousands of dollars to bring illegals across the border, money that none of those people had. Then the narcos would force the immigrants to work off their indenture.

There were a couple ways that could happen. For most people, it was through slave labor and drug trafficking. For young women, like the group that had been herded, none too gently, toward a third tent, it was prostitution.

Nick forced himself to watch and document as best he could, keeping his emotions strictly in check. He wasn't a father himself, but he had a little sister. Of course, she was in her thirties by now, but he'd always been protective of her, and he couldn't help but think about her when he saw those girls getting moved like livestock, fear and terror written in every line of their bodies as they were shoved through the flap and into the tent.

There was a deep-seated, killing rage building in his chest as he watched. Unfortunately, there was nothing he could do from a distance. Only watch, document, and report.

I think this confirms what that massacre was all about. Somebody was sending a message.

He put the binoculars down, picked up the camera, and started taking pictures.

***

Things quieted down after that, at least until about an hour before dawn.

The first vehicle that pulled up to the gate was a pretty new and flashy SUV, gleaming a dull silver in the light of the floods by the gate. Nick was supposed to go get Doug for the last watch before they switched out, but right then, there was intel to gather.

More of the gunmen came out from the gate and stood at right angles to the vehicle, while a spotlight was turned on it, and the doors opened. Nick kept snapping photos, hoping to get a shot of the license plate. He had some suspicions about what was going on right off the bat.

Two men got out of the vehicle and advanced toward the masked gunmen. As they neared the guards, both held their hands wide out to their sides, and they submitted to a quick frisking before being escorted inside the compound.

He lost sight of them briefly, but then picked them up again as they were ushered into the tent where the girls had been pushed. His eyes narrowed as he continued to take photos, hoping to get a clear shot of a face. The light was bad, despite the low-light capability of the camera, and the angles and distance weren't great, either. But if they could get enough identifying points, facial recognition software could do the rest.

Both of those characters were definitely Caucasian. He suspected, from the way they moved, that they were Americans. They were also clearly customers, not members of the crew.

And there was little to no doubt in his mind just what product or service they were there to purchase.

Slavery wasn't dead. It had just gone underground.

Doug had an almost preternatural ability to sense what time it was. He was suddenly at Nick's elbow. "Time to switch. You've been on glass long enough."

An extended time on observation could wear a man out. His attention got steadily dulled, and eyestrain was a thing, too. But Nick was on task at the moment. "Got some activity. Looks like our human traffickers have some customers."

"No shit?" Doug moved up next to him, hitching himself into a slightly better position, wedged between two boulders, with a small window of visibility between a cactus and a clump of sagebrush. He scooped up the massive binoculars and took a second to search out the tents. From his grunt, just before the two buyers—that was how Nick was naturally thinking of the pair—went inside.

They were in there for a while. Doug didn't push to get Nick off the camera. They had activity, and neither man wanted to risk losing sight of their targets just because of scheduling.

After about half an hour—Nick was trying really hard not to think about what might have taken that long in that tent— the two of them came out, laughing and joking. The masked gunman behind them didn't appear to be joining in their mirth, but Nick had seen his type enough to be able to picture the smirk behind the mask.

This time he was sure he got good enough photos for the computer to work with.

Doug, in the meantime, was on the radio. "Salt, Thumper. You guys awake?"

"Send it, Thumper." Saul, predictably, was awake. It was close to traditional stand-to time, so naturally he'd be up. Especially when they were in hostile territory, even if he and Mike were playing tourist.

"Got a silver SUV at the target compound, two middle-aged males in it. Need a plate ID."

"Roger. Talk us in when they start moving our way."

They were already walking out the gate and returning to the vehicle. "They're going to be rolling out any minute here."

Sure enough, they climbed into the SUV, pulled a three-point turn, and drove away from the compound, turning onto the nearest dirt road.

"Hell. Looks like they're going north." Nick was still watching through the telephoto lens, since Doug still had the binoculars.

"Looks like it." Doug keyed the radio. "Toe-Tag, Frog, this is Thumper. Silver SUV coming your way. Need plates on it."

"Good copy." Matt sounded fully awake, probably for the same reason Saul was. "On it."

The headlights receded into the dark, and Nick finally relinquished the OP to Doug. They had about another hour before Josh and Abaeze came up to relieve them. Returning to the hollow below the rocks, he set in to wait.

He'd barely lowered himself to the dirt when the radio crackled with Matt's voice. "Well, I'll be damned. They just pulled in here and have a room at the guest house. We've got plates, but we'll hold position and see what happens."

Nick glanced up at Doug, and was somewhat surprised to hear his partner say, "Don't let them get away from you, but keep your distance. They probably need to die, just not today."

CHAPTER
10

The next day dragged by. The contractors continued to shift in and out of the OP, though they needed to crawl up and down to it in daylight, to avoid exposing themselves against the skyline. They were a decent distance away from the cartel compound, but not so far that somebody couldn't look up and see a man standing on the ridgeline if he got sloppy.

Nick's prediction that a large portion of the illegals who'd been brought in the previous night were there for slave labor in the grow operation was confirmed at first light, as the narcos hustled a dozen or so of them out of the tents and into the greenhouses. Several more shuffled out of those greenhouses, heading for the tents under the watchful eyes of more gunmen.

When he and Doug got back up into the OP, the compound was quiet, almost as much as the rest of Shelter Valley. The lights had been turned off at dawn, and some of the guards were still visible, lounging around, smoking or looking at phones. He scanned the town beyond it, where a dog was barking in the distance, but the whole place looked about as dead. Nobody wanted to stir with the narcos that close, and Nick was starting to suspect that the locals knew that a shipment had come in the night before, and that lying low was a good idea.

It was also possible that this was just a typical desert town, where nobody wanted to mix with each other, anyway. Nick had been in a couple places like that. Unfortunately, if that was the case in Shelter Valley, then that might just have made it an ideal place for the cartel to set up, since everyone was *so* dedicated to minding their own business that they'd willingly turn a blind eye to the nightmare going on right in their own back yards.

That would need to be dealt with at some point, at least to Nick's way of thinking. In some ways, he was still an SF soldier at heart, and a part of him wanted to get down there and start organizing the locals against the cartel.

He knew that, as much as PGS stacked bodies, they were never going to be able to stop all the cartel activity, all over the country. That was simply impossible. They were too few, and the narcos were too many. The only way to finally put an end to them would be to shut them out, one local area at a time. That meant his old bread and butter, getting in with the local populace, arming, training, and organizing them against the bad guys.

He didn't know if or how Goblin would find a way to get them paid to do that, but as far as he was concerned, it would be a job he'd jump on in a heartbeat. He'd gotten used to this combination of close protection and intel gathering masking what amounted to a special operations unit, but some problems can't just be solved by kicking select doors and shooting select faces.

Their shift on the OP passed slowly, time dragging by as nothing much happened. Reconnaissance is ordinarily not a particularly thrilling activity. Surveillance even less so.

About an hour after they'd swapped out with Josh and Abaeze again, Manny came over the radio. "This is Frog. Our targets just linked up with two vans. No windows. Two men each. They're just hanging out at the guesthouse for the moment."

"Probably going to hang out until night, then go get their 'cargo.'" Disgust dripped from every word as Doug spoke.

"Do we want to interdict them?" Nick didn't look up, his boonie hat over his eyes as he leaned back against his ruck.

"I'd love to." Something about the tone of Doug's words made Nick lift his head, raising the brim of his boonie with one finger. Sure enough, his partner was on the main comm, a satellite puck linked to a smartphone. A carefully scrubbed smartphone, that shouldn't be linked to the local cell network at all. "Unfortunately, the mission isn't to stop these guys in particular."

Nick fought down the surge of resentment at that, and the accompanying memories of dozens of times when he'd been told by the command to stand down and let the bad guys have their way. More than once, that had resulted in people who'd helped the Americans ending up dead. Here, it would be almost worse.

There wasn't a man on that team that hadn't been around long enough to know with absolute certainty that there are some things worse than death.

"So, what the fuck are we supposed to do, then? I thought we were in this business to put the hurt on bad guys." Carl wasn't happy about it, either. Nick still didn't know too much about the man's background, but if he was a GWOT vet like all the rest of them, then the odds were good that he'd been through this dance before.

Doug looked up at him with a sardonic eyebrow. "If you'd let me finish, I'd tell you." He turned his attention back to the phone while Carl looked down at the dirt, abashed. "Goblin wants us to try to track them. This compound's not going anywhere, so he wants us to trace the chain. These bastards aren't the end-users. They're just another link."

"And how much are those girls going to go through while we try to trace the human trafficking network?" Durand's voice was low and quiet. "I've got a daughter that age."

"I know, man." Doug remained unperturbed. "But if we're going to shut this operation down—and I don't doubt that that's what the boss has in mind—then we're going to have to map it all out first. That means being patient." He looked up and pinned first Durand, then Carl with a stare. "This ain't the same thing as what we've all had to deal with before. 'Oh, that's not

85

the mission.' You think I haven't heard that a million times? No, we're going to get these fuckers. Count on that." Doug seemed awfully confident, but then, Nick couldn't see what Goblin might have sent over the satellite link. "The harsh reality of it is that we don't have the people or the position to stop them cold right now. We *might* help those girls down there, but at what cost to all the ones who come after them?"

The hide site went quieter for a long moment. Nick sat up, leaning his elbows on his knees, and stared at the dirt, the rocks, and the desert shrubs.

He didn't like the argument. Even worse, he knew that it was right. In the long term, it was right.

In the short term, it felt like a betrayal. Like cowardice. Like being one of the people who'd stood by and watched while Kitty Genovese was stabbed to death.

He knew that that story was more complicated than the common perception, but that didn't matter. What mattered was that their mission meant they had to leave those young women in the hands of those savages down there.

Some of them probably wouldn't survive it.

But Doug—and Goblin—were right, if he separated his emotions from it and looked at it coldly, clinically. They *might* be able to free *these* girls. But unless they could bring the network down, that wouldn't help all the others. Not short of a never-ending game of whack-a-mole that would use the contractors up before they ever got close to making a dent in this evil commerce in human flesh.

It was the same problem they faced with the drug traffic, and all the other forms of warfare that went along with it. They were one small company against a psychopathic juggernaut.

So, it had to come down to trusting Goblin. He hadn't backed down from a fight so far, and he'd always acted with strategic acumen.

And he'd never let expediency get in the way of what needed to be done. They either trusted him on this, too, or they needed to hand in their walking papers and look for a different place to work.

"This is Frog. Way ahead of you. We already got GPS trackers on all three vehicles. We can track them wherever they go, at least for the next week, or we can interdict if that's what we decide to do." Even over the radio, the tone of Manny's voice suggested just which course of action he'd be for.

"Good to go." Doug was already tapping out a message on the phone, probably letting Goblin, or whoever was on TOC watch, know. There was a pause, as all they could do was continue to watch, wondering if they'd be forced to only watch, as these evil bastards did whatever they pleased. "We'll have to see what the office says."

Nick had to think it over as he sat there, returning his boonie hat to its position over his eyes, his head back on his ruck. The truth was that there wasn't a whole lot that ten of them could do. Oh, they might stack some bodies. Might even do some real damage to the compound for a while. Would they be able to put it out of action permanently, though? That he wasn't so sure of.

He hated himself a little for even thinking through that math, but there was no way around it.

They *could* just take things into their own hands. There probably wasn't a law enforcement organ anywhere near Shelter Valley that could get to them, even if the narcos wanted to get them involved. As private contractors, they didn't need to worry about PGS trying to throw them in Leavenworth for going off the reservation. Hell, they probably didn't even need to worry about getting turned in, judging by what Nick had already seen of Goblin's character. If it had been any other company, he would have expected the rest of the staff to do something, but Goblin had kept a pretty tight hold on how the company was run.

The problem was, if they did go rogue—presuming everyone was on board—what then?

He sighed, closing his eyes beneath his boonie. It all came down to trust. Did they trust Goblin to make the right call?

Nick wasn't sure. But he was just as unsure that going off half-cocked was the right call.

Sometimes, this job could really suck.

***

The official word came down the pipe a little over an hour later.

"The office says to hold position and maintain surveillance. With a bit of an added note." There was a certain subtle, sardonic amusement in Doug's voice as he read the message. "It says, 'Stand by. Their time is coming.'"

There might have been a low rustle of nods around the hide site. So, Goblin was keeping it real. Or, at least, he wanted to assure his contractors that he was.

Given the lengths they'd already gone to, Nick had no reason to think that their boss was leading them on. They were committed. If he said they were going to put the hurt on the bad guys, then he meant it.

Nick closed his eyes and tried to get some rest.

CHAPTER
11

Three days of surveillance had started to feel like three weeks. We had a pretty damned good idea of Alex Bolus's pattern of life, and it wasn't what I would have called thrilling.

It also was more than a little sketchy, if I was being honest. The man usually started drinking at about ten in the morning—not that I found that all that surprising, given his former occupation and current surroundings. But he was also very clearly single, and equally clearly had a "type." And that type stopped at just shy of half his age.

And he wasn't that much older than me.

After about a day, I came to the conclusion that if we ended up having to put this guy in the dirt, it wasn't going to bother me that much.

He wasn't a target per se, though. Not yet. For tonight, he was an asset, willing or not.

Goblin had called everyone in, and we'd met in his room in the Chabil Mar Villas Resort. It was pretty swank, and hardly the place that anyone would have expected the ten men currently gathered there, surrounded by rich, dark wood and nice tile floors, to be planning what amounted to a break-in and interrogation.

"Okay, Kermit and Leprechaun have confirmed that he's called it a night, and he *doesn't* have a companion tonight." Goblin kept his expression and his voice composed as he said it.

I was sure there were a couple of us who didn't really see the problem with the age gap in Bolus's conquests, but Goblin wasn't one of them.

"We *could* keep watching, and see if we hit a better opportunity, but from where I'm sitting, I don't think we'll get one." He leaned on the kitchen table, where a detailed sketch of Bolus's house was laid out. Some of it was guesswork, since none of us had been inside, and getting plans had proved to be too likely to compromise us. The sketch was based on three days of external observation, including more than a few peeks through the windows.

Just not close enough to get exposed as a Peeping Tom.

"Chris, Ken, Custus, and Rob will come in with me. For the moment, I just want the numbers. Intimidation will help with this guy. As you've seen over the last few days, he's a hedonist who greatly values his own skin. I want the rest on the outside. Nobody should be bunched up; just singles and maybe pairs at most. Keep an eye on the roads and call out if anyone comes. Be ready to move in if I call for backup, though I don't expect to need it. Nothing we've seen over the last few days has led me to believe that Bolus is prepared for trouble, or even knows that any of us are in Belize." Goblin looked down at the sketch again. "Here's the plan…"

***

It was pretty dark in Placencia after nightfall, once you got away from the bars along the waterfront. There wasn't much crime, so there wasn't much need for external lighting. That provided us with more places to hide, without it looking like that was what we were doing, at least to the casual observer.

Let someone who wasn't drunk or high notice that several of us were just hanging out on the street, sandy though it might be, and that might change.

I hoped that Bolus sang like a canary, and we could finish this quickly. The only other alternative would be to hustle him out of town and to somewhere we could take our time, without being observed, but we really didn't have such a place set up.

That was an oversight, in my mind, but Goblin seemed to be confident that we'd get the answers we wanted out of Bolus that night.

I hoped he was right. He'd been on the money so far, generally speaking, but everybody miscalculates eventually.

Bolus's house was on the western coast of the peninsula, right across a narrow canal from a new housing development that was still in its finishing stages. Fortunately, not only was it dark, but there were a lot of trees around the house and the canal, and we could simply blend into the darkness as we worked our way toward the house.

We were still all in civvies, though we'd changed into clothing that was somewhat more practical for this than what we'd been wearing as tourists, watching Bolus and trying to blend in. Long pants, long sleeves, all in dark colors that blended into the night and the vegetation, were the order of the evening.

There were a few lights on in Bolus's house, though they were low and deeper in, only a faint golden glow coming to the back windows, none of which had the curtains drawn.

The house didn't have much of a back porch. Just some steps leading down into the shaded yard from the back door. So, most of us had to spread out, waiting in the shadows as Goblin and Custus walked up the steps to knock on the door.

None of us were armed. That was making me itch, but there was little help for it. If this turned into a fight, we'd already failed. As soon as Slobodian knew that we'd come looking for him—and Goblin was pretty sure that he'd make that connection if things got weird around Bolus—then he'd be in the wind, and we'd never find him.

Presuming this was all what we thought it was. We could well be barking up the wrong tree. Goblin didn't think so, but again…there's always that risk of miscalculation.

For a long couple of minutes, nothing happened. Goblin lifted his hand to knock again, and then paused. Maybe he heard movement inside the house.

I couldn't hear squat, in no small part thanks to all the nocturnal wildlife making noise in the bush.

The door cracked open. "Who is it? Do you know what time it is?"

"I know very well, Alex, but what we have to talk about isn't something I think either of us wants to be discussing in public." Goblin's tone of voice was much calmer than his words. He sounded like an old friend just dropping in, not a man who was willing and able to make the retired intelligence officer wish he were dead.

Not that playing it out that way from the get-go was a good idea. If Bolus panicked, we were up the proverbial creek.

Alex Bolus was not an impressive specimen of the human race, but I doubt any of us had expected him to be. Overweight, balding, looking like he was well into his sixties, even though he was only fifty-five—that added a few more questions about his retirement—his jowls and gut both sagged like wet sacks. That comparison was made all the more immediate and disturbing by the fact that he was currently wearing only a towel.

He squinted in the dark, the glow from inside the only thing illuminating Goblin's features, partially in shadow from Bolus's bulk. "Do I know you?"

"We worked together in Mali." Goblin motioned toward the interior of the house. "I remember you, Alex."

"Thad?" That wasn't quite the enthusiastic welcome that might have been the case among some of us, but then, we'd kind of suspected this sort of reaction.

The pieces we'd carefully put together seemed to be holding their shape.

"Yeah, it's me. Can we come in?"

Bolus looked at Custus, looming behind him, arms folded and dreadlocks cascading to his shoulders. A flicker of emotion crossed his face, too fast for me to really analyze it. I wondered at it as he stepped back and ushered us in, his expression now composed.

That hadn't been the panic I'd expected. There had been fear there, I didn't doubt that, but something else, too.

Relief?

That would be weird, but I'd seen some strange stuff on this job already.

Bolus padded into his living room, as the rest of us moved in behind Goblin and Custus, spreading out to check the house. Bolus glanced at us as we walked through his bedrooms, kitchen, and bathroom, but he didn't say anything. Didn't even look annoyed. It was as if he knew exactly what we were doing.

He probably did. If he'd worked for the people Goblin had implied that he had, he'd had a lot of experience with guys like us, and probably also knew that we were professional paranoiacs, who would only get harder to deal with if he raised a ruckus and tried to keep us from securing the area.

I was the last one in the living room. Goblin was sitting on the couch, the rest of the hit team spread out around the room, while Bolus puttered in the kitchen. "I know you guys won't take beers. Tea? Coffee?"

"Just sit down, Alex." Goblin was still playing it soft. From the look on his face as he watched Bolus, I could almost see the gears turning. What was the play, here? Bolus seemed a lot more collected than he should.

Bolus paused. "Can I put some shorts on?"

Goblin might have actually smiled, just a little. "Please."

When Bolus shuffled back toward his bedroom, Ken started to follow him, but Goblin raised a hand to forestall him. "Don't worry. He'll be back." He chuckled faintly, craning his neck to check that Bolus was out of the hallway. "He's not going through any windows anytime soon."

Nobody laughed, but there was a slight lightening of the mood. Only slight, though. This could still get ugly quickly, and none of us had more than a knife on him.

Of course, I was pretty sure every man there could do some serious damage with just a folder, but guns are usually preferable if it comes down to cases.

Bolus might have procrastinated, taken as much time as possible to change while he sent out a call for help. His phone was sitting on the coffee table, however, and the door was still open. While Ken hadn't followed Bolus into his room, he was standing right inside the hallway, where he could hear if our unwilling host tried to call for help.

After only about a minute, Bolus came back out into the living room, now wearing cargo shorts and a white, short-sleeved button down. It was a lot easier on the eyes than that corpulent former IC guy in just a towel. He sat down in an armchair across from Goblin with a deep sigh. "Okay, what brings you and your associates down to Belize?" He glanced up at us. "We've already established that this isn't a social call."

Goblin leaned forward and put his elbows on his knees. "I'm looking for Slobodian."

The reaction was subtle. I almost missed it. For the briefest of seconds, Bolus's face went completely still. Then he relaxed and reached for the water bottle sitting on the end table next to his chair.

We weren't especially tense at this point. Nobody was about to cut Bolus open if he tried to do anything with the water bottle. He was a retired intelligence officer, not a paramilitary. The movies' picture of deadly spies who would kill you at the drop of a hat if you gave them the opportunity is largely garbage. Spies deal in information and personal relationships—even if they're usually highly manipulative relationships based on ego-stroking and money.

Not that we trusted him, but violence wasn't on the table. Not with this guy.

"That's interesting. It's been a while, if I remember correctly. Why come to me?"

Goblin gave him the slow blink that told anyone who knew the man that he figured he'd just been asked a stupid question. "You were the closest thing he had to a friend when he was 'consulting' for the office, Alex. And I know that he kept in touch. You weren't *that* secretive about it."

This time the flicker of fear was unmistakable. Bolus *had* thought that he'd been covered. That brief widening of the eyes, quickly shut down, told me that he really had been in contact with Slobodian, and that he was both surprised and scared that Goblin knew about it.

"He's hit me up from time to time, yes." His eyes flicked from one to the other of us, the wheels turning. His answers were probably going to depend on what we wanted with Slobodian—and what the personal consequences to him might be. "What's the occasion?"

Goblin was still feeling things out as much as Bolus was, though. "He still trying to talk like a surfer?"

That threw Bolus for a little bit of a loop. A frown creased his brow. "Sometimes. You know him. His accent and his inflection change depending on who he's talking to and what he wants."

Goblin sighed, then looked over at me. I shrugged. It was his call.

"Okay, cards on the table." He fixed Bolus with an unblinking stare. "What I'm about to tell you doesn't leave this room. If it does, I *will* find out, and then I'll be coming back to ask you some *very* pointed questions." That the instruments that came along with those questions would be just as pointed was implied, if not said.

Bolus had mentally caught up, though, and had gotten over whatever fog he had put himself into with drink and sleep. "You know I can keep a secret, Thad."

Goblin might have snorted faintly. Bolus noticed, and flushed slightly, but he didn't say anything.

"Just so we understand each other. I wouldn't want a misunderstanding to make things unpleasant." The threat was more than just implied, there. Goblin leaned back on the couch and put one leg over his knee. "So, a few months ago, somebody murdered our client just before we started handling his security. Made it look like a suicide." He waved vaguely to indicate the other contractors in the room. "My boys started digging. Turns out that somebody was coordinating not only that hit, but a bunch of others, by encrypted email. We got our hands on some of those emails."

I was just as glad that Goblin didn't say exactly *how*. Phil and I had infiltrated that network, and in the process, we'd come awfully close to not only getting bound up in actual domestic terrorism, but also smoking a Federal agent. We might not trust the Feds as far as I could throw my truck, but that didn't mean we wanted to cross that line of putting one of them in the dirt any sooner than absolutely necessary.

"Whoever was sending them was being very careful. No location data, no signatures, nothing. There was nothing to indicate who was on the other end, calling the shots. Even the payment arrangements were all with crypto, and apparently run through half a dozen cutouts, at least.

"But there was one little thing that jumped out at me. A little tic of language that the author of the emails couldn't help but keep using. 'Most excellent.'" He was watching Bolus carefully.

There wasn't much of a reaction. Nor was there any attempt to misdirect. If anything, Bolus's shoulders slumped slightly. "He always has liked that line."

The retired spy looked down at the coffee table with a deep sigh. "While I can't say I'm all that surprised, you have to understand that I didn't actually know about any of this. My friendship with him has always been a personal thing. Once we no longer had a professional relationship, we never talked about work."

"That may be." Goblin wasn't convinced, and neither was I. From the looks I saw, most of the rest of the PGS contractors in the room weren't, either. "But I need to know where he is."

Bolus rubbed his chin. There was a hesitancy in his movements that told me, at least, that he wasn't just thinking over the information. He was thinking over the potential costs to himself and his lifestyle if he told us what we wanted to know.

"That could be difficult. He likes to travel."

I'll bet.

Goblin took a deep breath. "Let's clear the air a bit. I haven't told you the whole story. This son of a bitch—whether it's Slobodian or not—sent hit squads after several of my boys, *and their families.*" He let that sink in. "It's in everyone's best interest for us to find Slobodian. Whether it's to clear things up or... otherwise."

Bolus's eyes moved from Goblin to Custus, to me, then back to Goblin. There was a new note of trepidation in his gaze. "He does have a house here."

"Where?" Goblin was dropping the nice guy act, his voice as hard as his stare.

Bolus swallowed. "Look, Thad..."

"Where?"

Another look around at the flinty stares from professional killers, men he now knew had a personal stake in this hunt. Bolus seemed to deflate at that. He leaned forward. "It's over on the other side of the bay, just outside of Independence and Mango Creek." He proceeded to describe the address and the house itself. He looked up at Goblin finally, almost plaintively. "If this is real...if he really is what you think he is..." He gulped. "If he finds out that I told him..."

Goblin wasn't any more sympathetic than I was. "As a counterpoint, if he finds out that we're looking for him, and things go badly, just understand that we'll be back for a visit. And those pointed questions I mentioned before?" He stood up. "They're going to get even more pointed if we have to come back here."

CHAPTER
12

It was starting to look like our days of relative inactivity while we'd been watching Bolus might actually pay off a little. Despite the necessity of constant watchfulness that went along with an extended surveillance mission, when we'd been off Bolus, we'd been able to get some rest. And we were probably going to need it.

The superyacht that Goblin had, somehow, gotten as a company asset, had a launch that was able to come in and pick us up, bringing our gear along, without the sort of attention-gathering noise of the helicopter. We had to move down to the Municipal Pier and Plaza, at the southern end of Placencia, to meet up with the boat. It was past midnight when we backed water off the pier and headed for the mainland.

We geared up on the launch, though it was crowded and made for some uncomfortable maneuvering to change over from our civvies to camouflage fatigues, plate carriers, and helmets. We didn't know for sure that this was going to be a hit, but even if it wasn't, we were going to be in the weeds for a while.

"The primary mission for tonight is to get eyes on. If a target of opportunity presents itself, then we'll move on it." Goblin was in mission mode, already in his ATACS-FG combat shirt and trousers. "It could be that we end up making contact like we did with Bolus. If we see something that makes me think it would be advantageous, then we'll leave an element in the weeds, watching the house, while another comes back out to the boat to change over." He grinned, his teeth showing white in the green and brown camouflage face paint on his features. It seemed odd, a corporate leader like Thad Walker, who had the typical suit-and-tie, perfectly groomed photos on the company website, geared up to get some in the jungle. This was usually a task for much younger men. Goblin hadn't been a spring chicken when he and I had been partners in the Middle East, quite a few years ago.

He was a tough son of a bitch, though. I'll give him that. And he was driven, especially now.

"We might not be at our Sunday best, but we probably won't have time to go back to the yacht and take a shower, either."

He looked around at us. Most were already changed over and geared up. The tourists of the last few days were gone. "Insert in thirty mikes."

***

Big Creek was the unimaginative name for the stream that met the bay, south of Independence and Mango Creek. The launch could get upstream pretty easily. The problem lay in that the banks of Big Creek weren't exactly solid.

Most of the surrounding area was wetlands, essentially swamps with a few channels for boats to get to and from the larger estates to the north. Some lights shone from an industrial seafood processor to the south. Not many, and not enough for us to worry about, but it always pays to have awareness of your surroundings.

Unfortunately, the wetlands were going to limit our options when it came to surveilling Slobodian's house. The entire south side was inundated, and there was simply no place to set up an OP. Good insertion points were also limited, since there was a channel cut through the swamp to a dock at the back of the house, but the rest was shallow mire, studded with trees and dead logs. We *could* set up there, endure the discomfort, and hopefully spot either a covert entry or exit via the water. How long that could last, though, was another question.

Good recon troops can endure a lot and go where no one else wants to go. There are limits, though. There's only so wet you can get your gear before it fails, never mind the effects that it has on the human body. We were ready to put a two-man team ashore if we found a good sandbar with line of sight that might work, but if it was all just stagnant water and mangroves, that was going to be a non-starter.

The launch was moving slowly, mainly for noise reasons. The engine wasn't all that powerful, but even over the night noises of the swamp, it was still loud enough for the sound to travel through the swamps. And we didn't know what kind of early warning systems Slobodian might have put out.

I had to remind myself, once again, as I peered into the shadows beneath the mangroves and other tropical trees through the gray of my PS-31s, that we were still just gathering information. Sure, we were equipped and ready for a hit if it came to it, but that wasn't the mission. Not yet.

While we were operating under a lot looser rules than we might have had before, either on contract or in the military, and we weren't exactly law enforcement, either, I doubted that any of us really wanted to be the ones who went on a vendetta against a man who wasn't actually involved. Not only would it kill our souls, but it wouldn't help our families, or the other targets of the shadowy network we'd found ourselves at war with.

Making sure that we had the right target was important, in more ways than one.

The swamp slid by as the engine puttered. We were all out on the gunwales—not that there was much room in the boat for more than that—weapons in hand and scanning the dark through NVGs. So far, I hadn't seen any spot that would do for an OP, and if I was judging distances and speeds right, we were getting awfully close to the objective.

No one said a word, but we just watched and waited, even as the coxswain, a younger guy I'd only been introduced to

101

as John, turned us off the main channel and into a shallow waterway that curved toward the northwest.

We kept moving for another half hour or so, almost just drifting along. The more I looked around that swamp, the less I liked it. The vegetation directly to the north was *thick*, and would be a nightmare to thrash through, especially if we were trying to be quiet. The south was just water and scattered mangroves.

Finally, though, Tom pointed, and John started to bring the boat in toward shore. I turned my head and thought I could see the spot that Tom had picked out. A slightly thinner opening in the nearly solid wall of trees that loomed ahead of us.

John didn't beach the boat, though he probably could have. He just throttled back until the boat's slight drift was so slow that we were almost at a standstill. We were going to get wet, but that had always been a foregone conclusion in that place.

Tom and Brian went out first, since they were in the bow, splashing into the water though they kept their rifles high. In a time of aluminum and synthetic, keeping weapons dry was less urgent than it had been back in the day, but old habits die hard, both individually and institutionally.

Two by two, we moved up to the bow and got out, sloshing through the muck toward the shore where Tom and Brian had already moved into the trees and set security to hold the landing site. It didn't take long to get everyone on shore, at which point we pushed deeper in and formed a perimeter while John backed water and brought the launch around. He'd go back to the yacht and wait for word over comms to come get us.

Whether we'd be running for it, or slipping back out to sea quietly, depended on what happened next.

Not everyone in Pallas Group Solutions had been a recondo. There were a lot of us. The company probably had more Recon Marines and Ranger Recon Detachment guys than a lot of contract companies I'd worked for, but that didn't account for everybody. And of those of us who had been snake eaters back in the day, I'd be willing to bet a lot that most of us had let our greenside skills lapse a bit over the years.

Goblin hadn't had a concerted workup in mind to correct that, but it turns out that if you've had the training and experience, a lot of it comes back quickly once you put your mind to it, and a lot of the paranoia inherent in clandestine operations in urban environments also translates well enough to the bush.

The fact that a lot of us were hunters, and deer, elk, and moose can be more elusive than people, probably helped, too.

Sitting in the dark and the jungle, we waited for about ten minutes after the putter of the launch's engine had receded into the night, watching, listening, and trying to catalog the smells of the swamp so that we might be able to pick out any other people nearby. That was a long shot, since we simply hadn't had time to familiarize ourselves with the area, so we'd have to rely almost entirely on sight and sound.

Finally, Tom got up and started toward the north, after checking his compass. One by one, we all rose and followed, slipping into the dark like ghosts.

***

Two hours later, Ken and I lay in the weeds beneath a tree I probably couldn't have identified in daylight, watching the house that Bolus had fingered as Slobodian's.

It was a nice house, there was no denying that. Two stories, all in white and dark wood, which I could see better than the predawn should have allowed for since there were lights all the way around it. If not for the differences in real estate prices between Belize and the US, I would have thought that somewhere as big and nice as this would be an indicator that Slobodian was dirty. Anybody who "consulted" with intelligence agencies and had money to burn was probably either playing both sides against the middle, part of organized crime, or both.

Belize was a popular destination for expats, though, *because* real estate was cheap. The fact that Slobodian had a nice house on some significant acreage still wasn't a smoking gun.

So, we settled in to watch and wait.

CHAPTER
13

Traffic around Shelter Valley had picked up somewhat over the last couple of days. Nick noted it, wondering just what was up. While they photographed more vehicles coming and going from the cartel's compound, so far, none of them seemed to be bringing any new human cargo, though some were clearly taking drugs out. There wasn't a whole lot else to indicate what all the activity was about.

Word from the office—Goblin was away somewhere, probably down in Belize with the A Team—was sparse. Whoever was back there just kept acknowledging their reports and telling them to hold what they had.

Sooner or later, Doug was going to pull them off, just because batteries, water, and chow were getting low. None of them were young men, so they hadn't scrimped on any of the above, though they had packed light otherwise. That had led to some chilly nights, as the desert doesn't retain much heat after the sun goes down. "Pack light, freeze at night" was an old, old saw, but under the circumstances, Nick was just as glad he'd brought extra water and batteries.

The extra ammo he'd packed was starting to look like it might go unused. He had some decidedly mixed feelings about that, looking down at a cartel grow operation that was also a human trafficking hub.

He and Doug were about to go back up and take over the OP again when Durand hissed at them. "Hey. Message from the office. You guys gotta see this."

Doug slid over from where he'd been set up. They'd been in place long enough that they were going to leave a lot of trace when they exfiltrated. Nothing to do about it. Nick lowered his ruck back onto the rocks and duck walked over to join them.

The message was a pretty simple warning order. At 0230, they were to collapse on the compound and set up an exterior cordon for a D Team raid.

Doug's eyebrows were up. "Not the first time I've had to roll from recon into a raid."

Nick was feeling a bit more ambivalent. "I hope the D Team's got some reinforcements. Twenty dudes to take that place, ten of them on the outside, is going to be rough." They'd counted at least thirty shooters on site, and there was no way to predict just when the next group was going to show up with more illegals, or customers looking to buy said illegals.

There were any number of ways this could go sideways in a hurry, especially since they didn't have immediate backup, air support, or even any way to keep from getting arrested if it turned out that the California authorities found out about it before they could get back across the line into Arizona.

Those concerns weren't enough to make him want to back out, though. He just didn't think that keeping ten men on the outer cordon was going to work well. If they were going to burn that operation down—and he desperately wanted to, after what they'd seen and heard over the last few days—then they'd need every gun.

When overwhelming force isn't an option, speed, surprise, and violence of action was the next best thing.

"We'll hold position and continue to observe and report until around midnight, then we'll break down and start moving." Doug started moving toward his ruck again. "I'll pass the word to Saul and Manny.

"Gonna be a long night, boys."

***

The last light had died in the west two hours before. Rucks on, spread out into as close an approximation to a wedge as they could manage on the rough terrain, weapons in hands and eyes up behind PS-31s. While the rucks were considerably lighter thanks to almost four days of food and water being used up, they were still heavy enough that all six men were slightly hunched under their weight.

Doug had moved up to take point, and now he lifted a hand, sinking to a knee behind a boulder near the bottom of the hill.

Nick didn't close in but found his own slightly covered and concealed position a few yards off. It was plenty dark, but the terrain was open enough that they needed to stay spread out.

It took a second to see what had made Doug call a halt. There was a brief exchange of hand and arm signals—no IR; with the proliferation of NVGs on the open market, all of the PGS contractors had stopped flashing IR lights and lasers around a while ago—and then Saul and Mike got up from their position and moved to join up.

"Frog and Toe-Tag will move in from the north and take up positions on that hill." That had already been established by comms, but Saul seemed to want to make sure it was confirmed. There could be a lot of gunfire flying around the desert that night, and knowing friendly positions could easily turn into a matter of life and death.

Doug checked his watch, pulling back his cuff and carefully shielding the illuminated face from the desert. "We've got thirty minutes. Have you had comms with Disco?"

"Not yet." Saul, as generally unflappable as he was, sounded slightly worried. Nick could understand why. The D Team needed to be on the ball if they were going to make this work. If the cordon was sitting out there in the desert for too long, *somebody* would spot something and figure out that things were about to get exciting.

Doug sighed, the sound only barely audible over the whisper of the wind across the desert. "Well, we'd better keep moving." Timing on a raid was everything, especially one like this, and if they were out of position, and the D Team was just having comms problems, then things could go bad, fast.

Hefting their rucks, the contractors continued down into the desert, now moving along the wash that came down from the hills, using every bit of brush and rock they could find to hide from the compound. There weren't any guard towers, and they hadn't seen any cameras, either, but just about every man on that team had seen some op go bad because someone had gotten sloppy.

***

Nick fought the urge to check his watch. They'd been set in for what felt like a small eternity already, waiting on the D Team. Disco, the team leader, had finally made radio contact while the B Team had been moving to cover positions, but they were behind schedule. There was no explanation on the radio, but that was for the hot wash, anyway.

Now, though, he saw three vehicles turn down the road that they'd watched the human traffickers take to leave the compound several days earlier. They weren't showing lights.

"That's our boys." Doug was down in the prone next to Nick, also behind his ruck, watching the desert and the compound fence over his rifle.

Nick felt a lot of the fatigue and just general wear of the last few days sort of fall away. It was an illusion borne of the adrenaline rush, but he'd take it. He knew he was tired, stiff, and dehydrated, but they were about to get in a fight, and there was nowhere else he'd rather be.

Especially not given who the targets were.

He shifted his weight behind the gun, looking for the first sign of the cartel's response to the oncoming blacked out vehicles. The contractors hadn't observed any night vision devices on the compound, but those lights reached pretty far out into the desert—which was why he and Doug were as far from the fence as they were—and they had to be on the alert, from what they'd seen from the ridge. These guys weren't feeling casual, even tucked into the hills outside Shelter Valley, California. Given some of the cartel wars that had already leaked across the border, that was no surprise at all. It was just going to make the night's tasking that much more difficult.

He and Doug had worked their way along the southern fence, and now had eyes on the entire south side of the compound as well as the east, including the gate. They were well placed to hit any squirters, as well as lay down some cover fire for the assault force as they neared the gate.

It also meant that he got to watch the guards' reaction in real time.

There were three of them at the gate, all with their faces still covered. It almost seemed like a uniform to them. Two were carrying AK-74s, while the third had what looked like a Mini-14. The two with the AKs had them leaning against the shack that served as a guardhouse, while one of them sat on a crate and the other leaned against the wall. The guy with the Mini-14 was at least on his feet with his weapon in his hands, though he was still facing the inside of the compound, talking with the other two.

For a moment, Nick started to think that the D Team was just going to drive right up to the gate. That might have been doable with up-armored vehicles, but these weren't up-armored Humvees, and it wasn't 2005.

Fortunately, he saw them stop in the shadows, not far from the last house before the compound. That still gave them a sizeable distance to cross, all over open desert, but crossing that on foot, spread out, made the team much less of a target than if they'd just tried to drive right up. It might take more time, but it eliminated the risk of getting a third of the team wiped out when one truck went up.

Briefly, Nick turned his head and rotated one tube up out of his vision, blinking to try to restore his night adaptation. He could see how the old PVS-14 monoculars had a certain advantage over the binocular PVS-15s and PS-31s. With the older monoculars, if you needed to do something like this, you still had night adaptation in the off eye.

He was pretty sure that the figures that spilled out of the three vehicles and spread out in a wide V across the desert were still invisible to the guards, especially since those three were under a floodlight. That might change as they got closer, but that was what the rifles were for.

Rotating his NVG tube back down, he settled in behind his carbine and put the red dot on Mini-14's chest. He was the most alert, so he'd be the first to die.

Doug shifted slightly beside him, and he was pretty sure that one of the others was similarly targeted. Or, more likely, the same guy. Doug knew what he was doing, and it wasn't like they were coordinating with invisible lasers that only they could see. That was for movies and video games.

On target though they might be, they still had to wait. Open the ball early, and the assault force would be stuck in the open, having to adjust to the sudden gunfire. Nick kept his finger high and off the trigger for the moment, just to be on the safe side.

The wait seemed interminable as the D Team bounded forward, staying low and moving carefully. Nick knew that was just the adrenaline talking, and he kept his breathing even, resisting the urge to drop his finger to the trigger and end the guy with the Mini-14 right then and there.

He'd spent days watching these bastards abuse people and ship out poison that made them rich while it destroyed lives. There'd been a time when he'd been more open to at least the marijuana side. Unfortunately, after he'd gotten out of the Army, he'd seen too many lives irrevocably altered by the "harmless plant." Not in the typical way of sliding into squalor and addiction, like meth or heroin, but in a more subtle sort of way, an altering of personalities and perceptions. Some of the dudes he'd been at Group with were no longer recognizably the same people.

Now, he was on the verge of at least making this bunch pay, and he had to wait.

While the D Team weren't using the IR strobes that had been standard for friend or foe identification when Nick had first gone to Afghanistan, back in the early '00s, he could see well enough with his PS-31s on that he could pick out at least the closest operators as they neared the gate. *Any second now.*

Disco had execute authority. When the D Team started shooting, then it was game on.

As they got closer and closer, despite himself, Nick started to tense up more and more. It was only a matter of time before a stray noise, movement seen out of the corner of an eye, or something else gave them away. There's no such thing as pure stealth. If the narcos got the first shot off...

A suppressed gunshot snapped across the desert with a harsh, hissing *crack,* and the guard with the Mini-14 stiffened and dropped. Nick shifted his aim to one of the others as he grabbed for his AK, only to watch that one crumple as one of the D Team boys put a double tap through his head. The third was already down.

Nick took his finger off the trigger once more, as the D Team surged to their feet and raced into the gate, guns up and NVG tubes just above their sights. In seconds, the entire ten-man assault force had disappeared inside the fence. A few more suppressed gunshots snapped inside, then there was a long, rattling burst of AK fire, quickly silenced.

Just as Nick was starting to resign himself to the fact that this was going to be little more than external guard duty, a renewed storm of gunfire sounded, and the radio in Nick's ear crackled.

"This is Disco. Need some support, north side of the compound. They're trying to kill off the hostages."

Hostages. It sounded better than *slaves,* though the latter was more accurate.

"On me." Doug was already up and moving, leaving his ruck where it was. Nick followed suit. Letting his gear out of his sight went a little against the grain, but hauling a ruck into a close quarters firefight was a recipe for disaster.

They moved up along the fence. Just running in, when that fence was only chain link, wouldn't be smart, so they walked, though at a fast combat glide, as best they could over the uneven desert floor, guns up and searching for targets. Doug spotted one trying to get around behind some of the D Team shooters, and dropped him with a quick trio of shots, the suppressed *snap*s lost in the thunderous rattle of gunfire already shredding the quiet of the desert night.

Reaching the gate, they stepped over the bodies, though not before a quick, wordless deconfliction with Matt and Manny, as the other two PGS shooters came out of the dark from the north. Turning inward, they headed for the tents where the slaves were kept.

There was more cover inside that compound than would have otherwise seemed obvious, mainly piles of junk and vehicles. Little of it would stop bullets, but it provided some disruption and meant they weren't just running through an open courtyard with guns. Especially with half the lights already shot out—the D Team weren't allowing the narcos any advantage they could help, and the floodlights were whiting out their NVGs—there were a lot of places to hide as they moved in.

Unfortunately, the urgency of trying to save those people worked against a deliberate, cover-to-cover advance. At the same time, the narcos weren't dumb, and that meant they had to clear every bit of dead space behind those piles of detritus as they went.

There were half a dozen such piles, along with three beat-up pickups and an old Bronco, just inside the gate. Nick pivoted to check one as Doug blew another narco's brains across the already bullet-holed hood of the Bronco a moment later. Then they were through the entryway, Manny taking security toward the south end of the compound as Nick, Doug, and Matt moved toward the tent where the girls had been taken.

Another broken down car was parked between them and the tent. Several of the narco shooters had set in behind it and had good fields of fire to hold down the open ground between the shed and the tent. There were already some bullet holes through the canvas, though the D Team was keeping those shooters busy enough that they hadn't really been able to thoroughly hose down the tent. Nick hoped that the girls had had the presence of mind to get down on the ground as soon as the shooting started.

Presuming that they still had much of a sense of self-preservation left, after what they'd already been through.

Nick and Doug moved up next to the Bronco, Doug dropping to a low knee behind the front wheels and getting even lower to shoot underneath the old SUV. Nick, for his part, was about to do the same when he thought of something.

Vehicles don't make good cover, and they're not exactly solid, either.

Still staying low, keeping his head below the level of the windows, Nick wrenched the back door open, crawled across the back seat, threw open the next door, and threw himself out onto the ground. There was enough noise that most of the narcos didn't hear him, but one of them must have noticed something, because he turned and sprayed bullets at the noise, or movement, or whatever he thought he'd seen or heard.

Muzzle flash flickered in the dark, seemingly right in front of his eyes, and bullets hammered the sheet metal above him, shattering glass and covering him in fragments. Rolling to one side, he more or less just pointed his carbine and hammered a trio of shots at the muzzle blast. One of them must have hit, because the incoming fire suddenly stopped with a scream, and then he was scrambling away from the Bronco, half crawling, half running to get away from that position and to a spot where he could engage the *sicarios* without having the tent full of teenage girls on the other end of his muzzle.

He stumbled on a rock and went down hard, but it saved his life. Bullets *crack*ed through the air right where he would have been if he hadn't fallen. He crawled as fast as he could to get behind a boulder, throwing himself prone and bringing his rifle around to try to get a shot.

Doug, meanwhile, had shifted his own position as Nick had drawn the narcos' fire. Rising up over the Bronco's hood, he proceeded to put half a magazine through the broken-down car, taking full advantage of the fact that at least one of the narco shooters had exposed his head through the window as he'd turned to try to track Nick. The man's head jerked, and he fell. In that brief second that followed, as the final *sicario* hesitated, caught between two fires, Nick steadied his dot, craning his head to see through his NVGs in the prone, and dropped him with a tight, four-shot group to the chest.

The gunfire around the girls' tent went silent, then. "Croak! You good?" Doug hadn't moved, but still had his rifle trained on the car where the narcos had tried to take cover.

Nick had lifted his head, but still had his weapon aimed in and his finger hovering near the trigger. He wanted to be good and sure he wasn't going to get his head blown off as soon as he stood up. He wouldn't put it past these *sicario* bastards to play possum, just to get one more kill.

The first man he'd shot was still rolling on the ground, groaning in agony, and Nick had to suppress the urge to put a final bullet in him and silence him. As prudent as it might be, it would still be murder.

There was no way that the authorities would know exactly who had just hit this place, let alone that Nick had finished off a wounded *sicario*. But Nick would know. And so would Doug.

There were quite a few men in this profession who wouldn't blink an eye at it. Nick had to admit that he was borderline, himself. Yet something held him back, and he got to his feet, his weapon still trained on the moaning *sicario*, even as Doug came around the front of the Bronco, his own carbine leveled, and kicked the AK away from the dying man's hands.

Nick moved up to join him, his eyes and his muzzle lingering on the dying man, after he'd swept their surroundings quickly, determining that there weren't any more bad guys between them and the tent. Doug saw it.

"He ain't got long." Doug spared Nick a glance. "Don't need to finish him. Don't need to help him, either."

Nick nodded, though he didn't ever quite turn his back on the narco, even as the groans turned to fainter and fainter rasping breaths. Doug was right. The man didn't have long. Didn't make him any less dangerous.

The two of them didn't immediately make entry on the tent, but circled around it, making sure there weren't any more bad guys that might be in a position to come up and shoot them in the back. Only then did they move in. Behind them, a few desultory gunshots cracked over raised voices, mostly frightened, panicked pleading.

Nick wasn't sure how much of that pleading was the illegals who had been turned into slaves to the cartel, or *sicarios* who had suddenly discovered that they were far from the scariest motherfuckers in the valley that night.

The interior of the tent was dark, and with the gunfire having died down, now Nick could hear the panicked screaming and shrieking of nearly a dozen young women who were convinced they were going to die.

Doug triggered his weapon light, bathing the cramped quarters of the tent in stark white light. That seemed to trigger a renewed wave of screams, and Nick was glad he had his earpro on.

The first thing he noticed was the blood. Two of the girls were holding a third down, trying desperately to do something about the crimson fluid that was rapidly pumping out of her. She'd been unlucky enough to be standing up when the narcos had started shooting into the tent.

Nick went to her while Doug tried to get things under some control. "*Esta bien! Nadie te va a hacer daño!*" His bellow cut through some of the shrieking, even as Nick bent over the girl.

It didn't take long to see that she probably wasn't going to survive. She was already starting to look pale and waxy, and there was a *lot* of blood on the dirt floor. She'd been hit in the neck, and even as Nick plunged his hand into the wound to try to pinch off the jugular vein that had been opened, he already knew it was probably too late. Her eyes were glassy, staring at nothing, and her shudders were getting weaker. Nick gritted his teeth as he tried to find the blood vessel, but he could already feel the pump of blood slowing.

Then, just as he thought he might have found the vein, she just… stopped.

He still kept trying. He knew she was dead. He knew that there was no reviving her. Not from blood loss like that, never mind what other damage the bullet must have done. But he couldn't just quit.

Doug seemed to sense that, and didn't interfere, even as Disco and three more of the D Team came in. Disco was a big dude, with a bristling beard that reached almost down to the mags on his plate carrier. "What the fuck." It wasn't a question. It was just venting.

Nick finally pulled his hand away, and reached down to close the dead girl's eyes. "We need to get these people over the state line before sunrise. The Californistanis aren't going to look any more kindly on this than the cartels."

Disco nodded. "We've got a van just up the road. I'll call it in." He looked around at the girls, most of whom were barely dressed. It didn't take a genius to figure out what had gone on in that tent, and even the most shameless womanizer on that team would still be horrified.

Doug was looking around for something to clothe the girls with. It was probably going to be a long ride. "Make it quick. We're far enough out that I doubt local authorities will be here even by sunrise, but Croak's right. We need to make tracks."

It was a hell of a thing, Nick thought as he tried to wipe the blood off his hands. One of the single most unalloyed good things they'd done, and they still had to run to avoid being thrown in jail for it.

CHAPTER
14

Surveillance in a swamp is not pleasant.

Insertion was bad enough. Festering in the wet, getting eaten by bugs while it felt like my flesh was rotting away on my bones, was even worse.

Not that it was my first time. That probably accounted for how much it sucked. This had gotten old a few years back.

Still, it had to be done, so I kept my lip zipped and watched Slobodian's house when it was my turn.

And tried very hard not to slap the mosquitos that were trying to drain me dry. Not to mention all the other various insects that infested that place.

We could see somebody moving around inside, but so far, we had no positive identification. It might be Slobodian, but from the way Bolus had talked about this place, I doubted it. It seemed more likely to be a caretaker.

There was so much vegetation around the house that we were almost within spitting distance, almost perfectly concealed, and still couldn't see through the windows clearly enough to tell who was in there.

The longer this went on, the more likely it seemed that we were on a wild goose chase. This wasn't working. We were going to have to try something else.

Ken and I weren't alone in our hide, only a few dozen yards from the southwest corner of the house. Goblin had set in with us, which meant that we got a little bit more rest in between shifts of watching the windows. It also meant that we were on the ground floor when decision time came around.

I'd just laid down against my ruck, trying to stay quiet as I killed a couple more mosquitos that were trying to get at my dwindling blood supply, when Goblin sighed. "This isn't working."

"I could have told you that a day ago." I kept my eyes open, as tired as I was. If Goblin was talking in the OP, then something was about to happen. He'd been all but completely silent for the last couple of days.

"It was worth a shot." He was sitting back in the bushes, almost invisible from my position. I could see his eyes, though. He'd kept up on camouflage during the last couple of days. Years in the corporate world hadn't dulled him to the point of forgetting his priorities of work in the field. "I really don't know how walking up to have a conversation on his front porch is going to work out. It could be just like Bolus. It could be completely fruitless. It could turn violent in a hurry." He shrugged. "I just don't know. It would be better if we could get eyes on him here, then start to track him and get the intel we need that way."

"Whoever's in that house hasn't even stuck their head out the door for two days." I craned my neck to look toward the little bit of the west side we could see. "You're right, this is getting us nowhere."

Goblin sighed again. "Shit. If one of us walks up to that door, and Slobodian is what we think he is, then we're burned and he's going to run for it."

"Bolus said he likes to travel." As much as I had to admit that I wanted out of that swamp, I also wanted to solve the problem, and really *didn't* want to abandon the mission. "Maybe he knows where Slobodian does like to travel."

"Maybe." He squinted up at the house for a long few moments.

I studied my boss and former partner. We'd been through a bit over the years, but I still couldn't read his mind. Even so, I thought I could see when he started down another train of thought.

"Although..." He tapped a finger against his knee. "Maybe shaking the tree really *is* the right course of action."

"Is it?" I wasn't so sure. "Without being prepped and knowing more of his hiding places, he might just crawl into a hole and pull it in after him, then send more hitters after us."

Goblin chewed on it for a moment. "Bolus knows more than he told us. He's trying to sit on the fence, tell us just enough to keep the gun away from his own head. I know the man. He might be retired, and he might be playing that part up, living as hedonistically as he can here, but he's always going to have his ear to the ground." His voice got grimmer. "Even if it's only to make sure he doesn't get in trouble. The dude's got some serious skeletons in his closet, and I don't doubt that he's added more since he moved down here."

Given what we'd seen of some of his "dating" habits, I didn't doubt it, either.

"Hell, I guaran-damn-tee that that son of a bitch has been digging into whatever he can find about Slobodian ever since we talked to him, if only out of self-preservation. If he didn't know most of Slobodian's known haunts before, I'd be willing to bet he does now."

"So, we pull off, come back and knock on the door, if only to spook Slobodian, then go rake Bolus over the coals again?" I couldn't say I was against the latter. After watching him for three days, I really didn't like the man.

"Sounds like a plan to me." He leaned forward a little, his hand going to his radio's transmit switch. Before he could send anything, though, Tom came over the net.

"This is Scooby. Three vics just pulled up to the house. Four to five military age males per vehicle, most appear to be Hispanic, though I have eyes on two Caucasians, one blond and one brown haired. Casual dress, but this looks like a security or assault team."

Goblin's eyes were narrow slits. He had to be thinking the same thing I was. Bolus had called Slobodian as soon as we'd left. Or soon enough.

That threw the whole "knock on the door" plan out the window. And, I thought, even as I was already starting to shrug into my ruck, it accelerated the "go have a not-so-nice chat with Bolus" plan.

Ken was already slithering backward from our observation position. The fact that nobody needed to be told that it was time to leave meant that we'd all been thinking along the same, paranoid lines. None of us trusted Bolus, and he'd just confirmed our distrust.

"I'm calling in the boat." Goblin was about to switch frequencies. "Get everybody back to the water. Backwoods, you and I will be the last out."

I nodded. KG probably would have been the better choice, but he was up north, with Tom and Brian. I keyed my radio. "This is Backwoods. All elements fall back to the water for extract. Avoid contact if at all possible." Goblin hadn't specified that last part, but it stood to reason. Getting into a firefight there wasn't going to be a good thing.

Nobody acknowledged over the radio, probably because the rest of the team were getting their rucks on and fading back into the bush. There wasn't time for any chatter, and we were so damned close to the objective, because of how thick the vegetation was, that it was a risk no recon scout worth his salt wanted to take.

Ken was geared up and waiting, when Clint and Patrick came out of the weeds, still a little farther out from the house, and he moved to join up with them. If I strained my ears, hearing loss or no, I could just make out the sounds of more of the team moving back through the bush, even as the voices of the newcomers drifted through the weeds from the front of the house.

I couldn't make out words, especially since Goblin was murmuring into his radio to bring the launch back for extract—in the middle of the day, that wasn't going to be fun—but just going off the tone I could hear, it sounded like they were looking for something. Or someone. One of them knocked on the front door, and what I could hear didn't sound like a potentially hostile interrogation. It sounded more like checking in with a spotter.

That was my supposition, anyway, based on the vague mumble I could hear through the vegetation and the distance. It fit what we'd figured about this place. I seriously doubted Slobodian was on site.

We'd find out, if Bolus knew anything.

If he was smart, Bolus was already halfway to Europe. We had a line on him, though. We had more information about Bolus than he thought we did, and if he tried to hide, we'd find him. He'd be more easily run down than Slobodian.

This could be a long hunt. I could feel the urgency of it clawing at the inside of my chest as Goblin and I rucked up and moved out, falling in behind Tom, Brian, and KG.

We'd already had to fight to defend our families once. We'd gotten lucky, so to speak, since we'd had some warning. Sooner or later, if this kept up, they were going to get a hit squad through, and somebody we cared about was going to die.

You'd better run, Bolus.

CHAPTER
15

Extract actually went surprisingly smoothly. By the time we got back to the water, hearing no sounds of pursuit behind us, the launch was already there, John keeping it up against the bank with the motor. We clambered in, stashed our weapons and gear in the bags he'd brought along, and did what we could to look like just some dumb tourists out boating. That was a little difficult, with just thirteen dudes on a boat, but we didn't get too many looks, so we could hope that we'd pulled it off.

Our stop on board the yacht wasn't a long one. Just long enough to get a quick shower and change over. Then we were heading back into Placencia.

Picking up Bolus was, we thought, going to be a bit difficult. We'd been in the bush for almost three days, though Goblin had thought ahead and had some eyes in the city keeping tabs on him. I didn't know who, but Goblin *had* been expanding the company since its inception, and he didn't always tell us about everything.

As frustrating as it could be sometimes, "need-to-know" still occasionally applied to us, too.

We didn't take much care to separate on the way back to shore. Time was of the essence, so a certain degree of subtlety had to go away to make up for it. We headed back to the marina aboard the launch, looking and smelling a bit more human, though after three days in the weeds, I couldn't say we necessarily felt that way.

A good night's rest would have done wonders, but we simply didn't have the time, if we were going to intercept Bolus.

We'd barely hit the dock when Goblin's phone buzzed. He looked down at it, and his eyebrows went up. "Well, we've still got to move fast, but it doesn't look like Bolus has left town yet. He's not at his house, and apparently hasn't been for a couple of days, but we know where he is."

"We do?" Phil raised an eyebrow. I would have expected Brian or Jake to be the first to question things, as they were generally the most outspoken and pugnacious of the team, but Phil had probably the longest history with Goblin after me. "How is that, anyway?"

Goblin just smiled. "I don't tell you guys *everything*." He sobered. "It does look like he went to ground shortly after we inserted, which means he probably contacted Slobodian that night, then headed for a safehouse." He kept walking, heading off the dock and onto the beach. "The safehouse is up north. We should be reasonably secure down here. Everybody go to your hotel rooms, take five, then come meet up with me at mine. We'll have to move quickly, but there's no reason to get sloppy."

I traded glances with Phil and Ken. It all came down to whether or not we trusted Goblin. This wasn't the military. We weren't held by the UCMJ to obey him. We followed him because we were getting paid to.

And because he was willing to let us do the work that needed to be done.

We traded a nod. He hadn't led us wrong so far. We split up and dispersed into the crowd of tourists and expats, at least for a little while.

***

Bolus wasn't expecting us. That much became obvious when Goblin knocked on the door, backed up by Custus, and Bolus made a run for the back and the dock that sat on the bay.

Unfortunately for him, we'd kind of expected that.

I was waiting with Ken, Phil, and Marcos under the trees, while Tom and Brian had taken the launch around and were on the dock, just in case Bolus got past us. That was unlikely, but we needed to make sure there was no way he could wriggle out of this trap. He'd gotten complacent, figuring that Slobodian would take care of us, and that he just had to hide from any follow up that came looking for us. Seeing Goblin at his front door had thrown him into a panic.

He was looking over his shoulder, his mouth already gaping like a landed fish, as he half ran, half stumbled down the back steps and onto the sand. I'd already closed half the distance, not even bothering to run, by the time he looked where he was going and spotted me.

With a faint cry, he tried to change direction, almost as if he hoped he could get around me. He was already puffing, his flab flapping, and I barely had to break into a jog to close the rest of the distance, grabbing him by the upper arm as he just sort of gave up, gasping for breath.

"Should have kept your cardio up if you were going to make a run for it." I steered him back toward the house, my teammates closing in around us. "Let's go have a talk, shall we?"

***

Goblin was already inside with Custus by the time we got back into the living room. The safehouse was every bit as nice as Bolus's residence. Not that I found that terribly surprising. The man appeared to be the sort who liked his comforts.

He was sweating profusely by the time he dropped into a chair across from Goblin. "Thad…"

"Shut up." Goblin watched him, unblinking. "Let's get things out in the open, here. I told you that what we discussed was in confidence, and that if any word got to Slobodian, then we'd be back. Well, somebody came looking for us, and then you ran, so I think we can dispense with any pretenses here. You called Slobodian, which means you *do* know how to contact him, and you probably *do* have a good idea of where he is." He folded his arms as he leaned back in his seat. "You were too good an intelligence officer not to."

The backhanded compliment didn't seem to settle Bolus down much. He swiped a hand across his bow, and it came back dripping. Not all of that sweat was from the effort of just trying to run about twenty yards, either.

"So." Goblin let the word hang in the air for a moment. "You're going to tell me everything you know about Caleb Slobodian, whatever he's calling himself now. What you know about his network, his activities, and more importantly, his bolt holes. Everything." He smiled tightly. "And we're going to record every second of it, to be leaked where Slobodian can find it, if you cross us again."

Sweating, shaking, Bolus spilled his guts.

CHAPTER
16

By the time they got to Arizona, the rush of adrenaline and rage had worn off enough that some questions started to be asked.

"What the fuck are we going to do with these people?" Josh was the first one to raise the question, just before the Arizona border. He was driving, with Abaeze in the passenger seat, while Nick and Doug rode in the back. They were the heavy truck, running escort for the van just ahead, packed with illegals, recently liberated from the cartel.

When he didn't get an answer, he continued. "I mean, I'm not regretting getting them out of that shithole, but seriously, what the hell are we going to do with them? They're illegals. We can't just let 'em go. Hell, they'll either be scooped up or re-enslaved within a week. If we turn 'em over to the Border Patrol, then questions will be asked about how they got loose."

"You really think they're going to be able to identify any of us?" Abaeze asked. "It was dark, it was chaos, and most of us had NVGs on. Hell, they probably think we're *La Migra* as it is."

"No, they probably won't." Josh was still frowning. "Still, even if they tell the boys in green that it was BORTAC that got them, out, sooner or later somebody's going to put the pieces together."

"They will if they know we were operating in the area. Which they shouldn't." Abaeze was still looking on the brighter side. "The only people who know we were anywhere near Shelter Valley are PGS guys, and none of them should be talking about it."

"'Should' is the key word there." Doug's voice was grimmer than usual. "We've done pretty well so far, but no security is airtight, and at least *somebody*'s looking pretty hard at us. I wouldn't be surprised if this 'shadow network' tries to use the legit authorities against us, too." There was a long, heavy silence. Nick glanced at his partner, but Doug was looking out the window. They were all still in their ATACS AU-X fatigues, though the plate carriers, rucks, weapons, and helmets were all stowed in the back. They wouldn't stand up to a second glance, at least not in California, though in Arizona, they might not even get a second glance.

Finally, Doug shook his head. "We've got to do the right thing here. There's a risk, but we can't just put these people on the road and say, 'Good luck.' We've got to turn them over to the Border Patrol." He sighed. "Let's find a place to change over, first. At least keep *some* questions at bay."

***

It turned out to be simpler than Nick would have thought. They pulled into a truck stop just outside of Yuma, parking behind the line of semis. Nick was a little surprised how many trucks there were, considering the problems with independent truckers and California at the moment, but it was Yuma, and they were on the Arizona side. Maybe this was as far as these guys were going.

From there, it was easy enough to call the Border Patrol, report a van full of what looked like illegal aliens, possibly with some abuse involved, while the drivers from the D Team wiped down everything that might have had a print on it. Then, they just waited until the trail vehicle reported the green and white SUVs coming in, and they rolled out.

Nick looked back as they drove away. Doug caught the look. "I hope they're okay, too, man."

He turned forward again. "I mean, I'm kinda torn about it. On the one hand, they *are* illegals. They broke the law to get here, and they paid the fucking cartel to sneak in. I'm sure some of them are dirt poor and just wanted a better life, but that's the same damned excuse the narcos use."

"But on the other hand, nobody deserves to go through that." Doug nodded. "It's a complicated world. We can be sympathetic at the same time we have to make hard decisions."

Nick shook his head. He really did feel torn. Watching what those people had gone through, he couldn't help but feel that that they'd already seen enough hardship and agony. All the same, he knew a lot of people, legitimate, legal immigrants, who still hated the presumption inherent in illegal immigration, especially the drain it put on the system, not to mention the rampant crime there in the border areas. These people might be victims of the cartels, but they'd still broken the law, and still tried to cheat their way in.

"I guess that's why you shouldn't rely on feelings to make these decisions, huh?" Doug gripped his shoulder and shook him slightly. "They've got a better chance now. Even if they just get dumped on gen pop or come back over the border in six weeks, at least we've done our part. It might not have been entirely pleasant, but it was necessary. We don't know those people, and whatever they went through in the cartel's hands, that doesn't mean they deserve to get off scot free."

"Seems like you've got more trust in the rule of law than most of us do." Josh said what had just flashed through Nick's mind.

"Trust?" Doug should his head as he looked out the window again. "Not really. Like I said, they'll probably just be tossed out onto the street with a court date and no way to track that they make it. Even if they do get deported, then half of them will probably be back with one coyote or another within a few weeks. Hell, they'll probably get victimized again.

"But that's not up to us. We might be stepping outside the letter of the law from time to time, but we're not doing it because we're lawless. We're doing it because the people who are supposed to be stepping up *are* lawless, and they're not doing it. There's a difference. Some people might argue that it's a distinction without a difference, but they're wrong. Intent *does* matter.

"Everything we've done so far, if you look at it, has been in the service of the rule of law. Now, we're only so many dudes. We can't fix everything. But we can do what we can do." Doug nodded toward the dwindling truck stop behind them, and the flashing lights of the Border Patrol vehicles. "We did what we could do. Those people are better off than they were last night."

There was another long pause, as the freeway rolled away behind them. "I think that's the longest speech I've ever heard from you, Doug." Josh glanced in the back with the rear-view mirror. "Don't get me wrong, I'm impressed. Just…"

"Probably a good stopping point, there." Abaeze rolled his head to stare at his partner warningly. Doug didn't seem fazed, but Nick realized he wasn't the only one who felt a little awkward treating a man who'd spent seventeen years in a special mission unit like just another teammate.

Nick just leaned back in his seat as the desert flew by outside, mulling it over. Not everyone in the profession would think that way. Hell, Nick was pretty sure not everyone in *Pallas Group* thought that way. He wondered about even Goblin, sometimes. Sure, there was every sign that he'd carefully vetted his new hires, looking not only for skillsets but also for certain personalities, certain moral fiber.

Of course, that moral fiber had to have *some* flex in it, given their operations so far.

Or did it?

He realized what Doug had been getting at. There *was* a moral standard that Goblin expected them all to abide by. It was a moral standard that the authorities rarely ever observed these days, at least on a certain level. That was why Doug had talked so much about lawlessness. He wasn't talking about disobeying the government. He was talking about disobeying the *law*, and that meant something higher than some of the rules that politicians called laws.

It could turn into a slippery slope awfully fast. That was why they'd worked so hard to stay mostly within the confines of the law, even as they'd bent those confines as far as they'd go.

That raid might not have qualified as "within the confines of what's legal," but that didn't mean it was any less justified. Or that they'd had any other choice except to leave the people currently being picked up by the Border Patrol to their fates, as gruesome as those almost inevitably would be.

It was a lot to think about, but they had a long way to go.

***

They finally stopped in Gila Bend and got rooms in the Palm Inn. It wasn't a fancy hotel, but it would do. They needed to get some rest after the night before, and then figure out their next move.

Goblin was still off comms, presumably in Belize. Tim Coleman hadn't come with them, so Saul made the call. "I'll call Tim this evening. For now, let's everybody rack out. We're not all that far from the border, so keep your guns close and your doors and windows locked. The D Team's kept rolling; they're going to be in Phoenix tonight."

There was no argument. Nick had been fighting the sleep monster for the last hour on the road. He took a long shower, then was almost falling down by the time he threw himself into bed.

***

Despite the security risk, the team ended up eating dinner together at the little Mexican restaurant just down the road from the motel. They kept to themselves and were careful not to talk about their work, at least mostly. Abaeze had to rein Josh in a couple of times. Not that anyone seemed to notice. Most of the locals paid the ten athletic men, clearly military or law enforcement of some sort, little mind.

Nick wondered vaguely if it was out of respect, or if it was because some of the clientele worked for the cartels in some capacity, and didn't want the attention.

Finally, they called it a night and started back to the motel. The sun was going down over the desert, turning the hills to the north purple.

The beauty of the scene was slightly lost on Nick. He was watching their surroundings, glad he had his Glock with him but wondering if he shouldn't have found some way to bring a rifle.

When he'd just been in a balls-out firefight less than twelve hours before…

There are some things that just don't get turned off. Not easily.

The team all went to their rooms first. Saul had made that pretty clear in the restaurant parking lot. They *should* be clean, but it was best not to take chances. They'd expended some ammunition in the fight to clear that compound, so evasion was the best choice.

That was why they walked back in ones and twos, instead of all in one pack.

After about ten minutes dawdling around his room, Nick left, carefully locking it since he still had his weapon and gear in there, and headed around the L shape toward Saul's room. Matt, Carl, Durand, and Mike were already there.

Saul was sitting propped up on the bed, in his socks already, flipping channels on the TV. There weren't many chairs in there, so the others were either sitting on the floor or leaning against the wall. Saul didn't apologize, but just watched the drivel on the screen, waiting for the rest to get there.

Nick realized he hadn't actually watched TV in a long time. As the channels sped by, he realized he really hadn't been missing much.

A knock came at the door, and Durand turned to peer out the peephole, his hand next to his concealed Glock. After a second, he opened the door, and Doug came in, followed by Manny.

"Just waiting on Josh and Abaeze." Saul went back to flipping through channels.

Nobody seemed eager enough to get things rolling that they interrupted. Everyone just sort of stared blankly at the flickering TV screen, lost in their own thoughts and the fatigue brought on by a long field op, followed by a raid, followed by a nearly four-hour drive.

Five hours of sleep wasn't going to make up for that.

Finally, Josh and Abaeze showed up, and Saul sat up, swung his legs off the bed, and turned off the TV.

"Okay. I've talked to Tim. We've got some work ahead of us. I don't have a nice PowerPoint brief set up for you, so for now, it's going to have to be word of mouth.

"We're tracking those GPS pucks that Manny put on the vehicles. They're halfway across the country by now, and it looks like they're heading for the Northeast." He smiled, though it was a sour, humorless expression. "I hope y'all are ready to try to blend in with all the New Yorkers or Jerseyites."

Looking around, Nick realized that he didn't know of any New Yorkers in the company at all. Certainly not on this team. They were all gun guys, to one extent or another, after all, which didn't tend to play well in the Northeast.

"All New Yorkers hate each other and everyone else, so they do their damnedest to ignore everybody, anyway." Carl ran a thumb along his jaw. "Not too worried about the blending in part. The guns will be a problem."

There were some nods and quiet curses at that. New York was not a state friendly to the right to keep and bear arms.

"That's why we might be doing some more information gathering and reporting rather than direct action." Saul's demeanor was as deadly calm as ever. "Information can be a weapon, and unless this operation is entirely limited to New York, or New Jersey, or Massachusetts, or wherever the fuck they're going, then we should be able to find some other places to hit." A faint smile crossed his face again, though this time it was less sour and more feral. "Besides, we've seen already how much damage we can do just by leaking the appropriate information online. If this really is a human trafficking network we're following, then there will be more nodes we can hit, in more permissive areas."

There was a long pause. It was Doug, somewhat to Nick's surprise, who raised the question.

"I get why we're doing this. And I'm in favor. And I know that Goblin said that we're going to get paid. But the question needs to be asked. How is this within our mission? We seem to have left the primary contract to the C Team, and we *still* don't know what connection, exactly, this mysterious client has with these human traffickers."

"It's a fair question." Saul, of all the team, seemed the least in awe of Doug's background and demonstrated ability. It wasn't that he held the senior man in contempt. Far from it. Saul just recognized that at the moment, he was acting team leader, so he was going to act like it. "Unfortunately, it's one I don't really have an answer to. Mainly because I haven't been given that information." He looked around at the rest of the team. "For the moment, I'm willing to follow up on the human traffickers, since the boss has said we're still getting paid, and leave the grand strategy to the office."

"I hear you." Doug was packing a dip. "And I get it. I'm just going to throw this out there." He took a deep breath. "We don't have the cushion we used to. Leaving the grand strategy to the office could very well end up with us out here in the breeze. Just a word of caution, is all."

"And I can't say I disagree. I doubt any of us do. We've all been around. Not as much as you might have, Doug, but still." Saul got nods from around the room. "We've always known that we've got to sleep with one eye open."

"Fair enough." Doug worked the wad of dip into his mouth. "Just pays to have a reminder now and then. Anything else? 'Cause it's probably a good idea to get some more sleep before we hit the road again."

"Not yet. Tim said to hold what we've got for the moment, and as soon as we've got a target area, he'll get flights set up for us. It might mean a stopover to drop gear and weapons, but we've at least got a day to get some rest."

"No argument there." Carl was already heading for the door, yawning. "I'll see y'all for breakfast. At about noon."

CHAPTER
17

I hate New York. Nick had been forced to spend several days in the city several years before, when a flight overseas had been first diverted, then delayed. He wasn't quite as opposed to city living as some guys in the company, but he *hated* New York. He hated the squalor, the ever-present crime, the attitudes, and most of all, the fact that he couldn't legally carry.

Walking through the crowded streets, between brick and cinderblock commercial buildings covered in graffiti, his hatred wasn't getting any less.

There wasn't a good place in that area to set up surveillance. If you could drive in and find a parking spot, you might be able to set up in a vehicle and watch, but in a place like this commercial district, just sitting in a car was going to stand out. They needed to figure out something else.

That was taking time, though Tim had assured the team that he was working on it. The trouble with urban recon and surveillance was that it took a lot of preparation and careful planning, if you were really going to do it right, depending on the area. In a place with lots of tourists, it could be as easy as wearing casual clothes and going for a walk, switching out with another team or operator from time to time, rotating the whole team through in such a way that they shouldn't stand out.

In an industrial area, if you wanted to look like you belonged there, it took a bit more prep. There were a couple of angles that Nick had thought of, the most obvious being homeless guy camo. That took some time, too, though, if you were really going to be convincing about it. Just the smell had to be right, as well as some missed meals. Most of the homeless Nick had run into so far appeared to be far enough out of it from drugs that they might not notice.

Nick had known a couple guys who were now in the ground a lot of years because they'd assumed that the situation was fine, though.

In a combat situation—and Nick considered New York effectively a combat zone, regardless—assumptions get people killed.

The GPS trackers had paused for a significant amount of time on this block, before they'd moved not far away and then gone static. They didn't have much battery life left, but it looked like this had been the drop. So, while Tim worked on getting some sort of mobile hide worked up, they still needed to get eyes on and start to build a picture of what might be going on on the ground.

That meant getting boots on the street. Nick wasn't the only one, but he didn't have eyes on any of the rest of the team. That was deliberate. Footprint could get out of hand, fast, and if they alerted their targets, then either things could get ugly, or the traffickers—and their victims—could be gone in a heartbeat.

So, Nick was wearing jeans and a t-shirt, his hands in his pockets, walking down the street, taking in as much as he could on a single pass. They had a lot of territory to cover, given how imprecise the GPS tracking had been, and once again, there was that footprint angle.

As he moved past a parked box truck he crossed a gap in the line of parked vehicles on the curb, held open by orange traffic cones and yellow caution tape, probably because there was a hole in the street right there. How long it had been there, Nick had no way of knowing, but to his mind, the fact that there was caution tape, but no apparent effort to fix it, spoke volumes.

His eyes flicked across the street, just in time to see a door open and a fat man in a white shirt come out, followed by two Hispanic girls. They were dressed like ordinary teenagers, but both of them had their heads down and followed the man like they were on a leash.

His eyes narrowed, even as he made sure not to stare. Staring attracts attention. He just noted it, as the fat man opened the door of the van parked next to the building. One of the girls got in. The other balked, only to be grabbed by the arm and roughly pushed in.

Nick kept walking. It wasn't quite a smoking gun, but something about that little drama made him think that he may have just located their target building. There was more observation that needed to happen, and the rest of the area still needed to be swept, but this looked promising, for a certain grim definition of the word.

He kept going, digging out his burner phone and sending in a quick report. This bore watching.

***

"Okay, one question." Manny was looking at the box truck in the rental garage. "While the hide in the back is awesome, who the hell is going to drive this thing, and what are they supposed to do while it's parked?"

All eyes turned to Tim Coleman. There was a coolness there that there hadn't been with either Vern or Frank, even as Frank had increasingly isolated himself from the team out of a severe case of bruised ego. Tim had sent them on a long, difficult mission, and hadn't come himself. He was obviously more manager than leader, and the contractors clearly didn't really like it. Nick couldn't say he liked it, either. Not at all.

"We're working on that," was all he said.

Saul blinked slowly. Nick knew that expression, and it usually didn't bode well. Saul was slow to anger but once he lost his temper, it was bad. And that slow blink was usually a pretty good indication that he was about to lose his temper.

"We don't have a lot of time to get on this, Tim." Doug stepped up before Saul could blow his stack. "Find us some coveralls and some clipboards. We'll have to wing it." He turned to the rest of the team. "Coveralls and a clipboard can make a man invisible, if he's got the right attitude."

"Can also make him a target, if somebody thinks there's something in that box truck worth stealing." Matt wasn't sure about this idea.

"That's a risk we're going to have to take. Nobody's gotten mugged yet, but we were all prepared for that on the street, weren't we?" Doug was in problem-solving mode, Tim's apparent failure to plan no longer that high up in his thinking priorities.

Tim frowned. Dressed in slacks and a polo shirt, he was generally far more clean-cut than most of the contractors, down to his haircut and fresh shave. Nick found himself wondering just where Goblin had found this guy, and why he was in the position he was.

"That's still going to take some time, especially if we want to find something convincing, not just a random work coverall we got off ebay."

"Doesn't have to be an airtight disguise. It just has to look normal enough to let their eyes slide off. Hell, a coverall from Harbor Freight would be fine. Doesn't have to have corporate logos or anything." Doug turned an eye on their team manager. Nick couldn't quite bring himself to think of Tim as a team leader anymore.

Fortunately, Tim had enough presence of mind to nod. Saul was looming at the side of the box truck, his arms folded, his frown thunderous. The rest of the team didn't look all that much happier.

"Okay. I'll get something out here shortly."

Doug nodded in turn, then elbowed Nick as he headed for the garage door. "Come on. I want to do another drive through of that area. See if we can spot any *halcones*."

***

They were three blocks away, Doug behind the wheel, Nick sitting in the passenger seat and still feeling naked, unarmed as he was, before he broached the subject.

"So."

"So." Doug glanced sidelong at him. "What?"

"You seem a little more invested in the mission than before."

There was a long silence. Doug kept his eyes on the road and the mirrors, as if he was chewing it over. "Not more invested. Not exactly. This was the mission that Goblin gave us, and it's righteous. My concerns were more about whether or not we were going to end up way out in the cold, chasing the wind in a way that was going to leave us vulnerable. The A Team's chasing down this hitman network, the C Team is doing the contracted surveillance, so where does that leave us?"

He tilted his head a little, still watching traffic. "But I've been putting some pieces together. The client wanted eyes on that Wise dude, and they wanted him protected. Given what we found out, that almost certainly had something to do with his reporting on Shelter Valley, which seems to be about this human trafficking ring. The client has some interest in this network, and if they wanted us to keep Wise alive—which seems to have been the case, since they apparently bitched Goblin out for letting him get turned into pavement pizza—then it probably isn't because they wanted it covered up. They want something exposed, and/or shut down."

"You think this really is what we got hired for, just the client didn't want to show his hand by openly hiring a company of shooters to go nail a bunch of human traffickers?"

"It's a possibility." Doug rubbed his chin, his other hand on the steering wheel. "Makes me wonder who it is. That 'risk management firm' thing seems a bit sketchier all the time."

Nick leaned back in his seat, watching the traffic and the pedestrians on the street. It might not be as crowded here in this industrial part of town as it would be downtown, but it still wasn't a picnic. The street was supposed to be two lanes, but there were so many cars and vans parked on the curb that oncoming traffic had about the space of a hand's breadth between side mirrors and a wreck.

It made some sense. They'd started to get used to this shadowy war of information, hidden identities, proxies, and innuendos. That didn't mean they *liked* it, necessarily, but for those who had worked contract after the military, often in shady places for shady government agencies, it wasn't *completely* foreign. There was still something innately frustrating, almost dirty, about it. It was cheaper, in both money and lives, than open warfare, but it was far, far less honorable.

Despite the cynical, jaded sort of irony that many gunfighters adopted as a sort of armor against the bureaucratic bullshit they spend their entire careers dealing with, Nick thought there was a part of all of them that still craved that stand up fight. A warrior's form of warfare. As good as he was getting at the skullduggery side of things—and Special Forces had always involved some degree of that, being intended to go behind enemy lines and train proxies to fight the enemy for the US—he missed a straight-up sort of warfare.

Not that the cartels hadn't given them a taste of it. It was the shadowy, hidden movers and shakers in the background that pissed him off.

"So, you think we should hit this warehouse?" He brought his attention back to the here and now.

Doug, though, shook his head. "Not the time or the place. Sure, we could get our guns and gear in here, if we wanted to run the risk. Might even be worth it. But I don't believe for a second that this is the only hub. This is *a* hub. That compound in California was different. Out in the boonies like that, we could put some hurt on them and disappear. Here, there are almost guaranteed to be a lot more hubs, and they'll just shift if we only hit one of them."

He sighed. "No, we're going to have to do a lot of surveillance, and start mapping this out as best we can, if we want to do much more than offer the bad guys a couple of pinpricks."

Nick nodded, though he had to grit his teeth as he did it. "So, we've got to watch, wait, and stay cold."

"As always."

CHAPTER
18

"How sure are we that Bolus didn't immediately call Slobodian again as soon as we left?" I was sitting next to KG in the rental car we'd gotten from the AVIS in the Cartagena airport. The yacht was still on its way across the Caribbean, with our gear, weapons, and half the team, but Ken, KG, Phil, Marcos, and I had flown ahead to start doing preliminary reconnaissance.

"We don't, not for sure." KG was mostly paying attention to the road, which was absolutely necessary in Colombian traffic. Not that any of us weren't still somewhat used to Third World traffic and its utter chaos, even if some of us had been away from it for a few years. "We can hope that we put the fear into him, but there's nothing that's necessarily going to shut him up for sure besides putting him in the swamp. Which we couldn't do. However, even if he did rat us out, he can't know where we're going or when. That gives us something of an advantage."

I nodded. It helped that we'd flown into Cartagena, though there weren't any international airports—at least not that were open and legit—near the target area. It also put us far enough out that it was unlikely—not impossible, but unlikely— that Slobodian had eyes on us. As small as Colombia is compared to the US, it's still a big country, and nobody can have eyes everywhere.

That's a hard thing to get through your head. Some people go full paranoid, seeing hostile eyes and ears everywhere, to the point that they're paralyzed. Others get the idea that because no one *can* maintain surveillance over an entire country, that they've got nothing to worry about, so they get complacent.

Both ways are not what right looks like. You've got to find the right balance of alertness and realism. We'd had to learn that in places where the terrorist threat was high, but only rarely visible. Colombia was no different.

Bolus had spilled his guts and fingered three other locations where Slobodian had houses. From what Bolus knew, he rarely visited his place in the Hamptons, and was unlikely to be there at the moment. All of his recent contacts had been in Latin America.

The other two places, aside from Belize, were in Colombia and Paraguay. Colombia was closer, and from what Bolus had been able to gather—as despicable as the man was, he *was* a good intelligence officer—that was mainly where Slobodian was hanging out lately. Something was going on, though Bolus had no idea what.

I was starting to get my suspicions about Slobodian. Not that I didn't suspect before that he was a bad guy. But it seemed as if he was more than just a coordinator for a hitman network.

One of the things that you have to do, if you're serious about pursuing this profession, is read. The Marine Corps has a professional reading list, and I'd gone through half of it by the time I'd picked up Corporal. That habit had continued as I'd pushed into the close protection business, since you often get even less intel in the private sector.

So, I'd gone digging, trying to understand the threat environments I was going into. After that firefight in Atlanta that had really kicked off the kinetic part of my Pallas Group Solutions career, I'd really delved into more and more of the underground elements of what some people were calling 5GW. Some said it stood for Fifth Generation War, which is stupid, since some of this crap has been strategically used since the dawn of time. I tended to prefer an article I read that called them "Gradients" of war, rather than "Generations."

Anyway, along the way I'd discovered the concept of the "shadow facilitator." The sort of gold standard for this sort of character was the Russian arms dealer Viktor Bout, who'd connected multiple underworld entities and tyrannical warlords, all while running around as the legitimate CEO of an international air cargo company.

The "shadow facilitator" is the guy that connects all the networks of drugs, guns, money, slaves, and other contraband. I was starting to think, just based on his geographic range, that Slobodian might qualify.

Which meant a couple of things. One, he probably had a lot more resources he could call on if he was threatened than just the stable of unscrupulous shooters we'd already whittled down significantly over the last year or so.

Two, if we took him off the board, we could potentially put the hurt on this network for a while.

It wouldn't end anything. Not really. It wouldn't stop the corrupt politicians or the Chinese who were trying to get as many drugs as possible into the country while snapping up control of as much industry and natural resources as possible. It would only slow them down.

But that was better than letting them continue to sow as much destruction as possible.

And, if Goblin's suspicions about our primary client at the moment were accurate, we might be able to hurt some of those movers and shakers in their ivory towers beyond the mud and the blood where the killing was happening.

I was still watching our surroundings as I pondered all of this. Being the right seater meant that security was my primary responsibility. I leaned against the door and scanned the streets as KG took us out into the city.

***

What I'd seen of Cartagena so far reminded me a lot of places we'd been in Mexico. And the Middle East. Closer to the

149

airport, we saw a lot of the same crumbling sidewalks, slightly dingy look to all the otherwise bright, white and light-colored buildings, and the same rat's nest of power and telephone cables hanging far too low over the narrow streets. The humidity reminded me of Mazatlán, which made sense, since the city was right on the water, and we were less than a mile from the beach in any direction right then.

As we worked our way out from the airport, the grinding poverty got even more evident. The courtyards and concrete gave way to bare dirt, trash, and weeds off the road. The houses were smaller, more slapdash, and mostly made of red brick, partially plastered over with gray cement. Some of them had fenced compounds, though they were generally smaller than what I remembered seeing in places like Iraq, and there were usually bars over the windows on those houses, as well.

The main difference between that place and the Middle East that I could see, besides the culture and the red brick, was how green everything was.

It took a while to get out of the city. We finally started to get out into the countryside, passing the walled in compound of the Gobernación de Bolivar before finally getting out into the boonies. Even then, there wasn't that much of a view, as the vegetation still stood tall and green on either side of the highway.

I wished more than ever that I had my weapons. The violence in Colombia might have died down a bit since the days of Pablo Escobar, but that didn't mean the country was peaceful. Things between the government and the Gulf Clan cartel were flaring up again.

That wasn't even touching on the FARC, the ELN, the various splinter groups off of those groups, the Urabeños, Los Pachenca, the Comandos de Frontera, and plenty of others.

Unfortunately, we didn't have a contract as cover. Even if we had one—time had been a bit too pressing to do the necessary groundwork ahead of time—getting guns in Colombia was not going to fly, not openly. This was a country where civilian ownership is *extremely* limited, everything has to go through the Colombian military, and ammunition is rationed to about half my combat loadout per year.

If we were going to go kinetic, we were going to have to effectively invade Colombia and be ready to run like hell for international waters afterward.

That was another reason to go in as tourists, like this. Keeping a low profile, staying off the Colombian authorities' radar, we might be able to confirm or deny that Slobodian was even in the country before we started getting sporty.

Hunting a man isn't all just find, fix, and finish. We might just get eyes on him in Colombia and then do what we could to track him until we could corner him somewhere more advantageous to us.

Sometimes, as much as it might seem urgent to take a particular bad guy off the board, patience is still the name of the game.

So, I settled in for a long drive.

CHAPTER
19

Slobodian's Colombia house wasn't near one of the big metropolitan cities. Instead, it was up in the hills to the south of Capurgana, in Choco Department. That would make some of the infiltration a bit easier, at least so far as avoiding human detection went. We wouldn't have to worry so much about someone wondering why we were hanging out near a particular area. We would still need to be aware of our footprint, given that gringos weren't all that common in some of the more rural parts of Colombia. We didn't want to draw too much attention, but if we posed as hikers, we might be able to make it work.

The part that worried me was the fact that *somebody* was going to notice that these *Norteamericano* tourists were all physically fit men in their thirties and early forties. While we might have gotten better at the gray man model, looking less and less like special operations soldiers, the fact was that we all still fit a type, and in a place with a hell of a lot of human traffic, not to mention whatever cartels or ex-FARC mafias might be operating in the area, somebody might still finger us for gunfighters.

The human traffic was a large part of what made me nervous, trying to move through this part of northwestern Colombia unarmed, while attempting recon and surveillance. We weren't that far from the Darien Gap, the funnel through which thousands of refugees, slavers, drug smugglers, and terrorists had made their way from South America north, toward the US.

I didn't think it was a coincidence that Slobodian's Colombian residence was that close to the Darien. It only strengthened my suspicions about him. From what Goblin and KG had said already, I wasn't alone.

We gathered up at the Hotel Casa Costa, where KG had gotten a room. The rest of the recon team was spread out in various hotels and hostels around the town. There were a lot of other foreigners there, though most of them were African or Asian. Most of them were looking to make the trek through the Darien Gap.

While I might have expected that that would make us stand out all the more, there were an awful lot of gringos in town, too. A lot of them were tourists. There was still quite a diving and hiking industry in Capurgana, though tourism had taken a back seat to housing migrants lately.

I was pretty sure not all of them were tourists, though.

"We need to make sure we're keeping to ourselves." I glanced over my shoulder as Manny shut the door, the last one to enter KG's room. "I can't say for sure, but I might have recognized one of the palefaces out on the street this morning."

KG looked up at me sharply from where he was studying the map. It was a tourist hiker map, primarily for the El Aguacate-Capurgana trail, but it was still a good topo map, and therefore useful for what we had to do. "Who was it?"

I halfway regretted bringing it up. "I couldn't be sure. If it's him, he's lost some weight and grown his hair out. But it looked like Tang."

That raised some eyebrows. "Well, if the powers that be have finally started to take some interest in the activity in the Darien, then it makes sense that guys like us would be down here, too. The violence level might be a lot lower than it was during *La Violencia* and the Medellin Cartel days, but that doesn't mean it's exactly safe."

"It does mean that Chris is right, and we're going to have to be even more careful." Marcos had moved to the window and peered outside. It was raining, so the beach was only visible through a haze of gray. "Some of us haven't been away from that world for very long, and we all know dudes who are still in the business."

"Just be careful that you're not too obvious about avoiding anybody." KG turned his attention back to the map. "That can be as much of a target indicator as anything else."

"What are we supposed to say if we run into somebody we know here, though? A cover story for the locals is one thing. For somebody who knows what's up, it can be something else entirely." Phil had moved to the window across from Manny, looking down at the street as if he expected one of our old teammates to suddenly appear out of the gray like Bloody Mary when her name's called in a mirror three times.

Ken snorted. "Same thing you'd tell any of the locals, brother. We're here on vacation. Gonna do a bit of hiking, maybe some scuba diving." That slow grin spread across his face. "Come on, we all know dudes who got together half the team and came on some super yuppie tourist trip like this. Relax."

"We won't be in town for that long, anyway. Not today." KG straightened up and tapped the map on the table in front of him. "We've got about a three mile loop to cover to get eyes on Slobodian's house, and since it's in the jungle, I don't have to tell you boys how long it's probably going to take. I've let it drop a few places that we're planning to tramp all over this area, so nobody *should* be looking for us. Our extended absence from the hotel shouldn't be marked." He looked around at everyone with raised eyebrows. "I hope nobody left much of anything in their rooms that they can't stand to lose?"

"Not saying that there are any thieves around here, or anything…" Phil chuckled as he turned away from the window.

KG ignored him, pointing to the lines and notations on the map. "As you can see, this is going to be dead reckoning hell, so make sure everybody memorizes the route. We don't have a lot of time, but if somebody gets lost, it's so thick up there that we'll lose more time trying to get back on route."

He checked his watch. "The yacht is supposed to be within helicopter range tonight, so if we need support, extract, or even to hit the place, we should have it by then." He sighed. "Frankly, given the terrain we've got to cover, I doubt we're going to be in position before dawn."

Now with less than three miles to cover, that might seem overly pessimistic. When that three miles is through jungle and over hills, with the necessity to make damned good and sure nobody was following or watching us, then it can take an awful long time to cover that ground.

"Take some time to memorize the route, then we're stepping off within an hour."

***

The rain had let up by the time we headed out of the hotel and up into the hills. We got some looks, but those were unavoidable when the town was packed with migrants looking to go north, either for a better life, or for the sake of destruction and greed. I thought maybe I saw someone more familiar watching us from a hotel window, but I couldn't be sure.

For all the security measures that Goblin had put in place, I didn't doubt that certain federal agencies had a roster of Pallas Group Solutions personnel, and that they were *very* interested in our activities. We'd done a pretty good job of masking our more gray zone sort of missions, but nothing's airtight, and we'd already crossed the FBI once. It wouldn't surprise me if there were requests for information out to various intelligence agencies and their contractors about us.

It just meant that we needed to step carefully anywhere that we might be observed. For the moment, we had nothing to hide, not to the casual observer. We were just some dudes going hiking. None of us were wearing or carrying anything camouflage or overtly "tactical." Much like we'd done in

Panama, we were wearing civilian outdoor clothing and carrying drab but still obviously civilian packs.

Without looking up at where I thought I'd seen a face watching us, we headed up into the hills, starting with the trail to La Miel. We'd turn off once we were well into the jungle and out of sight.

***

Jungle movement just sucks.

The movies always show guys hacking a path with machetes, and sometimes that's what it takes, but it's generally a bad idea if you're trying to go unnoticed. If you look into the accounts of the MACV-SOG recon teams, they didn't cut their way through the jungle. It still took them all day to go five hundred yards, but they left less of a trace.

We weren't hacking our way through, either. That meant that within a few minutes of getting off the trail, we were already soaked with both the rain draining off the plants and our own sweat, and with a glance at my watch, I started to think that KG had actually been slightly *optimistic* about how long it would take us to circle around Capurgana and down to Slobodian's house.

I'm getting too old for this. I ducked under another low-hanging frond and got showered with water anyway. The wet wasn't bothering me nearly as much as the bugs, but it was going to start chafing before too long. Especially with the amount of plant matter that had already worked its way into my sleeves, my collar, and my beltline.

Doesn't matter. You're committed, and you have been ever since you shot those gangbangers in Atlanta. The fact that they came after your family *should have told you that. Mission is what it is. Suck it up, Brother Recon.*

I looked up, got eyes on Phil's pack ahead of me, and stepped over a fallen tree to close the distance. We had a long way to go.

***

It felt even longer than it was. The jungle fought us every step of the way, and we had to stop to rest and hydrate far too often. The day dragged on as we slogged our way through the thick veg, up and over ridgelines that would have been child's play back where I come from, but here, in this heat, humidity, and oppressively thick growth, wore us out fast.

The other reason we stopped so often was security. We might not have rifles or other weapons aside from pocketknives, but we still needed to make sure we weren't being followed. That meant sitting in place, as still as possible, dripping with sweat and listening to the jungle noises, staying as quiet as we could after we'd stopped trying to catch our breath and could just be still and listen.

Then we got up and got moving again, until the next point we had to stop and do it all over again.

The entire route wasn't through thick jungle, but we still stopped and conducted another security halt every time we came to an opening. Once again, while we were doing as good an impression as any of us could of mere tourists, out hiking through the jungle—because *that's* fun—we still didn't want to stumble upon anyone, whether they were local farmers, some of our former teammates in the intelligence and special operations communities, cartel *sicarios*, human traffickers heading for the Darien Gap, or Slobodian's security.

The sun had dipped below the crest of the mountains behind us as we worked our way down the last finger of jungle toward the house that Bolus had fingered as Slobodian's Colombian getaway. Everything hurt by then, in no small part because I was pretty sure I'd sweated every bit of salt out of my body about six hours before. I had electrolyte tabs, and was putting them down like crazy, but my legs were still trying to cramp.

It was *not* going to be a comfortable night.

The jungle was getting dark well before the light faded in the sky overhead. Nature of the beast. The noise of insects and other creatures actually got louder as the day slipped into night.

That was somewhat comforting, since it provided a nice noise screen to cover any extra sound we made moving through the vegetation.

Finally, though I could barely see him in the dimness, Phil raised a hand and then circled it above his head, as he lowered himself to a knee. I passed the signal back and moved up to join him, seeing the lights ahead that had made him stop.

KG was puffing as he caught up with us, and looked like he was just about ready to collapse. He was a big man, and a powerlifter. This sort of long-range movement, in this sort of heat, was not something he indulged in regularly. Still, he'd managed to keep up. Which was more than I could say for some contractors I'd known, back in the day.

Once he got his breathing under control, KG was able to take stock of our position, and the compound beyond. "Looks like this is our place." He lowered his ruck to the jungle floor. "Let's set in and start watching."

CHAPTER
20

The night got *dark*. There was no moon, and very little starlight could make it through the canopy overhead. We hadn't brought our PS-31s, either. They were with the rest of our overtly paramilitary gear, aboard the yacht. Those would have gotten confiscated in Cartagena, no doubt about it. Instead, we had some regular tourist optics. Binoculars, cameras, and a couple of Sionyx digital night vision cameras.

They were technically cameras, not NVGs. And while digital night vision had come a long way in a short time, I still wouldn't want to try to run them as NVGs, even though I knew some guys who said they worked decently well. There was still a delay that could be deadly if you were trying to shoot with them.

Not that we were doing that tonight. So, they were perfectly suited to what we were set in to do.

The spot where Phil had stopped turned out not to be ideal for an observation post to set surveillance on the compound. Yes, we could see the house from there, and some of the lights, but the bulk of the place was out of sight, and what we could see was still obscured by a lot of jungle. We had to adjust a couple dozen yards to the west and close in almost as much, hunkering down in the dark and the dripping vegetation to get a good view of at least part of the front of the house.

We broke things down into two sections. Phil, KG, and I would take turns watching the house. Ken and Marcos would switch out keeping an eye and an ear on our rear and flanks. Without weapons, we'd need as much warning as possible so that we could get out quickly if someone was about to stumble on us, but at the same time, we couldn't afford to get too spread out, either, so they were only a couple yards behind us.

I took first watch, leaning heavily on the Sionyx. It actually provided a pretty good picture, if grainy. The delay was hard to spot, though I knew it was still there. The picture was also in color, which took some getting used to. I'd trained with PVS-7Bs, PVS-14s, PVS-15s, and finally PS-31s. The first three were all monochrome green phosphor, while the PS-31s were white phosphor. Good contrast and clarity, especially with the PS-31s—the less said about the 7Bs, the better—and much more of an immediate image, but still monochrome. The color threw me a little.

The house itself had been built on the site of an earlier farmhouse, and had been built bigger, if not extravagantly. Slobodian seemed to eschew extravagance where he could. That made sense. The more ostentatious he was, the more likely he'd draw attention, and that's poison to somebody in his business. Just as much as it was to us.

There were two motorcycles parked out front. The only vehicles we'd seen in Capurgana had been motorcycles, bicycles, and tuk-tuks, which made sense when you considered that the nearest paved road was over a hundred miles away. This place was the back of beyond, right up against the Darien Gap, which is one of the wildest and most dangerous places on earth. We'd only gotten to Capurgana by ferry from Necocli, which was where most of the people and the supplies that kept the resort and migrant haven running came from.

Even the migrants came here by boat.

The house was dark and quiet, and after the first half hour I was starting to wonder if we'd hit another dry hole. It was even conceivably possible that Bolus had lied through his teeth and sent us on a wild goose chase. I knew that Goblin had asked some very pointed questions to head that possibility off, but if it turned out we were watching some Colombian rancher's property while Slobodian slipped away and sent another attack after our families, it was probably going to be almost as hard to find Bolus and make him pay.

Still, this was the target, and the bossman figured it was the right one. So, blinking hard to stay awake, pulling one of the high-caffeine energy gels I'd brought out of my ruck, I settled in to watch and wait.

***

We started seeing some movement about an hour after dawn. The house wasn't abandoned after all.

Unfortunately, the guy who came out onto the porch with a cup of coffee in his hand wasn't Slobodian. At least, he didn't match the description we'd gotten from Goblin. This guy was taller, broader, and clearly Colombian.

I was just waking up, not because it was my turn or even because I was rested, but just because a mosquito was trying to bore its way into my eardrum. I had a mosquito net over my face, but the noise was getting to me, despite the fatigue of a day's brush-beating and then several hours of observation during the night. I heard Phil muttering to himself, closed my eyes again after trying to crush the bloodsucker as silently as possible, then finally gave up and levered myself up to a sitting position against my ruck.

KG was racked out, his mosquito net over his face, and Phil was watching the house through binoculars. I didn't need the binoculars to see the source of his disappointment.

"Doesn't mean he's the only one here," I whispered. I sucked down some water, having lost a lot of it over the last day and the night. "Got to be patient."

Phil nodded slightly without taking his eyes off the objective. He knew the score. While not everyone in Pallas Group Solutions had a military reconnaissance background, we'd all done enough surveillance and counter surveillance on contract to know that sometimes—in fact, a lot of the time—it just consists of staring at nothing for hours or days at a time.

I retreated to my ruck again and dug out some chow. It wasn't my turn on the OP. The next day and night were going to be long enough as it was.

I'd barely gotten a bite in before Phil hissed at me, drawing me back to the narrow window we'd constructed through the greenery to give us a view of the house.

The Colombian dude wasn't alone. The man standing next to him was older than I'd gathered from the descriptions we'd gotten from Goblin and Bolus, but still trim and still with most of his hair. The streaks of gray near his temples were swept back with the rest of his hair, and he was dressed in a loose white shirt, shorts, and sandals. Slight of build, he didn't look like much, with a bit of a receding chin and a slightly bulbous nose.

Jackpot.

Except that there wasn't much of anything we could do to hurt him right at the moment. We could only watch and report.

I shook KG awake. I felt a little bad about it, but he needed to know that we had eyes on our objective.

He opened his eyes with a pained squint, looked up at the little bit of light we could see in the sky through the canopy, and looked at his watch before turning to me blearily and quizzically. I just pointed to my eyes, then toward the house.

That seemed to wake him up. He blinked, then sat up and reached for the phone and satcom puck that we were using to communicate back to Goblin on the yacht.

The sound of engines turned my attention back to the objective. Those were motorcycles, or four-wheelers. The latter would be interesting, since I hadn't seen any in town, just motorcycles and tuk-tuks.

They weren't four-wheelers that pulled up in front of the house, but regular motorcycles. The men on those motorcycles, however, drew my attention.

The six men could probably have blended into a crowd in Colombia, or anywhere in Latin America, for that matter, at least to the unschooled eye. There was something off about them, though. Most of the brown in Latin America comes from the *Indios*, the various native tribes who always have outnumbered the Spanish, and lent more of their genes to the local melting pot than the Iberian colonists did. These guys had the brown skin and black hair, but there was something different about them.

The beard on the last man gave it away. While beards weren't unknown in Latin America, few of them were as long or dense as this guy's. When the six of them got off the motorcycles, and the man with the long, black beard put his hand on his heart as he spoke to Slobodian, I was sure of it. These guys were jihadis of some stripe.

Slobodian came down the steps, his hand on his own heart, and then embraced the bearded man before shaking hands with all the others. I couldn't hear what was said, even as dangerously close as we were. But he'd clearly been expecting them.

While his Colombian associate watched the road leading back toward town, Slobodian ushered the six men, all of whom had that hard-eyed jihadi look that I remembered so well from Iraq, Afghanistan, and a couple other places, inside. I thought I heard "chai."

"Well, hell." KG had watched the little interplay, as well. "Phil, tell me you got photos."

"Of course I got photos." Phil looked back over his shoulder with a faint glare. "Not my first rodeo."

KG ignored Phil's crankiness and just held out his hand. Without any further complaint, Phil popped the SD card out of the camera and handed it across, quickly slipping a second card in so that he could still take more pictures if something else happened.

It was always a balance with surveillance. You had to get the information passed up the chain, but you also needed to keep eyes on and be able to record anything new that happened while that information was getting passed up.

Granted, if we had voice comms, we could generally just pass descriptions along, with photos or sketches to follow. There was a reason we were sending photos as soon as possible this time, though. We had facial recognition software, and our attached intel nerd, Noah Radford, was pretty good at using it to find people, even if only through news stories.

Something told me—and KG was apparently thinking along similar lines—that these guys were not just tourists or migrants looking for a better life in America. The fact that they were meeting with Slobodian, this close to the Darien Gap, meant we'd just stumbled on something bigger than just a vendetta against PGS.

If Slobodian really was a "shadow facilitator," of course, that meant he had his fingers in a lot of bad stuff.

I glanced at KG, but he was focused on getting the photos uploaded and sent via satcom to the yacht. I could feel the mission creep starting already, though all the same, if those guys were Al Qaeda or Hezbollah—some might object to my confusing the two, but they didn't exactly wear nametapes— then we probably wouldn't be *able* to just worry about Slobodian anymore.

Not that this was immediately or necessarily a case of "race to stop the terrorist attack that will bring the US to its knees." Not every threat has to be existential. That was a weakness I'd seen increasingly with the ever-escalating doomsday threats that never materialized during the GWOT. The fact that an enemy can't kill millions of people at the flip of a switch or push of a button doesn't make them any less of an enemy or any less of a threat that needs dealing with. To look at it any other way is to turn people into nothing but numbers and statistics.

I was fully aware that the same logic could be used to justify abject tyranny, but that wasn't what I was thinking about. Not all contexts are the same.

KG finished sending the photos and looked up. "You thinking what I'm thinking?"

I sighed. "That we just found ourselves a bigger target set? I'm afraid so."

He nodded. "Well, we weren't going to be able to take Slobodian down here, anyway. We just might have to expand our reconnaissance and surveillance efforts and get a better idea of what's going on here before we move."

"I just hope we don't take too much time at it, and one of his hit squads uses the opening to get to somebody we care about." Phil had turned his head to be able to speak without projecting toward the house, but he hadn't taken his eyes off the objective. "They only have to get lucky once."

"That's where trusting the team comes in, Phil." KG glanced over his shoulder toward the house. We couldn't see or hear much of anything, and I figured that KG was regretting bringing the entire R&S team out here. There was no way we'd be able to follow the jihadis on motorcycles, not when we were on foot and worn out from a day-long movement through the jungle. We might have to pull off that night, try to slip back into town, and reset. "Goblin's taken steps, and we've all got trustworthy friends keeping an eye on things back home. We're out here for a reason, and it looks like that reason might have just gotten expanded." He looked at his watch, then made the decision. "Pack it up. We've confirmed that Slobodian is here. I'm making the call that we need to do more of an area study and threat assessment before we can move. Let's see if we can get back to town and get set up before those assholes go north." He grimaced in the dark. "I think we all know that's where they're going, too."

Phil wasn't happy. Marcos and Ken held their peace. I could understand, and I had to admit that I felt the same way, myself. We'd come a long way, only to get confirmation that Slobodian was present and suddenly pull off. But KG was right. Slobodian was a facilitator, not the whole network. We'd just witnessed a meeting that could have far-ranging repercussions. We had a duty, even if one only self-imposed, to do something about it, or at least find out enough that we *could*. Besides, unarmed as we were, there wasn't much we could do to stop anything here, and it wasn't as if there were any friendly forces between here and the Darien that *could*.

So, we rucked up and backed off, heading back to the trail.

CHAPTER
21

"Okay, gents, bring it in." If Tim was aware of how alienated he was from the team he was supposed to be leading, it didn't show in his expression or his voice. "We've got some updates."

Nick glanced at Doug, but his partner was as studiously collected as ever. Whatever Doug thought of their "team leader," he was keeping it to himself. That was to be expected; the older man was vastly better at simply doing the job and keeping his opinion out of it than Nick was, and it was one more way that Nick sometimes thought he was still playing catch up. It wasn't enough that Doug was a machine he couldn't quite keep up with, he was also probably the most emotionally and professionally mature man on the team. Even compared to Saul, and that was saying something.

Nick had known a few special mission unit guys who were nothing like Doug. Guys who were every bit as petty as they were skilled at weapons and tactics. It was refreshing to work with Doug, as exhausting as it sometimes could be to try to keep up.

Saul was watching Tim with a blank, heavy-lidded stare that was about as neutral as the man could be, given how obviously frustrated he'd gotten over the last few days. The rest of the team was gathered in the hotel room in various attitudes of blank frigidity or sullenness.

Tim had not acquitted himself all that well over the last few days. Not that he'd necessarily been wrong, but he'd tried to micromanage the team's surveillance, all without setting foot on the ground. To his credit, he'd backed off when the guys on the ground—presumably more experienced, though when Nick had compared notes with Saul, none of them quite knew the man's background—had pushed back, but the problem was there, and there wasn't a lot of getting around it, short of Tim saddling up and joining them on mission, which he didn't seem to be willing to do.

"The surveillance of the last couple of days, coupled with some careful vetting of facial recognition based on some of the photos you've taken, have found us a potential target." He brought up a carefully prepared PowerPoint slide, with a photo that one of the surveillance teams, in the modified box truck, had taken outside the target building. It showed a young man, reasonably well dressed, stepping out of the door, already on his phone. Next to it was a much clearer and better picture, possibly taken from social media, of the same young man—at least, it looked like him—in a blazer and t-shirt, smiling widely.

There was something about the look of the man's eyes as he smiled. Something dead. Not that surprising, given that he'd been in that place, and clearly of his own free will.

"This is Robert Larkin. Publicly, he's a successful day trader. If you really dig into his finances, though, his day trading hasn't brought shit for returns. Judging by his appearance at the warehouse, twice in the last thirty-six hours, I think we can all ascertain what his real income comes from." Tim flipped to a different slide, this one with a couple of images of an apartment building entrance next to a map. "There are a couple of ways we can approach this. Ultimately, we want to have a long discussion with Mr. Larkin. The only question is how arrange that conversation."

He tapped the screen. "Larkin seems to be relatively careless with his personal security, and it was fairly easy to pinpoint where he lives. He's pretty flashy in public, and that includes social media. Once we had his identity confirmed with facial recognition, it was child's play to figure out where he lives and where he hangs out."

Another slide, with several points in the New York and Newark area picked out. "Again, the question is just how we want to make the approach. Since this *is* New York, a strongarm approach might not be ideal. We *could* break into his apartment and confront him there. Or someone could pose as a prospective customer and lure him into an advantageous position that way."

Saul looked around at the rest of the team, his arms folded. When he turned back to Tim, his face was set and hard. "'We?' Let's clear the air a bit here, Tim." He took a step forward, as Tim turned to face him, folding his own arms and watching the bigger man with a bit of a blank face of his own. He didn't look intimidated by Saul, but he didn't look all that comfortable, either.

"I get that there are different leadership styles. But some styles don't work with certain people. This is a small team, working outside the usual boundaries, and taking some pretty hellacious risks in the process. Most of us have been together for a while, even before this company. We've seen some shit together."

He wasn't yelling, wasn't even growling. His tone of voice was even and professional. Nick could still see Tim starting to stiffen, nevertheless.

"Now, none of us know you, but most of us have sort of figured that if Goblin decided you were worth the position, that we'd trust Goblin. However. You've sat back here and tried to direct the entire time, never once setting foot in the field with the rest of us. We might have had our issues with Casper, but even he went out with the team. Figaro could hardly be kept off an op."

Saul ran a hand over his jaw. "Now, I'm not saying you've got to be on each and every op. That kind of defeats the purpose of having a team leader. Just understand that nobody here is going to take a 'we' seriously when you're not doing anything but making PowerPoint slides."

Tim was looking a little white around the eyes at that point. Nick just watched him, wondering just which way the man was going to jump. He had to realize that this wasn't the military, and even if he'd been an officer—which Nick had to admit he suspected—that didn't matter one damn here. He couldn't just fall back on his imagined authority. These guys were contractors, not soldiers.

That was actually a bit more nuanced than that, but still.

"I understand your concerns, but we each have roles to play." Tim wasn't throwing a tantrum, but he wasn't backing down, either. "I can't coordinate everything from a vehicle or the middle of a stack. That's what I was hired for: to coordinate. That's what I'm doing. What your previous team leaders did is no nevermind to me. I know what *I* was hired to do, and that's what I'm doing."

Nick sighed. Somewhat to his surprise, it was Doug who took the next step.

"In that case, coordinate. You've tried multiple times to tell the guys on the ground what to do, when you need to be listening to the guys on the ground. Ground truth rules all in this business." He had fixed Tim with an unblinking stare. "You can pass word and make sure everyone has all the information available. After that, you step aside and let us do the planning and execution. If you're going to be a facilitator, then facilitate and get out of the way."

For a second, Nick thought it was going to be a fight. Tim's eyes were wide, and it wasn't with surprise or shock. He'd genuinely figured that, as an employee of the company and an appointed team leader, that he was the one who got to call the shots.

There was always that guy. It was entirely possible that Tim had a badass resume, not that any of the team knew what it was. But somebody always figured that his position extended to more expertise than it really did.

Fortunately, while he opened his mouth to say something, Tim stopped, seemed to reconsider, and then closed it. From the look on his face, though, this argument wasn't over.

Nick suspected that it wasn't going to be over for a long time, and that it was going to get very sticky before it was. Tim didn't seem like the type to let these things go, and if he wasn't going to hash it out with the team then and there, he was probably going to complain to the office, and there was going to be a lot of behind-the-scenes gossip and "he said, she said."

Nick hated that sort of garbage, and he knew that he wasn't alone. He didn't have enough of a history with Goblin to be sure what the boss's perspective on it was, but he could guess.

"All right, then. If that's how you want to work it. I'll just be the go between." He turned back toward the computer, tight-lipped. "Can I finish the brief?"

Doug waved a hand toward the computer as if to invite him to do so. Saul just stood where he was, arms still folded, just watching.

The thing was, there wasn't a contractor on that team who hadn't seen Tim's like a dozen times before. They were all over. It made it much less likely that Tim was going to be able to buffalo any of these guys. He might be able to with younger, less experienced operators, but not with this crew.

It only reinforced some of the questions Nick had about where Tim had come from, and why he'd been hired.

Tim proceeded, though not without a bit of a brittle chill in his demeanor, to finish going over the intel on Larkin. The man was a bit of a playboy, circulating through some of the higher-end clubs in New York on a pretty regular basis. Odds were, he had a pretty established clientele, and he was making the rounds to make connections for the new "shipment."

Pompous ass though he might be, Tim had made a good point. How *were* they going to approach this? Hitting him at home might be more straightforward, but it ran some pretty stiff risks. Somebody like Larkin was connected. He had to be, given the circles he appeared to move around in. That meant that he might well get a police response if he called for help, a response that a lot of New Yorkers really couldn't count on.

It was infuriating, but it was the way the world worked, particularly in places where the corruption went as deep as it did in New York. The bad old days of the 1970s were coming back in a big way.

Doug shook his head. "As much as I hate to say it, somebody's going to have to pose as a john. That's going to be the easiest way to get close to him."

"That's going to be a good way to end up in handcuffs for solicitation." Matt scratched the back of his neck. "We don't get qualified immunity, either. Arguing that we were running a sting probably won't fly. *Especially* not if this guy's connected."

"We'll definitely have to play it carefully. Keep things nice and vague, until we can get Larkin somewhere we can secure him and rake him over the coals." Doug smiled faintly. "After all, we can be pretty sure that *Larkin*'s not going to try to turn us in for solicitation. He'd have to turn himself in, in that case."

"Unless he's a Fed." Manny rarely added his opinions to these discussions, but his voice was low and dark now.

"That's a possibility we have to take into account." Saul nodded. "Chris and Phil ran into a Fed inside the network. Almost blew the whole thing." He chuckled dryly. "Out of four bad guys, two were our dudes and a third was a Fed. The only way it could have been any more perfect was if it had been Aryan Nation or something."

"Then it would have been *all* Feds," Matt said. "Then our guys never would have gotten in at all."

Saul sighed, ignoring the byplay. "As much as I hate to say it, I think you're right, Doug. Approaching as a prospective customer is probably our best bet. It'll be risky, but as long as we can do the wink and nod deniably enough, we should be able to pull it off." He looked around the team with an evil glint in his eye. "So, who gets the honors?"

"Too bad we don't have Bone on this team." Carl drew a chuckle. "He'd be a natural."

"We don't, so somebody here's going to pull the short straw." Saul kept looking around. "Come on, don't make me pick somebody."

"Why not you, Saul?" Durand asked.

"I've got my reasons."

There was a pause after that, which Doug finally broke. "I'll do it. It was my idea in the first place."

Nick was pretty sure it had been *Tim's* idea, but nobody was going to suggest letting their stuffed-shirt team leader screw it up.

"We'll have to have a tail on him to see where he's going." Saul knew what kind of trouble Doug could get into on a sting op like this. It wasn't the time to brood or angst over it. They needed to get a plan in place and move on it. There was something to be said for patience, but also something to be said for getting in and getting it done, without overthinking it. "We haven't had him under observation long enough to build a real pattern, if there even is one. That tail's going to have to act as Doug's backup, too." He looked over at the former Delta operator. "No offense, brother, but you're not walking in there alone."

"None taken." Doug flashed a grin. "Can't say I was looking forward to being the only poor dumb bastard trying to blend in with those clowns."

Saul rubbed his chin and looked around the team, calculating who needed to go where. "Matt, Manny, Carl, and Durand will be the backup element. You guys will orbit and be ready to move in to backstop and interdict if and when Doug makes the call. Nick?"

Nick knew what was coming, and as much as he didn't like it, he knew he had to say yes. He'd managed to stay in the car when Matt had gone into a DC area club to socially engineer their target a while back, but he wasn't going to get to play it that way this time. "I don't have clubbing clothes." It was a weak excuse, and he'd meant it as a joke, but it still sounded pathetic, and he hated himself for saying it as soon as the words got out.

It still got a chuckle, though. "We can work that out this afternoon. Since we won't know exactly where he's going until he gets there, then both of you will have to enter after him. Doug will go in first. Make sure you approach from a different direction and give him about five minutes. Under different circumstances, it wouldn't matter that much if you both went in together, playing wingman, but with this... I think staying separate would be a better idea."

Nick nodded. It would make things more difficult. He'd have to at least try to mingle, socialize, hit on girls. He'd never enjoyed clubs. They were distinctly artificial environments, and everything seemed fake and strained to him. Maybe it was because he'd never gotten into the drugs that made such things enjoyable.

But it was the mission, so he was going to have to swallow his discomfort and make it happen.

So, he nodded, though not without a faint sigh. Doug spotted it and gripped his shoulder, giving him a shake as he grinned.

They were all trying to look on the lighter side of what they were about to do. If they thought too hard about it, it was going to be supremely difficult not to murder Larkin before the night was over.

"Okay, let's get eyes on Larkin, starting now. We've got some prep to do, so let's get to it. Starting with getting Nick to look like an appropriate New York ladies' man."

CHAPTER 22

The Club Xtessi definitely *wasn't* Nick's sort of place. The walls that weren't covered with curtains displayed murals that looked like a cross between Salvador Dali and Hieronymus Bosch. The lighting was never clear, but kept fluctuating from red, to purple, to blue. The music was some sort of thrumming electronica, with words that he could never quite make out. It was distorted and strange, and probably sounded a lot better if you were on MDMA or ecstasy. Or something.

Nick had gotten past the bouncer, paying the exorbitant cover price, glad that it was coming out of PGS ops funds, and not his own pocket. The people who gathered here had money, and lots of it.

Which was probably why Larkin was there that night. Big money often meant big appetites and big corruption.

Nick found a table near the wall, where he could see most of the room and the expansive dance floor. At least, as much as he *could* see through the haze and the flashing lights. The entire aesthetic of the club seemed designed to disorient and distract.

Not many people in there had their phones out, but there were some. It still didn't seem to be all that prudent to bring his out unless it was absolutely necessary. He ordered a drink and settled in to watch the room, his elbows on the table.

He'd spotted Doug shortly after he'd entered. His partner, somewhat to his surprise, was already mingling, a drink in his hand, wearing an expensive collared shirt open halfway down his chest, and designer jeans that looked entirely out of place on the man Nick had watched tear a column of cartel technicals to shreds with a .50 cal, yet somehow, he was making it work.

Larkin was making the rounds, chatting people up as he moved from table to table around the dance floor. He seemed to know a large part of the clientele. Even if he didn't, he seemed to be the sort who could slide into a group and act like he was everyone's oldest friend within minutes. It was a talent, and one that he appeared to be using for some of the deepest evil Nick could think of.

As the party went on, more and more drinks—and probably some stronger stuff—circulated around, Larkin seemed to be filling his client list for the night. Nick was starting to wonder, as Larkin made his rounds, whether they were going to be able to get to him in time, or if he'd have enough names to make a night before Doug could catch his eye.

Doug knew what he was doing, though. The man had been around. After they'd been on site about half an hour, he caught Larkin's gaze, and after a moment, the facilitator broke off his current conversation and slid into the chair across from Doug.

Nick was much too far away to hear any of the conversation, even if there hadn't been the weird music trying to cave in his skull. He sipped his drink, just as an attractive woman wearing a glittering dress that left little to the imagination, matching the bangles of her earrings, slid into the chair across from him. "What are you doing sitting here all by yourself, baby?"

He forced a lopsided smile as he took another sip. "Waiting for you."

That drew a dazzling smile, as intended. He didn't know who the hell this woman was, and frankly, he didn't care. She'd make decent enough camouflage, provided he didn't let himself get distracted by her obvious charms to the point that he lost track of Doug and Larkin.

She leaned over the table, giving him an even better view. "Well, why don't you finish that drink and come dance with me, then?"

He tossed down the rest of the drink, momentarily glad that he hadn't become a teetotaler after the Army, like a few guys he'd known. If he had, he'd have been way too much of a lightweight to pull this off.

Especially since he couldn't afford to get too befuddled by alcohol or estrogen to lose track of the mission.

She grabbed his hand as he stood up and pulled him out onto the dance floor. It was a struggle not only to keep eyes on Doug and Larkin, especially as the woman in the sequined dress wrapped her arms around his neck, but also to fake as if he knew how to dance to this noise. It didn't actually take much skill, but he wasn't quite able to gyrate to the beat, as it never quite seemed to be "on," at least not to him.

The woman didn't seem to care. She also seemed to be oblivious to the fact that he was barely looking at her, even as she gazed up into his face with a dreamy smile on her own. He was trying to keep tabs on the night's business.

Finally, after about three sets on the dance floor, he was able to persuade her to go back to the table. She was clinging to his arm by then, and he had a bad feeling that she'd decided that she'd found her company for the night. He couldn't afford that.

They got to the table at about the same time Doug got up and walked out. Nick kept his expression blank as he observed that Larkin hadn't left yet but was chatting up another young woman at the same table where he'd been talking to Doug.

What just happened? Are we mission failure, or is Doug playing this out?

"Let's get some shots!" The woman had to lean in and almost yell in his ear, as the music continued to pound. If Nick was reading her right, the last thing this chick needed was more alcohol, but under the circumstances, he couldn't exactly say no.

Besides, it might deaden her enough that he'd be able to slip away.

"Great idea." He waved for the waiter, just as Larkin got up and headed for the door. *Fuck.*

He ordered tequila shots, mainly because that was what she was yelling for. The waiter nodded and started to walk away.

"I've got to go break the seal." He started to get up. "I'll be right back."

She grabbed onto his arm, though. "No! You can't break the seal yet! You'll be in there all night!"

"I'm about to explode, baby. I've got to. I'll be back in a second."

Reluctantly, she let him go. "You better not be running off." She wagged her finger at him with a seductive smile.

"Trust me." *You're damned right I'm running off, lady. Even if I wasn't working, there's no way I'd sleep with some New York club creature.*

He had to make for the restrooms, off to the side of the bar, if only to put her mind at ease and give him a chance to break contact. He couldn't move that fast to start with, but he was acutely aware that the time-distance gap was opening up while he tried to blend in.

Ducking into the bathroom, he went ahead and took a leak, since it would look weird to the other patrons if he just walked in and then walked out. Cover can be a bitch, sometimes.

Moving back to the door, he saw that his "date" was watching the dance floor, a pair of shots on the table in front of her. That was his opening. He slipped over to the bar, paid his tab in cash—glad that he could still at least do that; there were a lot of businesses going cashless lately, but it wasn't a big surprise that this wasn't one of them—and headed for the door.

He risked a glance over his shoulder just before he ducked out. The woman in the sequined dress was looking toward the restrooms now, still wondering when he was coming back.

He headed out into the street, pulling his phone out of his pocket. He hadn't been able to hear it inside, and the music had reverberated through every surface so much that he hadn't been able to feel the vibrations, either.

The first message was from Doug. *Jackpot.* He had their target. Nick grimaced as he headed for the rally point. He hadn't even been able to help out.

You were there as an insurance policy. You did your job. Now it's on to the next phase. He stepped it out as he headed for the pickup. They needed to move fast, to get Larkin out of the city before the rest of his network realized that he'd gone missing.

CHAPTER
23

It took entirely too long to get Larkin out of New York. They had rental cars, fortunately, as difficult as it was to get around in the city by car. Traffic was a nightmare, but they were able to get out and get down the road, heading for New Jersey.

New Jersey was every bit the nonpermissive environment that New York was, so they weren't going to stop there. Tim had arranged a safehouse just outside of Stroudsburg, Pennsylvania, using the company's go-to method of renting an AirBnB. It was just before two in the morning when they pulled up in the car, Doug and Saul in the front, Nick in back with their unwilling companion. The light on the porch was on, but the windows were dark.

Saul pulled the car into the garage, not even looking back as he got out and headed for the door leading inside, the keys jingling in his hand.

Larkin hadn't made a sound since Nick had gotten into the car at the rendezvous point. He'd just sat there, his hands in his lap, his face blank and pale, the entire two hours they'd been driving. He knew he was in a bad place. The fact that Doug had put him in a wrist lock and shoved him into the car as soon as he'd met up with him to discuss some "entertainment" for the evening should have told him that.

Doug got out while Nick stayed where he was. They didn't have guns yet—though Tim *should* have arranged for a cache there at the house, if he'd been on the ball—but he could still overpower Larkin easily enough if need be. They just didn't want to leave the man on his own without a PGS contractor within arm's reach. Not yet.

Opening the back door, Doug gripped their prisoner by the arm. "Let's go."

Nick glanced at the garage door as he followed them inside. This was extremely risky. Breaking into Larkin's apartment to interrogate him would have been slightly more easily brushed off, but this was technically kidnapping.

Granted, after what he'd seen in that compound in California, Nick wasn't that worried about what was going to happen to Larkin. He'd be perfectly happy to tie the man's ankles to a stack of cinderblocks and toss him into the ocean.

They would just have to step carefully and make sure they didn't get caught.

Saul was making sure all the blinds were drawn before they turned on any lights. Doug steered Larkin into a chair in the living room and forced him down into it, while Nick went looking for the promised weapons cache.

As he did so, going into the back rooms—which also served to make good and sure that they were alone and that the doors were all secured—he pulled out his phone and made a secure call.

"Send it." Carl had taken operational control of the surveillance in the other four men's absence.

"In position. No contact en route. Our guest has behaved himself so far." Nick tested the knob on the back door and was satisfied that it was locked.

"Good to go. There hasn't been any uptick in activity yet that might indicate they know that our boy's gone. Just same old, same old." Carl paused. "Actually, not quite. Money reported about an hour ago that there were five men who appeared to be riding along with the latest shipment of girls. They kept to themselves and didn't go into the warehouse. Just hung out on the street for a few minutes until another van came to pick them up."

Nick frowned. That did sound suspicious. "Any description?"

"All military age, dressed in jeans and t-shirts. All Asian. That's about all I can get you at the moment."

That was strange. And something about it raised Nick's hackles. He could understand why Josh would have noted it, and Carl have passed it on. "Roger. I'll let Saul know." He glanced over his shoulder. "I'll pass any info we get, as we get it."

"Good copy. I'll do the same." Carl sighed on the other end. "Gonna be a long night."

"Just like all the rest of 'em."

When he got back to the living room, Saul and Doug were standing to either side of the chair where Larkin was sitting, unbound but gripping the chair's arms and not trying to get up. The man looked sick, but that might just have been because of the surveillance photos that Saul was laying down on the coffee table in front of him.

"This really doesn't look good, Robert. We've got you at a place we happen to know is a human trafficking hub, multiple times. You've also got a reputation, though I have to admit that you're pretty good at keeping it out of the public. At least, the public that might be willing to see you put into a deep, dark hole for the rest of your natural life, given what it is you peddle." Saul was being quite conversational, while Doug just watched, unblinking, his arms folded.

"I don't know what you're talking about." The shake in Larkin's voice belied his words, though Nick had to admit that a normal person who'd been snatched off the street and hustled two states away to be interrogated might be scared enough to account for that shake. Not that they had any doubt that they had the right guy. "That's a mushroom shop. I get morels there."

Saul just sighed, tilting his head slightly, studying their prisoner. With his long black hair and sheer size, Saul looked a bit like some primeval barbarian, and Nick hoped that the appearance was enough to put the fear into Larkin.

Though, given what they already knew about this little scumbag, Nick reflected that he really wouldn't have any qualms about waterboarding the shit out of him. It was less than he deserved.

Shaking his head, Saul *tsk*ed. "This is not a good time to lie, Robert. Not a good time at all. See, we traced the last shipment of girls from Shelter Valley to that warehouse." He pulled a couple more photos, these showing the vehicles that had picked up the shipment of young women from the cartel compound. "That compound doesn't exist anymore, by the way. Everyone who was running it is dead."

Now just think real hard about what that means for you. Saul didn't say that part, but he didn't have to. From the way Larkin's eyes widened still more as he looked down at the photos, then back up at Saul, he'd definitely gotten the message.

"On top of that, you may not know it, but my associate here recorded your conversation in the Club Xtessi. We have you on video and audio pimping girls."

Larkin swallowed, then looked over at Doug. "Well, that means you were soliciting, doesn't it?"

The smile that crossed Doug's face wasn't pleasant, and Larkin's weak attempt at bravado crumpled in front of it. "I didn't explicitly say anything about girls. I just said that I'd been told you were the man to talk to when it came to high-end entertainment in New York. *Real* high-end entertainment. You were the one who took it to prostitution." That wolfish smile widened still further, though it never reached the older man's eyes, which were black chips of obsidian as they stared through Larkin's shriveled soul. "Besides, I didn't record anything *I* said."

Larkin seemed to shrink in the chair. "What do you want?"

Saul nodded. Now they were getting somewhere. "I want names, I want places. Everything you know about this operation

186

and who's running it, who's benefiting from it. Timelines. Schedules. Numbers. *Everything.*"

Broken, Larkin started talking.

***

"Holy shit." Nick wasn't convinced that Larkin wasn't still holding something back, but what he'd spilled was already a bombshell. The names on the client list not the least.

"You think this was why the client wanted us poking around this operation?" Saul looked over at Doug. "Not that they were open about it, but if Wise was digging into it, and the A Team was supposed to be watching Wise…"

Doug glanced at the door where they'd locked Larkin, after making very sure that he had no way to either get out—at least not in one piece; the room was on the second floor, and Larkin didn't seem to be the sort who'd be willing to risk a broken bone, even if it meant his own skin in the long run—or contact anyone. "It's possible. In fact, given that client list, I think it's probable. Unfortunately, I can't say that I have enough faith in the human nature of the sort of people with that kind of money to throw around to think that it's anything but a political ploy."

Nick nodded. "Use us as a stalking horse to expose a trafficking network that is servicing political rivals? Sounds about right."

"There's that extra bit you got from Gameshow, too, Croak." They were using callsigns as long as they were in the house with Larkin, on the off chance that he ever had the opportunity to say anything to anyone about this.

That part was starting to bother Nick, just a little. The primal part of his brain wanted to go upstairs and put a bullet in Larkin's head. The more rational part knew that they'd have a hard time justifying that. Even harder than kidnapping him in the first place.

He had an idea, though it might even be considered crueler than just drilling him through the skull and dropping the body twelve nautical miles offshore.

"The Asian dudes who got dropped off?" Nick brought his mind back to the problem at hand.

"Yeah." Saul rubbed his chin. "There have been reports lately of groups of military-age Chinese coming into the country illegally. The usual theory is that they're PLA, but it's just as likely that they're triad."

"Is there a functional difference these days?" Nick asked.

"Maybe not, though oversimplifying the issue isn't going to get us far." Saul wasn't the sort to look for an easy explanation to anything, while still avoiding the tendency to get overwhelmed by details and lose sight of the big picture. It was why most of the team—even including Doug—was looking to Saul since their "team leader" was barely there. "Did Gameshow say whether or not he got plates on the vehicles that picked them up?"

"He didn't, but I'm pretty sure that's not something either he or Train would overlook." Nobody on the team was an amateur when it came to surveillance. *Everything* was documented and reported on. While reconnaissance hadn't been Nick's bailiwick in the Army, he'd had to learn it on the private side of the house. Reconnaissance and surveillance were all about information gathering. While a certain degree of discernment was necessary, for the most part they were creating as thorough a picture as possible and dumping the information, leaving the filtering out of anything that might be irrelevant to the analysts. Otherwise, given the immediacy of the situation being reported on, they might actually miss something important, just because it might not *seem* important at the moment.

"Fair." Saul frowned, thinking things over.

His phone buzzed. His frown deepening, he looked down at it. They were running with burners, throwaway pre-paid phones that only a handful of their teammates should have the number for. And from the look on Saul's face, he didn't immediately recognize that number.

Doug shrugged. The fact that nobody was *supposed* to have that number didn't mean it was impossible. There were always scammers who were scraping hundreds, if not thousands, of random phone numbers. On the other hand...

Almost on impulse, Saul picked up the phone and answered it. "Yeah." He listened for a second, then, instead of hanging up on some scammer or canvasser, he set the phone down on the coffee table and pressed a button to put it on speaker. "You're on speakerphone, Val. Start over from the beginning. Thumper and Croak are here."

"Hey, Thumper, what up?" Bill Devens was one of the C Team contractors, and one of those guys who'd been kicking around the contracting world for a long time. "So, I was telling Salt that we seem to have suddenly had some overlap in our surveillance. Cricket thinks he saw Gameshow while we were following our client's person of interest yesterday. We've started to do some thinking, and I *know* I spotted Frog, though that's only because I know the guy."

Saul looked back and forth between Doug and Nick. Doug had an eyebrow raised but didn't comment. "Who's your target?"

"Some guy named Brown. He's a former tech CEO, finance guy, who seems to mostly go on expensive trips and lobby politicians. Got to New York just two days ago, and he's mostly been hobnobbing with Broadway actors, finance people, and New York politicos. He's also been indulging in the city's drug traffic, as well as high-end call girls. We've got most of that documented, though the latter requires identifying the call girls as such. We haven't been bugging his room, though Booger, the sick bastard, keeps wanting to.

"Anyway, tonight he apparently thought the call girls were too tame and started doing some digging. We don't know who he called, but he was waiting around some club for a while, checking his watch, then tried making another call, started to freak out, and then came down into the industrial area around Bushwick. I think you can see where I'm going with this."

Nick and Doug traded a look. Saul was still watching the phone, his expression impassive.

"That was when we spotted Gameshow and Frog. This guy tried to get into a commercial building on the corner, one that your guys seem to have under observation. He was turned away, though he seemed pretty agitated about it, but there does appear to be a connection between your target and ours."

"So it would seem." Saul glanced up toward the floor above, where Larkin was ensconced, unwillingly. "I think I know why your boy got a little upset. We may have thrown a wrench into the operation tonight."

"Good." Bill was usually so indecently chipper that it got aggravating, but even over the phone there was a note of weariness in his voice. "This entire thing reeks."

"No kidding." Saul paused, thinking over what he wanted to say over a cell connection, even if it was encrypted. "We got a lot of information tonight. It's going to take some time to unravel this thing, but we've got a good start."

"Well, judging by this guy's connections, watch your backs," Bill said. "He's got friends, and from what we've seen, their moral compass is about as fucked as his."

"We'll be careful. Don't get complacent because you're just watching this shithead."

"No worries there. I'd be happy to drop him like a bad habit, but the contract says, 'watch and report,' so that's what we're doing."

"Good copy. Keep us posted if you see anything that might be of interest. We'll do the same."

"Roger that, brother. Out." The call ended.

There was a long moment of silence, as the three of them thought over what they'd just heard.

"Well." Doug straightened up and stretched. "I think our theories about why the client wanted us to run surveillance on these randos are looking more solid."

"Yeah." Saul ran a thumb along his jaw, his arms folded. "The question is, what do we do about it? Even if they haven't come after us, we already know we're on the FBI's shit list. We can't just turn these clowns over, especially not if the Feds are just going to pay more attention to how we got the evidence than what these fuckers did."

Doug looked a bit amused. "Simple. We've been taking a master class in information warfare, along with all the other shit we've gotten up to. We use what we've learned to fucking destroy them. One at a time."

CHAPTER
24

Capurgana didn't look like anything had changed while we'd been in the weeds. Nobody gave us a second look when we came out of the jungle on the El Aguacate-Capurgana trail, even though we'd left going *north*, toward El Miel. Maybe we *weren't* being directly observed, and nobody really paid a bunch of tourists any mind.

I didn't believe that for a second. There were eyes everywhere, especially in a place like this, where illicit networks from all over the world were converging to push drugs and people north, through Central America and into the US.

It might seem like a bit of hubris to assume that the US was the target, but most foreign actors involved there weren't looking to destabilize Mexico. They couldn't do much more than the cartels and the *maras* already had done. No, the US was the cash cow and the target. The biggest drug market in the world for the cartels, the biggest sugar daddy for those migrants just looking for cash—which the more nefarious actors would use to their advantage, as well—and the Great Satan—or whatever the chosen pejorative was, depending on the faction—to the terrorists and saboteurs who wanted to get into the country without any record of their having entered.

And among them might just be men hired to put a bullet into one of our family members. With Slobodian there, doing deals with jihadis, it was a possibility that we couldn't discount.

Getting back to our hotels, we cleaned up and then met back at KG's room again. He had a somber look on his face, that didn't bode all that well.

"Got an update. The B Team and the C Team crossed the streams last night."

"No shit?" Phil stuck his head in KG's room's fridge, and came out with a beer, a red can of Prima. "What happened?"

"Not a whole lot, on the surface." KG had his own can of Prima open on the little table. "The C Team spotted the client's person of interest trying to get into the target warehouse. He was turned away, but his agitation seems to have started when Salt, Thumper, and Croak snatched up the local facilitator."

We were being careful with our choice of words, even in a place where we were supposed to be alone. There were eyes everywhere, and I suspected ears, too. Capurgana was hardly the most high-tech place, but if Slobodian was there, and he was as deep into the underworld as we suspected, then he'd have listeners out and about. It didn't have to be technical surveillance. All it needed to be was someone on the other side of the wall with a damned water glass.

Some people in this business tend to forget that the old-fashioned, low-tech methods still work just as well as they ever did. Sometimes better than the fancy stuff that requires batteries and wireless networks.

"Did those guys get anything?" Marcos asked.

"They got a ton. They didn't even have to push very hard, from what Salt said in the report. I've barely scratched the surface, but it looks like they confirmed that Slobodian has his hands in a lot of human trafficking as well as hired murder. His name didn't come up specifically—at least, not any of the aliases we're aware of—but some of the contacts that this guy spilled apparently match up." KG took a sip of his beer. "On top of that, it looks like our tasking really *is* related to the current contract, since the guy that the client has the C Team on was trying to make use of the same human trafficking network."

"All this shit converges, eventually." It was a part of this shadowy sort of warfare that I was starting to wrap my head around. Crime leads to instability and rot, and that means that bad guys with a vested interest in weakening their target country will feed that crime as much as they need to. Usually, they'll enrich themselves at the same time, of course.

Let's face it, the sort of people who will knowingly and willingly use such psychopaths as the cartels, the *maras*, and the kind of lost souls who made up Slobodian's hitman network are the sort of people who really should be dangling from a fucking gibbet.

This wouldn't get us to those people. But we might be able to hamstring their strategy, at least for a little while, if we took Slobodian out, along with as much of his network as we could locate.

Sometimes, that's the best you can hope for.

"That's not all we got, though. Radford's been busy with the photos we sent him. I doubt that boy's slept at all for the last few days."

"He sleeps?" Phil acted shocked. "I thought he just ran on caffeine and sugar."

"He might." KG shrugged. "I've got to admit that *I've* never seen him sleep. Anyway. He ran the photos we sent through facial recognition software and then dragged the whole internet for a match. And he found one." He brought up the phone that he'd been using to send data while we'd been in our OP. The screen was pretty small, but we all crowded around the table to see.

The photo was of one of the visitors to Slobodian's house. "Now, we still don't know exactly who this guy is. No name, nothing. What we *do* know is that Radford's facial recognition software is about ninety percent certain that it found him in an old AP photo of a Hezbollah march in Beirut about thirteen years ago."

Phil let out a sigh. "Hezbollah. Well, that could be all sorts of bad news."

"Maybe." Ken shook his head. "There are Hezbollah cells all over the country. These guys might not be much more than errand boys. If they *really* wanted to hit us—and I don't think they do, not yet—then they could, just about any time they wanted."

Phil frowned. "They're jihadis. Why *wouldn't* they want to hit us?"

Ken's smile was as slow as ever, but there was a chill behind it. "I ran into a couple guys who broke down outside of a Hezbollah headquarters—in Beirut, no less—a few years back. They could have been hostages, guns or not. But the Hezbollah guys just told them they had two hours to clear out." He shook his head. "They want a war. Make no mistake about that. They just want it on *their* terms, not ours."

"That doesn't mean we won't throw a wrench in their operation if we can." KG had no sympathy for the jihadis, and neither did I. "And I'd like to make *sure* that they're just errand boys. Things have been getting a bit more heated with the Iranians lately, and they've got one hell of a presence down here. So, I ran it past Goblin, and he agrees. We'll get eyes on the Hezbollah operatives and follow them. If they were meeting Slobodian, then they *probably* weren't planning on heading north through the Darien right away. Even if we don't get the go-ahead to take them down, surveillance on their movements might give us some more immediate targets."

There it was again. The hard truth about working this way. We couldn't get all the bad guys, and we couldn't save everybody. We just had to do what we could to disrupt the bad guys, even if only for a little while.

That could be a hard pill to swallow sometimes, but as I got older, the more I saw it was just the reality of human nature. Nothing men do lasts. There is no saving the world permanently.

And anybody who thinks that he's going to save the world needs to have his head examined in the first place.

"Do we have any idea where they're staying?" I knew that was a long shot. We'd barely just gotten back, ourselves, and there was no way we'd beaten them to town, unless they'd really dawdled at Slobodian's place.

"Not yet." KG smiled faintly. "So, we get to go for a stroll and look for these motorcycles." He tapped the photo. "Not to mention any of these goons." With some shifting, he brought the photos Phil had taken up. "Memorize them as best you can. Then do your best to look like some harmless, dumbass *norteamericano*."

***

It can be amazing, the things you see when you just take the effort to really *look*. On the surface, Capurgana was just another Latin American tourist town, despite the large numbers of African, Asian, Middle Eastern, and Latin American migrants crammed into shantytowns around the parts of town that weren't specifically intended for Westerners. That barrier was far from airtight, though the more touristy parts of town took their security a little more seriously. It was still Latin America, and you didn't take stuff you couldn't afford to lose.

Once you started to watch some of those migrant movements, though, interesting patterns started to emerge.

Now, this probably wasn't something that a regular guy could necessarily pick up right away. It took years of professional people watching—read: reconnaissance and surveillance, or sitting in a hole, an abandoned building, or a vehicle for hours or days at a time, watching people who don't realize they're being watched—to really start to see some of the surreptitious stuff that professional bad guys don't want anyone to see.

So, as I wandered, seemingly aimlessly, through town, I spotted a few things.

Like the Anglos who seemed to be holding court in a house at the north end, with groups of migrants coming through every hour or so. I didn't get close enough to hear what was being said, but from observing body language, I could guess. These guys were giving instructions. Judging by the range of people I saw coming in and out of that house, I guessed that they were bleeding hearts who were giving medical and survival advice. The Darien Gap is one of the most inhospitable places on the face of the planet, and that's just talking about the wildlife and the terrain. There are a lot of ways to die in the Darien.

On one hand, I could respect what those guys in that house were doing. Not all of the people trying to get north were bad guys. They were still human beings, and I could appreciate someone who was just trying to help people.

On the other hand, an awful lot of those people really *were* bad guys, and most of these people, if they made it through the Gap, were going to die or be exploited on the way north. The B Team had already found and destroyed a graphic example.

How much were these guys really helping?

They were still a lot more benign than the guy staying in the place where I finally found one of our Hezbollah targets.

While I couldn't say that all Chinese were necessarily in service to the CCP—they definitely aren't—this guy was shady as hell. My first glimpse of him, he was lecturing some obvious Chinese nationals who looked like they were getting ready to head north. I couldn't speak a word of Mandarin, but he had a video presentation up on a projector screen in front of the house, and from the looks of it, it was all about the inevitable collapse of the United States.

When two of the Hezbollah operatives came and greeted him, and got ushered inside, I was even more convinced that this guy was part of the network.

That didn't mean he answered to Slobodian, or even knew of Slobodian. That's not how these networks work. Often, they're loose webs of people who know about each other, but never meet, and coordinate via secure comms or simple signals.

One dude I'd known a while back put it well. It's less a matter of conspiracy and more a matter of converging methods and interests. That makes these networks harder to crack, because each node is still effectively isolated from the others.

KG had been smart, setting us to finding the Hezbollah operatives. Sometimes the best way to map the web is to follow a drop of water as it slips along the strands.

I did my best to stay unobtrusive, drifting along the side streets and taking what I hoped were suitably touristy pictures, while also getting the house, the Chinese coordinator, and the Hezbollah types. I had to be careful. I still didn't have any of my weapons. They were a security risk that we couldn't take at the moment. There were still Colombian police in Capurgana, and getting caught with guns would not go well. Not only would it derail the operation as a whole, but it would also mean time in Colombian prison, where none of us really wanted to go.

Unfortunately, I wasn't quite careful enough.

It wasn't anything so obvious as the Chinese facilitator pointing and yelling, but I thought that he might have looked up as I was taking a photo. It was time for me to leave.

However, either he'd noticed, or else somebody who was working security for him had. I didn't get a block before three men, all locals from the looks of them, stepped out into the street in front of me.

It only took a glance behind me to see two more stepping out to close the ring. They weren't big men, but I wouldn't expect big guys in this backwater, dirt poor corner of Colombia. That didn't make them any less vicious, though. All five were wiry and carried themselves with the attitude of guys who thought they were tough. One had a lazy eye that seemed to be staring off at something over my right shoulder, and another had a hook-shaped scar on his cheek.

I didn't see any guns, but I was pretty sure they all had knives, and had probably used them more than a little. This was the country that had introduced the idea of the "Colombian necktie," in which the victim's throat was slit and his tongue pulled out through the gash.

The one with the scar pointed at me. "*Dame tu teléfono!*"

His accent was thick enough, and my Spanish poor enough, that it took me a second to realize that that was what he'd said. He wanted my phone. He probably didn't know who or what I was, but he knew that I'd probably taken a photo of his boss.

There was no way I was giving him my phone, but at the same time, even as big as I was compared to any of these, and the fact that I still had a knife in my pocket, five to one is not good odds.

So, despite the fact that it stuck in my craw, I ran.

There wasn't a good escape route available to me, but there were two behind me and three ahead, so I spun on my heel and threw myself at the smaller guy behind me. His eyes widened as I pivoted and bull-rushed him, and he grabbed for his beltline, confirming my suspicion that he had a knife.

I was on him before the blade cleared his waistband, and I threw an elbow at his head. I was moving fast enough that it connected, even as he tried to rear back to avoid it. It wasn't a solid hit, but it grazed him and made him stumble, and then I was past and sprinting for the corner.

Leaning into the turn, I left the five of them out of sight behind the low, blue-roofed building and the surrounding trees, and poured on the speed. I was nowhere near as fast as I had been in my twenties, though I was definitely stronger. I had to rely on length of stride and endurance if I was going to lose these guys.

With shrill yells, they came after me, but the sheer surprise of my sudden breakout had bought me time. They'd expected me to freeze, like some dumb tourist.

Unfortunately, I was still by myself, had only a three-and-a-half-inch folding knife to fight with, and they *were* going to close the distance if I didn't act fast.

I still had my phone in my hand. It's not easy to manipulate a smart phone's touchscreen while you're running for all you're worth, but somehow, I managed it. I couldn't exactly text, but I managed to speed dial KG.

"Need some backup. Just north of the Hotel Jessimar Capurgana."

That was about all I got out before one of the little bastards burst out of an alley just ahead of me and lunged for me.

I dodged him, jumping sideways and inside his rush, making him overextend and stumble past me. I kept going, sorely tempted to aim a kick at him, but I'd lost some momentum getting around him, and two more were around the corner behind me and closing fast.

Almost missing a step on the sandy road, I corrected and kept going. I needed to get south and east, fast. There was more security presence in the east, entirely too far away as things stood, and in the opposite direction I was going. I'd picked that turn around the corner purely to put something, anything, between me and the bad guys.

I took the next turn, heading down the road between hotels and back toward the airstrip. Behind me, over the rasp of my breath and the pounding of my heartbeat in my ears, I could hear one of them closing in, his feet beating against the road and gasped curses in that heavily accented Spanish getting louder.

After another ten yards, I knew he was going to catch me. He had me on weight and age. I wasn't going to outrun this guy.

Which meant that if I wasn't going to take a knife in the back, I was going to have to turn and fight.

I just had to avoid getting cornered and dogpiled.

There was a narrow alley just up ahead, between a green, two-story hostel with bars on all the windows and a low, but larger, red-roofed building. That was going to be my opening.

Ducking into the alley, barely two yards ahead of my closest pursuer, I skidded on the gravel as I turned, shoving the phone into my pocket.

He wasn't expecting the turn, and almost overshot, catching himself at the corner of the red-roofed building and dashing into the alley. It put him off balance just a little bit, and that was all I needed.

I wasn't the greatest MMA fighter, and I'd never say so. I suck as a grappler, but I can hit people, and my brain had gone into combat mode, judging angles and targets, as soon as those three had stepped out into the street in front of me. Which meant, despite the breath burning in my throat, the pain in my legs from the run, and the pounding of my heart, I was tuned in and ready when he rounded the corner.

The truth is, if you're going to get into a knife fight, you're going to get cut. That's a hard thing to wrap your brain around, at least the part where you have to expect it and wade in, anyway. He had a knife in his hand, but he didn't have it up in a defensive or fighting position. He'd been concentrating on running, which meant the knife was out by his side as I moved in on him.

I closed the distance fast, my hands up and fists poised. Punches aren't the greatest blows for this sort of thing, but I'd boxed some, and that was what I fell back into in the heat of the moment.

My first jab caught him coming in. I was a lot closer already than he was expecting, and I was facing him, when he'd expected me to still be running. It wasn't my most powerful punch, but it still caught him in the eye socket and knocked him off balance, ringing his bell just enough that he momentarily staggered, not even trying to bring the knife around to stick me with.

I was already following up with a hook, and caught him in the temple, snapping his head around and throwing him against the wall. He hit hard, losing his grip on the knife as I kept hammering him, throwing two more blows to the head, then another to the solar plexus. The knife clattered to the ground, but then two more of my pursuers appeared in the opening, knives in hand.

We were deep enough into the alley that they hadn't seen us until they rounded the corner, and they clearly weren't ready for what they saw. Unfortunately, they didn't freeze. These men were used to violence. If anything, seeing their buddy on the ground, bleeding from his mouth and nose after I'd beaten him half senseless, only seemed to piss them off more.

Wherever Phil, Ken, Marcos, or KG were, they hadn't caught up yet. I had no recourse but to run again. Turning back down the alley, I poured on the speed, knowing already that this wasn't going to last long, as a snarled Spanish curse sounded behind me.

They were coming up behind me fast. This was going to be a knife fight in the next few seconds.

I just had to hope and pray that I got through it without losing too much blood or having anything vital cut or punctured.

I was almost to the exit and the next road, about to make a try for the right, when KG pulled up on a motorcycle. He almost rode all the way past, but he happened to glance down the alley in time to see me and the two bad guys behind me. He braked hard, almost putting the bike down on the gravel and the sand, as I kept moving, though this time, when I came around the corner, I turned to face the two knife-wielding thugs, pulling my own folder as I did so.

The two of them slowed, dropping their knives to their sides as they reassessed the situation. While he'd very nearly crashed the motorcycle when he'd braked, KG had recovered quickly, and now he swung off the bike and joined me, a wrench in his hand. I didn't know where he'd gotten it, but I was glad as hell that he had.

I really wished I had my Glock. The yacht should be offshore by then, with all my gear and weapons aboard. Except that we still couldn't quite afford to go full retard with the guns. Not just yet.

"Hey, *putos!*" Marcos was in the opening at the other end of the alley. He wasn't visibly armed, but Marcos could project some serious savagery, and just the fact that there were now three of us to their two gave them pause. "Drop the knives!" When they didn't react right away, except to look from us to Marcos and back, he stepped forward and repeated himself, in Spanish, and from the length of it and my admittedly limited knowledge of the language, there were a lot of extra curse words in the tirade.

KG took a step forward, into the alley, hefting that wrench. I followed, my folder held low and flat to the ground, poised for a thrust that would disembowel one of them.

That decided them. With a glare, first one, then the other let their blades fall to the ground. Marcos stepped toward the wall. "*Largo de aqui!*"

Not without one more poisonous glare, the two of them quickly walked out of the alley and disappeared up the street.

I turned to KG. My chest was still heaving, and my throat burned. "Thanks, brother. Thought I was about to get scalped, there." I checked my pocket. The phone was still there. "Come on. Got some intel we might be able to use."

CHAPTER
25

"The body has been tentatively identified as Robert Larkin, age thirty-six, a day trader who has lived in the New York area for several years. While police have been unwilling to speculate as to the motive behind the brutal murder, sources have told this news station that it may well be connected to a viral recording purporting to outline parts of a network in the greater New York metropolitan area, dedicated to providing drugs and prostitution to some of the state's richest and most politically connected. The recording has not been corroborated with any official sources, and the NYPD continues to refuse to comment."

"Well, I gotta say, as cold as it was, it worked." Matt was leaning back on the couch. The team was gathered in a motel cabin in Milford, Pennsylvania. It was a really nice place, with wood wainscoting and old-fashioned furniture. It seemed far too nice for the current clientele and the stacks of weapons, ammunition, and tactical gear scattered around the rooms.

"It was bound to." Saul was pretty matter of fact. "Operations like this can't stand daylight, and they're closely enough associated with the cartels that it was inevitable that they'd make an example out of anybody who talked."

There were some slightly absent-minded nods. Most of the team were getting ready for that night. Nick didn't think that Larkin had spilled everything, but he'd given them enough targets to put some serious hurt on the human trafficking network in the northeast. The last few days of surveillance had confirmed enough that they were going to move on at least a few of those targets.

Operating where they were meant they had to get in and out fast. Pennsylvania was the most permissive environment for firearms in the area, but even that state wasn't great. Most of the northeast was gun control hell, not that it had slowed down the violent crime rate.

So, they were staging in Pennsylvania and getting ready for two lightning raids into New Jersey and New York.

They hadn't been able to hold Larkin. Even if there hadn't been serious legal ramifications if they got caught, the company simply didn't have the resources to make a man disappear, short of murder. So, they'd done the next best thing. The same night that they'd turned him loose, on foot, on the outskirts of New York City, they'd also uploaded a highly edited version of part of his interrogation to several social media video platforms, framing it like more of an interview, where he'd named a few names. Mostly names they weren't going to be able to hit.

It hadn't taken the network long to track him down and silence him.

Nick wasn't sure how he felt about that. On the one hand, given Larkin's known connections—and he had them, some going all the way to the state and federal levels of government—the odds that he'd be punished for what he'd done were pretty long. In some ways, the process can be the punishment, but it seemed awfully likely that he'd get off with a slap on the wrist. "Time served," or some such bullshit. They'd seen it before. If nothing else, the way the feds had reacted to their uncovering Devon Archer's corruption had taught them never to trust the system past a certain point. And given some of the names Larkin had dropped, they were way past that point.

What they'd done had been to sign Larkin's death warrant almost as surely as if they'd pulled the trigger themselves. Yet, on a certain level, their hands were still clean. While it had been almost certain that he'd be murdered for the information he'd let out, none of the PGS contractors had killed him.

It was a gray area that Nick wasn't sure he was really that comfortable with, but he had to admit that it was part and parcel of this form of warfare. Better to turn the bad guys against each other and let them tear each other apart.

It wasn't as if they didn't all deserve it.

Saul checked his watch. To no one's surprise, Tim wasn't there. He was ensconced in a makeshift TOC, somewhere in Upstate New York. He would "coordinate."

Nick was pretty sure that Saul and Doug were going to have a long talk with Goblin, whenever they got a chance.

"Wheels up in thirty. Make sure everything's in, easy to grab, and out of sight in the next fifteen."

***

Not all of the targets that Larkin had fingered were going to be within their reach. For one thing, the sheer geographical spread of the operation was prohibitive. There were stash houses and miniature networks in every major city, and there seemed to be more and more connections with multiple organized crime networks, as well, from the cartels, to the triads, to the Russian *mafiya*, even to what was left of *La Cosa Nostra*. And the politically connected client list just got longer and more untouchable.

But the thing about network-centric warfare—the real stuff, not the tech-heavy version that was being talked about in the 1990s and 2000s—was that you didn't have to hit *every* node to disrupt things. Just the right ones.

So, not that long after dark, two blank, featureless white rental vans sped down I-280, heading for their first target.

Both vans had been stripped out, intended for commercial use rather than passengers, but while they might be in trouble if they got pulled over—which was why Carl and Durand were both being very careful to stay under the speed limit, despite the cars zipping past them, some honking furiously—each had four men with duffel bags full of weapons and gear in the back, sitting on the floor in the dark, thinking things through as they rocked with the motion of the vehicles.

Nick wasn't really letting his mind wander. There were too many dark, dark rabbit holes he could go down at that moment. Instead, he was recalling the imagery of the target and going over the plan in his head, visualizing each step, hoping that it would go as smoothly as he was thinking it through in his mind once they got on target.

He knew that it wouldn't, but better to go over the plan mentally as many times as possible, anyway.

The trip was only about an hour and a quarter, though sitting in the back, in the dark, it felt far longer. Despite the thoroughness of the plan, and the fact that they'd already worked up some decent misdirection, there was always the chance that things could go badly wrong. Plans, training, and rehearsals only go so far. Sometimes, Murphy himself decides to take a hand, and then the plans go out the window.

Nick had been on enough ops like that that he was starting to tense up, the adrenaline already flowing, the anxiety eating at him. He kept his breathing slow and even. What would come, would come, and worrying about it wouldn't help.

"Five minutes." Durand twisted his head to call out the time hack. They were almost there.

There wasn't a lot of movement at that announcement. They were ready. All they had to do was grab the bags and go.

The vans didn't come screaming up to the front and brake. They lumbered up to the house like a delivery that was late, coming to a smooth stop that barely jolted the men in the back. "This is our stop, gents."

Doug swung the back doors open, and the four of them got out. Durand would stay with the vehicle. The driver drives, and they might need to get off the X with a quickness.

Pulling their bags out, the hit team moved off the sidewalk and quickly passed into the narrow, darkened alleyway between buildings. The entire block was made up of two- and three-story buildings, mostly duplexes, with lots of red brick and light-colored siding. It was almost a designer neighborhood, which made the presence of one of the network's money houses that much more disturbing.

Of course, it *was* New Jersey.

The porch lights were all on, but the van was blocking most of the streetlight's glow. That gave them some shadow to work with as they hustled down the alley and toward the side entrance.

Surveillance on this place had been difficult, due to just how tight the neighborhood was. Not that they were socially tight—this was New Jersey and an urban area. Most of the people probably didn't know their neighbors in the other half of the duplex. No, the difficulty had been how to get eyes on the house without alerting the men inside, or those coming and going at all hours.

If anything, though, the fact that there were guys coming and going, moving money in and out—at least according to Larkin—was their best bit of cover. Carl and Durand had gotten eyes on one of these visits, and they'd picked the bags the way they had for just that reason.

Those bags might be their ticket inside. At least, at first. Once they were in, speed and violence would be the order of the day.

The windows were lit, indicating that someone was still up—not a surprise after the pattern of life Carl and Durand had, if briefly, established. There was no sign that anyone thought there was anything amiss, though, and as the four of them reached the side door, they still didn't hear anything like raised voices or movement.

Doug glanced at the other three contractors, then nodded and knocked on the door.

Nothing happened at first. There was only silence—or, as close to it as a residential neighborhood in the middle of Harrison, New Jersey could provide. Dogs barked, cars drove by, horns honked. Somewhere in the distance, Nick could have sworn he heard gunshots.

Then the door rattled, as if someone was unlocking it, and creaked open a crack. An eye appeared in the crack. "Who the fuck are you? We weren't expecting a drop for another two hours, and you didn't call ahead."

"Yeah, everything got fucked up." Doug didn't miss a beat. The guy on the other side of the door didn't seem to notice that all three of them had their hands inside the bags. "Not my problem. Come on, this shit's heavy."

The guy on the other side of the door wasn't buying it. That wasn't mission failure, it just meant that they might have to go loud a little earlier than planned. After all, he'd unlocked the door. The hard part was done, whether he knew it or not.

"Look, there's a procedure..."

He should have just slammed the door and called for backup. Doug interrupted him with a front kick that knocked the door into his chest and sent him staggering back.

Nick drove in on him, already yanking the Glock out of his bag, shouldering the door aside as he stomped on the man where he'd fallen on his ass, rotating around the door to clear the other side. A gunshot sounded right behind him, loud enough to hurt even through his electronic earplugs, but he had to trust the three men behind him, and the lack of further gunfire told him that one of the other contractors had eliminated their greeter, even before he pivoted back toward the center of the little entryway and saw the man who'd answered the door twitching in a growing pool of his own blood.

They were in a small hallway, with a door onto the first floor immediately to their left and steps leading up to the second floor just ahead. Doug and Manny headed up the steps, while Matt and Nick briefly stacked on the door, Nick waiting for a slight squeeze to his tricep before he burst through.

The door opened up on another short hallway, with a bathroom on one side and a bedroom on the other. The hall was dark, with the only light in the kitchen and dining room down at the end. There was movement out there, and a voice was raised, cursing in a language Nick couldn't quite catch.

The bathroom door was open, and Nick quickly pied it off as Matt held on the closed bedroom door. There was no sound there, even as more gunshots slammed upstairs, and the voices down the hall got even louder.

"On me." Nick made the call to bypass the bedroom. The door was shut, and all the noise was coming from up ahead. Matt brought his own Glock up just past Nick's shoulder, and the two of them pushed down the hall.

The sounds from the living room got steadily more frantic. The pair of contractors paused just short of the end of the hall, and Nick started to lean out, hoping to get a better picture of what they were facing. It had proved impossible to find a floor plan for the house, so they were running on guesswork. That was par for the course in some of the places they'd worked, where they might well have needed to go into a building they'd never seen before to get a client out, under fire, so it didn't bother him that much, but since the second van was outside, ready to intercept anyone trying to break out through the front, he wasn't in that much of a rush.

The kitchen counter was piled with cash and what looked like drugs, several bags on the floor and chairs nearby. A pair of bill counters were still shuffling through hundreds, even while three men desperately tried to shove more into a pair of bags, one of them with a pistol in his hand.

Nick didn't hesitate. He lined that one up and dropped him with a single shot to the head, the report a sharp *clap* in the enclosed space. The man stiffened and fell on top of a bag of money, as the other two recoiled, one of them grabbing for a sawed-off shotgun with a curse. Nick pushed out into the kitchen while Matt turned the corner, his Glock leveled, and blew the would-be shotgunner's brains all over the dining room table.

The third guy could have surrendered, though Nick wasn't sure what they'd do with him if he did. Instead, he threw himself on the floor and grabbed for a pistol that had fallen off the table when the first man had fallen. Nick took a long step around the counter, leveled his Glock, and double-tapped the man in the head from about ten feet away.

"Clear." Matt's voice was flat and faintly muted in the sudden quiet, despite Nick's electronic earplugs, which were supposed to amplify the quiet sounds and deaden the loud noises.

"Clear," Nick agreed. He turned to the table and took in the piles of money. "Damn."

"Clear. Friendlies coming down." Doug was at the door.

"Bring it in." Nick glanced over as his partner and Manny came in, their pistols still in their hands, bags still slung over their shoulders. They'd brought a lot more hardware than they'd ended up needing, but sometimes it was better to have and not need, than need and not have.

"That's a lot of cash." Manny was eyeing it, and Nick couldn't say that he would especially object to taking it. It wasn't as if this was getting reported to the IRS.

"We'd have to be damned careful if we took it." Doug didn't sound like he was all that opposed, either, but he was cautious. "This shit's dirty as hell, and if the bad guys get a *hint* that it didn't go up in smoke with this house, then we're going to have a whole new set of complications."

"Who gives a shit?" Matt holstered his Glock. "They've already tried to kill us. What are they gonna do? Try to kill us deader?"

"I get it, but think." Doug wasn't upset, he was just trying to get through. "You heard that client list, same as I did. You think they'll hesitate to get the FBI involved if they think they can nail us with this cash? The Feds won't care whether we were righteous. All they'll give a damn about was that we busted in, shot seven people, stole a bunch of cash, and then committed arson. All of which are illegal and will put us *under* Leavenworth for the rest of our natural lives. Never mind that if we reported this place, at *best*, nothing would happen."

He shook his head. "As tempting as it may be, we're getting paid well, and this haul isn't worth the trouble. Torch it and let's go. We can expect a response to get here soon. They didn't get a call off, I don't think, but we need to get the hell off the X."

Nick nodded, turned on the stove, and grabbed a pile of cash. For a second, he looked down at it and wrestled with himself. What would one wad of hundreds matter, out of the millions that were in that house? It wasn't like it was drugs.

He could feel Doug's eyes on him, though he knew his partner well enough to expect that even if he decided to shove those bills in his pocket, he wouldn't say anything. He'd know, though.

"Damn it." He tossed the bills onto the pile, grabbed one of the cigarettes from the pack sitting on the counter, lit it, and sent it after the wad of bills.

The fire started small. It was just a cigarette on a pile of cash, after all. They'd brought a few party favors in those bags, though, and soon enough they were having to fall back to the side door as the room became fully involved, flames crackling and the heat already getting oppressive. The stench was already getting noticeable, too, as human flesh began to sizzle in the fire.

They couldn't count on the bodies being so destroyed that an investigation wouldn't realize they'd been shot. The fire would still wipe out most of the useable evidence of the fight. There'd still be an arson investigation, but they intended to be a long way away by that time.

The important thing was, one of the network's major cash hubs—along with millions of dollars—was gone.

They hustled out of the side door, back out onto the street, and into the van.

Behind them, as Durand started toward the next target, flames began to blow out the front windows, as sirens wailed in the distance.

CHAPTER
26

The final approach to that warehouse was going to be tricky. The streets were tight, and even late at night, there were a lot of cars parked out there. Furthermore, traffic at the warehouse appeared to increase sharply after dark. From the surveillance they'd already conducted, they'd seen vehicles coming and going all night, with clientele either going in and coming out an hour or two later—and many of those faces and license plates were in a growing database/target deck—or picking up and driving away.

That traffic was going to make the approach that much more hazardous. Most of them probably weren't armed, but they had phones and eyes, and for some of them, they were going to be highly aware of their surroundings, if only because of the vestiges of a guilty conscience. They'd notice the vans, and probably alert the bad guys.

Fortunately, the C Team had detached Cricket and Jumper to monitor the warehouse, and they were sending real time updates to the assault force as they moved in.

"Cricket says they just observed a drop, and there's a pair of Subs waiting while the traffickers unload." Doug was reading the latest message. He looked up, his face faintly illuminated by the phone screen in front of him, the only source of light in the back of the van. "If we get there fast enough, we might be able to stop some of these kids from getting destroyed for the rest of their lives."

Nick doubted it. He could only imagine, based on what they'd seen down there in Shelter Valley, what had been done to those girls—and probably a few boys—on the way to New York. Even if they'd intercepted them at the border, there had been a long way through Mexico, or wherever they'd come from.

No, they couldn't undo anything that had already been done. They couldn't take that trauma away. But maybe, if they moved fast enough, they could stop anything more from happening to those kids.

Tim had already covered their bases. They'd tried to get the NYPD to investigate the place. They were so overwhelmed by the ever-escalating crime wave, however, that they'd done nothing.

They'd even tried contacting the federal human trafficking task force, and it had even looked like an investigation might have been started. It had quickly died, however, without explanation. There was no telling whether or not it was because of connections the network had, or simply the fact that the Feds had figured out that the tip had come from Pallas Group Solutions.

Nick's money was on the former. They'd been careful.

"We'll have to hope that they're taking their time. We're still at least thirty minutes out." Durand didn't sound happy about it, and Nick could imagine why. They were behind schedule. They'd gotten out of New Jersey cleanly, so far as they could tell, but they wanted to be back in Pennsylvania and sterilizing everything by dawn. That was going to be tight, especially depending on what went down at the warehouse in the next hour.

They'd crossed the Hudson via the George Washington Bridge and were working their way down from Astoria. The traffic was still bad enough that it had slowed them down considerably.

There had been some discussion, before they'd even left Pennsylvania, of trying to pass themselves off as a SWAT team, much like the A Team had done in Atlanta some time ago. It would have alleviated some of the locals' concerns and kept the cops off, since nobody was likely to call the cops on what they thought were cops. However, that operation had also partially depended on a used armored vehicle, which hadn't been in the cards, not at the moment. It also would have been an absolute nightmare to drive through some of the urban areas they'd needed to traverse to get to their targets. Not just because of size and bulk—though those were definitely concerns—but also because there was no way they'd fly under the authorities' radar. Getting pulled over in a pair of modified Bearcats—or whatever they'd managed to find—with guns, armor, and gear, particularly in New Jersey or New York, would have ended the entire operation immediately, and landed the whole team in prison.

So, they'd gone with the blank-sided utility vans, but those weren't getting them there any faster.

The warehouse was a different target from the money house, so, as they got closer, the bags came open and the gear started to come out. They weren't going to be able to bluff their way in with pistols in duffel bags this time.

"Two minutes." Everyone was geared up, weapons in hand, by the time Durand called out the warning. They were passing a baseball field, gone dark as the late hour had sent the players and their families home.

Doug's phone vibrated, and he pulled it out, checking the screen. "Drop is still on site. So are the Subs. Looks like the clients from the Subs are making their picks."

As generally collected as he was, Doug couldn't keep the anger and disgust out of his voice. Nick gritted his teeth. Even though he was single, and had no kids that he knew of, he still felt the same rage at what was being done. He had friends who had kids, even a few who referred to him as "Uncle Nick." All he had to do was think of a few of them, especially the girls, and

217

it was enough to make him want to murder everyone who even thought about getting involved in this trade.

Minutes later, Durand pulled the van over into a parking spot and turned around in his seat. "Okay. The warehouse is just ahead, on the other side of the street. Cricket and Jumper are a block ahead of us, in the box truck OP. The Number Two vic is pulling around to the other side of the corner. We've got another box truck parked right in front of the warehouse, and I can see those two Subs across the intersection, parked on the corner facing us. Looks like they've got driver and passenger still sitting in the vics."

That could be a problem if those drivers and passengers decided to intervene when their principals were threatened. Which they were about to be.

"All right. On me." Doug, plate carrier on under his shirt, his carbine in his hands and slung around his neck, threw the back door open and went out fast.

He didn't rush in, though. The four contractors spread out as they got on the street, Matt covering their six for a moment, Doug starting across the street, his rifle held low along his leg to conceal it from the guys in the Suburbans. Nick loitered at the back of the van, keeping an eye on the Subs, even though Durand—who was just as armed to the teeth as the rest of them, had a clear line of sight on those two vehicles.

Manny followed Doug, similarly keeping his weapon as low profile as possible. None of them could completely conceal the long guns. They were the wrong size and shape for that. The idea of using AR pistols or short-barreled rifles had been brought up, but not everyone had had them. They weren't using company weapons—that would have been a bad idea and could completely destroy any plausible deniability that PGS might have if one of the weapons was captured on an off-the-books operation like this—but most were still running with full-length carbines, that weren't on any ATF paperwork.

At least, they weren't supposed to be.

A voice was raised on the other side of the traffickers' box truck. It was a challenge, though Nick couldn't quite make out what was said. He did hear Doug reply, his voice low and reasonable. The answering yell was a bit more understandable, and profane. They didn't believe that Doug was there to examine "merchandise," and wanted him to get lost.

That might be because the traffickers had a known schedule, as dangerous as that might be if it was on paper or electronic copy anywhere. They should see if they could get that.

Doug kept advancing. From where Nick was, he could see that the guys unloading the box truck couldn't see Manny, where the smaller man was moving up alongside the cars parked on the side of the street, his weapon already at the low ready.

Nick started across the street to join Manny, Matt falling in behind them, and that was when the guys in the closest Suburban realized something was wrong.

Both front doors opened, and the two men in the front vehicle ducked out, AR pistols in their hands, the weapons coming up and around the open doors fast. Nick and Manny, however, were slightly faster.

Their weapons were slightly longer, thanks to the suppressors on the ends of the barrels—though they weren't registered and weren't legal, having been machined somewhere in Texas, off the books—but they didn't have car doors to get around, and they'd both seen the movement immediately. Muzzles snapped up and shots *cracked* down the street, Nick dumping the driver with a hammer pair that took him high in the chest, the second punching through his clavicle at the base of his throat. Manny dropped the other one with four shots, following him to the ground with his muzzle until his fourth shot cored out the man's brains.

More suppressed gunfire snapped at the back of the box truck, and high-pitched screams rent the night. A flurry of shots smashed into the back Suburban, as the secondary team popped the corner and eliminated the backup shooters in that vehicle.

Nick and Manny turned and moved on the box truck, fast. The shooting had stopped, though the screams were just as shrill and panicked. The two of them fell in behind Doug and Matt, who had pushed onto the loading dock.

There were four bodies on the ground, one on the sidewalk and one just inside. The rollup door was still open, and half a dozen young women and girls huddled on the concrete, their hands held over their heads, crying in fear. Doug and Matt were already pushing inside, guns up, and Nick and Manny joined them as Saul, Mike, and Abaeze fell in from across the street. Josh, apparently, was holding their exit, along with Carl and Durand.

The loading dock, such as it was, was a fairly small space, though it hadn't always been that way. The sheet rock wall just ahead was clearly a later addition to the brick structure. The lights weren't bright, which made sense, given the fact that there were another dozen girls, ranging in age from about ten to seventeen, huddled on the floor, their faces tear-streaked and fear in their eyes.

The three men who'd been guarding them were down, their blood spattered on the drywall—and a couple of the girls— and the woman with the clipboard, who didn't look like she belonged, was sitting against that wall, holding a shaking, bloodied hand to the hole in her abdomen, the subcompact 9mm on the floor next to her forgotten as she stared in shock at the red on her other hand.

Matt kicked the pistol away from her, but otherwise left her alone. No one was going to lift a finger to try to treat her while there were still bad guys in the warehouse.

Probably not even after they were secure, either.

There was a slippery slope there, and Nick knew it, in the back of his head. The lure of vengeance was pretty strong. They had to keep their innate savagery under control, or this was going to turn out badly, like so many other vigilante organizations, including many of the *autodefensas* south of the border.

But right then, looking at what was being done to those girls—even in the dim light, the cuts and bruises were obvious, never mind the harder-to-see scars—he couldn't bring himself to give a damn.

As they pushed deeper, that hatred only got stronger.

The door off the loading dock led onto a hallway. It looked like the whole place had been gutted and reconstructed. The front appeared to still be the mushroom shop that it was supposed to be, but the back had been turned into a series of cubicles, most of them only closed off by curtains.

More screaming and wailing was coming from inside, some of it being shouted down by harsh voices. The hallway, however, was currently empty.

Doug and Matt took the first doorway. There was no shooting, but Nick could hear the curses as he and Manny swept toward the next door.

They burst through the curtain, guns up and looking for targets. They found one quick enough, too.

The man had a girl who couldn't have been more than nine or ten by the throat, holding her in front of him, while half a dozen others cowered behind him, crying.

"Shut up!" The man was well-dressed, his hair slicked back, and looked like he had quite a bit of money. He looked like the type who might bring two Suburbans of armed security into New York to pick up some of his latest conquests. "Don't take one more step, or else…"

Manny shot him through the eyeball, a fraction of a second before Nick's bullet split the bridge of his nose.

Only the fact that there were seven girls in the room kept Nick from canoeing the man's head. He was already dead, a substantial portion of the contents of his skull painting the back wall of the room—and a couple of the already traumatized girls. It still took a lot of self-control not to mutilate the corpse further.

"Stay here, stay low, and don't move." Nick put a finger to his lips, lifting his muzzle slightly as he did so. "We'll be right back. It's all going to be okay."

He couldn't be sure that any of them understood a word he'd said. There was one Caucasian girl, but the rest were Hispanic or Asian. It didn't matter. There were more scumbags to kill.

Another pair of shots barked up ahead, as he and Manny rolled out of the room, just as the Caucasian girl screamed, "Please don't leave us here with them!"

The others had just cowered away, just as afraid of the men with guns as they had been of the slick-haired bastard who was leaking the contents of his skull onto the floor.

Nick paused, just for a moment. He needed to move, but he couldn't leave them in a panic. Keeping the hostages calm was part of a hostage rescue, because often a panicky hostage could end up getting a lot of people killed. "We won't. We just have to make sure the place is safe. Then we're going to take you out of here."

Then he had to go, following Manny on the hunt.

More voices were raised at the back corner, and a flurry of unsuppressed gunshots sounded. As they came out into the hallway, they saw Saul and Mike fall back from the bullet holes getting punched through the drywall. Someone in the last cubicle was spraying fire through the wall, screaming epithets in what sounded like Spanish as he did so.

The fire ceased as Nick and Manny caught up with the lead pair, and then they poured through.

This room was slightly bigger, with a filthy mattress on the floor. Nick only had to catch a glimpse of the two toughs looming next to the mattress, and the second well-dressed man with his pants around his ankles huddled on it to see what had been happening.

The toughs were both reloading, having gone dry at the same time. The burst of gunfire practically tore the two of them and the half-dressed man apart. Blood, brains and hair spattered the walls, as the girl on the mattress screamed her lungs out.

Doug came in behind them, already pulling his cover shirt off. It would mean wearing his plate carrier in the open for anyone on the street to see, but the girl needed it more than he did. He covered her up, murmuring that it was going to be okay, despite the blood that had splashed on her face.

"The place is clear." Saul's voice was the voice of a man walking through a graveyard. "Get photos of those motherfuckers, get the girls in the vans, and let's get the fuck out of here."

CHAPTER
27

"Okay, from the top." Goblin looked more rested than the rest of us probably felt, but I suspected that appearances were deceiving. The man had probably been up for all but four hours a day, max, going over every bit of information we'd been sending back, and looking over Radford's shoulder while our resident geek and intel weenie dug into whatever he could find.

"Slobodian's coordinating a lot down here, but he's not the only one, and from the looks of things, he's primarily working on these Hezbollah guys and another team of Chinese. We haven't been able to identify them, but they don't look like refugees, and while they've met with Zhang Shihong—whom we *have* identified as working for a Chinese cultural organization that appears to primarily be a propaganda and intel arm of the MSS—they didn't get the full lecture, the one that Chris got some photos of." He spat a stream of brown juice into a water bottle. "They smell like PLA to me, though I won't even begin to speculate as to which unit." He sighed. "Which makes our next move a bit more complicated."

The next slide was a tentative flow chart of the network around Capurgana. "Slobodian has a house here, but he doesn't appear to be a linchpin of the local trafficking network. He's just plugged into it. Whether that ties in with the hitman network or not, we don't know. But there does appear to be a group heading into the Darien Gap soon, just judging by the interactions you guys have documented, and Slobodian has a vested interest in it.

"Without more information, we can only guess what that interest is. What's pretty obvious, at least to me, is that we have confirmation that Slobodian's dirty as fuck, and therefore, I'm greenlighting the hit. At the very least, we can, hopefully, get intel on just what Slobodian's up to with these guys, and why he's coordinating human trafficking from Iran and China, via the Darien Gap."

He brought up imagery of the house and the surrounding area. "Since we've got a limited lift capacity, then we'll have to offset insert, so the bird can make two trips. We could do it all in one if we were closer in, but I want to make damned good and sure we're in international waters for this one." He spat into his dip bottle again and grinned slightly. "Not that that'll save us if we attract the wrong kind of attention. Our saving grace here is that there isn't much Colombian Army presence up here. Any response is probably going to be from the local illicit networks, particularly whoever Slobodian's got on call. The recon team didn't see heavy security, but there are a lot of weapons around this place, just where the tourists can't necessarily see them.

"So, since KG and the recon team were out for a while, they'll get another hour or so to rest and prep. The rest of us are going wheels up in three hours…"

***

The helicopter came in low over the coast, miles south of Capurgana. There had been some discussion of trying to fake flying into the airstrip, but that had been decided against, since it was still going to be early enough that there would be tourists out and about, enjoying what night life they could while trying to avoid the crime. And that was assuming that Slobodian, Zhang, and half a dozen other bad actors in the town didn't have eyes on the airstrip at all times.

So, we were inserting in the jungle, in the pitch dark. To make matters worse—or better, from an infiltration point of view, it was raining. There wasn't much we could see out the windows, and I only knew we'd passed the coast when the pilot called out, "Feet dry!"

I'd had my NVGs down since shortly after we'd left the yacht, not that there was much to see with them outside. The bird was flying below cloud level, but the rain had been coming and going all the way in. It was just getting heavier as we flew toward the mountains, and I hoped the pilot could see better than I could.

Flying in adverse weather is always dicey. Flying into darkened, jungle-covered mountains in adverse weather is worse. I didn't know where Goblin had found our helicopter pilot, but the guy was nuts.

Our kind of nuts.

"Thirty seconds!" We pulled the doors open, and as the rain spattered inside the helicopter, I found that I could see the darker jungle below easily enough. There was no moon or stars, and the rain kept the visual range unfortunately short, but the PS-31s were good gear.

The bird was already low, almost skimming the treetops. I once again took a second to appreciate our pilot's combination of brass balls and mental illness just before he flared, bringing the helicopter almost to a standstill before lowering it toward the LZ.

The trees loomed blackly on all sides, and then we were hovering only a couple feet above the tall, waving grass. "This is your stop, gents!" The crew chief seemed completely unfazed by the flight through a storm, or the fact that the jungle seemed to be close enough in the small clearing that we were about a couple feet away from pruning tree branches with the rotor.

I went out first, since I was right there by the door. I had to admit that I was going to be glad to get the hell away from the bird. Not because I didn't think it was safe—though I've never ridden on a helicopter and entirely trusted it—but because even as a contractor, when I'd done helicopter inserts, we'd had door gunners. Here, in what was arguably an even more dangerous place, where the people we were coming to hit were part of a ruthless international crime and terrorism syndicate, we had only our rifles.

The drop was longer than it looked, and I hit hard, stumbling a little under body armor and assault pack. We weren't nearly as heavy as some of the patrols I'd done in Iraq or Afghanistan, but we had to have enough contingencies covered that we could sustain in the jungle for a while. The plates were because we were about to hit a house.

Moving away from the LZ, I scanned the jungle to find the rest of the team. The plan had been to rendezvous on the LZ, then proceed in toward the target, but it had been an hour and a half since they'd inserted, and we were trying to keep comms to a minimum. A lot can happen in a combat situation in an hour and a half.

Fortunately, Goblin and the rest were watching and waiting, and as I moved away from the bird, heading for the treeline, I spotted a faint flash on IR off to the side, just past the helicopter's nose. While we'd been trying pretty hard to avoid shining a bunch of IR around—we all knew special operators who'd been picking up NVGs from the battlefield for over a decade—there was a time and a place.

I skirted the edge of the clearing and joined the rest under the trees. The LZ was small and tight, and I had to hand it to the pilot all over again that he'd managed to bring the bird into it, under those conditions, without crashing or smacking a rotor blade into a tree.

The team was assembled in a small perimeter about ten yards under the canopy. The rain dripped off the leaves and some of it was bound to find its way down the back of a neck or two. The guys who'd come in first must have been miserable.

After the amount of time we'd spent in that wet, doing our advance recon, I wasn't *that* sympathetic.

We held our positions after I'd counted in the rest of the team, confirming for KG and Goblin that we had everybody. Twelve shooters on a knee in the steaming, dripping jungle, waiting for the helicopter to depart.

That didn't take long; the pilot didn't want to stick around, and I couldn't blame him. Insert on this sort of mission was always dicey, and while we were pretty sure the Colombians didn't have much of a military presence in the area, we'd seen enough to expect that there were far too many paramilitary, narco, and terrorist organizations that did. Despite the weather, the noise of a helicopter was bound to attract attention, especially since we were within a mile of the target.

That might seem far too close—and it did, to me—but we were limited by the amount of darkness we had to work with, and the terrain and vegetation we were going to have to fight through to get to the objective.

We held our position as the snarl of rotors faded into the night. It wasn't replaced with quiet, but with the various night noises of the jungle, along with the dripping of water and patter of rain. Fortunately, we didn't hear any human noises that might suggest that any security forces were coming out to look at what had brought a helicopter in.

Finally, after about ten or fifteen minutes—though I was sure that Goblin was getting damned impatient by that time, after already sitting in the jungle for the better part of two hours—we finally got up and started out, fading into the dark and the wet in single file, heading for Slobodian's Colombia house, and what we hoped was a reckoning with the spider in the web.

CHAPTER 28

Things had changed at Slobodian's little getaway, and now we were going to have to rethink the whole plan while crouched in the dripping jungle.

There were several generator-powered worklights spaced around the outside of the compound, and in their glare, we could see not only several more motorcycles, but a couple of four-wheelers and half a dozen shooters, all watching the perimeter, even on the jungle side.

We didn't think that we'd been compromised when we'd been observing the house, Slobodian, and the Hezbollah operatives who'd come to meet with him. Yet, here were at least six guys on external security, armed with a mix of AKs, M4s, a couple of Tavors, and what looked like a VHS-2. They were Caucasians and Hispanics, from what I could see, though there might have even been a few Middle Easterners in there, as well. My guess, from where I crouched in the weeds, soaked to the skin and chafing, was that these guys were part of Slobodian's international network.

Had we given ourselves away, especially with that little dustup with Zhang's security in the north of town? It was possible, which meant that we had to either fade into the dark, figuring that the enemy was alerted and warned, and that we'd face too hard a fight to win, or we had to go *now*, before Slobodian disappeared.

From where I knelt, not far from Goblin and KG, who were watching the objective and conferring in low murmurs that didn't even travel far enough for me to hear, I couldn't say which was the more prudent course of action. We sure as hell didn't want to let Slobodian slip away, but when we could *see* at least six shooters, there might be more inside.

This could easily turn into a meat grinder, without more intel.

Unfortunately, while we had *some* advantages of stealth and mobility, we *were* still up against a bit of a time crunch. It was only a matter of time before Slobodian sent someone else against our families, or some other target that was calculated to try to take Pallas Group Solutions off the board. I had to hand it to Goblin that he'd managed to maneuver people and information so that PGS didn't appear to have the legal or financial weaknesses for the bad guys to take us out by those means—despite some of the stuff we'd done—but that had only driven them to find some other way to come at us.

Or, maybe, Slobodian was just that kind of guy.

I glanced over at Goblin and KG, though I had to turn my whole head and take my eyes off the objective to do it. It had taken us almost two and a half hours to get to where we crouched from the LZ, and we were burning through the night fast. A decision had to be made soon.

And it was. Goblin circled a hand over his head, and the four of us who had pushed forward to get eyes on just before the hit fell back to our attack position, barely fifty yards away through the jungle, which was thick enough that it felt like it was a lot farther away than that.

"Okay, listen up." Goblin kept his voice pitched low. "There's more security on the objective than we were expecting or planning for, but that doesn't change much of anything. Kermit, Leprechaun, Ziggy, and Drizzle, you're on exterior security. Set up on the northwest and southeast corners. Those should be the easiest to get to undetected. First shot you hear, drop any external security you see. I don't give a shit whether the assault team is in yet or not. Kill 'em, and drop anyone who comes out of that house who isn't us."

He looked around at the rest of us, though most of us were still watching the surrounding jungle. We were less than a football field away from the target house. We couldn't afford to let our guard down for a brief.

"The rest of us are going in. It looks like we'll have to go over the fence, but it's a cyclone, so we can cover each other through it. Then we hit the back door and clear that house. If we can take Slobodian alive, that's fine." I wondered just what we were going to do with him if we *did* take him, but hopefully Goblin had a contingency plan in place for that. "If not..." He shook his head. "Well, then we tried."

He stood up. "Brian's on point."

Without another word, and with as little noise as possible, what rustling we did make partially masked by the sound of the rain and the dripping water, we slipped through the jungle toward the compound, even as I thought I could hear raised voices coming from the house.

It took a few minutes to cover those fifty yards or so. Clint, Patrick, Phil, and Marcos had vanished into the gloom and the vegetation on the flanks, moving to their cordon positions, each pair setting up where they could cover two sides of the compound. The rest of us converged on a spot at the fence where the jungle was almost growing through it.

That vegetation was working for us and against us at the same time. Our visibility was every bit as limited as the bad guys'. And the veg was so thick next to the fence that we actually had to move farther over, closer to one of those lights, to get to a spot where we *could* get over it.

Unfortunately, that put us a little too close to that light.

Brian and Tom were on the fence, halfway up, Tom already hooking a leg over the wire, when one of the security, a short, bald-headed guy carrying a VHS-2, came around the corner and stopped, squinting in our direction. We were still in some shadow, but he had to be able to see the fence shaking as our two teammates climbed over it.

I was right next to where Brian was climbing, covering that corner. I snapped my rifle up and put two rounds into the man's chest, just before either Clint or Patrick shot him in the head, from somewhere off to my right.

The guard dropped, and Brian and Tom jumped down to the ground. Tom landed heavily, losing his footing for a second, but then all hell broke loose.

Gunfire snapped and thundered around the house, as Ken and I threw ourselves over the fence. We weren't alone, either. With Tom and Brian running to the wall, facing opposite directions, Brian dumping rounds toward someone I couldn't see, everyone who could fit on the fence at that point raced to get over it. More gunfire sounded from the other side of the house, and Clint and Patrick were hammering away as well.

Getting over the fence didn't take that long, but when you're off the ground, clambering over a chain link fence that's waving like a flag in a storm because there are five or six guys, each weighing over 200 pounds with armor, weapons, and ammo, a couple of seconds feels too long. I got over the top and practically threw myself on the ground, landing hard and rolling away from the fence as KG came over it behind me.

Scrambling to my feet, I quickly joined Tom at the back door. Two more bodies were on the ground near the corner, but it looked like we were still all on our feet. The gunfire out front hadn't slackened, though, and that was a bad sign.

I gave Tom the squeeze, and he hit the door hard, pushing through with his rifle up, hunting for targets. Three shots hit him in the chest, and a fourth punched into his shoulder, even as I came in on his heels, Ken right beside me, our muzzles dropping level past his shoulders as he staggered and stumbled to a knee. I shot the first silhouette I could see, just past the muzzle flash that was now pumping bullets into the jungle behind us, the rounds *snapping* past my head and through the door as the recoil made the AK climb toward the ceiling. Two more rounds went into the ceiling overhead as the man dropped, one hand going to the new hole in his throat as the other still spasmodically jerked the Kalashnikov's trigger.

With Ken beside me, Brian dragging Tom out of the doorway while the older man protested that he was all right, that it was just a nick, I drove deeper into the house. It wasn't a large house, and I quickly cleared the kitchen and the rear entryway, Ken turning left while I turned right. The kitchen was small and fairly dirty, somewhat odd for a rich guy's home, even in northern Colombia. No one else was in the room, not even hiding behind the small island in the middle, so we pushed, now joined by Jake, Rob, KG, and Goblin.

The gunfire out front had died down some. I didn't know if that was a good sign or a bad one, but now I could hear voices and movement out in the main living room.

I really, really wished I had a frag grenade. Clearing with frags hadn't been something we'd trained, but sometimes you'd rather just blow the hell out of the room, especially when you're reasonably sure there aren't any hostages in it, rather than risk your own neck charging in. But all we had at the moment were rifles, so, pausing just before the opening, I dipped my muzzle slightly, got an answering dip from Ken, who was set up to cross cover through the door, took a deep breath, and went through.

The front was a mess. Bullet holes were scattered across the front wall, and two men were already down, one near the door, another in the middle of the living room itself. I only took those in somewhat peripherally, though, as a bright muzzle flash erupted seemingly right in front of my face, and I *felt* the bullets go past my ear and tug at my helmet.

I responded instinctively, reflexively slamming about ten rounds into the man. I was barely aiming, but at that range, with my weapon in my shoulder already, all I really had to do was point and shoot. I blew a chunk out of his heart, and he fell over backward.

More suppressed gunfire was hammering through the room as I swung back toward the front door, catching a figure trying to hide behind a couch, a pistol in his hand. The only reason he hadn't been shot yet was that I was the only one in a position to see him. He caught my movement out of the corner of his eye as I advanced and pivoted toward him, and he tried to turn and bring the handgun to bear, but I was already ahead of him, and blasted a chunk of his skull and its contents across the upholstery.

Then the gunfire stopped, as there were no more targets. At least, none that were moving.

"Find Slobodian." Goblin's voice was a harsh rasp over the radio.

"This is Ziggy. Slobodian's gone." There was something about Phil's voice that made my heart skip a beat. Something was wrong. Very wrong. "We got two of his security on the way out, but we missed him." There was a pause, but nobody filled it right away, I thought because we all sensed what was coming next. "Dizzy's down."

"Fuck." Goblin stood in the center of the living room, his face set, his weapon slung in front of him, looking down at the bodies on the floor. "Get him in here if you can." He looked around at the team, though most of us were already moving. "Get security on the doors and windows. I don't know how much time we have, but we need to toss this place before we pull off. Photos of all these assholes, too." He took a deep breath. Ken and I were already on the door, as Phil appeared out of the jungle, Marcos over his shoulders. From the way he was carrying our buddy, I knew that Marcos wasn't just down.

He was gone.

Flashes flickered behind me as photos were hastily taken. Looking out the door, I could see that several of the motorcycles out front were gone. That must have been Slobodian's escape plan.

The odds were good that he was gone. There was no way we were going to be able to exfiltrate and get back on the trail before he was out of the country. Somebody like Slobodian would have half a dozen escape routes, over land, sea, or air. It wouldn't surprise me if there was a private plane landing on the strip in Capurgana at that moment to pick him up.

We lowered our muzzles to let Phil through with Marcos, blood dripping down a limp arm to leave wet craters in the dirt as he headed inside. We'd have to drag the body back to the bird. We'd had to leave our dead behind before, but not this time.

Not this time.

CHAPTER
29

The white bus that was waiting for the B Team in Pennsylvania was relatively nondescript, and aside from a small logo near the door, it might have been mistaken for an ordinary, Blue Bird commercial bus, the sort that just about every PGS contractor remembered shuttling them around military bases during training. This one belonged to an organization dedicated to rescuing trafficked girls. Not as high-profile as an outfit like Operation Underground Railroad, the Coat of Many Colors Foundation was also a little less intent on making sure they dotted their i's and crossed their t's, as long as the kids got liberated and returned to their families, or put into a home that would be as good as, if not better. They were more willing to look the other way when it came to making sure those girls got rescued, rather than waiting for law enforcement to get rolling.

Nick hadn't heard much about them, but he was hoping that their lack of worry about the methods used to get the girls didn't extend to not worrying about security. There was something to be said about an anti-human trafficking organization that was willing to entertain some vigilantism, but if they got sloppy, it was going to come back on everyone.

Doug seemed to think highly of them, though, and when they pulled up in the vans and a slender woman with long brown hair came down out of the bus, she gave the former Delta operator a quick hug before turning toward the vehicles.

The girls had mostly endured the ride in shell-shocked silence, some of them huddled and hugging themselves, staring a thousand miles away, faces blank and eyes dead, while others had cried quietly the entire way. As traumatic as their captivity had been, their rescue had been pretty rough, too. While Nick didn't doubt that some of them had seen some pretty savage violence on their way north, the brutality that he and his teammates had unleashed on their captors in their rage had probably not helped the girls' state of mind. Some of them had been spattered with blood and brains as the men who had enslaved them had been cut down, often with a few more bullets than had really been necessary to do the job.

Doug was speaking quietly to the long-haired woman as she walked toward the nearest van, parked in a field out in rural Pennsylvania. They'd wanted to do this quietly, with as low a profile as possible, for a few reasons. The last thing these kids needed was a bunch of cameras and lights in their faces, for one thing. Of course, keeping PGS's involvement in their rescue a secret was one of the other big ones.

Matt and Manny swung the doors of their van open. They'd been riding up front, along with Mike and Saul, all the way from New York, doing what they could to give the girls some space in the back. It was difficult, since there had been about twenty-three girls on site when they'd hit the warehouse, but they'd done what they could.

It was a good thing they'd managed not to get pulled over anywhere in New York, New Jersey, or Pennsylvania. Ten men with weapons, body armor, and tactical gear, transporting twenty-three mostly underage girls in vans with no seats, would not have gone over well.

What else were we going to do, though?

Doug hung back as the woman approached the open doors. None of the girls had gotten out, and a few of them had shrunk back from the opening. "Girls? My name's Martha. I know you've had a really hard time, but I promise that it's going to get better now. These men just made sure of that." She

240

repeated herself in Spanish, then in what sounded to Nick like Russian. *Probably Ukrainian. Heard about a lot of kids getting trafficked from the war through Mexico.*

It took more soothing words and offers of water and clothing before the girls finally started to get out of the vans and onto the bus. Several other people were waiting there, speaking gently and careful not to make too much physical contact. Watching them, still geared up except for his helmet and NVGs, his hand resting on the Glock at his side, just in case, Nick reflected on just how much better the people from Coat of Many Colors were at this than the contractors.

Most of the girls avoided eye contact as they filed hesitantly onto the bus. One of them balked, but the man at the steps just got down onto the ground, crouched next to her so that he had to look up at her, careful not to touch her, and spoke softly to her.

Nick found that Martha was standing next to him, watching the procession of young kids who had seen and been subjected to evil that they never should have been exposed to. "It's going to take a long time, but they'll be all right. We've gotten pretty good at helping them through this."

Nick could only nod, even as one of the girls, a little blond who looked like she couldn't have been more than eleven or twelve, walked up to Doug and, in a little, hoarse voice, just said, "*Dyakuyu.*"

"*Nema za sho.*" Doug smiled at her, and she hurried away, looking down as she turned toward the bus. Doug moved to join Nick and Martha, as the last of the girls were finally coaxed onto the bus.

Martha looked around the team, then up at Doug. "Are *you* guys going to be okay?"

Doug glanced at Nick, then turned to the woman. "We will be. As soon as we can put more of these fuckers in the ground."

***

"Well, well, fucking well." Bob Grayson reached down and scratched the stump of his leg where it met his prosthesis. "Guess who those two fancy boys you guys smoked worked for?" He pivoted his laptop around so that Nick, Doug, and Saul could see the screen. Most of the rest of the team were dispersed to various hotels in western Pennsylvania, getting as far from the scene of the massacre they'd unleashed as possible.

The picture on the screen was of a trim, smiling, perfectly coiffed, deeply tanned man in a suit. Nick frowned as he studied it. Something was familiar about the face, and not just because he saw the dead, shark's look in the man's eyes.

"*That* is Simon Badeaux. Formerly *Congressman* Simon Badeaux. Currently the CEO of Alchemical Finance, LLC, as well as the Vision World Foundation." The look that Grayson shot at the screen was pure venom.

"I wonder if that's actually our target." Saul rubbed his chin. He'd calmed down since the raid, and was back to his usual icy, calculated self. Not that he'd been particularly emotional during the hit, but there wasn't a man on that team who hadn't been affected by what they'd seen. "If the client was interested in this specific trafficking network, and Badeaux is a client..."

"That's hard to say without more information." Doug had his arms folded. "It's a possibility, but we don't have any definitive proof that they were there on his say-so, either."

"Except that we do." Grayson smiled, though it never reached his eyes. He changed files. "Manny was smart enough to grab some hard drives on one of the desks in there. Turns out, these fuckers were keeping a client list. Guess who's pretty high up on the list?"

"Why am I not surprised at this point?" Saul sighed. "Seems the more money and influence they've got these days, the dirtier they are."

"It's probably always been that way," Doug mused. "Some temptations are baked into the wiring." He rubbed his chin with a thumb, studying the screen. "Here's the question, though. We've got the information. But, given *how* we got it, what are we going to do with it?"

None of them had an answer. It was a problem with acting as vigilantes, which was largely what they'd been doing on this job. The authorities were unlikely to accept their evidence.

Of course, Nick was aware of a few times where the authorities had been unwilling to accept evidence *they* hadn't collected, even though it had been collected through nonviolent, open-source means. So, that was still a problem. Even if they hadn't broken a bunch of New York and New Jersey gun laws and conducted unilateral raids on two organized crime houses— which they'd been pretty sure the local cops were aware of— then they *still* might not get any movement.

And that was even without a very rich, very connected former Congressman being involved.

"That's going to ultimately be up to Goblin." Saul turned toward the door. "I know he's busy as hell right now—probably more than the company's fucking *CEO* should be—but I'll give him a call." He paused at the threshold. "I just hope he's got things worked up so that we *can* use this." Looking back at the other three men, he breathed a heavy sigh.

"You know there *is* a way, right?" Nick asked, knowing just what he was suggesting. Still, after what he'd seen in that camp at Shelter Valley, and even worse in the warehouse in New York, his concerns about following proper lines of law—in the more bureaucratic sense of the word—were fading into the burning need to see these monsters brought to justice.

"Oh, I know." Saul glanced down at the floor, thinking. Doug had, so far, held his peace, but that was Doug. "It's been a possibility ever since we started to go kinetic. I just... I'm not sure we really want to go all the way over that line, yet."

"Why not?" Nick wasn't usually the type to confront guys like Saul or Doug. He respected both men, but in this case, he wasn't going to back down. He pointed, even though he was pretty sure he wasn't pointing in the right direction, but still indicating New York by implication. "We sure as shit didn't hesitate to waste those motherfuckers back in that warehouse, or the cartel scumsacks in California. Or any of the MS-13 savages we've killed. Or even the hitmen who came after our families. If those cocksuckers are fair game, why the *fuck* do we have to go hands off on the sons of bitches who are calling the shots?"

"Ideally, there is no difference." Doug's voice was quiet. "Practically, we gain nothing by tilting at windmills. The blowback from knocking off a former Congressman—and huge campaign donor—is going to be far harsher than scragging a few gangbangers and human traffickers. This son of a bitch is going to have an entire PR machine devoted to defending him and painting him as the greatest, kindest man who ever lived, and anyone who goes after him as an absolute monster. *We* might know the truth. *We* might know that Badeaux is lower than a rabid dog and needs to be put in the ground for all the lives he's destroyed. But if we go off half-cocked and just go ham on this, then *we'll* be the ones who get buried, while he gets canonized a saint, if we even get to him."

The former Delta operator shook his head. "This is heavy, dangerous shit. As much as it pains me, we've got to be cunning, and we've got to be strategic. Be patient. Let's see what Goblin's got in mind. He hasn't led us astray yet."

Nick nodded, though he didn't like it. He looked down at his hands and took a deep breath.

You're letting your emotions get the better of you. Doug's right. Saul's right. We've got to be smart about this, or we're just going to play right into the bad guys' hands.

He still didn't like it. He probably never would. The idea that enough money and influence might allow an absolute monster, who exploited slaves in ways that Nick didn't really want to think about, to walk away scot-free, untouched by the misery and death he'd already wrought, only to spread even more without a care in the world, enraged him.

You don't have to like it. Just got to adapt and figure out a way around it. I just hope that our faith in Goblin isn't misplaced.

CHAPTER
30

Adrenaline is a hell of a drug.

I was too wired as we flew away from Slobodian's house to even blink, it felt like. I was tired, but there was no risk of falling asleep on security. The feared backup hadn't arrived, so we'd had a little more time than we'd planned to toss the house, as well as the bodies. That had netted us quite a haul. Those bastards had had phones, SD cards, and even handwritten notes, though most of those seemed to be in Farsi. That wasn't even getting into the stuff that Slobodian had had on site. We'd dragged a full duffel bag of shit back to the LZ, along with Marcos's body.

By the time we got back to the yacht, however, I was *dragging*. The adrenaline had worn off and I was ready to crash. It took an awful lot of effort just to take care of my weapon and gear before I threw myself into a bunk—which was pretty luxurious, thanks to the yacht's origin as a high-end billionaire's toy, rather than an operational platform for paramilitary shooters—and passed the hell out. Even the grief of losing Marcos wasn't enough to keep me awake at that point.

Not that the fatigue kept the nightmares away.

So, I was still dragging when I walked into the salon that had been turned into our mobile TOC, late in the morning, looking for coffee. I was one of the first ones up, though Goblin had beaten me to the operations center by some time, it looked like. He had a steaming cup of coffee in front of him and already had a dip in, too.

He looked up as I went to the coffee pot, which was already down to about a quarter full. Goblin had, indeed, been there a while. There was no sign of Radford—maybe the kid really did sleep, occasionally—but he didn't drink coffee, anyway. He preferred energy drinks. By the gallon.

"Well, we've started to scratch the surface." He reached for his spitter. "And boy, things are already getting interesting." He pointed toward one of the phones, sitting on the desk nearby, wired up to one of Radford's little gadgets that was designed to get past a lot of digital security. Probably illegal on some level, but we weren't exactly playing by the rules these days.

When the bad guys have turned the rules to their advantage, sometimes you've got to step outside of them.

I sipped my coffee. Goblin had sprung for the good stuff. "What kind of 'interesting?'"

He raised an eyebrow over his spitter. "How's 'assassination of a sitting Congressman' sound?"

That made me blink. "Really?"

"Really." He glanced past me at the door. "Ah, hell. The rest are going to have to get the briefing, but we should have some more information by then.

"So, our client, who wanted you guys to shadow *and* protect Wise—but neglected to mention that last part—is Congressman Jacob Aller. I had to agree to keep his identity confidential, and he was already working through a risk mitigation firm, anyway, so that kinda worked. But now that confidentiality doesn't seem to have paid off for him, I think that you guys should know, especially given what comes next.

"Apparently, Slobodian told those Hezbollah guys that Aller was instrumental in the targeted killing of Qassem Soleimani a few years ago. I have no idea if it's true or not, but it doesn't matter. The Qods Force has been vowing revenge for that killing for years. If they can get *anybody* highly placed and call it vengeance for Soleimani, it's a victory. They just have to do it in such a way that it doesn't invite open war between the US and Iran."

I snorted. "We've been at war with the Iranians for decades. It's just not nice to say so, no matter how many Americans they put in the dirt in Iraq."

"Still, because of that 'can't say that' bullshit, as long as they can maintain some insulation between them and the hitters, they can keep their asses covered."

I nodded, thinking it over as I sipped my coffee and got my brain back on track for the day.

Then I frowned. "Why do I suddenly suspect that Slobodian wasn't just doing this as a favor to Hezbollah?"

"Because he quite obviously wasn't." Goblin leaned back in his chair. "We're reasonably sure that it was his network that took Wise out, and Aller was interested in Wise. There's a connection there. Somehow, Aller's security has broken down, and the bad guys know that he's the one who hired us. Or, possibly, we're just right in the middle of the perfect storm, and the hits on our families were just because of the undercover work you and Phil did, while the hit on Aller is only coincidentally connected to our contract with him. It's possible. I'm not sure I believe in that kind of coincidence, since I know what kind of intel collection capabilities these assholes have, but it's possible."

I had to admit, it made sense. There *was* still a certain degree of coincidence involved, but that became almost inevitable when you get deep enough. It's a small world, especially in the dark places we tended to go.

"I guess that raises the question of what he's going to do now." I took another sip of coffee. It was starting to cool. "I doubt that he's done, even if we shut down the hit on Aller." We'd confirmed that night that we'd killed all the Hezbollah operatives in that house. Only Slobodian and perhaps one of his security guards had gotten away.

"Oh, I guaran-damn-tee he's not done." Goblin scratched the stubble on his jaw. He hadn't bothered to shave for a while, since we'd been out Colombia way. "He can't *afford* to be done. This isn't like back in the military, where if something goes wrong, the command can just decide to declare victory and pull back. His life's on the line now. If not from Hezbollah, then from anyone else who might smell weakness. He *has* to follow through and fix this, or he's dead, and I know him just well enough to be sure that he knows it."

Phil, looking drawn and hollow-eyed, had come in while we were talking. KG wasn't far behind him. I was a little surprised, to be honest, that KG hadn't beaten us all there, even Goblin.

As I turned to our teammates, my eyes lingered with concern on Phil. He didn't make eye contact, but just went to the coffee pot. I might have dismissed it—I'd done the same thing—except that Marcos was currently in the yacht's freezer, below decks, awaiting transport back home, where he'd have a quiet, closed-casket funeral.

Phil and Marcos had been partners for a long time. Like most of us, they went back to before Pallas Group, but they'd gotten to be tight as actual blood brothers. Phil was hurting with Marcos gone, and as much as I missed the guy, I worried about Phil. I knew *him* well enough to strongly suspect that he was blaming himself that Marcos had gotten hit.

It was bullshit. Even Phil had to know it. Combat is inherently dangerous, and the longer you go where the bullets are flying, the greater the chance that you're going to catch one. From the brief hot wash we'd stumbled through once the bird had set down on the yacht's fantail, there had been no fewer than four shooters, and they'd come out shooting.

It had just been Marcos' time.

Try telling that to his best friend, though.

I wasn't the only one watching Phil at the moment. Custus had come in and was standing by the hatchway, his big arms folded, his eyes on our teammate, something different from his usually sardonic expression on his face. But before anyone could say anything—not that it would have helped much at that point—a phone buzzed.

Eyes searched for the sound. We were well offshore, far from any cell towers, so it had to be satellite. And there weren't too many people who had the company sat phone's number.

Goblin scooped it up and frowned at the screen for a second before he answered it. "Yes?"

His eyebrows climbed toward his hairline as he listened, turning toward the rest of us. Then he set the phone down on the desk beside him and put it on speaker.

"What do you want, Caleb? Or what should I call you, now?"

"Caleb's fine." The voice on the other end had no significant accent, aside from a sardonic edge to it. He was trying hard to sound cool, but there was something about his tone that struck me as a very nervous man.

There was a faint rasp over the speaker, as if he'd just taken a deep breath and blown it out. "I need to do what I should have done months ago, instead of listening to the client. I'd like to buy you out, Thad."

Goblin just looked down at the phone—which was really just an ordinary smartphone tied into a satellite communications puck—with a faintly bemused expression on his face. "You want to run that by me again?"

"You heard me. I want to buy Pallas Group Solutions. I'm good for it. It will be a lot less expensive, in many ways, for all of us."

"Buy me *out*, Caleb?" Goblin hadn't lost a faint smile. "Or buy me *off*?"

"Out. This is business, Thad. We're both spending a lot of money and blood, and for people who really don't give a shit about either of us. Five hundred million for PGS. Cash. Or sixteen and a half thousand Bitcoin, if that's more your speed. Should be plenty to take care of the rest of your contractors and give you a nice nest egg. You can retire, and we can put all this unpleasantness behind us."

Goblin looked around at the rest of us, that same faint, sardonic grin on his face. "Well, that's an awfully generous offer, Caleb. Hezbollah must be almighty upset with you."

There was a short pause, though I thought I could detect the anger on the other end of the connection. "They've got nothing to do with this. It's just good business."

Goblin turned back to the phone, his expression shifting. Even though the call was audio only, his face turned set, hard, and there was a deadly fire in his eyes. "Except that it's not 'just business,' Caleb." His voice turned into a snarl. "You sent killers after my boys and their *families*. It wasn't 'just business' before that, but now, it's far, far more personal." He reached for the cutoff. "Be seeing you, Caleb."

He ended the call. Quiet fell over the salon while we all sort of processed what had just happened.

"Not sure that was all that smart, boss." Custus hadn't moved from where he'd been leaning against the bulkhead. "He's going to be even more desperate, now. And if you'd strung him along a while, we might have gotten a better idea of where he's hiding."

Goblin shook his head, already leaning forward and pulling something up on his computer. I'd seen that look before. Our boss was well into problem-solving mode. "He wouldn't have given anything away. This was a Hail Mary, but he's still way too cunning to allow for that kind of a slip." His frown deepened. "I do wonder what he thought he was going to accomplish. Hopefully he didn't manage to trace the call."

"That's what we've got VPNs and shit for," KG pointed out.

"True, but there are still tricks." Radford had come back from wherever he'd been hiding. "I don't necessarily know of one that can trace a VPN'ed up satellite call, but that doesn't mean that it doesn't exist."

Goblin had stopped paying attention, and was peering at the screen, leaning on one hand, lost in thought. Finally, though, he leaned back. "I think I know where he is."

I glanced at Custus, who shrugged. "Where, and based on what?"

He tapped the desk in front of the screen, which was now showing overhead imagery of what looked at first glance like one city split three ways by rivers. "Bolus told us that he had a place in The Hamptons, Belize, Colombia, and Ciudad Del Este." He pointed to the screen. "My money's on him running for Ciudad Del Este."

When he didn't immediately elaborate, Custus prompted him a little. "Why there?"

I thought I was starting to get the picture, but I waited for Goblin to explain.

"Ciudad Del Este is smack dab in the middle of the Tri Border Area." He got a couple of nods, but when he also got a couple of blank stares, he grinned lopsidedly. "It's only probably the biggest hub of organized crime, terrorism, and everything else bad and illegal in the Western Hemisphere. Cartels, human trafficking networks, Chinese operatives… You name it, they've got a presence there. It's the confluence of borders between Paraguay, Argentina, and Brazil. There's very little law there, mainly because anyone can pretty easily skip over the border. Here's the kicker, though: Hezbollah has their biggest fundraising operation in the Western Hemisphere right there in the Tri Border Area."

"You think he's headed there to try to smooth some ruffled feathers and assure them that he didn't get their boys killed." KG was nodding.

"It makes sense. Notice he didn't deny it when I suggested he was a bit desperate about Hezbollah. He's a little off his game, no matter how hard he's working to keep it together." He glanced at Custus. "That's about as good a slip as we're likely to get."

"Are we going after him?" Phil asked. It was the first thing he'd said that morning, and while his voice was that of a man walking through a graveyard, he was still solid. Still committed to the mission.

"I am." Goblin looked around at all of us, meeting each man's gaze. "I'll put it to the whole team once everyone's up, but I fully intend to put Slobodian in the ground, along with as much of his network as possible. Whether you come along and join me, or go back and protect your families, I will leave up to each of you. As for me...

"I'm going to end this."

CHAPTER
31

Grayson was waiting when Nick came back into the temporary TOC they'd set up in Morgantown, West Virginia. It was a long way from New York, where their presumptive target was, but for the moment, Tim had agreed that getting some distance while the heat died down was probably their best bet. They weren't going to get to Badeaux overnight, anyway.

The C Team was still in New York, still gathering what information they could. Nick couldn't say he envied them, even though he knew they were probably going to have to go back into that hellhole if they were going to take down Badeaux.

He was torn. It would be just to put a bullet to the man and end him. But it would probably be better for the company— and the individual contractors—in the long run if they could sic the law on him and take him down that way.

He was thinking about all of that when he noticed that Grayson was leaning against the desk, his prosthetic crossed over his good leg, arms folded, looking down at the floor with a frown.

"What's up, Bob?" Something was wrong. Given everything they'd seen over the last few weeks, the first thought that popped into his head was, *Oh hell, what now?*

Grayson looked up, though he was still kind of staring off into space. "Oh, hey, Nick. Hm." He propped his chin on a fist, as if he was thinking over how much he really wanted to say. "So, I got a call last night, from an old buddy. We were at 2nd Ranger Battalion together. Anyway, he joined the FBI after he got out."

Nick felt himself go very still. "Do I need to call Saul in here?" It struck him that he probably should have said, "Tim," but Tim was a manager, not a leader. The team looked to Saul.

"Probably." Grayson seemed to shake himself out of his reverie a second later. "Oh, it's not that they're investigating us, or anything. At least, not that he knows about. No, it's... well, it's a little more complicated than that."

Nick sighed. "I'll get Saul." He turned around and headed down the hall. They were using an AirBnB as a team house again. It had worked out in Atlanta and a couple of other places, and it was working here, though the company hadn't rented it. That had been Tim, who was actually staying in the master bedroom with his wife. Without a contract in Morgantown, they'd needed to get a little more inventive with their cover story. The team were just friends of the family who were in the area, which had necessitated most of them finding lodging elsewhere around town. However, they were mostly hanging out in the house at the moment, waiting on the final word from Goblin as to just what, exactly, they were supposed to do next.

Saul was in the living room, watching TV, or at least pretending to. From the bored look on the man's face, he wasn't really paying attention to the inanity on the screen. He looked up as Nick entered the room. "Something going on?"

"Might be." Nick tilted his head back toward the team room. "Bob says he got an interesting call last night. Might be significant to all of us. Seems he's got an old buddy who's a Fed."

That got Saul's attention. "Sounds like something we need to hear, all right." He turned toward the back. "Doug! Josh! Matt! Front and center!"

The other contractors filtered out of a couple of the side rooms. "What's up?"

"Sounds like Bob has a story for us." Saul was already on his feet, as Nick turned back toward the TOC.

Grayson hadn't moved and seemed to be waiting for them. "What's up, Bob?" Saul asked. "What's this about a Fed?"

"My buddy Blake Givens joined the Bureau right out of the Army." Grayson wasn't apologetic and seemed to be a lot more at ease than he had been a few minutes ago. "He wanted to go to work with HRT. Seemed up his alley. He didn't get there, and he's been working racketeering cases for the last few years. He's in a dead-end rut, he knows it, and I think he's still bitter about it.

"All that's background. Point is, I still talk to the guy from time to time. No, I haven't told him about this job, or what I've been doing for PGS. None of his business, even if he *wasn't* a Fed. But he *does* know that I work with PGS, at least from our conversation last night. And that's actually why he called me.

"From what he said, he knows that we're working for Congressman Aller." That raised some eyebrows, and he looked around. "Oh. You guys didn't know that part yet? Shit." He rubbed the back of his neck. "Well, we are. Goblin knows. He had me do some of the initial digging. Aller went through Harper's Shield Services to keep some distance between us, but it's definitely him. And, apparently, the reason the FBI thinks he's digging is because of a former congressman and big-time political donor, that Blake's found popping up in one of his recent investigations far too often."

"Badeaux." It wasn't a question.

"Bingo." Grayson nodded. "Thing is, he says that every time he's started to try to get a warrant to look into Badeaux, he's been stonewalled, up to most recently, when he was flat-out told by his superior to drop it."

"So, what's he want?" Saul was clearly feeling a bit ambivalent about the whole thing.

"He wants to meet." Grayson shifted his weight, seemingly a little more on balance now that he'd gotten going.

"He didn't want to put any more details on the phone. Given who he works for, I can't imagine I blame him."

"Maybe not." Doug was thinking, and turned to one of the two laptops on the desk, pulling up overhead imagery of the surrounding area. "Given who we're dealing with, I'd say somewhere out in the open. Long lines of sight. No crowds for Feds to hide in."

"What if they have a crop duster, though?" Josh asked.

Nick frowned, trying to remember the reference. Doug just chuckled.

"I doubt the kind of Feds we're worried about would have the taste to have seen *North by Northwest*."

Saul stepped closer and looked over Doug's shoulder. "Here." He pointed. "There's not a lot of open farmland around here, but that should do. We can have overwatch in the woods up here."

Doug nodded. "Good a place as any." He shifted the laptop so that Grayson could see. "Give us a couple hours to get set up, then call your boy." He straightened up. "Let's go have a talk with a Fed."

***

"He's late." Nick glanced at his watch. He and Doug had taken separate vehicles, and Grayson was sitting in the passenger seat of Nick's truck. He couldn't say he was a big fan of the rental Nissan Frontier. His Tacoma was generally better than the midsize Nissan pickup in just about every way.

Grayson was looking out the window, his elbow propped up on the door. "You trust this guy?" Nick asked.

"About as far as I'd trust anybody in the Bureau, which is a low bar, I gotta admit." Grayson was still watching the road, lost in thought. Finally, he turned back toward the front. "Blake was always an idealistic kid. He was the kind of guy who genuinely joined up with the FBI because he wanted to help people and catch bad guys." He laughed faintly. "How disillusioning that job has to have been."

"Unless they turned his idealism into a weapon for their own agenda," Nick suggested. "Seen that happen before."

Grayson shook his head. "Nah. You didn't hear him. He's an angry, angry man. And he was never much of an actor."

Before Nick could comment, a dark green sedan pulled into the parking lot of the Circle K, and Grayson straightened in his seat a little. "That's him." He pushed open the door and got out.

Nick stayed where he was for a moment, sending an alert text over the encrypted app that they'd been using for text comms for a while. Then he got out, falling in behind Grayson, leaving a couple yards between them. He'd be close enough to listen in and intervene, if necessary, but this was still Grayson's show.

Blake Givens was a heavier man, who actually looked older than Grayson, despite the PGS intel guy's calling him a "kid." His face was lined and a little jowly, and it looked like he could stand to lose a good thirty pounds. He hadn't kept up his fitness in the Bureau, that was obvious.

He shook hands with Grayson. "Thanks for coming, man." His eyes flicked to Nick, the question there, and Grayson glanced over his shoulder.

"This is Nick. We work together." He turned back to Givens. "You wanted to talk. Let's talk."

Givens' eyes lingered on Nick for a moment before turning back to Grayson. He gusted a sigh. "Look, I *could* get in a lot of trouble over this. Just so that's clear. I'm trusting you guys."

Grayson just nodded, folding his arms. Givens looked up at him as if trying to gauge what he was thinking, then continued. "Like I told you, I keep running across this Badeaux fucker. So far, it's all circumstantial, and that's given everybody above me enough of an excuse to not only sweep it all under the rug, but to tell me to leave it alone."

"That sounds suspicious all by itself," Grayson commented.

"Ya think?" Givens was obviously bothered, and he looked around again. Nick followed the man's gaze, wondering if he was looking for threats, or looking for backup. "They might object to the characterization, but let's face it. The leadership isn't interested in investigating Badeaux because he doesn't check the right boxes for them."

"Ain't that the way of the world?" Grayson sounded sympathetic. "So, what do you want from us?"

Givens swept the parking lot with his eyes again, and when he spoke, his voice was low. Nick watched him carefully, eyeballing his clothing for anything that might indicate he was wearing a wire. That was going to be hard to tell, and he desperately hoped that Grayson's trust wasn't severely misplaced.

"Look, I know that you guys do a lot of intel work. Hell, it's on your website. And I know that your current client has some interest in Badeaux's less-savory activities." He rubbed his nose. Nick felt every nerve on edge. Was that a signal? The timing wasn't great, if it was. Nobody had said anything that might be remotely incriminating.

"All I'm asking is for is any information on Badeaux's illegal activities that you can get. Any attribution can be scrubbed. I'm sure you guys can figure that out. Give me *something* to nail this guy. Something that they *can't* just shrug off. I've been forbidden to open an investigation. But if an informant *gives* me something that can't be ignored…"

Grayson squinted at the other man with a mixture of bemusement and skepticism. When he glanced over at Nick, Nick could only shrug. He wasn't sure what to make of it.

"I thought that evidence in a criminal case had to be collected by the law enforcement agency bringing the charges," Grayson said.

Givens shook his head. "Only if the law enforcement agency doesn't want to bring charges, usually because of this very sort of thing. It's all politics. The thing is, the Bureau isn't so much a law enforcement agency as it is an intelligence agency with law enforcement powers. That's why we do so many sting operations and have so many scumbags as paid informants."

Grayson nodded. "See, here's the problem. Even if we *can* get the information you want by open source and legal means, what guarantee is there that it won't *still* get swept under the rug, for those same political reasons? We could give you a fucking dossier, with names, dates, photos, video, DNA, and a full forensic breakdown, but if your bosses don't want it to see the light of day, it goes bye-bye and vanishes. And then we probably get investigated, in case they can find any way we *might* have skated close to breaking some obscure law in gathering it." He gave Givens a half-smile that was more of a grimace. "We've seen a thing or two."

Givens seemed to deflate a little. Either he was a much better actor than Grayson had given him credit for, or he was genuinely crushed, thinking that his attempt to get a case built on an absolute monster who seemed to be politically untouchable had failed. "I can't give you a guarantee. It's a chance, a hope, that maybe we can build enough of a case that it can't be ignored." He was almost pleading. "Look, I *know* this guy's dirty. His name's come up too many times, in association with some really, really heinous shit. If it was just me, maybe a team, then you're right, there's no way it would ever see the light of day. But you guys work for a private company. You can dig things up *and* find a way to make it public enough that it can't be ignored. Trust me. These assholes are all politicians, on some level. They get embarrassed hard enough, and they'll have to move."

Nick and Grayson traded a glance. *Oh, you poor, naïve kid.* Both men had seen that very scenario play out in exactly the way that Givens seemed to believe it wouldn't. Politics ruled all, especially the higher the echelon you dealt with.

Still, it was worth a try. None of them *trusted* the US government any longer, given the sheer weight of incidents where the government—to include the Department of Justice— had overlooked some blatant crimes and tried to fabricate others.

But they all knew that there were still *some* decent people in those institutions, and if they *could* leverage them against the bad guys, it would be better than going in guns blazing, and further painting a bullseye on their backs for whoever eventually put together what they were doing.

The problem wasn't even that everyone in the government were bad guys. It was that because there were bad guys in government, there were a lot of ordinary people in government who would side with the bad guys just because they *were* in government.

"We'll run it past our boss." Grayson was studying his old friend closely. "You understand that he's going to have to sign off on it. I'm not going to go around his back. That would be a good way to get my ass fired."

Givens looked a little crestfallen at that, but he nodded. "You know how to reach me."

"I do." Grayson raised an eyebrow. "Though I think we'd probably better keep the electronic communications limited to arranging meets like this. We're playing with fire, here. People have already been killed over this."

That prompted a blink. Givens must not have heard about Wise's murder, or else he hadn't connected it. That was an interesting oversight, considering that he'd identified PGS's involvement with Aller's investigations into Badeaux...or his associates.

"Well, I guess it's the best I can hope for." He looked down at his hands, then back up at Grayson and Nick. "I joined the Bureau to hunt bad guys, not to sit on my hands because they're friends with the right people."

"Welcome to the real world, buddy." Grayson turned back toward the Frontier. "Just watch your back. The wrong people figure out that you're digging, and you'll be a target, too."

Givens watched them go, standing by his car with a look on his face as if he really wondered what he'd just gotten himself into.

CHAPTER
31

"There's our boy."

In the old days, either in the military or working for the various shadowy government agencies that most of the PGS contractors had worked for, it would have taken a long time to get authorization to do what they were doing, if they could have even gotten authorization at all.

Goblin had listened to the brief on what they'd found in the trafficking warehouse, and then the meeting with Givens, had thought for about five minutes, and then had told Saul, "Go with it. Dig up what you can. If you can leverage the FBI against him, do it. Let them take the heat." He'd taken a deep breath. "There's another reason for that, too. It's just going to be you and the C Team handling that end. I'm going to need everyone else down south." He'd outlined what they'd figured out about Slobodian. "If you can get this Stateside thing wrapped up before we need to move, I'm going to pull you down to join us. This is going to get hairy, so the more guns we've got, the better."

So, now Nick and Doug found themselves waiting to pick up Badeaux's car on surveillance. They'd been skipping ahead for a couple of hours, as Josh and Abaeze had been following Badeaux since shortly after he'd left his house on the north side of Long Island, just outside the Hamptons. He'd taken a long, meandering route, staying out of New York City proper and heading north, into Connecticut. Now, though there was no sign that he'd spotted the tail, Josh and Abaeze were handing surveillance off to them.

Hours on follow was taxing as hell, anyway. It was time for a fresh set of eyes.

"Looks like you were right. He *is* the type to drive himself." Doug was watching the gleaming Bentley as it rolled past, Nick swinging their nondescript Ford Focus in behind it.

"Told you. Even when he was a Congresscritter, he still had a rep for liking to drive. Including using his position to get out of speeding tickets." Nick had been doing some research on their target, and he really hadn't liked what he'd seen. There had been some credible accusations of influence peddling just before Badeaux had left office, and before he'd moved to New York. If anyone had an airtight case on the man, they were keeping it quiet, but there were a *lot* of indicators that he was as dirty as it got. He appeared to be a gangster in all but name.

Badeaux had run for office at the last minute, yet he'd flooded the field with so much money that he'd managed to cultivate one hell of an impression in only a few months. With some of the best PR that money could buy, he'd further polished a public image that he'd been burnishing for years as the CEO of Circe Tech Solutions. He was the ultimate corporate activist, pushing millions—if not billions—at all the right causes for his chosen political side. He'd made friends with dozens of the highest-level people, in both the government and private sectors, and the number of photos online of him shaking hands with CEOs, giants of finance and entertainment, Congressmen, Senators, judges, and foreign dignitaries, were legion.

Those friendships had only been strengthened after he'd left office, becoming one of the biggest political donors around. The thing that Nick had noticed—and he was sure that a lot of other people noticed, too, but were afraid to point out—was that the sheer dollar amounts were a little bit bigger than just the returns from Circe Tech Solutions could account for. There was probably a lot of financial legerdemain going on behind the scenes, with other stock portfolios, but that same legerdemain could also apply to money laundering for illicit activities.

"Looks like he's heading for New Haven." Doug sounded a little grumpy, but that was probably only because he'd lost the bet. Now that they'd observed Badeaux driving his own Bentley, he owed Nick fifty bucks.

"Long drive." Nick glanced over his shoulder and changed lanes. He didn't want to hang out behind Badeaux's car for too long. He needed to use distance and traffic to disguise their presence for as long as possible. "Wonder what's in New Haven that he can't find in Long Island or New York."

"I know you're not objecting to not having to drive in New York."

Nick laughed. "I'm not as much of a country boy as some guys in this company, but no. New York, LA, and DC are three places I'd rather not have to drive much."

He wondered a little if Doug had detected the brittleness in that laugh. He was feeling himself tense up as they continued to follow their target. Knowing what kind of business Badeaux had indulged in, he was wondering just where this was going.

Sure, there were probably legitimate business interests for the man in New Haven. Probably. They'd caught a glimpse behind the mask, though, and it was hard to see anything else after that.

The follow into New Haven went quietly and smoothly, passing over the West River before getting off the interstate and heading north, into the city. They watched the increasingly run-down surroundings while Nick backed off as much as he dared, and Doug sent updates via encrypted text. Away from the interstate, it would be far easier for their quarry to spot them. Correlation over time and distance is far harder to hide when there's less traffic to get lost in.

Finally, Nick took a turn that they'd just watched the Bentley go through, only to see the luxury car parked on the side of the street, not far from the intersection, right in front of a three-story white house with blue columns on the front porch.

Nick drove past without hesitation, accelerating just enough to make it appear that he'd simply made a turn and kept moving.

Doug noted the house as Badeaux, dressed in slacks and a polo shirt, every silver-gray hair perfectly in place, got out of the car and looked up at the house. He didn't pay any attention to the white car driving past, but stood there on the sidewalk for a moment, his hands on his hips.

Doug pointed. "There's a package store on the corner. Pull over here." He was slumped down in his seat, where he could see the right-side rear-view mirror. "Somebody just came out, and they're talking on the porch." He already had the camera running, pointing at the mirror. It wouldn't be the best quality video, but Radford had some downright magical tools that could clean it up a lot. Almost enough to get a positive ID on the guy on the porch.

Nick pulled over and parked. "You going inside, or am I?" If this was a trafficking network house where Badeaux had parked—and there didn't seem to be much else in the way of justification for a man of his standing and wealth to be stopping at a residential house in the middle of New Haven, and not a particularly high-end neighborhood of New Haven, for that matter—then they probably had lookouts. Cover for status necessitated that they do more than just park and sit there.

"I've got this guy." Doug was still watching, his eyes narrowed. "This looks sketchy as fuck, bro."

"I ain't arguing." Nick opened the door, making sure that his shirt still covered his Glock 19. He was carrying illegally; none of them had Connecticut carry permits. The company didn't have a contract there, and there sure as hell hadn't been time to try to run paperwork for even a few of them, even if the state hadn't been a "May Issue" state. They all had permits with as expansive reciprocity as they could get, but that didn't extend to Connecticut, which didn't honor *any* other state's permit.

Not that Nick gave a damn. If they had to dump somebody in Connecticut, they were getting the hell out as fast as humanly possible, leaving as little evidence behind as they could.

He forced himself not to even glance over his shoulder as he walked toward the package store, thinking up a legend as he went. The problem with this kind of mobile surveillance was that there was no way to lay the groundwork needed to justify any sort of long-term presence. Without a pattern, they were subject to the whims of the target's movement, and this had put them *way* outside of their operational bubble.

He went inside, looked around a bit, chatted with the staff about potentially setting up for a new drop-shipping business, and then, with promises to be back, he stepped back outside. As he started toward the car, he slowed, his eyes unavoidably locked on the scene unfolding on the sidewalk.

Badeaux stood just outside the gate, holding a girl by the arm. She wasn't trying to pull away, but even from a block away, Nick could see that he had a tight grip on her. Her head was down, but he could tell that she was far too young for what she'd already been through.

If he'd had any doubts about what this house was, they were gone now. Some people might call it all circumstantial, but Nick had seen too much not to trust his gut on this.

The man on the porch was leaning against the railing, and while voices weren't exactly raised, the tension was palpable. Nick slowed, easing toward the brick wall of the package shop next to him while he watched, hoping to go unnoticed.

He couldn't overhear much, but he did see Badeaux jabbing a finger at the man on the porch. There was something about the gesture that seemed off. Like this wasn't an upset customer. This was someone demanding accountability.

Nick couldn't be sure how he knew that, but there was just something about the body language involved that told him there was more going on here than just Badeaux picking up a new toy.

After all, most predators like Badeaux didn't get demanding with the sort of hardened criminals who ran trafficking operations. Most of them, as evil as they might be, didn't have that sort of guts. Either Badeaux was ballsier than Nick had expected of someone like him, or he had some sort of leverage over the traffickers.

Leverage, or authority.

This was looking darker and darker.

Realizing that he was probably going to attract more attention by loitering and watching, he forced himself to walk over to the car and get in. Just before he rounded the back, he overheard a bit of what Badeaux was saying.

"I'm going to call Yan tomorrow. There had better be some movement by then. This is unacceptable."

Nick slid behind the wheel and closed the door carefully. He didn't want to draw any attention.

Doug was still watching the byplay behind them through the camera, using the mirror to record. It didn't look like he'd moved since Nick had gotten out.

For his part, Nick closed the door and pulled out his phone, bringing it to his ear.

"What are you doing?" Without moving the camera, Doug glanced over at him.

"Talking to our business partner about drop shipping. Just like I told those guys in the package store that I was going to do." He was still keeping his eyes on the rear-view mirror. He couldn't see the guy on the porch, but he could see Badeaux, and the girl, who was still standing there with her head bowed, her hair fallen in front of her face, her arm still gripped in Badeaux's manicured hand.

"Ah." Doug returned his attention to the camera. "Good point."

"Did I miss anything?" Nick was almost afraid to ask.

"What looked like it might have been a briefcase full of cash that got put in Badeaux's car." Doug's tone was light, but Nick turned to stare at his partner.

"No shit?"

"No shit. It looks like our boy's not just a player. He's an *operator*."

In their line of work, that latter word had a different connotation, but Nick got what Doug was saying. Badeaux was more than dirty. He might well be an active coordinator.

It fit, somewhat. He was an influence peddler with access to massive amounts of money that exceeded even his considerable declared resources. They'd assumed it was more a matter of bribery, the criminals using his influence as a big time CEO, activist, and former Congressman to escape legal scrutiny of their activities. But what if it was worse than that?

"Givens is gonna love this."

"Maybe." Doug sounded a bit skeptical.

Nick didn't have to ask why. Even with what they had, it would still be extremely difficult to open an investigation into someone as connected as Badeaux.

Badeaux got into his car, pushing the girl into the back seat, and then pulled away, though not without yelling something through an open window at the house. Nick couldn't make it out, but he wasn't sure he wanted to.

"We've got to give it a try, though. Like Goblin said, let the Feds take the heat." Even as he said it, he wondered whether he was just trying to reassure himself about their course of action. He was no more convinced than Doug that this was going to go anywhere.

After all, it had taken a local sheriff to move on Devon Archer, and that had still ended in a firefight.

"Hmm." Doug was, as was his wont, keeping his thoughts to himself. "We gonna follow him? Or should I call in Gameshow and Train?"

"Better get Gameshow and Train on him. I might be burned, after that little walk." Nick reached down and started the car. "I'm not sure how long I'd be able to keep following him without trying to PIT his car into a bridge abutment, anyway."

Doug could have pointed out that such a maneuver would probably just hurt the kid in the back seat, but given what she was probably in for, a car wreck would be better.

That continued to nag at Nick as he pulled away from the curb. "We've got to do something." He didn't need to say what.

Doug didn't answer right away, sending the information for Carl and Durand to pick up surveillance on Badeaux. "I'm not against it."

Now that he'd broached the subject, though, Nick didn't have a plan, aside from the aforementioned PIT maneuver. Goblin wanted them to gather information and sic law enforcement on Badeaux if they could. An ambush in broad daylight, with weapons in a state that essentially forbade their carry, would cause all sorts of problems down the line.

But the problems for that girl were far, far worse.

"I've sent the information to Givens and the New Haven PD." If Nick hadn't gotten to know Doug better, he would have thought that his partner was talking about leaving it at that. "Let's see if we can switch off with Gameshow and Train. Keep eyes on him and look for an opening. He's got to stop somewhere. He hasn't filled up since he left the house this morning."

"Do billionaires use regular gas stations?" Nick realized he was making the quip to try to keep from thinking too much about that girl in the back seat of Badeaux's Bentley.

"When they're trying to keep a low profile because they've got a trafficked kid in the back, I imagine so." Doug shrugged. "We'll see." He looked down at his phone. "Gameshow has the follow. He's heading back to the interstate. Let's see if we can get ahead of him."

***

"It can't be this easy." Nick watched Badeaux walk into the Mobil station, leaving the girl in the back seat.

"If we didn't have Noah's little toy, it wouldn't be." Doug was already getting out, a small box in his hand. "Get ready to drive fast."

270

Nick had "combat parked" the car two spaces over from the Bentley, backing into the space so that he could quickly pull out in a single, smooth movement. He already had the car in drive.

The little box in Doug's hand was designed to capture RF signals, as well as decode them. He'd had it on while Badeaux had locked the car and had captured his remote's signal. Getting into the Bentley would be the matter of a tap of a key on the screen.

Getting the girl out might be a bit more complicated.

Nick didn't doubt that Badeaux had the car child-locked, but if the girl really wanted to get out, she could reach forward and unlock one of the front doors. The predator of a CEO had probably thought of that, as had the traffickers who had passed her to him. Which meant the girl had probably been brutally conditioned not to run. Nick knew of a few tricks, mostly explained to him in SERE school. Let the prisoner attempt to escape, think that they had, and then intercept and punish them severely. That was one way.

He was sure that the traffickers had some even more inventive methods.

His fingers tightened, his knuckles whitening as he gripped the steering wheel, staring at the Mobil station with barely restrained, molten fury. He wanted nothing more than to walk in there and put a bullet in Badeaux's skull.

But Doug had made a good point. They couldn't touch Badeaux yet. If they'd tried to hit him, things could have gone badly wrong. They hadn't *seen* any security following their quarry, but that didn't mean they weren't there. Not to mention the possibility of intervention by a local Good Samaritan, who wouldn't know just why the two hard-looking men with illegal guns were going after the nice-looking older man in a gas station.

If they just got the girl out, it might damage some of the short-term evidence they were gathering, but it might spare her some of the suffering, and what was Badeaux going to do? Call the police and report that his underage sex slave had been kidnapped?

Nick glanced over. Doug had the door open, but he was still crouched next to it. Probably trying to talk the girl down. She was probably every bit as afraid of Doug as she was of Badeaux. Maybe even more, depending on what her captors had done to her to teach her that escape was not only impossible, but the ticket to a lot of pain.

Finally, Doug was hurrying back to the car, the girl in tow, held by her wrist, her head down just like she'd held it at the trafficking house in New Haven. He might have had to resort to some force, but it was better than the alternative.

Doug opened the back door, pushed the girl in, and shut it before quickly getting into the passenger seat. "Let's go."

Nick already had the car moving before Badeaux came out of the gas station, a soft drink in his hand. The girl hadn't said a word or made a sound yet.

"Gameshow and Train have him, now." Doug turned to look into the back seat, already dialing his phone. "Let's get some distance. I'm calling Martha." He looked at the girl, who finally lifted her head to meet his gaze. "We're going to get you somewhere safe. I promise."

And then we're going to make those fuckers pay.

CHAPTER
32

Brazil was different, but not so different from Panama, Colombia, or Honduras to be completely alien. Sure, everything was in Portuguese instead of Spanish, but when you don't speak either language well, they blend together at first glance. The green was much the same, the red earth wasn't unfamiliar, and the houses were mostly plastered and painted bright colors.

The poverty was just as obvious, too.

Foz do Iguaçu was the Brazilian part of the Tri-Border Area. Only one of the most lawless areas on the planet. It wasn't as openly violent as that description might have made it sound, but I'd been in enough places like it to know that the violence was just below the surface. Always.

And worse.

Clint was driving. He and Patrick had gotten there first, and they had already handled the rental vehicles. They'd flown commercial, though that had to have been a nightmare. The Foz do Iguaçu International Airport wasn't that big, and there weren't a whole lot of flights going in. They'd had to fly to a larger airport in Brazil, then catch a connection. All while keeping as low a profile as possible and flying without any of our usual gear aside from some basic survival stuff and comms.

The rest of us had flown in on a charter. I had no idea how much that had cost the company, though the fact that, somehow, Goblin had worked his magic and gotten us a contract in the area must have made a difference.

Security contracting was big business in Brazil. Officially, especially with the current government, all security was supposed to be the responsibility of the Federal Police, but violence was so endemic in the country that armed security was one of its fastest growing industries.

I didn't know all the hoops, paperwork, and red tape that had to be gone through to get a foreign contracting company permission to work there, but the other possibility was that Goblin had just concentrated on the local—and presumably corrupt—authorities.

"Let the others continue on to the hotel." Goblin was in the front seat, next to Clint. "We've got another visit to make." He held out the tablet with a route on it and propped it on the center console. "This should get us there with minimal delays."

Knowing Third World traffic the way I did, I doubted just how "minimal" those delays were going to be. You could rarely accurately predict traffic patterns in a place like this.

Clint just looked at the route and turned off at the next intersection, though. He'd been there, done that. He knew the score as well as any of us.

Goblin turned around in his seat. "I do have a contact down here. He was one of my mentors on the program, way back when. He went into all sorts of black-bag stuff after that, and ended up down here, keeping an eye on about half a dozen narco and terrorist groups that are using the Tri-Border Area as fundraising, recruiting, and coordinating grounds." He smiled faintly. "If there's anybody who has his finger on the pulse of things, that we can—mostly—trust to be on our side, it's him."

"Does he know why we're down here?" Ken asked. It was a good question, and the answer could have far-ranging consequences.

"If he doesn't, he'll figure it out." Goblin turned to face forward again. "He's a smart dude. He's also about as close to a rogue operative as we're going to find, who's still somehow part of the fold. I think his bosses would be just as happy to forget he existed, but he's a long way from where they can touch him, and he gives them good information."

"How likely is he to actually share that information, once he figures out the kind of havoc we're down here to wreak?" I asked.

"We'll see. It's been a long time since I've seen him. But I think you might be surprised." He glanced over his shoulder again. "Remember, this is a people business, and I've been working on making connections for a *long* time."

"You always were a social butterfly." That prompted an even wider grin. It had been a fact that, when he and I had worked together, he'd always been the one to do most of the talking with the client. I just drove.

We were all armed, though the Glocks were all property of Pallas Group Solutions, as per Brazilian law. I wasn't sure if the Brazilian government would be thrilled that we were carrying those Glocks at the moment, since we hadn't linked up with the client yet, and thus we weren't "on duty." There were very strict rules as to what armed security in Brazil could and couldn't do.

We were going to ignore pretty much all of them.

The route wasn't all that long. The contact didn't live in the city proper, but in a small village just outside, to the north of the airport. Goblin talked us in, almost as if he'd been there before.

He probably had. He hadn't been kidding about setting up contacts. I didn't know how long it had been, but he'd definitely met with this guy in Brazil before.

Clint parked outside, and Goblin opened the door. "We might want to leave a guy or two on the vehicle. Chris, Ken, I'd like you to come in with me."

We didn't ask questions. He wanted backup, and while I wasn't the top dog in the team, let alone the company, Goblin and I had worked together before, quite a lot.

He led the way up to the front door. The house wasn't the most impressive, but it wasn't a hovel, either. One story, the walls painted a light green, surrounded by nicely kept-up landscaping. The house was dark, with no movement in the windows, but Goblin seemed unconcerned.

I hung back just a little, ready to snatch my shirt out of the way and grab for my Glock. Goblin knew and trusted this guy, but I didn't. From the way Ken sort of fanned out to Goblin's other side, he was thinking the same way.

Goblin didn't even glance at either of us, but just walked up to the door and knocked.

The man who answered it was thoroughly unremarkable, which was one of the chief advantages a man could have in this business. While most of us contractors were pretty good at the Gray Man thing, there was still only so far we could take it. We all kept in good shape, and there was a way we carried ourselves, mostly unconsciously, that the trained eye couldn't help but notice.

This guy was short, slightly overweight—at least at first glance—and just looked kind of dumpy. He had a heavy-lidded, sagging sort of look on his face, and his beard was just scraggly enough not to draw the eye much. He was wearing an off-white collared shirt, open to the second button.

Yet the eyes that swept over us were careful and observant, and when he saw Goblin he just smiled. "About time. Come on in."

"Holy shit." Ken was staring at our host, who waited inside the door with a Cheshire cat grin and an extended hand. "Tick?"

"Long time, Rip." The dumpy-looking man grasped Ken's hand and pulled him into a one-armed bear hug. "I'm surprised you remembered."

"Damn. It's been... How long has it been?"

"Longer than I've known him." Goblin had gone straight to the minibar in the back and was fixing himself a drink, uninvited. "I didn't even know you knew each other."

"It's been a long, long time. Back in the early days, in Afghanistan. Just after Mazar." The older man picked his own drink up off the coffee table in the middle of the little, pastel blue living room an took a sip.

"How the hell did you go from Afghanistan to this place?" Ken found a seat, though not without keeping his back to the wall and facing the door. Old habits. And it *had* been a long time since he'd been around the man known as Tick.

Those hooded eyes took on a hard squint. "I followed the money and the drugs." He sat down with a sigh. "There was a lot of heroin going out of Afghanistan, at the same time that there was a glut of it on the streets back home. I did the math, jumped ship where I needed to, and followed it. All the way across Africa and over to South America." He took another sip. "The pipelines are more complex now, especially since the triads have found out just how useful fentanyl is—and more economical—but there's still a lot to keep tabs on. That's why I'm still down here, mostly tolerated by the powers that be back home." He turned to Goblin. "So, I got your message. I can read between the lines pretty good, but I'm going to need some more specifics. Who are you looking for?"

When I raised an eyebrow, he smiled. "Not my first rodeo, son. I know that Goblin himself wouldn't be coming down here just for a close protection gig."

Goblin leaned forward, putting his elbows on his knees. "Slobodian."

Tick's eyebrows went up. "You don't fuck around, do you?" He looked around at the three of us. "I hope you brought more than just this. He's a dangerous man."

"We know. He's already sent people after our families."

"Ah." Tick leaned back in his chair and steepled his fingers in front of him. "So, I take it you don't exactly have a mandate for this."

"Got all the mandate I need. I know you understand."

Whatever history Goblin and Tick had, it must have been just enough. With a deep sigh, the older man nodded. "He's not here."

"Not in Foz do Iguaçu, I know." Goblin nodded. "Bolus gave up his bolt holes. But he's here in the Tri Border Area. I'm sure of it."

Tick tilted his head to one side, his face still expressionless. "What makes you so certain?"

"Because we whacked the Hezbollah hit team he was sending north through the Darien." I noticed that he didn't say anything about the connection with our client. "It only made sense that he'd come to one of the main Hezbollah fundraising spots to try to smooth some ruffled feathers."

Tick studied each of us in turn. I could almost see the wheels turning behind those deceptively tired-looking eyes. "Well, you're right. He is here. He got to his lake house about two days ago." Another long, studied moment. "What do you need from me?"

"Weapons, ammo, optics. And any intel you can give me on his place, his movements, and whatever security he's got."

"M4s, AKs, SG550s, what do you want? I can get most of it, though the SIGs and the AKs are probably going to be the easiest."

"M4s if you can get them. Twenty-two. Make it twenty-five, so we've got spares. With optics and suppressors, if that's doable. Five hundred rounds per. Plate carriers and Level III+ plates. Full combat loads of magazines. Helmets. Any trauma gear you can dig up would help, too."

Tick didn't write anything down, but just listened and nodded as each item was rattled off. "You want NVGs? Or did you bring your own?"

"If you can get 'em."

Another nod. "They'll be PVS-14s. Probably not as fancy as you've gotten used to." When he didn't get any objections, he smiled faintly. Most of us had done at least one

278

combat deployment with 14s. They might not be as nice as the PS-31s, but they'd do the job. "What else?"

"Transport across the river, along with all the intel you can give us."

"Well." Tick stretched. "If it brings that son of a bitch down, finally, I got all you can stomach. How much time you got?"

***

One of the drawbacks of having an actual client as a cover for action is that we still had to dedicate at least some of our guys to protecting that client. Granted, I was starting to suspect that Ignacio Munoz was read in. I didn't know how Goblin had worked it, but he happened to have a reasonably wealthy client looking for protection while he was on a trip to one of the most lawless areas of the world, ostensibly to see the Iguazu Falls.

Of course, when I'd asked about that staggering coincidence, Goblin had just grinned.

The good part of having a wealthy client as cover was that it meant we got pretty nice hotel rooms, at least for the prep phase.

Now, we couldn't exactly haul the weapons that Tick was getting for us in there, but we could get some rest in between shifts ferrying Munoz around. We still used KG's room as an operations center, at least when he was up.

"You know, for a guy who's here to look at the falls, he sure as hell is a lot more interested in Lake Acaray." Brian came in to check in and drop off the photos and video they'd gotten on their latest run out into the city. "Second time we've gone through Customs, across the bridge, and over into Ciudad del Este. I thought he wanted to go down to Argentina?"

KG looked up from his laptop with a slow smile. Brian looked at the expression for a second, looked over at Phil, who was now working as KG's partner, and his shoulders slumped as he slapped a hand to his forehead. "Fuck. He's one of us, isn't he?"

"I don't know the whole story, but yeah. His wealth is all corporate, and I don't think I even want to know what sort of off-the-books accounts Goblin tapped to create it. But yeah. He's here to support us, which means he's running surveillance as much as we are." There was a wry twist to KG's grin.

"So, why the hell didn't we get told about this?" Tom threw himself onto the couch. "I swear, sometimes Goblin is the best boss in the world, and sometimes he plays things so damned close to the vest that it's impossible."

"He probably didn't think it was that important. The cover is just that—a cover. He's not counting on Munoz getting us close enough to do what needs doing. That comes after we've got all the gear and weapons together, and we can handle this our way." KG shrugged. "It's not something I'm all that worried about. He's been damned good about pushing the word down. This is just a detail."

"Details get important, especially when we're downrange." Tom wasn't letting this go.

"I get that. But if you get so lost in the details that you lose track of the mission, that's not good, either." KG turned to face him. "Okay. You didn't get told that the client is a stalking horse. Big fucking deal. He's *on our side*. Why is this an issue?"

Tom looked around. Most of the rest of the guys in the room were at least staying neutral. We were all tired. We'd been on the go for a long time, and the threat to our families didn't seem to have lessened much. Slobodian was, apparently, worried about Hezbollah at the moment, but none of us doubted that he knew full well who had hit his place in Colombia. And Belize. Revenge was coming, if we didn't take him out, soon.

I wondered if he didn't have contingencies set up. Dead man's switch sort of shit. Well, we'd have to deal with that when we came to it.

Tom didn't have an answer right away. Brian was looking between him and KG, almost like a kid who'd just heard his mom and dad start yelling at each other. Maybe it was just shock that Tom, of all people, was bitching. It was *Brian* with the callsign "Scrappy."

Finally, Tom just looked away. "We need to be in the loop, that's all." He was muttering more than anything else. "If he doesn't tell us about this, what else isn't he telling us?"

"That's bullshit, and you know it." It was KG's turn to get irate. "We've been working for the man for how long? And he hasn't screwed us over or played any stupid games yet." He looked around the room. "Are we really having this conversation? Here? Now?" He pointed toward the window. "The man who sent hitters after our *families* is only a few miles away, and we're going to start bitching about the boss?"

Tom looked down at the floor. He didn't want to admit that he'd been out of line, but he knew it, and so did the rest of us. "Okay. I'll shut up. Forget I said anything."

He got up and left, heading for his room. I watched him go, frowning. Ken was leaning against the wall, watching the door shut behind Tom with a pensive look on his face. When he saw I was watching him, he shrugged. "We all got our limits, cuz. He'll be all right. This has just been a rough job, and every once in a while, this shit piles up and a man has to let off some steam."

"Yeah, well, I'd rather he let off steam on the bad guys." KG turned back to his laptop. "We've got plenty of them to worry about." His phone buzzed next to the satcom puck we were all using to stay off the local cell network. "Get set, boys. Goblin just confirmed we've got all the gear. We're going in as soon as Goblin gives the word."

CHAPTER
33

"We might have a problem." Grayson looked a little pale. Doug frowned as he and Nick walked into their TOC. They were back in Pennsylvania, as it was closer to New York and their target's stomping grounds.

"What's up?" It had been two days since they'd rescued the girl from Badeaux's car. They hadn't collected much more since then, though they'd maintained surveillance. The calm hadn't been relaxing. Knowing the kind of monster he really was, waiting around for the FBI to do something—they'd sent Givens the take from the New Haven follow immediately—had just rankled.

Grayson glanced down at the phone on the table next to him. "I just tried to contact Givens. No answer. Multiple times." The worry was written plainly on his features. They might have gone their separate ways, but there was still the brotherhood between Grayson and Givens.

And given the context, and some of what the PGS contractors had seen over the last year or two, that sudden silence was concerning.

"You think he was a stalking horse? That they're about to hit us?" Nick couldn't help but jump to the worst case. If the worst case didn't turn out to be the real one, then you were already better off.

Grayson shook his head, his eyes haunted. "No. Not Givens. He's a lot of things, but the kind of guy who'd try to cover for a predator like Badeaux isn't one of them. Not even if the Bureau held his entire career over his head. No, I think something worse has happened."

"You know where he lives?" Doug was already pulling the keys out of his pocket. Under different circumstances, they might adopt more of a wait and see approach, but given the stakes... Nick understood, and was already slinging his go bag over his shoulder.

If the bad guys were already moving, then they didn't have long.

"Yeah. It's going to be a bit of a drive, though."

"Then we'd better get on the road."

***

Givens had worked for the Long Island field office, so his home was an apartment in Freeport. It took a couple hours to get over there from Pennsylvania, but they still didn't get there before the police had cleared out.

There was only one cruiser outside the brick, four-story apartment building, and it was no longer flashing its lights. Nor was the ambulance parked next to it. The EMTs wheeling the gurney out of the apartment building weren't in any hurry.

The cop stepped out to stop Grayson as he crossed the street in a hurry, Nick not far behind him. Grayson was trying to crane his neck to see who was on the gurney. "I need to get in there."

"Just give us a minute, sir." The policeman didn't seem to be too worked up. He just looked and sounded tired. "We'll be out of the way here shortly."

"My friend hasn't been answering his phone. I was expecting to hear from him." Grayson might have been exaggerating the situation just a little, but something told Nick, as he watched the gurney come closer, that there was no exaggeration involved. He suspected that he knew just who was on that stretcher.

The cop picked up on it, too. "What's your friend's name?" He was trying to find a gentle way to approach this, hoping that maybe the ambulance call and the clearly worried man in front of him weren't connected, but knowing that the coincidence was too much to be real.

"Blake Givens. He's an FBI agent." Even as Grayson said it, Nick saw the cop's shoulders slump, just a little. Most cops developed a certain emotional armor plating, separating themselves from the pain that was most of their careers. They saw humanity at its worst, which Nick suspected was a large part of why some of them became complete assholes.

"Sir, can you step over here for a moment?" The cop beckoned Grayson toward the cruiser. "I'm afraid I have some bad news."

Grayson went very still for a moment. He closed his eyes, then opened them with a sigh. "That's him on the gurney, isn't it?"

The cop nodded. "I'm afraid so, sir. It appears to have been a suicide. Pills and alcohol. Sometime last night. There was no note, but that's what it looks like." He grimaced faintly, knowing that he might be picking at an open wound. "Were you aware of any problems Agent Givens was having, recently?"

Grayson just looked at him for a heartbeat. "No. Nothing that would make him do something like this."

Nick knew that while it was technically the truth, it wasn't the whole truth. They all knew what had happened here. They'd seen it before.

Grayson continued to ask questions, doing a better job of keeping the vital information from the cop while still trying to come to grips with the fact that his friend was dead. Nick faded back toward the car.

"We've got a new problem." He leaned against the vehicle next to where Doug had the window rolled down. "Give Saul a call. We're going to have to get in touch with the boss."

***

"You're certain about this?" The encrypted video call was slightly blurry and a little pixelated, but it was still clear enough. Goblin looked tired. As well he should be, given what he was trying to do. Operational command of the mission against Slobodian while also trying to coordinate the company as a whole...Nick wondered that the man hadn't collapsed yet.

"One hundred percent, sir." Grayson's voice was still slightly hoarse. Givens' death had hit him hard, harder than Nick had expected after the coolness of the meeting in West Virginia. "Agent Givens was murdered, and it can't have been a coincidence that it happened the day after we sent him all our evidence."

Goblin nodded, lowering his eyes as he thought. Grayson waited, fidgeting a little bit. "I know who his boss is, sir." The question—the request—was obvious, if unspoken.

But Goblin shook his head. "No. Not yet. He'll get what's coming to him, but hands off, for now."

"That cocksucker had Blake killed, sir." Grayson's voice was starting to rise. "He had one of his own guys murdered to cover for a pedophile human trafficker."

"I get that, Bob. And like I said, he'll get what's coming to him." Goblin leaned toward the screen. "You have to understand that we *have* to think strategically right now. We go to open war with the FBI, and we're *never* putting that genie back in the bottle. I'm not saying the time's not coming, but it's not *now*. We're not ready for that. And if we take out the head of the Long Island field office, then the entire Bureau is going to come after us, including some good dudes who aren't a part of this. I'd rather lay the groundwork first. Patience."

"So, what are we supposed to do?" Saul was calmer than Grayson. Tim, predictably, wasn't around, so Saul had taken over. Nick was really starting to wonder what they were going to do about their new "team leader." So far, he just seemed to be detached and kind of incompetent, but that could turn out to be every bit the liability that active malice might have been. "Sit on this?"

There was a hard set to Goblin's features, visible even through the faint distortion of the encryption and the internet connection, as he shook his head. "Fuck no. This Badeaux's highly connected enough that he's got the FBI either doing his dirty work, or sending him the information to get a man murdered? Fine. He goes down. Be smart about it, keep it deniable, but put that fucker in the dirt."

Nick felt a faint chill that had nothing to do with the air conditioning in the room. He glanced at Saul, then at Doug. Both men were expressionless, but he knew that they had to have reached the same realization he had.

They'd taken down Devon Archer with the help of the local sheriff. Hell, Sheriff Hernandez had deputized nearly a dozen PGS contractors for that attempted arrest. This was different. This was taking unilateral action against a well-connected American citizen. They'd certainly eliminated some enemies on American soil, but those had all been within the context of defending a protectee or conducting a rescue. Going after a former Congressman and captain of industry, going full vigilante, was a Rubicon that Nick realized he'd always expected they'd have to cross, but just not quite so soon.

"Good copy." Saul didn't have any other comment. Doug said nothing. He didn't ask if the other teams down south were going to need more backup. They had their mission, and it was going to be hairy enough as it was.

"Make it happen, gents. I'll be in touch." Goblin cut the connection.

For a moment, the TOC was silent. It was Matt who spoke first.

"Well, it's about fucking time."

CHAPTER 34

Our initial recon had to be a little complicated, because we needed to get eyes on the target from two directions. We had imagery of the landward side of Slobodian's getaway, though Munoz's cover wasn't quite enough to get solid, long-term surveillance on it. We had photos and a good idea of the layout, but a pattern of life was still pretty damned sketchy.

What that reconnaissance, coupled with overhead imagery, had established was that a landward approach wasn't going to work that well. Escape routes were limited and would force us to move through the nearby town, where Slobodian was sure to have backup. That backup hadn't been identified, but he was simply too careful not to have someone out there, especially not after he'd had two houses hit within the last few weeks.

So, our best bet was going to be to approach from the lakeside. That presented quite a few problems as well, and our first reconnaissance patrol was intended to figure out good routes in and out as much as to get eyes on the lakeside part of his estate.

We were also going to be crossing international borders to do that, and so we were going to have to be even more careful. The general lack of enforcement on those borders formed the reason the Tri-Border Area was as sketchy as it was, but that didn't mean that border guards were *nonexistent*.

They were just mostly paid off.

So, it was late at night when we launched the boats on the Parana River, just downstream from the Itiapu Dam. They weren't overtly paramilitary—no Zodiac clones here—but the pair of trawlers had all of our gear, along with foldable kayaks, hidden under the gunwales. We were still going light at that point—no rifles, just Glocks, and no body armor or chest rigs—but we still needed to be discrete, since the Federal Police were out on the river, patrolling regularly.

Tick had assured us that we didn't need to worry about them, but complacency kills, as we'd all gotten used to seeing stenciled on every concrete barrier on FOBs halfway around the world away and half a lifetime ago, it felt like.

I found my thoughts drifting back to some of those ops, in places far drier than central South America. It had been a long time and a long way, and it never seemed like we'd gone enough places or done enough. Everything just always seemed to be getting worse.

I knew that it was the fatigue and the stress eating at me. I'd managed to talk to Julie a little bit before we'd launched. She was worried, though there hadn't been any more movement to hit the house. Strangers were getting some extra scrutiny in our area after that incident. Hopefully, we'd put enough of a dent in Slobodian's American network that he simply didn't have the manpower, coupled with the pressure we were putting on him personally.

Deep down, I knew that that pressure wasn't enough by itself. If he was as connected and savvy as we thought he was, all he'd need to do would be to send out an anonymous posting and he'd get plenty of takers. He was biding his time, I didn't know why, and it bothered me.

I just hoped we could get to him before this all blew up in our faces.

We drifted down the river, staying dark and keeping low. We weren't wearing our camouflage fatigues, but we were all still wearing brown and green, that should blend in well enough with the vegetation when we got across into Paraguay. We kept our eyes out for the Federal Police, of either Brazil or Paraguay, as we crossed the bend in the river and approached the low, dark line of the far shore, swathed in trees.

There was a small inlet that led back into the jungle, and we brought the two boats puttering into it. Jake and Rob would stay with the boats, while the rest of us moved through the jungle and onto Lake Acaray.

It took a few minutes to get set, the biggest of us shouldering the foldable kayaks. While they only weighed about twenty-six pounds each, they were bulky, and part of the night's operation was also to pre-stage them so that we wouldn't have to insert with them while weighed down with ammo, weapons, armor, gear, and UDT vests.

The UDT vests weren't optional. Paddling somewhat unstable foldable kayaks with all of our gear, there was a non-zero chance that somebody was going in the drink, and even with the lightweight armor we had, the ammo, weapons, and other gear would drag us down.

Nobody wanted to drown in a lake in Paraguay, before we'd even made the hit.

Matt took point, forcing his way through the veg, and we started to cross the nature preserve that stood between us and the lake.

***

It was a long, grueling movement. The jungle sucks to move through, and as much as I might have bitched about the desert, during all those years working the Middle East, the desert is paradise to operate in compared to the jungle.

We had less than a mile to go, but it still took well over an hour to cover the distance. We were drenched in sweat, covered in bits of vegetation, and already dragging by the time we reached the shore. Fortunately, it was dark as pitch under the trees, despite the lights on the lakeshore on the far side, only about six hundred yards away, so we weren't going to be observed as we hunkered down to take a short break and catch our breath before putting the kayaks together and launching.

That took longer than it should have, despite the fact that we'd rehearsed boat setup for several hours previously. Everything always takes longer in the field, between fatigue, the need to hold security, and the fact that you're always doing it with less space than you'd like to have. Crammed under the trees, the kayaks just didn't want to take shape without snagging on *something*.

We finally had them all together, though, and launched.

Actually, only Ken and I launched. The rest held what they had back on shore. This was reconnaissance, and the smaller the footprint we had out there on the water, the better.

We'd have to approach in force if we made the hit from the lakeside, but for the moment, less was more.

I was increasingly glad that we had as much darkness to work with as we did. Everything was taking longer. Getting off site after a hit was going to get interesting, to say the least.

Ken and I hugged the shoreline as we paddled north. Most of the entire eastern side of the lake was forested, part of the *Reserva Natural de Acaray*. That provided us some concealment, especially in the dark. We had to get a little farther out onto the water as we approached the target site, since there were more and more houses—with docks—the farther north we got.

After about half an hour, I laid my paddle across the gunwales and let my kayak drift, my eyes on the posh house on the shore just ahead. I had my NVGs on, wearing a skullcap mount instead of a helmet, but now I lifted them and raised my binoculars to my eyes. I wouldn't be able to observe for all that long before I had to correct the boat's drift, but I could get eyes on for a bit.

The back lawn and the dock were pretty well-lit, though there was a line of trees along the southwest part of the property, just above the shore. That might be an advantage to us, or to someone on the shore.

Even as I watched, I caught a glimpse of movement under those trees. It took a second to identify what I was looking at, but soon enough I figured out that it was a man with a rifle.

From there, it was easy enough to spot the others. Four men on shore. No idea how many inside. I *could* get closer to see if I could spot anyone through the windows, but I had to decide whether the juice was worth the squeeze. If I got compromised out there on the lake, Slobodian might very well fade before we could even get anything together to hit him.

I wasn't taking photos. We'd talked about it, but few cameras are really made for operating at night, without showing any glow, anymore. Sure, some had night vision mode, but we didn't have any of them.

So, I was going to have to fall back on an old Recon skillset. I was going to have to memorize as much of the picture I could see through my binoculars as possible and sketch it out once we got back.

That was why we'd played Kim's Game over and over and over again in Recon. Sometimes the tech will fail you, or just won't be available, and then you'd better be able to rely on your eyeballs and your brain.

Of course, some of the shit the military had put us through was hardly conducive to solid memory. I was lucky that I hadn't had the TBI that some dudes I'd known.

Finally, though it was an awfully short period of time for what I was trying to do, I put the binoculars back in their waterproof case and took up my paddle again. I couldn't see Ken until I lowered my NVGs again. He was farther out, holding a wide enough dispersion that one of us wasn't likely to compromise the other if we did something stupid, like fumble-finger optics into the water. He was already heading back.

I dipped my paddle into the water as carefully and silently as I could, bringing the bow around and heading back the way we'd come. There was still a long way to go that night.

***

"So, at least four shooters outside, and more inside. Those trees will provide some cover and concealment in the dark, but not a lot, and we'll have to get past the outer security some way or another. And there's really no place where we can offset insert and move in from the flanks." I tapped the sketch with my pencil. Ken had helped add details, so it was now about as complete as two old guys' memories could make it, after another half-hour paddle, hour and a half march through the jungle, river crossing, and then a roundabout drive back to the hotel. We were all still sweaty and filthy, though we'd used towels in the vehicles to get most of the plant material off.

Goblin was studying the sketch intently, unblinking, his chin resting on his fist. "What I wouldn't give for a couple of helicopters right now. And air support to make sure we didn't get shot down."

Jake snorted. "What *I* wouldn't give for a Reaper with a couple of Hellfires right now." He dropped a fist toward the sketch, then splayed his fingers with an explosion sound. "Problem solved, problem staying solved."

Goblin didn't look up. "Except that we wouldn't be able to rifle through the house for intel afterward. We'd have half the Paraguayan Army on the place in an hour." He shook his head. "Just taking Slobodian out isn't enough. I need whatever records he's got in there, too. Otherwise, who's to say that he doesn't have a designated successor to run that network? No, we've got to go in there after him. Even if the Reapers and Hellfires were a possibility, which they aren't. May as well wish for a tactical nuke, while you're at it."

"Oh, I can wish for it, and I am." Brian was absent-mindedly twirling a knife between his fingers. It was interesting, sometimes, some of the more feral habits that come back in situations like this. "Fuck this place."

"I can commiserate, but this isn't the time to waste mental energy thinking about things that can't be." Goblin had to be tired. He wasn't usually that short. "We're going to have to see if a diversionary attack on the landward side can draw the shoreline security away, then hit from the water." He finally looked up and around. "We'll need to insert the D Team somewhere to the north. Tick has told me he's got a way to get everybody across…"

CHAPTER
35

"This motherfucker sure is confident." Grayson leaned back from the screen and stretched. His grief over Givens' murder was still there, but he'd buried it in work and the search for vengeance. Nick wasn't sure how healthy that was, but he wasn't going to gainsay it, either.

After all, they weren't in the therapy business.

Nick looked over his shoulder. Most of the team was gathered in the Pennsylvania TOC. Matt and Manny were still on surveillance in Long Island, still sending periodic updates, but Saul had decided that it was time. They had enough to plan the hit. And the longer they waited, the more damage Badeaux could do.

And the more the FBI could look into who had provided Givens with the evidence that had gotten him killed.

That was a threat they were going to have to deal with eventually. Nick didn't know how or when, but he knew the time was coming.

"He's had people over every night. Caterers. Drug dealers—yeah, we've got that on video. That was interesting."

Saul nodded. "Mike was ready to call the cops. Probably should have, but unfortunately, it wouldn't have done anything, and would have just tipped our hand." That was a slippery slope, and every man there knew it, but they'd already seen what calling the law on Badeaux resulted in.

"So, what *is* the plan?" Grayson looked up at Saul. "He's got plenty of security on that house. At least four guys at any one time. And all they've got to do is hold what they've got and scream for the law. We already know that the cops will be told to look the other way at the sex dungeon in his basement. Or whatever he's got going on."

Saul's eyes were still fixed on the screen, and the photo of the sprawling, two-story white house just off the water. "We'll have to find a way to get in quietly." His eyes narrowed. "He obviously doesn't like to cook. He's had a van delivering food just about every night, especially when he's got company."

Josh nodded. "And they're using the same route, at the same time. Why wouldn't they? It's fucking Long Island. It's not like these people have any training to avoid crime, never mind an ambush."

Saul straightened a little. "Okay. Two teams, two trucks." He looked at his watch. "If the schedule holds, the next delivery should be headed his way in about two hours. We've got that long to get into position. Better step it out, gents."

***

Operating in an urban—or suburban, which was often worse—environment presented some challenges for this sort of interdiction. They had to make it happen somewhere that they were less likely to be observed, which had been difficult even before the days of near-ubiquitous CCTV cameras. They also were constrained by the route the target took, which in this case was a fairly straightforward west and then south.

Nick was waiting in the box truck that they'd been using in New York City for a mobile hide. They were parked in front of a vacant house that was a little smaller than most of the rest in the neighborhood. Maybe the owner was on vacation, maybe they were moving out because they couldn't afford the property taxes anymore. He'd seen a surprising number of apparently

298

empty houses, even in affluent Long Island. The exodus from New York continued apace.

The back was mostly dark, though the fiber optic camera ports they'd installed were doing a pretty good job of keeping them aware of their surroundings via a pair of screens mounted at the front. It was also quiet, since none of the contractors felt much like talking.

"Eyes on. Five mikes." The radio was low, because they didn't want anyone walking by to suddenly hear radio traffic from inside the parked box truck.

Nobody moved, except for Carl, who shifted just enough to ease his back. It wasn't comfortable back there, but given what they were doing, Nick didn't feel like comfort was at the top of the list of priorities.

The seconds seemed to crawl by, and Nick could hear his heartbeat and his breath in his ears. Had they taken another route? Had someone's timing been off? Were they going to have to go back and replan the whole thing? What would happen while they were delayed? How many kids would get hurt during that time?

Then he heard the squeal of tires as someone braked hard just outside, followed by the same sound a few seconds later. "Jackpot."

Doug rolled up the back door, and Nick, Saul, Mike, and Doug piled out. They were all in black, with plate carriers, helmets, balaclavas, gloves, and carrying black printed FGC-9s. There wasn't a law enforcement entity on the face of the planet that carried those weapons, but they'd be completely untraceable if somebody got their hands on one. They were also dirt cheap to make, so when they went in the ocean after the op, no one would weep.

The van was stopped right next to the box truck, a rental car pulled out in front of it, Durand behind the wheel and gesturing at the van's driver as if he was out of his mind. The driver, for his part, looked like he was about twenty at the most, and was also apparently completely unaware of the second car that was right on his rear bumper. If he tried to back out, he'd hit it. He was leaning out of the window, yelling at Durand, who was doing a creditable job of acting as if he didn't understand.

Nick and Doug moved up on the driver's side, while Saul and Mike circled around to the passenger's door. The kid still didn't even realize that there was anything else going on until Saul yanked the passenger door open.

The driver suddenly snapped his head toward the far side as Nick came up to the driver's side door. "What the fuck?"

Nick pulled the door open and almost brought the driver with it. The kid squawked as he started to fall, grabbed for the steering wheel, then got snatched out by the shirt and thrown on the street. He yelped, started to scramble to his feet, then the yell died in his throat and his eyes widened as he looked up and saw the black well of a 9mm muzzle pointed at his face, cold eyes between a black balaclava and black ballistic helmet staring at him just above it.

"Get lost, and keep your damn mouth shut." Nick paused, about to grab the kid's wallet to check his ID, but he had a company badge hanging around his neck. "If you talk about this, Troy, or post about it on social media, we'll find out, and then we'll come to have a talk with you."

"I didn't see nothin'." The kid was scared stiff. In fact, he was about to start to cry. "What am I gonna tell my boss?"

"Tell him you got carjacked." Doug was already climbing into the driver's seat, as Durand moved the rental car out of the way. "It's the truth, after all. Don't worry, you won't get blamed. It's not like they let you carry around here, do they?"

Nick kept his eyes and his weapon on the driver as he moved around to the back. It was going to be a tight fit, but it would get them inside. He squeezed in next to Mike, then pulled the door shut, the smell of the food in its boxes filling his nostrils. Mike banged on the side of the van, and then they were moving.

Next stop was Badeaux's house.

***

300

Surveillance had noted a vehicle that was always parked at the end of the road, where it dead-ended just before the beach. There were always two men in the car, though it wasn't always the same vehicle. Badeaux had security, all right.

The good part was that they'd noticed over time that the two men weren't all *that* alert. They'd look up when a vehicle approached, but they didn't seem to look all that closely at who was in it. They'd watch where it was going if they didn't recognize it, but that was about it.

Like Badeaux himself, it looked like his security had gotten complacent. Why wouldn't they? They were in Long Island. They were in one of the richest neighborhoods on the island. And who was going to dare cross Badeaux? He had his fingers in politics, finance, *and* organized crime. These guys might not know about that last part, but they apparently were just there to cash a paycheck.

At least, Nick could *hope* that they didn't know about that organized crime angle. He'd seen the photos, and the security looked like the standard executive protection detail. They didn't look like thugs or hoods. Just kids—mostly in their late twenties, the usual age bracket when guys got out of the military and tried to find a new career in the security industry—in suits and carrying guns.

Guys not unlike the PGS contractors, at least on the surface.

Nick didn't want to believe that these guys knew what was going on inside that house. Because if they did, then they deserved to die every bit as much as the man they were on their way to kill. And the hard truth was that the whole op would go better if they *didn't* kill anyone else.

They might have to make someone else disappear. But they'd keep the heat off more if this all went according to plan.

Nick suppressed a shudder at the thought. Nothing *ever* went according to plan.

He couldn't see the security vehicle from the back of the van, but as he felt them make the turn, he heard Doug say, "Well, that worked. No reaction. They recognized the van and didn't bat an eye. Even with two dudes in black in the front seat." Of course, with the headlights on, given the time of day, that shouldn't be that surprising. They probably hadn't been able to see anyone in the front.

Nick held on as they went around the curve and turned into the driveway in front of Badeaux's garage. Time to focus on his part of the raid. Durand and Carl would take care of the lookout vehicle, if necessary.

He had to admit that this was probably going to be the hairiest hit he'd ever been on.

The van came to a stop with a faint lurch. They had arrived.

If this had been Iraq or Afghanistan, this would have been the place where they'd rush out, kick in the door, and go to work. However, they needed to be a little more subtle this time. This was Trojan Horse stuff.

He and Mike had to wait, unable to see anything, wondering if the security was going to come out and check the vehicle before letting it in the garage. That could mean a gunfight right away, but it was a real possibility. Their disguise had gotten them this close. It all depended on just how untouchable Badeaux thought he really was, and how much that had rubbed off on his security.

The rollup door rattled into the ceiling, and a moment later the van started to move again, slowly rolling into the garage. It went about a full vehicle length, then stopped. Nick could hear the door rolling down again. Doug must still have the headlights on, or else nobody had come down to take a closer look.

Once the garage door was shut, it was time. He pushed the doors open and he and Mike jumped out, quickly clearing their sides of the van.

The garage wasn't that big. The van filled almost one entire half of it. The Mercedes that was parked next to made Nick think that either Badeaux had another garage somewhere…

Or he wasn't at home.

Surveillance should have picked that up. He gritted his teeth as he padded around the van, heading for the front, as the door to the inside of the house opened up, and a voice called out. "You might want to unload here. This isn't a good time to be hanging out inside."

The man sounded bored at first, but Nick thought he detected a bit of something else. Discomfort, maybe. Like he really didn't want to be there.

Picked the wrong client, bud.

The warning ended with a faint strangled noise. Nick came around the front of the van, behind Saul, to find Doug holding a man in a black polo shirt and khakis at gunpoint. The man was armed, with a pistol at his side, but Doug had the drop on him, easily. Younger, probably in his late twenties, the security guard was watching the muzzle with wide, fixed eyes, his hands held well away from his sides.

"Close the door." Doug's voice was faintly muffled by the black balaclava over his face. If they were careful, none of them should be identified that night.

When the younger man did as he was told, Doug stayed where he was, his FGC-9 still pointed unwaveringly at his face. Saul stepped around the front of the van and relieved the guard of his sidearm and phone. "You've got a choice here." Doug's voice was neither patronizing nor particularly threatening. He let the gun handle that part. "I'm going to give you the benefit of the doubt, given what you just said, that you're doing this just for the paycheck, and doing your damnedest to look the other way. That's not much of an excuse, but we're not here for you. So, you can take the flex cuffs, keep your mouth shut, and never, ever breathe a fucking *word* about what goes on over the next thirty minutes, or we can smoke you right here and now, and you can answer for your cowardice in the next life. We'll worry about cleanup later, but you'll never be found, and no one will ever know what happened to you."

Saul had pulled the man's wallet out of his pocket. He was apparently too scared of Doug's rock-steady aim to object. "Same goes if you talk about this later, David." Saul stuffed his wallet back in his trousers. "We know who you are, and where you live. What happens here never happened, or else someone will pay you a visit, and you'll disappear."

It was a degree of ruthlessness that the PGS contractors hadn't quite displayed yet, though Nick found that he was entirely comfortable with it. This wasn't terrorizing innocents. This was giving a man a second chance when, in a way, he deserved to die for what he'd allowed to happen.

The truth was, every man who had ever carried a gun for a living had that streak of ruthlessness in them. Most men do. That violence, that savagery, is only ever held back by honor or the threat of punishment.

When honor demanded, it was all too easy to let it out.

David looked up at the cold, hard eyes above dark balaclavas then, and read what was there. He gulped, then nodded.

Saul grabbed him by the upper arm, hauled him the rest of the way down the steps, twisted him around, and quickly zip-tied him before pulling out a black sack and putting it over his head. A quick and detailed search produced a handcuff key and a couple other useful tools for escape and combat, which disappeared into Saul's gear.

"Who else is in the house? How many on security? Weapons? Staff? Guests? I need to know numbers, where they are, and what the plan for the night is." Saul was almost whispering next to the kid's head.

The kid hesitated, but Saul was still holding his arm, and increased the pressure, just enough to remind him where he stood. He started talking.

"Kevin and I are the only security in the house. Mr. Badeaux didn't want the full four tonight, and he told us to stay in the kitchen and the back rooms. He's got a couple of guests." Something about the short hesitation before he said "guests" told

Nick that the kid knew exactly what was going on but was trying very hard to avoid facing it. "That's it."

"Define a 'couple.'" Saul wasn't letting up.

The kid winced, visible even through the hood over his head. "Three. One adult male and two girls."

Nick felt the icy fury start to build again.

"Stay quiet, don't move, and you live." Saul kept his voice low. So far, there was no sound from deeper inside the house to suggest that they'd been made. Music could be heard faintly through the door, but so far there was no other commotion. They'd gotten in cleanly, at least for the moment.

Doug was already stacked on the door. Nick and Mike joined him, crowded into the narrow space between the side of the van and the wall, and then Saul quietly pulled the door open. Weapons dropped level as they stalked inside.

CHAPTER
36

So far, so good.

The movement back to where we'd stashed the kayaks on the shore of Lago Acaray had gone more smoothly than even our exfil the night before. That wasn't because we'd used the exact same route, either. That had been considered, for reasons of time, and had been rejected. The risks were too high. We *thought* that we hadn't been observed, but there was always a chance, especially in a place where we didn't have eyes everywhere that could note reactions and pass the word along. So, just to make sure that we didn't walk into an ambush, we'd taken a different route, crossing the road and the powerline cut some distance away from where we had the night before.

We were armed to the teeth this time, though it felt awfully old school. The M4 in my hands, with its battered old CompM2 Aimpoint—that still ran like a champ—wasn't much different from the one I'd carried in Iraq, almost twenty years before. Peering at the jungle around us through the single tube of a grainy, ancient PVS-14 monocular only made it seem even more surreal.

Of course, the jungle wasn't the environment I'd gotten used to back then, and the body armor I was wearing was *far* lighter and more comfortable, but there were still just enough similarities to trigger some flashbacks.

Jake was on point, with Goblin right behind him, and Ken and I coming up behind Goblin. Phil had wanted to take point, but Goblin had vetoed that, probably because, despite the rather desperate situation we were in, he was worried that Phil was going to do something stupid to try to make up for losing Marcos in Colombia. It hadn't been his fault, but survivor's guilt is a hell of a thing.

I couldn't see Jake through the vegetation, but I saw Goblin put up a hand to call a halt. We all had radios, but under the circumstances, I was fine with sticking to hand and arm signals. We needed to be close enough to see each other anyway, just to keep from getting lost, and radios made noise, even when you had earmuffs on. The human voice can still travel, and so silent communication was paramount on an infiltration.

Goblin went down onto one knee, his M4 across his raised leg, and I followed suit as I passed the signal back to Ken. We waited, the bugs buzzing around our heads and faces, sweat dripping from every pore, while Jake worked his way forward just to make sure that the kayaks were still there, untampered with, and not currently being watched by an ambushing force.

What felt like hours later, even though it was only a couple of minutes, Goblin gave the all-clear signal and stood up. I followed him, and we moved down to the kayaks.

We might have broken them down again, making them easier to conceal, but that would have meant more time right there on the shore, getting ready to move, when we had a limited amount of darkness to use to get to the target, make the hit, and get out. So, we'd left them assembled, just shoved under trees and covered in as much vegetation as we could find. It took a matter of a few minutes to get them uncovered and shoved out onto the water.

Riding lower in the water because of the added weight of men, armor, ammunition, and weapons, we slid out onto the lake, two men per kayak, and started to quietly paddle our way up toward Slobodian's last refuge.

***

While there's definitely something to be said for silence on an infiltration, including radio silence, sometimes timing and coordination suffer from it.

Without using the radios, we had no way to communicate with the D Team. That meant that timing would be entirely dependent on everyone hitting time hacks.

That had, in fact, been considered. Silence right up until the point we started shooting was damned important. But the risk of something going sideways because we couldn't coordinate had been deemed too high.

It still didn't go according to plan.

I was dipping my paddle, watching the nearest lights slide closer as we moved out into the middle of the lake, when the radio went live.

"This is Dice. We are behind schedule. Got held up going around a checkpoint. Estimated time on target now 0125."

Shit. We were going to be in position almost fifteen minutes before the D Team could do their diversionary drive-by shooting on the front of the glorified mansion where Slobodian was holed up. That meant either we had to go to ground in the jungle that was now behind us, float out there on the lake for an extra fifteen minutes and hope we weren't spotted, or else take the chance that we could overwhelm the security on the shore and get in before Slobodian bolted again.

I didn't have a good feeling about either of the latter two options. Fortunately, neither did Goblin. Within a couple of minutes, we were steering our way back toward the tree-shrouded shore, looking for a spot to hole up until we could—hopefully—take advantage of the D Team's diversion.

I was sweating, and it wasn't just because of the heat and the humidity. We hadn't even fired a shot yet, and things had already gone wrong. *What's next?*

Even as I thought it, bringing the kayak in to slip under the overhanging branches, I knew I was probably going to regret asking that question.

***

Time crawled. We were so close that I could look across the water and imagine that I could see Slobodian's security moving around the trees on the shoreline. We were just a little too far away for that, especially given the apparent age of my PVS-14s, but just sitting there as the kayak rocked a little on the slight waves of the lake was nerve-wracking.

Once you get nerved up to go, sudden interruptions and delays like this can only weigh on the mind. You start thinking about everything else that can go wrong, and if you're not careful, you can start to lose in your head before you ever put a finger on the trigger.

That just made it worse when gunfire erupted to the north. It wasn't quite coming from Slobodian's place, but it was fast and intense. A moment later, Dice came over the radio again. "Just took contact from what appears to be a security patrol we didn't spot earlier. We have to fall back."

Well, Murphy was well and truly bending this op over. I looked over at Goblin's kayak, wondering which way he was going to jump.

My worry was that if we called it off, then Slobodian was going to disappear. There was no way he wouldn't, not after the last two attempts we'd made. From what we'd learned, he was no fool, and he'd find a deep, dark hole and drag it in after him. And while he vanished, he'd send more bad guys after our families.

They wouldn't necessarily be the sort of hitters we'd faced before, either. Not if he was trying to use Hezbollah against Congressman Aller. He'd find some other way to get to us.

Goblin started paddling. And he wasn't heading back the way we'd come. He was moving toward the objective.

It took a minute to get the whole team moving. Nobody lagged or complained. Everyone was all in at that point.

The only question was how we were going to approach this. The D Team was supposed to draw the security toward the front of the property, opening up the back to us. Instead, it looked like we might have to land opposed by an alerted security force, and if Colombia was any indication, Slobodian surrounded himself with some guys who knew what they were doing.

Goblin wasn't going straight for the target, though, I saw as we continued moving, keeping as low to the water as we could while still being able to see through our NVGs. Night vision goggles aren't really designed for use in anything but an upright posture, so you really have to crane your neck to see in a crouch or in the prone.

As we got closer, I could see and hear the activity on the compound. Everyone was alert, and even as we paddled within a hundred yards of the shore, a vehicle pulled away from the front, rushing toward the gunfire. I hoped that was just their react force, as much as it was going to suck for the D Team guys. If it was Slobodian, I doubted that he'd be going *toward* the gunfire. Not after what we'd seen him do in Colombia.

We still had a chance.

Goblin picked up the pace, aiming for the thicker trees slightly to the west of the house, where the shadows were thickest. Ken and I followed, closing in as we approached. We still needed to maintain some dispersion, but we also needed to get on the ground as fast as possible.

If we'd hoped that all of Slobodian's security would shift their attention toward the D Team, those hopes were dashed a moment later, as I looked up and saw movement under the trees, and heard what might have been a radio call drift out over the water. Slobodian had hired pros. They were watching their sectors and leaving the fight to the guys who had that responsibility.

So, it was going to be a fight from the get-go.

IR lasers flickered out from the treeline, searching for the source of the little bit of noise we were making. It was really dark, with no moon, so even with NVGs, I doubted they could see us clearly. That would change, as soon as they got a flood or an IR illuminator on us.

I put down my paddle, letting the kayak drift, and brought up my M4.

The reason a lot of units had stopped using active IR several years before was because the bad guys had been getting their hands on more and more NVGs. If you're the only one with night vision, like we'd been in Iraq and Afghanistan for years, then you could flash all the IR around you wanted. If the bad guys had NVGs, though, then IR lasers were subject to the same ironclad law as tracers:

And tracers work both ways.

The suppressor on the end of the barrel made the rifle a bit muzzle-heavy, but I braced it against my knee despite the rocking of the kayak, put the red dot as close to the end of one of those bright lines of green light as I could, flipped the selector to "burst," and squeezed the trigger, trying to keep the dot as steady as I could, though the bobble was even more unavoidable on a kayak than if I was on dry land.

With a hissing series of *crack*s, I sent three rounds at the source of the IR laser. At least one of them connected, because the laser suddenly waved wildly over the lake, while Jake and Goblin dug in and hauled ass for shore. I kept up the fire, dumping the rest of the magazine in a series of three-round bursts as I shifted my fire back and forth across that treeline.

My bolt locked back on an empty mag, while Ken pulled hard on the paddle and the rest of the team pushed past us. More gunfire erupted from off to my right and behind us, as either KG or Phil opened fire, picking up the suppression after I'd run dry.

I reloaded quickly, stuffing the empty mag into the dump pouch at my hip. I didn't want to get to shore with an empty weapon, and Ken was still keeping us moving toward the bank. The IR lasers had shut off, and more suppressed gunfire was crackling from the shore near the trees. Goblin and Jake, at least, were on the ground.

We had less than fifty yards to go, but over open water, with paddles, that can feel like an awful long way. Some sporadic gunfire was starting to stab out of the dark at us, but we'd caught them just enough by surprise that they were off balance and falling back toward the house, those who had survived the initial burst of fire.

I had to set my M4 across the gunwales, or else the suppressor would have melted a hole through the kayak. That slowed me down, but I was able to get my hands on my paddle again, and gave us a bit more of a shove toward the shore.

The kayak scraped on the grassy bank, and I jumped out, gun up and looking for targets as I sprinted to where Custus and Rob were on a knee next to one of the trees. Clint, Patrick, Tom, and Brian had already started to push up through the yard, past the gazebo and the pool, trying to cut off the front, if only by fire.

Ken dragged the kayak a little higher on the bank, his M4 slung across his back, then he brought it around in front of him and moved up to join us.

There were two bodies on the ground not far away. One was slumped on its side under the trees, while the other had collapsed on its face halfway to the house. Whoever it was, he'd died fighting, facing us.

I was pretty sure, from a cursory glance around me, that both bodies belonged to the bad guys. Goblin was already up and moving, dashing to the next tree, while Jake was down in the prone by the gazebo.

Movement in the back of the house caught my eye, and I snapped my weapon toward it. It was hard to see in the glare of the lights by the dock, off to my right, but I could see enough to identify the shape of a man pointing a weapon.

Custus and I both opened fire at the same time. Suppressors coughed, glass shattered, and the man fell out onto the back porch.

Then we were up and moving, driving toward the house, even as a ripping crackle of suppressed gunfire sounded from up near the front.

CHAPTER
37

There were no flashbangs, kicked in doors, yells, or any of the other sound and fury that was often associated with a raid, particularly one where contact had already been made with the opposition. So far, they appeared to be in without alerting Badeaux or his guests, so they'd keep it that way as long as possible.

The end goal here wasn't bullet holes and bloodstains, not if they could help it. This had to be more subtle than that.

The four of them padded down the hallway from the garage, quickly clearing the kitchen, the laundry room, and the first bedroom. The floor was carpeted, and their boots made no sound, especially over the music that was playing from the living room. It was something poppy and nauseating, but it was just loud enough that no one inside had noticed the takedown at the garage.

The second security man was watching a movie in the first room. He looked up as the door swung open, probably expecting his buddy with chow, and his eyes widened as he found himself facing two men in black, pointing guns at his face. He didn't resist, though he looked over at the Glock sitting on the end table nearby. The threat of those suppressed 9mm submachineguns overrode any thought of heroics, though. As Mike zipped him up and hooded him, he got the same warning that David had in the garage.

If anything, the young man seemed almost relieved, though he was shaking a little as he was secured. He probably figured he was a dead man either way, but he must have seen enough to figure that he didn't want to give his life to protect Badeaux if he could help it.

While Badeaux seemed like the type to have a cook of his own, there was no one in the kitchen. The food van had probably been meant to drop off the cartons and leave them for the former Congressman and his guests to serve themselves.

Nick had found himself next to Saul, moving up the hallway, slowly and quietly. They could hear voices ahead, over the music. They were coming from just around the corner. They could see to the far windows and the little nook by the front door, but the bulk of the living room was out of sight.

Saul held up a hand, and Nick slowed and stopped, listening.

"...unfortunate, but with your connections, you could help get them through with minimal trouble." The voice sounded faintly accented, though Nick had to search his mind to try to place the accent. Whoever it was probably wasn't an American, but he was well-traveled enough that his English was pretty good. "I assure you that compensation will be appropriate. Their mission is extremely important."

"I don't really care about their mission." That was identifiable as Badeaux. He sounded slightly distracted, and when he thought about what might be distracting their target, Nick's blood started to boil. "What happened, though? You usually haven't needed my network to bring any of your people in."

There was a pause. Saul had his phone in his off hand, though his rifle was still pointed at the corner, held in his shoulder with his right. He was recording this. Good call.

"There was an...incident...in Colombia, before they could depart through the Darien Gap. The facilitator was forced to flee, and with the amount of chaos and scrutiny that followed, the team leader saw fit to call off the movement and find another way." There was a faint sound like something moving on a seat, and then he spoke again. "There are concerns that the facilitator's network may be compromised to the point that we will have to shift our resources."

"Slobodian's not indispensable, no matter what he thinks." Badeaux sounded both distracted and dismissive. "We've had backup networks for years. That's why these things are *networks*. No one individual is indispensable." He laughed. "Present company excepted, of course."

Another pause. "That is good to hear. We would not want it to turn out that our investment had been squandered." There might have been an implicit threat there.

Badeaux certainly seemed to think so. "Don't get it twisted, Yan. We have a mutually beneficial arrangement. If one of us goes down, we all go down." Another laugh. Something about that sound just made Nick white-knuckle his weapon a little more. "That won't happen, though. We're covered. Trust me. All the right people are watching our backs."

The other man didn't seem to be entirely convinced. "That is good to hear." There was a coolness in the man's voice as he continued. "Can you get them into the country?"

"If you need passports and a wave-through at Customs, that *can* be arranged." Badeaux sounded unconcerned with his guest's coldness. "It's simpler and carries less risk."

"No. There can be no record of their entry into the country. You do not need to know why."

"Fine. I'll make some calls." Badeaux might have been trying to be conciliatory, but he still didn't sound terribly concerned. "Where are they now?"

"Still in Colombia, though they have returned to Cartagena for now. The team leader is concerned that they may have been identified in Capurgana, so he does not consider it prudent to attempt another trek through the Darien from there."

A dry laugh. "Nobody's keeping tabs on the Darien. You know that as well as I do. It's what makes it such a useful pipeline."

Saul had apparently heard enough. He shoved the phone back into his chest rig and put his off hand back onto his 3d-printed submachinegun. Together, the four-man team pushed down the hall and into the living room.

The two men weren't really paying any attention and didn't immediately notice the men in black who glided into the room, muzzles quickly tracking in on both of them. The girls noticed first, eyes widening, as one of them let out a faint squeak. Fortunately, both girls were still clothed, for certain values of the term, though their places on the two men's laps was all that the four PGS operators needed to see.

Badeaux looked just as slick as his photos, even in his own house, with an underage girl on his lap. The other man was significantly younger, Asian, with his hair slicked back. He turned and saw the guns, the gear, and the balaclavas before Badeaux did. His eyes widened, as the threat of the 9mm muzzles registered. There were liquor bottles and bags of drugs on the coffee table, but he didn't seem to have partaken. His hands moved away from the girl, spread wide to show that he didn't have a weapon and wasn't a threat.

Badeaux looked up, annoyed, and it took him a second to realize what he was looking at. "What the fuck?"

"Shut up." Doug was already pulling the girls away. His voice lowered as he herded them toward the breakfast nook. "Stay down, look at the floor, and don't make a sound. We're not going to hurt you. This will all be over soon."

Saul motioned with his muzzle. "Down on the floor. Both of you. You make a sound, you die. You move wrong, you die."

Even as he did as he was told, keeping his hands up, Badeaux still didn't seem to understand the gravity of his situation. "Do you idiots have any *idea* who I am? Do you have any idea just how badly you just fucked up?"

"We know who you are." Saul's voice was ice. He glanced at Doug. "Do we want to toss this place?"

"Might be useful." Doug's voice was emotionless as he turned his eyes toward the two men on the carpet. "Might also put us in possession of stuff that is rightfully a felony to possess."

"I don't want to see any of that shit." Mike sounded almost strangled, like he was struggling with himself not to just mag-dump into the two scumbags on the carpet. Mike was one of the most straight-arrow of the PGS contractors, and this was some dark, twisted shit.

This almost made the horror show they'd found in that MS-13 destroyer house in Honduras look tame. Almost. This was a different kind of evil, not that the *mareros* had shrunk from it.

"Take phones, at least. We need contacts." Doug was unwavering. It was grim work, but it had to be done. Just taking Badeaux off the board wouldn't be enough. They had to disassemble as much of his network as possible, even if that meant leaking names and incriminating evidence.

Nick wondered just how well that was going to work. Connections had trumped evidence every step of the way, so far.

"I'll take care of it." Saul lifted his muzzle and turned toward the stairs. "You guys just keep an eye on them."

As Saul headed upstairs, the seriousness of the situation seemed to start to get through to Badeaux. This wasn't just a robbery, or even a rival trying to make a play. This was something much, much worse. The four men who had entered his house with weapons, silently getting past his security, were faceless agents of vengeance. Through the fog of drugs and alcohol, the fear started to creep in. Even so, he couldn't get past the illusion that he was untouchable.

"Look, I don't know who put you up to this, if you just walk out of here, then I can promise that it will all be forgotten. I'm sure you were given a bad deal by somebody. There's nothing valuable enough in this house to make it worth your while to go through with this. Just walk out, and nobody will look for you." It was a lie, but none of the contractors had any intention of listening to it, anyway.

"You were told to shut up." Doug's voice was dead and flat.

There was a sudden, venomous curse from upstairs, and somehow that seemed to convince Badeaux to keep his mouth shut. The Asian man hadn't said a word or made a sound, though he was trembling on the carpet.

Saul came back down with a bag of cell phones and a handful of actual, old-school polaroid photos. "That motherfucker had fucking *polaroids* in his fucking sock drawer." He threw them on the carpet in front of Badeaux, and after the briefest glimpse, Nick averted his eyes. He didn't want to see that shit any more than Mike did.

Saul wasn't just going to stand there indulging in righteous indignation, though. He was already hunting around the living room, then turned and stalked back toward the garage. Nick glanced after him with a frown. Saul was a man on a mission, and under the circumstances, Nick suspected that it wasn't going to be good for somebody.

Badeaux was really starting to understand, now. "If you kill me, you have no idea the world of shit that's going to come down on your heads. I don't give a fuck how much you hide your faces. We'll find out who you are, who your families are, everybody you've ever cared about and loved. Their lives will be completely destroyed if you do this, and it'll be your fault."

Saul came back down the hallway. He had an extension cord in his hand. "We're not going to kill you. We were never here. You're going to do that yourself."

Strangely, he was starting back up the stairs, twisting the cord in his hands as he went. It took Nick a second to figure out what he was doing.

Badeaux's living room had a vaulted ceiling, with a bit of a railed balcony above it, leading onto another hallway to the upstairs bedrooms. Badeaux himself was almost directly under the balcony, on his stomach, and he couldn't see above and behind him. He started to crane his neck to look, but that only put him in a better position for Saul.

The noose dropped neatly around his neck and tightened as the big man gave the cord a ferocious jerk, yanking Badeaux up off the floor. He scrambled to his feet, grabbing at the cord, trying to take the weight off his neck, but Saul was already hauling him up, hand over hand, until his feet were off the floor, kicking wildly. Only then did Saul hitch the cord to the railing, securing it quickly while Badeaux clawed at his throat, his feet still trying to get some purchase on the chair.

Doug walked over and kicked the chair away.

"Those photos will be explanation enough, when he's found." Saul was coming back down the stairs. "Bag that other fuck and get some clothes for the girls. We're out of here."

As it turned out, the girls did have clothes in the house, though they still weren't enough, to Mike's way of thinking. He found two of Badeaux's coats and wrapped both of them in them. The girls allowed themselves to be led out, their eyes haunted, their stares hollow, even as Badeaux's final convulsions slowed and ceased.

The security guard they'd bagged in the garage was still on his knees, his head bowed under the sack, shaking slightly. It was doubtful how much he'd heard, but he had to know something had gone down. The other one, Kevin, towed by Doug, had clearly heard all of it, and he was shaking like a leaf.

Nick bent down close to David. "We're going to go for a ride, now. What happens at the end of it is entirely up to you." He picked the man up by the arm and propelled him toward the back of the van. They still had a long way to go that night.

CHAPTER
38

I outpaced Custus to the door by a couple steps. Pausing just short, I waited until I felt his squeeze to my upper arm, then I went through the shattered glass fast, stepping over the body on the threshold. I didn't have the time or the attention to spare to kick the weapon away from his hands, mainly because I was more concerned with the two dudes wearing plate carriers coming in around the corner from the front of the house.

I shot at the first one as I practically threw myself through the door and toward the corner, coming up short on the kitchen counter. Custus was right behind me, and I heard him grunt as they both opened fire, but he was shooting back, so he wasn't down. Everyone was using suppressors, so it was an eerily quiet gunfight, even as I caught my rush just enough to take a knee and steady my aim. I felt a bullet snap past my ear just as I dumped the guy on the left with a double-tap through the teeth. He went down like a sack of rocks, and his buddy tripped over him, at which point Custus painted the floor with his brains.

"Hybrid, you all right?" Ken, Jake, Rob, and Goblin were pouring through the opening behind us, spreading out between the two of us and the doors, giving us some cover, if only plates.

"Yeah." He was getting up, dark fluid on the tattered shreds of the shoulder of his jungle fatigues. "Got a little trimmed, is all."

I almost hesitated. The mission was paramount. But if Custus bled out in the next five minutes while we were trying to clear the house, the mission was going to be jeopardized, anyway, and we had four gunmen between us and the rest of the bad guys. I quickly crossed the open doorway, ducking down to retrieve the dead man's weapon as I went, and quickly checked him over.

"I'm fine, Backwoods." He was back on his feet after going down onto his side, having thrown himself flat as he'd gone through the door. His teeth were gritted, but he also didn't pull away or shove me away as I checked him for bleeds, either.

"Shut up." I finished quickly. He'd lost a chunk of meat on his shoulder that would need to be bandaged, but he wasn't leaking badly enough to try to pull him out of the fight. We needed to move. "You'll live."

"Glad to hear it." He flexed the shoulder and winced. "Damn, that hurts."

Goblin and Rob were already moving, pushing around the outside of the room. Custus and I fell in behind Ken and Jake and kept pushing.

More gunfire sounded from the front of the house. It was getting more intense. Slobodian had to know he was cut off, and he was trying desperately to get out. He might have headed for the boat that had been tied up on the dock as we'd come in off the water, but we'd kiboshed that plan as soon as I'd opened fire on the shore security. Now he was trying to break out the front, but the cordon team had the front locked down.

Goblin and Rob had pushed around the sectional in the middle of the great room at the back, moving toward the door leading into what might be the master suite right behind it. Ken and Jake had posted up on the kitchen island, covering the stairs, the entrance, and the two rooms off to that side of the house.

Both of those doors were shut, though we could hear muffled gunfire coming from what might have been the front room.

There was no one in the entryway. If Slobodian had been trying to get out that way, he'd either managed to break out, or he'd fallen back to the front room.

"Cover those stairs." I moved around the island, behind Ken, and started toward the nearest door. There were too many angles for me to really feel comfortable with any of it, as I had to keep my eye and muzzle on the stairs, the front door, and the two doors ahead of me. Off to our right, Goblin kicked open the master suite door with a crash, and he and Jake went through fast, guns leveled.

I was too focused on my part of the mission to tell if there was any shooting from in there or not. My concern was that room right in front of me.

We'd all trained to the point that we didn't really stack up anymore. As the One Man, I paused just long enough to feel a squeeze to my tricep, then I threw the door open, riding it to the stops as I hooked through the opening, sweeping my muzzle across the room as I went.

Halfway through the doorway, I spotted a man crouched in the window, trying to get a shot at the guys outside. I put a bullet in him as fast as my red dot crossed his back, finished clearing my corner, and pivoted back toward him, just in time to put another round through the top of his skull as he fell, two of Custus's bullets already in him.

He was the only one in there. Custus led the way out of the room.

We repeated the process with the next door, though this time I gave Custus the squeeze. More gunfire was hammering throughout the house, and I caught just a glimpse, as I went through one door and toward the next, of Ken and Jake shooting up the stairs from behind the kitchen island.

Custus went through the second door like a bulldozer. He barely unlatched the door before he had his shoulder to it and was slamming it toward the wall, his weapon dropping level as he moved, already spitting bullets at the two men crouched by the window, one of whom was reloading as the door burst open. He looked up just in time to catch Custus's first round through the eyeball, spattering red ruin on the wall behind him and slumping against his buddy, who was still trying to get shots at the cordon, until I went through behind Custus and shot him five times, stitching rounds from his armpit up to his throat.

Custus moved quickly to clear the remaining dead space, then we were moving out.

The exchange of gunfire up and down the stairs had stopped. Jake and Ken were covering the rear and the front of the house, now, as Goblin and Rob started up the stairs, muzzles high as they did what they could to cover every angle on the way up.

I moved to join them, unfortunately forcing Jake to lift his muzzle as Custus and I crossed the entryway. We moved as fast as we could, joining Goblin and Rob, adding our own muzzles to the work.

That allowed us to climb the stairs marginally faster, but there's no easy or quick way to go up stairs in close quarters combat. It's a nightmare any way you cut it, so we had to climb one step at a time, opening up a little bit more of the hallway and the landing at the top with each step.

Only when Goblin got high enough that he could see pretty much the whole hallway, including the two of three doors that stood open, did he suddenly move faster, all but running up the steps, Rob right on his heels. Custus and I moved a little bit slower, mainly because we were still covering the landing and the last door.

I heard commotion in the room just off the landing, but Custus and I had to deal with the other two. We *could* have just covered them, but with the way the night was going so far, I didn't think we had that kind of time.

We cleared them both quickly. Neither one was occupied. We rolled out of the last one and headed for the door that Goblin and Rob had entered.

"Coming in!" Deconfliction was something that none of us could afford to ignore, not when we'd already done as much shooting in that house as we had. And there was more still going on somewhere to the north. If Slobodian had called for his react force to come back and cover him, the D Team was doing a pretty damned good job of keeping them too occupied to break contact.

How long that would last was anyone's guess.

We came through the door to find ourselves in the actual master suite. The big room downstairs must have been something else. The king-sized bed dominated, with a large picture window across from it that would give a great view of the lake if the sun had been up. A plasma screen stood against another wall, with a desk just beyond it, and the lavish bathroom opened up on the corner.

Slobodian was standing by the desk, his back to us, his hands spread, Goblin's and Rob's rifles pointed at his head.

"I don't suppose now would be a good time to revisit a financial arrangement?" Slobodian kept his voice light.

"No." Goblin's own tone was far calmer than mine probably would have been. This man had facilitated terrorism, kidnapping, murder, narcotics, and human trafficking, and had sent hitmen after our families. And that was just the stuff we *knew* about. "I'm afraid it's far too late for that."

"I thought it probably was, but I had to try."

I'll give Slobodian this. He was fast. He threw himself sideways and down, hitting the floor in a heartbeat, and rolled to his back, snatching a pistol out of his waistband. Goblin and Rob hadn't had a chance to close in and disarm him yet.

He was fast, but you can't miss fast enough to win a gunfight.

His first shot went high, blowing a pit out of the ceiling, as Goblin flung himself to one side, dropping to a knee with his weapon already tracking in toward Slobodian.

I knew I was taking a risk, but I jumped up onto the bed and ran across it, fighting to keep my balance as I tracked in on Slobodian on the far side.

He saw me coming and tried to twist around and bring his handgun to bear on me, but Goblin and I shot him at the same instant. Well, Goblin shot him. My first round went just past his ear and into the floor, but my second shot took him in the clavicle. Goblin had already hit him in the guts, and his follow-up shot, as Slobodian jerked a second round into the ceiling, caught him just under the chin and blew the top of his skull off.

My momentum wasn't so easily arrested on the mattress, and I kept going, stumbling off the edge of the bed and almost landing on the ruin of Slobodian's skull. Goblin got up with a faint groan as I caught myself with a hand to the wall, and he turned toward the computer.

"Good. We got to him before he could erase anything, it looks like. He's got his digital shredder app right there on the desktop." He started checking a few things. "Nope. He didn't get it started. Thought he could break out, his security would take care of us, and then he could come back and get back to it." He looked down at the dead man. "More fool him."

Another burst of fire crackled from not too far away. "This is Dice. We're seeing reinforcements coming our way, and it looks like the Paraguayan Army might be on its way, too. A military helicopter just went overhead. We need to go, now."

CHAPTER
39

"Grab whatever we can carry." Goblin was already pulling the cords out of the laptop. "We've got two minutes to snatch up every bit of intel, waterproof it, and get off the X."

"What about the D Team?" I asked. "We can't just leave them hanging."

Goblin went still for a second. "We'll move to the front and see if we can give them covering fire. But their exfil is to the north, and we don't have the platforms to get them across the lake."

There'd been a time when I might have said that that was why we had contingency plans, but he was right. We were on a shoestring, *way* outside of any support except what we could get through Tick. Contingency plans are often constrained by just how many assets you really had to draw on, and without months of groundwork, we had *no* assets in the Tri Border Area.

We just had to get back across the line and into Brazil one way or another.

Goblin had his assault pack off and was stuffing the laptop into it, followed by everything that looked like it might be electronic storage of some form. The rest of us looked for anything else for a moment, then, with a nod from Custus, the two of us headed back downstairs to hopefully give Dice and his boys a bit of a helping hand.

"Friendlies coming down!" The last thing I wanted was to accidentally get shot *after* the target was dead.

"Bring it." Jake was still at the island, covering the front. Custus and I hustled down the steps.

"We need to push out and see if we can give the D Team boys some fire support." I pointed toward the northeast corner of the house. "They're getting hammered, and it looks like we might have the Paraguayan Army showing up to the party, too."

Slobodian must have had local connections that he contacted as soon as the shooting started. There's no other way the army would be responding this fast, in this lawless shithole, otherwise.

Ken joined Custus and me as we headed out through the smashed glass of the back door, hooking around the corner of the house. "This is Backwoods. We're moving up to the northeast corner." I also didn't want to get accidentally shot by any of the guys on the other side of the house.

"Copy. Moving up," Tom replied.

There was some landscaping at the corner of the house, and though it wouldn't provide us a lot of actual cover, it would conceal us, and with our suppressors, it might keep the bad guys from figuring out where we were altogether.

Of course, if they were paying even the slightest bit of attention to events of that night, they already knew.

I moved up, prying my PVS-14 back down in front of my eye, and as I reached the corner itself, I saw the shapes of four gunmen in plate carriers, helmets, and NVGs coming across the front of the house. I recognized Tom from his build and the way he ran, so I knew it was our teammates.

Unfortunately, I couldn't see the fight up by the town nearly so well.

A few muzzle flashes flickered in the dark, but they were visible more as strobes of light against the buildings and under the trees, and then only on NVGs, rather than actually visible muzzle blasts. There were too many trees, and even a few buildings, between us and the fight.

Custus pointed. "There's a treeline over there that should get us up onto the flank."

"Let's go," Tom said, crouching next to me while the other three stacked up behind him, muzzles trained out into the open ground around the target house. We were still far from out of the woods, even though the shooting where we were had stopped, for the moment.

Custus started moving, and I fell in behind him. The rest of the team—except for those still in the house—formed a bit of a wedge as we moved toward the trees, keeping low and moving quick. It was a short movement, while the gunfire up north of us only continued to intensify.

As soon as I settled in behind one of the trees, on the far side from Slobodian's house, I saw some of what was going on.

Three vehicles were stationary on the road that stretched north from our position. What might have been shattered glass glinted on the ground, even as half a dozen or so gunmen crouched behind the vehicles, taking the occasional shot at the houses.

Those weren't our guys. None of them were running suppressed, unlike the bad guys in the house, and they weren't wearing the right gear. I hoped that the bodies lying on the street were theirs, too.

Another burst of fire hammered the nearest vehicle, and two of the shooters ducked, almost as if they were trying to get into the fetal position behind the tires. Those guys were not having a good time.

But they were between our teammates and exfil. It was, frankly, a credit to their professionalism that they hadn't broken as soon as the shooting from the house had stopped.

Several of the shooters at the middle vehicle started to open fire around the front and back, flame stabbing into the night from their muzzles. They must have had more than just a paycheck hanging over their heads, if they were that determined to hold the line for Slobodian.

Too bad for them it was far too late. They were about to die for nothing.

Brian opened up first. He double-tapped the nearest man, who was still crouched by the tire as the D Team kept up their fire, and then we were all shooting. The vehicles provided the bad guys some cover, but not enough.

The two at the nearest vehicle went down hard, torn up by almost a dozen rounds each. Then we were moving up, driving forward, guns up and shooting on the move as we spread out and raked the remaining vehicles with bullets. It wasn't the most tactically sound approach, but between us and the D Team, those guys were pretty pinned down already, and we were short on time. I could hear the helicopter overhead, and it was only a matter of minutes before that bird was going to get authorization to either land and put troops behind us, or just open up with the door guns and lay waste. Not to mention what forces were coming from the north.

Caught between us and the D Team's fire, four more of the shooters went down. The last one decided that if Slobodian wanted to come after him for abandoning his post, then he'd have to find him first. He jumped into the vehicle, even as bullets punch more holes in the bodywork and the already smashed windows, revved the engine, and sped away into the night.

"Dice, Backwoods. Status?"

"Cornhole and Sand are down. We can hear vehicles coming from the north, and another helicopter."

"The way to the house is clear. Move down and link up with us. We're at the rear of the southernmost vehicle you were shooting at." With the opposition down or fled, we'd spread out and tried to find some cover, even though there wasn't a whole lot to be had.

"Roger. Coming to you."

The night seemed oddly quiet after the gunfire had died down. The helicopter, an old Huey, was now the chief source of noise, and it was circling. That it hadn't opened fire yet was a relief, but that might just be because they couldn't tell who was who down on the ground.

Not that that had stopped many Latin American militaries that I knew of.

Figures came jogging out of the nearest side street, pausing only to trade IR flashes with us. With the amount of time we had left, we had to take the chance. Two of the D Team had bodies over their shoulders—Cornhole and Sand.

Dice was puffing as he skidded to a halt and dropped to a knee next to where Custus and I were on a knee in the bushes. He glanced up at the helicopter. "Taking his time, isn't he?"

Custus followed his gaze. "He's well within rifle range. I think he wants to be sure, or to have someone else be the focus of attention before he opens fire."

"That's cheerful." I didn't know Dice that well. Only by reputation. We'd always worked different AOs. "There's a problem, though. I don't think Tick's going to send the bird back in directly here, especially not if the Paraguayan Army's in the vicinity, and we don't have boats."

"Slobodian did." Custus had hit on a plan. "It might be a bit higher profile than the kayaks, but it'll get you to the other side of the lake. Come on."

We stayed under the trees as much as we could, while that helicopter continued to circle. I glanced up as we moved, catching a glimpse of it through the treetops. We were going to have to do something to discourage the pilot before we got out on the water, or else we'd be sitting ducks.

I wasn't the only one thinking that, either.

The rest of the team had fallen back to the dock and the shore by the time we came out of the trees. Goblin was already on Slobodian's boat. "Load up. We're going to make a run for it."

I stepped onto the dock, but I wasn't going to leave Ken without a second paddle. "Big target."

"It is. But we've got guns, and we've just got to make it a mile and a quarter to the jungle. The Paraguayans won't pursue us across the line into Brazil." He sounded a little like he was trying to convince himself.

"Hope you're right." I spotted Ken and joined him as we ran for the kayaks. "See you in the jungle."

The helicopter rumbled by again, but for some reason, the pilot still seemed reluctant to engage. I wasn't complaining, but I was wondering.

Then I didn't need to wonder anymore.

The helicopter must have gotten new instructions, or else the pilot figured that the people leaving Slobodian's house by water while his official reinforcements approached weren't friendlies. Dipping lower, it started in toward us, and when I looked up, as we shoved the kayak out into the lake, I could see what looked like a door gunner leaning out of the open side door.

Goblin had been waiting for it, though. As Slobodian's boat started to putter out onto the lake, half a dozen M4s opened fire from the stern, sending a wall of bullets up at the helicopter.

They'd taken their suppressors off, too, so the pilot got a good look at six flickering muzzle flashes, as our guys mag-dumped on full auto at him. With a sudden wrench of the controls, he dipped the nose further and banked sharply away. The Paraguayans didn't have many helicopters—I was frankly surprised they'd brought one out for this—and it would probably be his hide if it got shot down.

Except...

Something about the way the bird was flying told me that the sudden maneuver wasn't just evasive action. A moment later, the pilot tried to correct, lost control, and the Huey slammed down onto its side in the fields on the far side of the house.

Somebody had hit the pilot.

We had our opening.

As Slobodian's boat sped away, the rest of us, on kayaks, paddled into the deepest shadow we could find, and endeavored to vanish into the night.

***

We got a pretty good look at what was going on at Slobodian's house as we followed the arc of the lake around the point to the southwest. Lights flashed and swung around the house, as the Army descended on the abattoir we'd left behind. We were already too far away to make out a lot of details, aside from the lights. I wondered just how big an army unit an international shadow facilitator of drugs, guns, murder, and human flesh rated.

There was no sign of pursuit at the moment, but I was sure there would be, as soon as somebody got word up the chain about the lost Huey. They weren't going to just shrug at the loss of an asset like that.

That was why Ken and I were fading toward the eastern shore as fast as we could. If we could get lost in the shadows, we might avoid the inevitable pursuit, at least long enough to get ashore and link up with the rest.

Worst case, we'd ditch the kayak, get into the jungle, and link up on the river.

Fortunately, I'd overestimated the speed at which the Paraguayans could coordinate such a response. The Lago Acaray was actually pretty damned big, and the Federal Police didn't have a base close enough to intercept us.

Just over half an hour after we'd cast off, we slid into our landing site, covered by darkness and the trees. Tom, Brian, Clint, and Patrick had beaten us there, while I thought I could just make out the rest of the kayaks hugging the shadows near the shore, still coming. There was no sign of the boat, though Goblin was on the bank waiting for us, with the rest of the D Team higher up and deeper into the woods behind him.

"Sent the boat along toward the dam," he explained. "Let 'em chase that."

We clambered up out of the water, hid the kayaks under the vegetation, and waited for the rest.

***

335

The speedboats were out on the lake, sweeping the water with spotlights. Custus and Rob had gotten ashore and their kayaks hidden just in time.

"Time to go." Jake and Goblin led out, disappearing into the dark under the jungle canopy in a few moments. The rest of us followed.

Behind us, we left the body of one enemy. I wondered how many more we were going to have to leave on the ground before this was all over.

If it was ever over.

EPILOGUE

The middle of a corporate headquarters, as modest as Pallas Group's headquarters was, seemed like an odd place to have this sort of a conversation. But, given the fact that we didn't have a SCIF—Sensitive Compartmented Information Facility—of our own, it was probably about the best we could do, unless we were going to convene out on the yacht.

We'd been back Stateside for about two weeks. So far, while we knew that the repercussions of our actions were reverberating around the world, we hadn't seen them. Our families were unharmed and being left alone, from everything we could see. And we'd looked. We'd done some serious counter-surveillance work as soon as we'd gotten home, as exhausted as we'd all been after the hits in Colombia and Paraguay.

What the B Team had done...that could have some serious implications down the road.

"Investigations have begun into the apparent suicide of former Congressman and philanthropist Simon Badeaux, who was found hanging in his house, surrounded by drug paraphernalia and what appeared to be photographic evidence of sex crimes. Everyone who knew Badeaux has expressed their shock and disbelief, both at his apparent suicide, as well as the alleged evidence of sex crimes.

"Simon Badeaux was a great man, with one of the biggest hearts I've ever known." The actor on the screen was dabbing at his eyes. *"It's absolutely unconscionable, what*

they're trying to do to him after his death, when he can't defend himself anymore."

"Check that motherfucker's hard drive." Under different circumstances, that crack might have drawn a grim chuckle, but after what we'd seen, nobody laughed. Jake was dead serious.

Goblin shut off the news program. "So, you can see that the narrative is already spinning as hard as it can. But we knew that was going to happen."

He leaned on the table at the head of the conference room. It wasn't a big facility, but it could fit the four teams that weren't on assignment right at the moment. "We took out two monsters out of a legion. *But.* Most importantly, we got a lot of intel. A *lot*. Not the least from Mr. Yan, who has been our guest for the last couple of weeks."

"Is he PLA?" Tom asked.

Goblin nodded. "Through and through. We haven't gotten the mission of the team he was talking about out of him but, given the fact that he wanted them smuggled into the country with no records, that kinda narrows it down. Even most of their illegal activities are run by people who are here legally. My guess is, they were supposed to be a sabotage squad."

"What are we going to do with him?" That was a question that had been nagging at me for a while. We couldn't keep him. He'd been shuttled around the country in a trailer for two weeks, but that couldn't last forever. And there really wasn't anyone we could trust to hand him over to.

"We're going to let him go tomorrow." There was a deadly chill in Goblin's voice. "If he can walk out of where he's getting dropped, he deserves to get back into circulation."

There were nods at that. The desert is wide, as was sometimes said in the Southwest.

"So, what's the next step, boss?" Saul was standing near the back, his arms folded over his chest. "Like you said, we got two, but there are a lot more."

"There are indeed. And thanks to Slobodian and Badeaux, we have names, receipts, and addresses.

"Get some rest gentlemen, because we're going hunting again soon."

AUTHOR'S NOTE

While the title *Frontiers of Chaos* was initially planned as referring primarily to the Tri-Border Area, as this story took shape, it became more and more about every frontier where lawlessness starts and spreads. While the events and people in this story are fictional, the congruence between these sorts of crimes and heavier security concerns is very real.

There are enemies of the United States, both foreign and domestic, who seek the erosion of the US via any means necessary. One of those means is, simply, crime. Lawlessness weakens a society, and while this series has touched on more immediate strategic concerns as well, it's largely what these books are about. In *Frontiers of Chaos*, the crimes have taken more of a center stage than the strategic picture, but it still remains, and will continue to do so.

This is a long, quiet, never-ending war. That's the nature of *Unrestricted Warfare*.

I hope you've enjoyed this book, as dark as it got.

To keep up to date, I hope that you'll sign up for my newsletter—you get a free American Praetorians novella, Drawing the Line, when you do.

If you've enjoyed this novel, I hope that you'll go leave a review on Amazon or Goodreads. Reviews matter a lot to independent authors, so I appreciate the effort.

If you'd like to connect, I have a Facebook page at https://www.facebook.com/PeteNealenAuthor. You can also contact me, or just read my musings and occasional samples on the blog, at https://www.americanpraetorians.com. I look forward to hearing from you.

Also By Peter Nealen

Brave New Disorder (Pallas Group Solutions Thrillers)
Gray War
The Dragon and the Skull
Silver or Lead
Frontiers of Chaos
Non-State Actor (Forthcoming)

The Brannigan's Blackhearts Universe
Kill Yuan
The Colonel Has A Plan (Online Short)
Fury in the Gulf
Burmese Crossfire
Enemy Unidentified
Frozen Conflict
High Desert Vengeance
Doctors of Death
Kill or Capture
Enemy of My Enemy
War to the Knife
Blood Debt
Marque and Reprisal
Concrete Jungle

The Maelstrom Rising Series
Escalation
Holding Action
Crimson Star
Strategic Assets
Fortress Doctrine
Thunder Run
Area Denial
Power Vacuum
Option Zulu
SPOTREPS – A Maelstrom Rising Anthology

The Lost Series
Ice and Monsters

Shadows and Crows
Darkness and Stone
Swords Against the Night
The Alchemy of Treason
The Rock of Battle

The Unity Wars Series
The Fall of Valdek
The Defense of Provenia
The Alliance Rises

The American Praetorians Series
Drawing the Line: An American Praetorians Story (Novella)
Task Force Desperate
Hunting in the Shadows
Alone and Unafraid
The Devil You Don't Know
Lex Talionis

The Jed Horn Supernatural Thriller Series
Nightmares
A Silver Cross and a Winchester
The Walker on the Hills
The Canyon of the Lost (Novelette)
Older and Fouler Things

Printed in the USA
CPSIA information can be obtained
at www.ICGtesting.com
LVHW050929170823
755410LV00025B/274/J